THE ELECTRIFYING DEMISE

BY
James and Joy Munson

Matchstick Literary
1-888-306-8885
orders@matchliterary.com

FOREWORD

I've had this story in my mind for 40 years and tried to find some one to write it for me since my handwriting is illegible. Then I decided to learn to type but I'm not a good student and that didn't work out, so one day I decided to punch it out, hunt and peck style on the computer, which worked better because I think faster than I type; therefore, I didn't have to go back and change too many ideas.

What I learned was, "writing" is fun and it amazed me how I would introduce a character in one place and they would show up later as an integral part of the story. If you have a desire to write just sit at your word processor and start. The story will flow out by itself. At least that's the way it happened to me. My wife asked me who wrote the book because the grammar and descriptions didn't sound like they came from me.

The story is set in The Dalles Oregon. I had an uncle who lived there. His ranch was west of town with an enormous pine tree in the front yard. In the early 40s my dad and I (I was 14 at the time) spanned the tree. As I recall it took us 4 or 5 times to go around that tree. We started at a chalk mark stretched finger tip to finger tip until we reached the original chalk mark.

I remember also, the migrant Indian fruit pickers who would come into town and sit on the side walk. They never blocked a business entrance or caused any trouble. When they bought any thing, including groceries, they would pay for each item and put it in their car or truck and go back for more until they had all they needed or ran out of money. The first soft ice cream I ever ate was there and still is the best and was served at the Siberian Cafe. It was whiter and smoother than "Dairy Queen or any of the others. The closest I've had since is in a "Truck Stop" on I-86 in New York.

If you looked west you could see beautiful Mount Hood in Her mantel of white. The green of the trees and the pure blue of the sky was a sight I will always remember. This was before pollution reared its ugly head. I hadn't been back since then until I started driving a semi coast to coast. I was going West on I-84 and saw a sign with an arrow pointing to Mount Hood. It was just a gray form on the sky line. I had looked forward to seeing her in her glory and was so disappointed I cried like a baby. How could we let this happen?

The ranch mentioned in the story is at the foot of the "Loops". I swam in the river there and fished for sturgeon and salmon. Unless you have taken your fish from the river to the oven you have never eaten good fish.

There is a lot of what I wanted to be in the story and my own philosophy about a lot of things. I have too many people to thank for their encouragement so in fear of leaving some one out I won't mention any names with one exception. I love you Maudie.

CHAPTER 1

It was a beautiful Saturday in April. His CPA had filed his returns earlier in the month and the business was doing very well. He felt glad that he could give his employees a bonus and pick up more of the tab for their insurance. The only thing clouding his life was his marriage. *It's a good day to bore holes in the sky,* he said to himself. *I'm going to fly over Mt. Hood and go to Troutdale for lunch.*

The antique Piper Cub, his father had given him as a high school graduation present, sat in the corner of a barn that had been converted to office and storage space for "Michael Murphy and Son Electrical Contractors." Mike had restored the Cub and had taken his first flying lessons in it. That seemed a long time ago.

Since his first lessons, he had been constantly upgrading his skills. After graduating from Oregon State, he was accepted by the US Navy for flight school at Pensacola, Florida. He had flown with the Blue Angels, was "Top Gun" and was checked out and certified to fly every aircraft the Navy had in its massive arsenal, including choppers. When the "Angels" were in Omaha doing an air show he managed to be certified for the US Air Force 747. It was said, "If it's supposed to fly, Murph can fly it."

His heart had been set on a career in the Navy with dreams of commanding a carrier, which came with the rank of admiral, but "Murph" senior had a mild heart attack and was forced to either sell the business or take on a partner--neither of which he was willing to do. While he was recovering, he and Mike discussed the options. Mike decided it was time to give back as much as he could to his dad for all the sacrifices he had made for him, like working on Saturdays and long days so he could watch Mike, Jr. play ball. Mike's wife, Agnes had been miserable while he was at sea so he had decided to come home and be his dad's partner.

When he told Murph Sr., what his decision was, tears welled up in his Dad's eyes and he said, "Son, I've been wishing you were a part of the business since the day you were born. When I bought you that old airplane, I watched your eyes light up whenever you talked flying. I knew in my heart that I could not compete with flying so I let my dream go. Please don't make the same mistake." "Dad," Mike had responded, "this is not a snap decision. I will miss the thrill of high-speed flight, but it is getting harder and harder to take the flack from Agnes when I've been deployed. I honestly believe she thinks the only reason I'm willing to get shot at is so that I can screw around with other women. I've had plenty of opportunities but have never been unfaithful to her. She is not convinced, so this will help quell some suspicions but it won't eliminate them. I have already turned in my resignation, so I will be on board in a week or two. There will be no debate--I have your Irish stubbornness as well as your temper."

He had then told his mother what he and Dad had discussed. When he told her he was resigning his commission, he could see the relief in her eyes, and the look only an adoring mother has for a child who has really pleased her.

Agnes was non-committal and only sneered, "The whores around the world will miss you."

CHAPTER 2

The Piper whined, stuttered, and purred into life. Once airborne, he climbed to 3000 feet and followed the Columbia River heading west for Troutdale. Mt. Hood was still snow-capped to the lower elevations and he could see the skiers maneuvering down the slope to Timber Line Lodge. As always, the waterfalls along the gorge were impressive.

He landed in Troutdale and was lost in thought over a cup of coffee when he overheard, "You drunk son-of-a-bitch. My granddaughter will die because you are too drunk to fly her to the hospital. I've put up with your bullshit as long as I'm going to. You are fired as of right now. We will mail you your check. If you ever again set foot on this place, you will be arrested for trespassing and anything else I can think of. I will report you to the proper authorities and see that your ticket (license) is lifted and you never fly again. Now you have a good reason to get drunk."

Mike walked over to the upset grandfather and asked if he could be of any help. The grandfather snapped, "Only if you can fly a Gulf Stream jet."

"Sir," Mike replied, "my name is Michael Murphy. I've been flying since I was seventeen. I am certified to fly anything, including 747s, so your Gulf Stream would be no problem. Let's quit talking and get your granddaughter to the hospital. Where is she now and where does she need to go?"

"Lizzie is in the plane with a nurse and we need to get her to the Galveston, Texas hospital as soon as possible," he answered. "She has a heart problem and is having a severe episode and needs a doctor. "The plane is fueled and ready."

"Then why are we standing here? Let's burn some holes in the sky."

Mike made the walk-around preflight inspection and noticed the name over the door, "Henderson Manufacturing". He paused to look at the child asleep under sedation, blonde curls and an innocent smile. He thought to himself, that if ever there was a model for an angel, she was the one. "Strap everyone in," he ordered. "We are heading to Galveston." The jets whined and roared to life. Mike asked the tower to hold all landings and departures. "We have a five-year old girl in a life and death situation and cannot afford any delays."

"No problem. What is your name?" the tower asked.

"Michael Murphy; this is Angel flight one. I had to leave my antique Piper on the tarmac. Would you please see to it 'til I get back?"

"Be happy to, Mike. Godspeed, we are all praying for your passenger. Let us know the outcome; the airport is yours."

The grandfather had strapped himself into the co-pilot's seat and was watching with interest as Mike eased the throttles to full speed and soon had the plane airborne and climbing to the assigned altitude. Mike then set his course for Galveston, 2400 miles and five hours away. The Gulf Stream had all the bells and whistles, so Mike set it on autopilot.

Grandpa cleared his throat and spoke, "I'm Walter Henderson and this jet is my toy. My only child, my daughter, was killed by a drunk driver; my granddaughter is all I have left of her. My wife is still in mourning and never leaves the house. I honestly believe that if anything happens to my granddaughter, Elizabeth, my wife, would give up and waste away. Maybe now you can understand how I felt when my former pilot was too drunk to fly. The thought of a drunk killing my daughter is hard enough, but to have a drunk responsible for Lizzie's death because he couldn't fly, was more than I could handle. You seem to know what to do in a crisis; would you like to be my pilot?"

"I can't think of anything I would rather do, but I have a company to run." He told Walt about being partners in a contracting business with his dad. "I'm just getting my feet wet in the business and it wouldn't be fair to Dad to jump ship."

"This is a beautiful bird and I would love to fly it anytime you really need a pilot. I will do my best to be available. When your little Angel is ready to come home, I would consider it an honor and pleasure to fly her home."

"Son!" Walt exclaimed, extending his hand. "You've got yourself a deal."

CHAPTER 3

Time and miles passed quickly and Galveston was soon on the horizon. Mike called air traffic control for instructions and was advised he had priority clearance and to follow Fed-Ex heavy plane and then follow the escort to the helipad where the chopper was waiting. The medics were fast and efficient and in a matter of seconds, Elizabeth was on her way to surgery.-"From here on, Walt," Mike remarked, "it's out of our hands and in the hands of the Almighty. Remember that we pray, 'Thy will be done', so we have to prepare for the worst, expect the best, and take what comes. I just remembered--I was having a quiet cup of coffee when you so rudely broke my chain of thought. The least you could do is buy me a replacement cup," Mike added jokingly.

"I guess you're right," Walt agreed, "but what do I owe you for your services?"

"You don't owe me a thing, Walt. The feeling I got seeing your little Angel in distress and knowing I had the ability and opportunity to help is worth more than money. I wish I could do more of this kind of flying."

"Mike", Walt said, "you have given me an idea. Hear me out, think it over, and then let me know what you think. You heard me say the jet is my toy and it is just that, a toy for me. I've got more money than I could use in five lifetimes. I need to give a lot away or Uncle Sam gets a bunch of it. I'm going to form a non-profit corporation called "Angel Flight." Its purpose is to transport children to the Shrine Hospitals. You will be the President and CEO. I will transfer title to the Gulf Stream to you after I have it refurbished to your specifications. I have enough people on hand to get us up and running quick, but it will take some time to work the kinks out. Think about it and feel free to make suggestions, especially in regard to the refurbishing and get back to me. Now, I'm going to see Lizzie; want to come along?"

In the cab, on the way to the hospital, Walt remarked, "With all the excitement and confusion at Troutdale it never occurred to me that you may be the son of an old faithful customer of mine. You are Michael Murphy, the contractor, aren't you?"

"Yes I am, and damn proud to say it."

"Your father changed my business practices years ago. I had written one of my biggest orders and gave him the contract for signing. He said if my handshake wasn't good enough to do business on, there was nothing left to say. He took out his checkbook, added up the order, including tax and wrote the check commenting; 'A contract only protects the crooks.' You may be sure we filled his order and shipped it the next day. He later told me that by shaking hands he could look the other party in the eye and see into their soul. If there is any wavering on their part that is the last time they are *received*, and I have discovered him to be right. We both have been stiffed a time or two, but the word gets around and the company or person involved goes broke. Earlier when I said, 'Son, you've got a deal', that was a contract."

"I feel the same way, Walt," Mike replied.

"When you get back to the office, may I send a sales associate to call on you and show you some new, state-of-the-art, electrical products? Since you are fairly new, there are probably a lot of changes in the industry you're not aware of and my associate can help bring you up to speed."

"Great idea, Walt. I can use all the help I can get."

CHAPTER 4

The hospital waiting room was close to the ICU and they could see, but not hear what was going on. The nurse that had accompanied them from Oregon was red-eyed and sobbing. Mike had noticed her eyes when they were taking off from Troutdale. She had a surgical mask on but her dark brown eyes could melt your heart, even with the redness they were still overpowering. Walt rushed to her to know the prognosis--fearing the worst. "Susan, please tell me the truth, don't leave anything out."

"Okay, but sit down and wait until you hear the whole story. I didn't want to tell you, but when we got into the chopper, we lost her. Then the young intern with us said, 'This little Angel loves Jesus more than she fears the Devil so I say to you Satan, get thee hence.' Almost immediately, she responded and the rest is history. Elizabeth is still in surgery but the doctors expect a full recovery with no long-lasting side effects. She will need to stay here for at least two weeks while they monitor her progress. We'll be able to see her in four or five hours but she won't be fully conscious and without sedation until Tuesday morning. There is nothing that we can do but wait for now."

Walt suggested they all check into a hotel, freshen up, have a quick dinner and figure out the next move in the morning.

"Sounds like a plan to me," said Susan.

"Good idea," Mike agreed. "I'll call my secretary at home to let her know where I am and the circumstances that brought me here, then I have to get a complete change of clothes and some shaving gear."

"I am so relieved Lizzie is in the doctor's care at last. We'll wait while you make your call and then we'll all go shopping, because it seems that we're all in the same boat," Walt commented.

The cab let them out in front of a downtown department store.

"Let's meet back here in an hour," Mike suggested, "that should give us plenty of time."

They went their separate ways and then met as planned; loaded down with packages, they were in front of the store waiting for a cab when three, tough-looking hoodlums challenged them with a gun. The street was deserted and the hoods thought they would be easy pickings.

Mike, standing 6 ft. 2 in., was broad-shouldered with a narrow waist and weighed in at a solid 215 pounds. Placing himself between the hoods and Susan and Walt, in a very calm voice said, "We have had a very long and stressful day; this is my dad and my wife. We just left the hospital where our little girl is having a heart transplant, so just put your gun away and we'll forget the whole thing."

"What if I don't?" the hood asked. "What are you going to do about it?"

"Please excuse the profanity, honey," Mike said to Susan. Turning to the hood, he said, "First I'm going to take the gun away from you. If it is candy, you will eat it, if it isn't I'll cover it with Vaseline and stick it up your ass and maybe pull the trigger. As for your two friends, if they are still here when I finish with you, I'll just break a leg or arm or maybe both, I haven't decided yet."

"What are you," the hood asked, "some kind of superman?" "No," Mike answered, "but I have earned four black belts in the martial arts."

"Don't try any of that jujitsu crap on me," the hood said defiantly. "I'm going to blow you and your old man away. Then we will have a party with the broad."

"That does it," Mike said softly. In one motion, he took the gun away and tossed it to Susan. She deftly caught it, and it was quite obvious she knew exactly what to do if the need arose. The other two hoods stood there in open-mouthed disbelief. Before they could run, Mike planted his number 11 hard-toed boot squarely in the jewels of one, came down hard with his doggie-heel and all of his 215 lbs. on the right instep of the other. He grabbed the gun-toter by the throat, squeezed until the hood's eyes were ready to pop out, released the pressure and asked, "Can you hear and understand me?"

The hood, gasping for breath, nodded his head "yes."

Mike said, "I never write a check I can't cash. When I told you what I was going to do, I meant it, and since the gun isn't candy, you know what comes next. I'll give you a minute to make your peace with God. Susan, honey, cock the gun and hand it to me please. Susan, you and Walt better go around the corner, this is going to be messy. Okay, mister tough guy, drop your drawers and spread your legs. I'm sorry I don't have any Vaseline, but it will only hurt for a second."

The hood cried and said he was sorry. His two friends were in no shape or position to help him. He was all alone and helpless. When Mike placed the cold hard steel muzzle of the gun against his anus, the hood screamed and fainted dead away.

Handing the gun to the cop who was watching in silent amusement and wonder, Mike said, "He wasn't so tough, was he?"

The cop asked, "Where did you learn those moves? They were so fast I could hardly see them."

"I took some training in boot camp at Parris Island, and the rest I just picked up in martial arts classes with some improvising." "Semper Fi, Mac," the cop said.

"Sorry officer, Navy pilot's survival training," Mike responded. "Do what needs to be done with this trash. Here is my business card. If you need any information, get in touch with me."

Susan and Walt came from around the corner. "What is that smell?" Walt asked.

The cop answered, "It seems Mr. Murphy literally scared the shit out of them because they all shit all over themselves. We will hose them down and they can ride in the back of a pick-up on their way to jail."

"Mike Murphy," the cop continued, "it was a pleasure to watch you work. I may use that gun-up-the-ass trick myself. Would you really have gone through with your threat?"

"If they had touched either of these two, I definitely would have, and without remorse. I know this to be a fact from a past experience, and that is all I will say. If there is reward money, put it in your police officers' relief fund. Good night officer."

The ride to the hotel was in total silence; each with their own thoughts about the events of the day and how fate had drawn them together. They still hadn't realized how much they needed each other, in ways yet to be discovered.

CHAPTER 5

The trio checked in and agreed to meet in the dining room in one hour. Mike let the hot water drain the stress and weariness from his body. After a shave and brushing his teeth, he changed into his new jeans and western-cut shirt. Looking at himself in the mirror and combing his hair, he was satisfied with the way he looked and went to meet Susan and Walt. Walt was already there, sipping coffee and reading the paper. He folded it as Mike joined him and said, "My boy, you put on quite an exhibition of self-defense today. I have read about such things and watched demonstrations but I have never seen it used in real life. Can you explain some about it so that an old fart like me can understand?"

"It's just like anything else you learn. You learn and practice, practice and learn, and practice until you react without thinking and the moves just happen naturally. I used the arts for exercise and to keep in shape. I also try to run a mile or two twice a week. While I am running, I'm also thinking. Since I am alone, there are no phone calls or other interruptions. I will think about your proposal when I run on Wednesday. Also, the Chief of Police in my hometown is my very best friend and we have an ongoing pistol shooting match. We shoot at his pistol range every Thursday at 10:30 a.m.; loser buys lunch. It's not a very exciting life, but it suits me and to fly your jet was just the tonic I needed."

Susan made her entrance a few minutes later. She wore a red silk, floor-length dress with a Mandarin collar. A slit up the side went just far enough to create interest but quit before revealing anything except her long, shapely legs. Her raven black hair reached her waist, with a simple black bow at the nape of her neck to hold it in place. Her flawless complexion, a golden tan color, was set off by deep brown eyes that could look into one's soul. Mike gasped at her beauty and was instantly aroused, a feeling he hadn't had in years. All eyes watched her as she seemed to float across the floor. The men admired her beauty. The women mostly felt jealousy; in full knowledge of the fact that she had it, they didn't, and there was no way they could ever have what she had.

They were almost through with dinner when the orchestra started playing soft, slow, romantic music. On the spur of the moment Mike asked Susan if she would like to dance.

"I haven't danced in years," she said, "but I would love to." After a shaky start, they found each other and danced the whole set. When they got back to the table Walt said, "You young folks make a handsome couple. Enjoy yourselves. I'm picking up the tab for dinner and rooms; as you said Mike, there will be no debate about it."

Mike and Susan danced as long as there was music and each dance was like neither had ever experienced before. Mike felt Susan snuggling closer as the night went on. When they had danced the last dance, Susan asked Mike if he would share some wine with her. "I use it on occasion to help me to get to sleep. After all the stress of the day, I definitely need it tonight."

When they got to her room, she excused herself and returned shortly with the wine. She had changed into a long lounging robe and poured the wine and took a seat on the couch. Mike sat directly across from her in the recliner. Their conversation covered subjects from politics to religion, business and sports. Mike poured another glass of wine for each of them and sat beside Susan on the couch. She seemed to be inviting him to be a little aggressive, without being obvious.

"Susan," Mike said, "I have never enjoyed dancing, but tonight I could not get my fill. You seemed to anticipate my every move and you are the most beautiful woman I have ever seen." He reached over, kissed her neck, and unintentionally put his hand on her knee. She opened up and Mike found home, warm and moist.

They continued their foreplay into the bedroom. Mike untied her sash and her gown dropped to the floor. There she stood as God made her—the only thing that dropped was the robe. The nipples on her perfect breasts stood out, waiting to be kissed; Mike obliged while she undressed him. Mike laid her gently on the bed, and they began to do what they both wanted. Susan moaned and groaned and Mike stopped to ask if she was okay.

"Mike, you are in places I didn't know I had. Please don't stop until you can't continue. Pay no attention to my moans—they are moans of ecstasy." Susan had several orgasms and they finished together. They lay in each other's arms for several minutes.

Susan broke the silence. "Mike, you said you called your secretary. Be honest with me, do you have a wife?"

"Yes, Susan, I am married. But do I have a wife? I don't think so. You are the only sexual experience I have ever had except for Agnes. When I felt the need or wanted to be romantic, she would ask, "Do you want to diddle?" I'll get up and get ready."

When she came back to bed she would spread her legs, then often she would imagine my back was a piano and proceed to play. I was constantly accused of being unfaithful but tonight was the first time I broke my vows. The reason I was at Troutdale was to figure out what to do about my marriage. After tonight, I could never go back. Now, tell me about yourself."

"My name is Susan Romaine. I fell in love, or so I thought, with a Cuban who charmed me with attention, gifts and promises of a good life. He was wealthy and seemed sincere in his intentions. We were married and sadly, it wasn't until I became pregnant with our second child that I realized he had only wanted the status of being a happily married family man, not at all that he had ever intended to carry out the promises of the good life he had made in the beginning. I truly believe he only wanted my body to shell out kids. I was a virtual prisoner, but he has connections clear up to Castro himself. His power is derived from drugs. All the drug dealers go through him. Some have tried to circumvent him but they are found with their throats cut. I escaped but had to leave my children behind. Many nights I cry myself to sleep over them. I have a doctor friend who tied my tubes without Ramon knowing it so I can't have children. We keep in touch and sometimes when Ramon is out of the country, he calls me and I can talk to the children. I went to work for Walt as a secretary. One day a customer came in and the sales people were not available, so I took over. He placed the largest order Walt had ever had. The customer called Walt and congratulated him on his new sales associate, so from then on I was in sales. He has been giving me more responsibility and I sit in on the board meetings. He often asks my opinion on a decision the board has to make and they listen. Sometimes it makes a difference and sometimes it doesn't, but the point is, they listen and respect my opinions. I was awarded a nursing degree from a Florida Extension Course I took while in Cuba. There are some parts of nursing I'm not qualified for, so I don't go there, but by and large, it works.

I had a wonderful evening, dancing and everything. When those hoods challenged us and said what they were going to do to me after they shot you and Walt, I was terrified. I have seen the results of a gang rape, and it is horrible. If the woman survives, she is emotionally scarred for life. If they kill her, they mutilate her in the worst way and often she is alive when this happens. I need you near me tonight. Would you please stay with me?"

"How can I refuse such an invitation? Of course, I'll stay, but I think I'll shower again. I seem to have worked up a sweat." The hot shower felt good. As he was about to lather up, a pair of hands started washing his back and legs. He took a washcloth and started washing her back and legs, first the outside, then the inside, then home. He turned to face her and they realized Mike was ready for action, so this time they dried each other. They climbed between the sheets and made love like it's supposed to be done—not like some horny kids, but gently and tenderly. Mike kissed her breasts, rolling the nipples with his tongue, and then slowly slid into her warm and waiting cavity.

CHAPTER 6

Mike woke at 6:00 a.m., slipped on his clothes, and quietly left. The phone in his room was ringing. "Good morning."

"Where have you been?" asked Walt.

"In the shower," Mike lied, "with the door closed steaming some of the stress out of my system. What's up?"

"Nothing in particular, I thought we might have coffee and plan the rest of our adventure. I know you have to get back and Susan should go to the office and keep things running. She has been a blessing to me since the first day she started working for me. I honestly believe without her I would be forced to retire because I can't run the shop by myself. She will be named Executive VP and CEO of Henderson Manufacturing at the next board meeting, which is May 15. This is to be a surprise, so don't breathe a word of it to her. Come on down when you are ready. Bye."

Mike put the phone back in its cradle and decided he'd better shower and shave because he normally started the day that way. He dressed quickly and was almost out the door when the phone rang again.

"Good morning, this is Mike."

"I was hoping it was you," Susan said. "I woke up and you weren't here; for the first time in years I am lonesome."

"I was sorry that I left like a thief in the night but something happened to me last night that I have to sort out. Walt called just as

I got to my room and is waiting for me to discuss plans for the rest of our adventure, as he called it, and I was just going to meet him."

"He called me too, that is what woke me up. I'll be down as soon as I get dressed. Bye."

They were on their second cup when Susan glided into the coffee shop. Her raven black hair in two braids with Turquoise beads on rawhide thongs tying them off, western-cut denim blouse over denim jeans. With her skin tone, she gave the appearance of a Native-American maiden you used to see in the Spring Maid linen ads--in a word, gorgeous.

"Susan," Walt said, "I've known you for ten years or more and I have never seen you as radiant or beautiful as you are this morning. What happened?"

"Last evening I thought I was about to be gang raped and mutilated. Then in the blink of an eye I held the gun and the hoods were out of commission, thanks to this man, who was a total stranger until yesterday morning. The things he has accomplished for us are miraculous. I have been reborn, thanks to him, and I am going to kiss him good morning." With that, she placed a sweetheart kiss full on the lips and said softly, "Thank you."

"I'll be staying here for a few days, at least long enough to speak to Lizzie. Mike has to get back to his business and Susan; you have a full plate at the office. I've called the airport and the jet is being serviced as I speak, so you can leave whenever you are ready. Mike, Susan said it all. You have been a blessing to us and I would like to call you friend."

"Walt," Mike interrupted, "you've called me son a time or two already, so I consider you more than a friend."

"Thank you Mike. Getting back to business, Susan will direct you to our hanger at Troutdale. Susan, make sure his Piper is properly serviced and fueled on our company account. When I am ready to come home, I'll call you Mike. If possible, I would like you to fly me back when Lizzie can come home. We will wait for you. You are Lizzie's angel and the only person that I would give that responsibility. You've not left yet and I miss you already. A *R.fames* handshake is not enough; a hug is better," he said as they hugged. "Be careful son," he said, as a tear formed. "I love you."

CHAPTER 7

As promised, the Gulf Stream was ready. Mike made his walk-around inspection while Susan secured their luggage. Climbing aboard, he invited her to sit in the co-pilot's seat. "This is a better view and we will be crossing over some incredible scenery. If you have never seen Mount Hood or Crater Lake from the air you are in for a real treat." The jet roared into life, and after the checklist was through, he taxied into line behind a 737. The 737 turned left onto the runway and after a little hesitation for final clearance, the airliner roared down the runway and into the air. Mike waited for a UPS freighter to land, turned left following the 737 and was airborne. The control tower turned him over to air-traffic control, saying, "Thanks for stopping and have a safe flight." Mike went into a climbing turn and set his course for Troutdale. After reaching altitude, he eased back on the throttle and set the autopilot.

He unfastened his seat belt, took a deep breath and said, "Susan, about last night. I apologize for the way I acted. I came into your room for a glass of wine, you were so beautiful, and sensuous I could not control my animal instincts. I'm not sure what I would have done if you had offered resistance. I'm going to blame the wine for your behavior because you are not the kind of woman who goes to bed with a stranger."

"Mike," Susan responded, "the wine had nothing to do with my misbehavior. You rescued me from a fate worse than death or maybe even death itself. You are my hero. All damsels in distress who are rescued fall in love with their knight in shining armor. I seduced you and I don't know what I would have done if you had refused to take the bait. Last night was the most incredible sex I have ever had; not that I have had a lot. At times, I get so lonely and am vulnerable. When I wake up, I'm still lonely, still vulnerable and thoroughly pissed off at myself for getting into the situation. After last night there can be no other but you."

"Susan, like you, I have never had sex so totally draining and wanting more, but at this time it can't be. We are not going to sneak around. I can never even try with Agnes again, and I'm not going looking for a one-night stand. If what we had is all we ever have, I will at last know what love is; thanks to you. It's too soon to tell whether I'm in love or in heat. When I know, you will know. You are a very special person, and should any one harm you, I will pull the trigger."

Susan oohed and aahed over Mt. Shasta, Lake Mead, the Hoover Dam, Crater Lake and Mt. Hood like a little girl watching Fourth of July fireworks.

Air traffic control called him several times to verify his flight plan, but when he explained this was a sightseeing mission, they let up.

"Troutdale just ahead, fasten yourself in," Mike ordered. He wasn't used to the Gulf Stream, so his classic touchdown was slightly harder than he liked. "Damn," he said under his breath, "I almost had it, maybe next time."

"What are you mumbling about?" Susan inquired.

"I normally touch down so soft you don't realize you are on the ground until you feel the bumps in the runway, but I'm not used to this bird yet. I have a feeling I will be flying her a lot in the future."

"That is our hangar to the left of Beaver Air," Susan directed. "Park in front of the office; the crew will take over from there."

Mike did as he was told. The two of them went into the office to settle up and Mike asked about his Piper.

"Yes sir, she is all set to go. The paint is dry," the mechanic said.

"Paint, what paint?" Mike demanded.

"The logo on the door. We were just following Mr. Henderson's orders," answered the mechanic.

Mike went outside with Susan at his heels. There on the door was an angel with the words "Angel Flight One."

"That looks like it belongs there, don't you think, Mike?" Susan commented.

"Yes it does," Mike replied, "that old fart is making it tough for me to say no to his proposal. What do you know about it, Susan?"

"Absolutely nothing," said Susan, "he has never mentioned anything except that I am to send a sales associate to an old account. She gasped, slapping her forehead. What a dummy I am! That old customer must be your father!"

"No, Susan. I am the new, old customer," Mike grinned. "Does that mean that you will be calling on me?"

"You can definitely count on that, Michael Murphy, and it will be strictly business, for two reasons; number one that is the way I operate--strictly business. I leave my personal life at home. Reason number two: Walt wants you to be successful. He loves you like the son he never had, plus you also will be buying more of our products and increasing our income so that we can give more to charity. Ten percent of our net goes to charity: He has never mentioned anything other than that, so what proposal are we talking about?"

"On the way to Galveston, he came up with an idea. He wants me to spec out modifications for refurbishing the Gulf Stream. He will form a company whose only mission is to transport children to Shrine hospitals and he wants me to be president and CEO. The Gulf Stream would be donated to the non-profit corporation called, are you ready for this? "Angel Flight". I would be chief pilot and recruit other pilots and corporations to donate time and equipment that would all be tax write-offs."

Susan was impressed and listened intently as Mike continued to describe the proposal and his experience.

"I can't describe the feeling I had inside when that little angel was lying there and I knew that I had the God-given talent and opportunity to help. I've just convinced myself to do it. I have to go,

Susan. Call on me early on a Thursday morning. I want to show you off to my friend the Police Chief, and stick him for two lunches."

"Remember what I said about business, I buy my own lunch. The loser of the shooting match can get the tip. Have a safe flight home. I'll see you a week from Thursday at 8:30am at your office." Giving him a kiss on the cheek, she walked back into the office of Beaver Air.

The ride home was uneventful and there was a nagging loneliness inside that he had never felt before. It was a race against darkness to get to his field and he made it with about a half hour to spare.

CHAPTER 8

Julie, the faithful secretary, had left the office for the day, and he didn't want to talk to Agnes, so he drove into town hoping to find his friend, Hawk Phillips, the Police Chief. He stopped at Mary's Good Time Café and the fates were smiling on him. There sat Hawk in his usual spot where he could see out and observe without being noticed. He waved at Mike and motioned for him to join him.

"Where have you been, old buddy? Your absence has been noted by quite a few folks, including myself."

Mike told him about Lizzie and Walt; not mentioning Susan. He went on to explain "Angel Flight."

"Have you been home yet, Mike?" "No, why do you ask?"

"There is something going on around here and it seems to be centered at your place," Hawk answered.

"Any ideas what it is? Agnes and I are about to split up. I haven't told her yet but I can't go on any longer like we have for the past fifteen years."

"I don't think it has anything to do with that, Mike. I think there are drugs involved in some way. Anhydrous ammonia is being stolen at an alarming rate. Drug stores and their warehouses are being broken into and the things stolen are mostly drugs like Sudafed. That points to a meth lab somewhere."

"You just gave me an idea. There's a base operator in Klamath Falls with a chopper that he calls "BOO", because it can be put it in a silent mode and it is almost totally silent. If we had that here

I could fly it and maybe we can see from the air what we can't see from the ground."

"I would deputize you so it would be legal. What do you say?" "Anything I can do to help stomp out drugs and their dealers and manufacturers I am more than willing to do," Mike replied. "Just don't schedule it for Thursdays. You set it up and we'll get it done," he said, as he dialed Julie on his cell phone. "Julie, I'm back in town and I need to talk to you. A lot has happened this past weekend, and some, if not all, is going to affect you. Do you have time to talk now or is it too late?"

"Michael, it is never too late to talk to you. I'll brew up some coffee. Why don't you pick up something to go on your way over?"

The waitress had just cut into one of Mary's world-class banana cream pies, so he bought the rest to go. Julie met him at the door in her pajamas and robe with her hair up in curlers.

"If I had known that you were coming courting, I'd have made myself more beautiful," she teased.

"Julie, you are always beautiful-sometimes more than others-but always beautiful," Mike answered.

"Flattery will get you everything. Come on in, the coffee should be done. Is that one of Mary's pies?"

"Yes, it is, and your favorite, banana cream." He followed her into the kitchen and put the pie on the table.

"Go on into the den and I'll bring the coffee and pie," Julie said. "Then you can tell me what is going to happen that I don't already know about."

Julie served the pie and coffee on her favorite informal plates; tan colored with large red apples and vines on the rims. "I just love using these," indicating the dishes, "they seem to bring calm and class to the party no matter how many guests you have. Oh my, this is gooood stuff," she said. "Since you brought so much I'm going to put the rest in the fridge and save it for later. Now I'm going to freshen our coffee and you start talking. You didn't come here at this hour for pie and coffee or for sex, so talk; starting at the beginning and don't stop until you get to the end."

"Julie, I'm so tired of being married and not having a wife. I decided Saturday morning I was going to leave Agnes." He continued on about the unexpected flight to Galveston with the little angel, Elizabeth, and Walt and his proposition about Angel Flight.

"Julie, I love flying but I've never had such a warm feeling about it until I saw this child who desperately needed help. At the time she needed it most I could and did step up to the plate, and hit the game winner. Walt wanted to pay me but I had already had my reward. Read Matthew 6:1,4, and that brings us up to date."

"I'm going to go ahead with Angel Flight, promoting you officially to executive secretary with a substantial raise. You already run this company, so you should be paid for it. I'm sorry that we, Dad and I, didn't realize this sooner."

Julie started to cry. "Oh don't Michael; I love you and your dad. I have always felt like you were the son I never had, and your dad is the dearest and sweetest man I have ever known. I probably would have worked for nothing, just to be around you two. What do you mean, being married and not having a wife?"

Mike explained as best he could about he and Agnes' marital problems.

"In plain English she did not like screwing," Julie blurted out, much to Mike's surprise at the language. "I thought she was a cold fish the first day I met her. What are you going to do? Is there another woman?"

"Julie, this is the honest truth, I have never lied to you and I never will, so listen to the whole story before you say anything. I had already decided I was going to leave Agnes before I left for Troutdale Saturday morning. I thought about trying to get my commission back but that would have left dad in a tough spot so that wasn't an option. Then Walt Henderson entered the picture and every thing changed. The attempted robbery at the house is hard to figure out. The nurse on the flight, who is also Henderson's secretary and sales manager, is the most beautiful woman I have ever seen. We checked into a hotel and freshened up for dinner and Julie, I had never cheated on Agnes, note the past tense, but when she invited me up for a glass of wine that is what I went for. But as it turned out, we seduced each other. I had never known such ecstasy. First, it was two horny people and after that, it was two lovers. I spent the night with her and slept like I hadn't in two years. I don't feel guilty; I feel I have been completely loved. The sessions lasted for almost an hour each."

"If they lasted that long it wasn't sex; it was complete love. You are going to marry her, aren't you? Not to make an honest woman of her but because you two are hopelessly and helplessly in love!"

"The thought of marriage never occurred to me. I don't know if she'd marry me if I asked."

"Michael, take it from me, all she is thinking about now is how soon you are going to propose. It seems you have already made up your mind, so get a lawyer and split. If you have no place to stay tonight, use my guest room. In fact, why go through hell any more? Move in here until things are finalized; I'm tired of cooking for one person. It would be nice to talk to someone instead of a cat for a change. I promise that I won't try to seduce you if you promise the same." That brought a laugh from them both.

"Julie, if we were closer in age I couldn't make that promise; not that you are too old. You are a beautiful woman and I don't think that I could keep up with you. I thank you for the invitation and I will take advantage of it for tonight at least. We will have to see how it plays out in the daylight."

They visited the night away and watched the late news. Julie showed Mike to his room, said good night and left Mike to ponder his next move.

Julie knocked on his door at 6am, "Coffee is done, and bacon is cooking. You have five minutes before I throw it to the dogs," she announced.

"I want my eggs basted easy," Mike replied.

"Fine, basted easy it is, but they may look scrambled."

Mike stumbled to the table, fastening his shirt and buckling his belt, he needed a shave, and his hair was still uncombed.

"You are a handsome dude this morning," Julie joked. "Supper will be at 6:30 whether you are here or not. I don't know of anyone ever, who looked their best first thing in the morning. The nice thing about real love is you see the other person from the inside out."

"That's what I was saying about you, Julie. You are beautiful from the inside, as well as on the outside. I'll be a little late today. I'm going to see the folks and break the news to them. I want them to hear it from me, not rumors and innuendos. Supper at 6:30 is just fine. I'll stop by my house and get some of my things and get settled in, at least temporarily."

CHAPTER 9

On the way to his parent's house, he was trying to form the words he wanted to say, but nothing seemed right. Oh well, he thought to himself, why not let it all hang out and then work from there?

He parked in front and Mom met him at the door with a big smile and motherly hug. "So good to see you son. Your Dad is out back getting some sun. He is doing quite well and the doctor said he could work a few hours a week now. He will probably ask if there is anything he can do. He is so tired of just sitting."

"As a matter of fact there probably is, but I have to talk to you two. I have some news for you, so let's join Dad."

"You go on out, it's time for his milk break. As I recall, you and he always had a regular milk break so I'll bring two glasses."

"Okay, Mom, and if you have any of your applesauce cookies left, bring a couple. I haven't had one in a long time."

"As a matter of fact, son, I just made a batch this morning, Dad's outside. Send him in if he would like a cookie." his Mom replied.

"Hi Pop, you're looking good-how do you feel?" Mike asked. "I feel great son, and I was about to ask you for a job."

"Well, Pop, I am going to have an opening for someone with your experience. It will be part-time at first, but will soon develop into full-time, and then we'll probably have to hire more help. I came over this morning to break some news; I want you to hear it from me first. As soon as Mom gets here I'll lay it all out for you."

"Sorry I took so long, that gossipy Mrs. Bird was on the phone, and you know how hard it is to get away from her. The cookies are still warm and I'll send some home with you. Now son, what is the news?" his Mom asked.

"I'm not going to beat around the bush," Mike said. "After a sleepless Friday night I flew to Troutdale to think things out. I've said this many times to myself, now I don't care who knows it. I'm tired of being married but not having a wife, so I have decided to leave Agnes. I had never been unfaithful to her but she was constantly accusing me of sleeping around. I've had plenty of opportunities but never took advantage of the situation."

"Michael, your father and I knew you have been unhappy with Agnes for sometime," his Mother said. "We have talked about it a lot and were worried you might do something stupid that you would regret for the rest of your life. You said you've thought it out and decided that divorce was the answer. If you are sure, you have our support. Whatever course you take, within reason, we will support."

"Okay son, now that we've settled that, what is this position you think I may be qualified for?" his Dad asked.

"You remember Walt Henderson?"

"Of course I do, is that old fart still around?"

"Yes, he is and still going strong." Mike related the story to his folks who hung on every word. He didn't mention Susan; he would leave that for later. "Dad, that is the kind of flying I want to be a part of. Up until now, my flying and training were intended to kill or destroy. If you could have seen Walt's granddaughter, an angel on earth, if there ever was one, you would understand."

"Your mother and I understand more than you know. The Lord put you two together for a purpose. You just said it--now you can help save lives instead of taking them. If you hadn't had that experience, you probably would have wasted your God-given talent of flying. Go for it son! How do I fit into the picture? I am so excited, just thinking of working again and to be a part of Henderson's plan. Mother! Get my clothes laid out; I have work to do! I feel twenty years younger!"

"Not so fast, Pop, we haven't even gotten started yet."

"Well, pick up the phone and call Walt, tell him that we are ready on this end and to get off his butt. No, on second thought, I'll call the old fart myself. What's his number?"

"He is not at his office. He's in Galveston at the Hilton or at the hospital," Mike said calmly, trying to settle his Dad."

"Both of those places have phones, don't they? I'll try the hospital first. Now get out of here and let me get some work done. Wow, I feel great!"

Mike followed his mom into the house. She was smiling and humming to herself. She stopped, turned to face Mike and gave him a motherly hug and kiss and said, "That was the best medicine that he could take. The doctor said he is as good as new, possibly even better because he now sees the doctor regularly and monitors his vitals. Don't worry about him working too many hours. He may be a little nutty, but he is a long way from stupid. Go tell Julie another wild Irishman will soon be driving her crazy again. By the way, how is Julie?"

"She is fine, Ma. I'm staying at her place until things are sorted out. Gotta go, thanks for the cookies, bye-bye."

Mike stopped near the crest of the hill overlooking his house. Agnes probably thought he wasn't home since he didn't buzz the house last night as he usually did, but she would be expecting him home soon. Hawk said there was something going on here so he walked to the crest of the hill behind some trees. He took his binoculars with him so he could get a good look at the situation before he barged in and gathered up his clothes and other personal gear. Being careful not to skyline himself, he picked a spot in the shade so the sun would not reflect off the lenses and give away his position. There were several strange cars and a Hummer in the driveway. Some men stood around like they were looking or waiting for someone. "By God, they have guns," he said to no one.

"They are sentries. I'd better cover my butt before I barge in there or I might get it shot off."

He walked back to where he had parked and drove to town to find Hawk. It would be lunchtime when he got to Mary's Café; that would be the likeliest place to find him. Hawk had more or less a regular routine, but he made certain he was at Mary's at noon. That way if anybody needed to see him they would know where to find him.

Sure enough, his patrol car was parked at the curb, and he could see Hawk talking to someone inside. He and Hawk had worked out a simple sign for "don't come near." Mike would wait until Hawk saw him, if Hawk brushed his hair back, that was a brush off, it meant, stay away. Mike walked in and as in most small-town cafes, people looked to see who came in. Hawk brushed his hair back and looked at his watch. That meant, "Go to my office after you eat lunch." Mike took a stool at the counter and joined in the conversation. He was still full of his Mom's cookies so he just had coffee.

The customer on his left was a young man in his early 20's, talkative and interesting. Mike focused most, but not all of his attention on him. The one on the right was short and swarthy with a moustache and Latino accent, but spoke perfect English. When he left, Mike saw a bulge in his waist in the back. He caught Hawk's eye, and shaping his hand like a gun, put his hand behind him to indicate where the Latino had his gun and nodded in the man's direction. Hawk acknowledged the sign, brushed his hair back and continued his conversation. Mike paid for his coffee and went to wait for Hawk.

Hawk's real name was Warren. He earned the nickname "Hawkeye" at an early age because of his uncanny ability to spot deer or grouse or anything else young boys hunt long before anyone else. It was shortened to Hawk later. His father was Yakima and his mother was Shoshone. Hawk was proud of his heritage. His parents were migrant fruit pickers, traveling from crop to crop; cherries, peaches and apples as they ripened. When they got paid and went to the grocery store, his mother would pay for each item individually because she, like most of her peers, had no idea how to add. Of course, some unscrupulous merchants had taken advantage of them.

A rancher's wife noticed a grocer taking advantage of Hawk's mother. She took his mother and the groceries to the manager and said, "These people shop in your store once a year. We ranchers shop here year round, but if you are going to take advantage of these people because they aren't educated we will take our trade elsewhere and let folks in town know what kind of a son-of- a-bitch you are. The choice is yours."

The grocer blanched, gulped and asked what he could do to make amends. "I'll even give her the groceries," he offered."

"That would be an insult," she said. "These are proud people, poor but proud. They work for what they have and don't want charity. It's damn time you paleface bastards quit screwing them and I will start as a committee of one to see that it stops here and now. My mother is an Aztec from Mexico City and my father is Amish or as you people call them, Pennsylvania Dutch. You will treat these people with dignity and respect and charge them the same price you charge me including items on sale and a small sack of candy for the children--on the house of course--would be nice. "Madam, I think that is more than fair and I thank you for pointing out my short-sightedness. You have my word there will be no more of that kind of treatment." A sizable crowd had gathered including employees. The grocer got on the PA and announced, "if anyone does not understand the new policy that started ten minutes ago, I will be more than happy to explain it to you. If you continue to take advantage of people, any people and it is brought to my attention, you will be fired on the spot and given ten minutes to clean out your locker. If there are no questions, let's go to work." Turning to the rancher's wife, he offered his hand and asked her name.

"Gronberg, Rosalie Gronberg. Mr Otis, thank you. I didn't like the idea of driving 20 miles to buy groceries, but I would have. That's how strongly I feel about the way Indians have been treated."

Hawk's mother and Mrs. Gronberg bonded that day, and Rosalie taught her to read and basic math. Mother decided her son was not going to be a cherry picker. She asked Rosalie if Hawk could work for them, go to school and save enough money for college. They hired Hawk and later said they would like to have more hands like him. He was always on the job doing more than was asked, volunteered for all the dirty jobs, and never complained. At the same time he received A's and B's in school as well as earning varsity letters in wrestling and track. Instead of college, he enlisted in the U.S. Marine Corps and trained in Police Work. He came out as a sergeant, came home and joined the Police Force, and went to the Academy--graduating with high honors. A very proud mother and father sat in front beside a proud Gronberg couple. Hawk wore his hair long and sometimes in braids, as a sign of pride in his heritage.

"Did you pick up my sign on that Latino with the gun?" Mike asked as Hawk came in the door.

"Yes, I did. You make a pretty good Injun the way you spot things and pass signs," Hawk answered. "The car he is driving is a rental car from Troutdale. They are checking the name on the credit card."

Mike reported what he had seen at his house. "I want to get some of my things out of there, but I don't want to go barging in unannounced. Any suggestions?"

"How about this? Mike, if you are serious about divorcing Agnes, get your lawyer to draw up the papers. Then, you go over to Klamath Falls and check out the chopper. Before you leave make a list of everything you want now, like clothes, shaving gear and golf clubs. Have your lawyer put it into legalese. I'll call Agnes and tell her you have filed for divorce and I am to serve the papers and pick up your personal things. I'll ask her to set the time; that way any thugs that are at the house can get out of sight. I suggest you go to the bank and cover your ass so she doesn't write a lot of checks and break you."

"Brilliant, Hawk," Mike said, "for a 'dumb injun' you can come up with good plans. I'll cut her a check for five grand; you tell her that's it until the divorce is final. We can let the lawyers work out alimony and property settlement. While you're there, hook onto my boat and take it to your place. We might get some fishing in this year. We are still going to shoot Thursday aren't we?"

"Absolutely, I'm not going to let a bunch of drug-heads stop me from beating you out of lunch. Speaking of the drug situation, if that chopper is as silent as the man says, we could use one of those fancy night vision cameras and get pictures of the night traffic. There is a lot of traffic up there at night. They don't stay long, almost like at a whorehouse. But from what you tell me, Agnes DON'T like screwing and I don't think she would consider being a Madam, so the next conclusion is drugs. Get out of here and get your divorce started. Don't forget to go to the bank before you leave. Take off, and don't use your Piper; just sneak out of town. Give me Aggie's check and go. Call if you run into a snag and I'll see you Thursday morning at 10:30."

Mike passed Mary's on his way to the bank. He noticed a "Hummer" at the curb so he swung around and parked on the opposite side of the street. By now, Mom's cookies had been about digested and he was hungry. He took a booth at the back so he could observe without being obvious. Mike had been in town only a few weeks, so the chance of someone calling out his name was pretty remote. The first thing that caught his eye was the big table in the center of the room. There were four or five unshaven and generally unkempt men and one woman. The only thing that indicated she was female was her large breasts and deep cleavage. She had a man's voice, a man's biceps and a man's manners. They were careful about what they talked about, but he did hear her say they had to increase production because Ramon had recruited more mules for East coast delivery and wanted things buttoned up before he went back to Cuba.

Mike had finished his burger and fries and was sipping coffee when Hawk came in. Hoping Hawk would catch the sign; he brushed his hair back and sat down at his regular spot. The five or six at the big table got up and left, giving the Police Chief a good once over. They knew who he was, but not what he knew about them. After the quintet was gone, Hawk motioned for Mike to join him.

"Did you pick up anything?" Hawk asked.

Mike related what he had heard and said, "You were out of earshot. Who was your lunch partner?"

"Undercover Fed, Mike. This drug thing is not a small operation, its part of a cartel that goes to Cuba and disappears. They have high-powered clout, but that's all we know at this point."

"Hawk," Mike said, "let's put our surviellance on hold. I met someone in Galveston who may be able to put a floodlight on the cartel. That's all I can say right now, but trust me on this. I've got to go, see you Thursday."

Mike stopped at the bank and closed his personal account and opened a new one. There were law offices on the second floor and he was soon sitting across from Ross Dillon, Attorney at Law. He explained what he wanted and asked if he could get the necessary papers to the Police Chief so he and the Sheriff could serve Agnes before Thursday.

"It is unusual but can be done," Ross stated.

Mike cut him a $500 retainer check and left to call Julie about his unexpected trip. Don't hold supper for me, I won't be back until- hell, I don't know. Get set though-Pops is coming to work and he is as excited as a stud in a pasture full of mares in season."

"He's already here and you are right," Julie reported. "I don't know what may be going on, but you be careful. Love you, bye."

He called Susan and asked if he could pick her up Wednesday afternoon. "I think you can fill the Police Chief in on a problem we have here and at the same time, help you out with a problem you have. That's all I can say at the time except that it's important."

"Of course I can," Susan answered. "I'll pack some traveling clothes and we may be able to get to the airport and wait at Beaver Air. Can you give me an ETA?"

"Not at this time, but if things work out, I'll be flying a chopper and can pick you up in your company parking lot."

In his Piper, it wouldn't take very long to get to Klamath Falls, but with his old truck it would take several hours. He called Hawk and told him he was going to leave his truck at the truckstop and have Julie come and get him. "You can have one of your deputies find it and drive it out to the office and start looking for me. When I call Julie, I'm going to have her get the Piper ready like normal, leave it in the shed idling, but clear. When she gets back to the office, she will call everybody in and tell them to be on the lookout for anything suspicious and report it to you. I'll be flying in the back covered up so nobody can see me. When they are all inside, I'll sneak out and "steal" the Cub. That will creat some diversion. When you show up with the truck and serve the divorce papers, Agnes will think I"ve run off with another woman. Do you see any obvious holes in my plan?"

"No but how about our shoot-out Thursday-it's still on isn't it?" "Of course. I"m not going to let a drug dealer beat me out of a chance to get lunch at the expense of some redskin. I"ll hide the Cub at Klamath Falls, show up Wednesday with the chopper and be totally surprised and pissed off that some bastard would steal her. I'll file a report with you and do everything I can to make it look real. Gotta call Julie. Bye."

Julie picked Mike up as a hitchhiker down the road away from prying eyes. "Your Pop is as happy as I've ever seen him," she commented. "What will I tell him about this caper?"

"He can be as closed mouth as anyone I've ever known," Mike said. "Tell him all you know and not to worry. But make it clear he is to tell nobody, including Mom.

"Office coming up-get down and cover up. Where do you want me to park?"

"In your normal place, nothing should be out of the ordinary. Call all the help into your office and tell them what I told you to say. After I get in the Cub, I'll idle to the door then punch it. At that point, you can give them hell about leaving a fully fueled aircraft unattended. I'll straighten it out Thursday; in the meantime find some place for Susan to bunk for a day or two."

"What's wrong with sleeping with you? It's not like it's the first time, or strangers to each other. Just don't make a lot of noise while you are not sleeping," Julie stated.

"If that's okay with you it's more than alright with me," Mike answered, "and I don't think Susan would mind. Thank you Julie."

Be careful" she whispered, as she shut the car door. Mike heard the bell ring to call all hands in. When he was certain the coast was clear, he took a quick peek and ran to the shed about twenty yards away. Once inside, he saw that the fuel gauge on the Cub registered full. Then he made his walk-around visual inspection. With everything okay, he pulled the chocks, climbed aboard, strapped himself in and eased the throttle forward to taxi. As soon as he cleared the doors of the shed he gave full throttle and went roaring down the strip and into the air. Making a climbing bank and turn, he looked back at the office and saw the whole crew staring after him in disbelief. He thought he saw Julie in the background giving him the thumbs up, but at this distance he couldn't be sure.

CHAPTER 10

The flying time to Klamath Falls was a little less than two hours. By the time he got checked out in the chopper, it was obvious it would be dark when he got to Portland. He radioed Troutdale from the chopper and had them patch him through to Susan.

"I'm running behind schedule. Could you meet me at Beaver Air? I'm about an hour out."

"Beaver Air it is," Susan answered. "See you soon."

He set the chopper down in front of the office and went inside. Susan wore the same jeans and shirt she wore on their trip from Galveston, with the addition of custom-made boots with high "doggin'" heels, long dangling turquoise earrings, and a turquoise trimmed, buckskin headband. She was surprised at seeing Mike.

"I never heard the chopper," she remarked.

"I guess the silent mode works," Mike grinned. "Susan, I've decided to go with Walt's plan so while I'm here I'll talk about refurbishing the Gulf Stream, if he wants to go ahead with the project."

"He definitely wants to go. In fact, when I called him and told him I was meeting with you he said, 'Get that stubborn Irishman off dead center and let's get moving. It's too important to delay any longer.' He has a blank check to get you started and I mean a *blank* check!"

Turning to the clerk, Mike asked who he should talk to about refurbishing the Henderson jet. The clerk became very alert and said, "That would be Mr. Jenson. He is not here at the moment, but for a client like Mr. Henderson, he wants to be called. If you will excuse me I'll call him.

Mike looked at Susan and said, "You are so beautiful you take my breath away, I've got some things to tell you later. I can't believe how much has changed in less than a week."

"Mr. Jensen is on his way, which will take about thirty minutes," the clerk said. "If you folks are hungry, I suggest the dining room at the terminal. You are to use our car and he will meet you there."

"That sounds like a plan to me," Susan said. "I'm starved." "Me too," Mike echoed. "Let's go."

They were halfway through dinner when Mr. Jensen arrived. "You must be the Henderson party" he said. "Robert, the clerk, said I should look for a beautiful Indian and you were easy to find. Now what can I do for you?"

"Mr. Henderson wants his jet converted to a Medivac-type aircraft with all the latest equipment. We want everything necessary, but nothing extra. Besides the patient there will be a nurse, one or two parents, and the flight crew. We want the latest and fastest jet engines, Mr. Rolls and Mr. Royce make installed and fuel capacity to go 3-4000 miles. We will have the hospital help you pick the proper equipment, but, I repeat, nothing extra to run up the bill. This whole thing and probably more aircraft, will be non- profit. In fact, the patient and parents are guests of Angel Flight. I almost forgot, a little blonde, curly-haired 5-year-old angel will be our logo, so put them wherever you see fit. The aircraft colors will be sky blue and cloud white. The decor is up to you. Have I missed anything?"

"I believe you have covered it all sir. What is your name?" Mr. Jensen asked.

"Michael Murphy," Mike replied.

Jensen looked closely at Mike with a faint smile and asked, "Were you top gun and fly with the Angels?"

"Guilty," Mike said. How did you know?"

"I was a crew chief on the Angel missions and your skills are legendary. Is this your wife?" he continued.

Without thinking, Mike responded, "I haven't asked her yet." Turning to Susan, he said, "How about it, Susan Romaine, will you marry me?"

"I thought you were never going to ask. Yes, I will."

Mike turned back to Jensen and said, "Thanks for the nudge. That wasn't very romantic but it was sincere. I really love this lady."

Susan said, "Let's get back to business before I cry."

Jensen said, "Since this is going to be an ongoing charitable project, we will donate the labor and furnish all parts at cost. Mike Murphy, Miss Romaine, it's a pleasure meeting you. I've got to go and hear my little angel's prayers."

"It's been a long day Susan, and I don't feel like flying back tonight. Let's find a hotel and get an early start in the morning." Mike said.

"Paleface Brave make plenty smart talk. Let's find teepee and sleep." Susan joked.

Mike called the Holiday Inn shuttle bus to come pick them up. He registered as, Mike and Susan Murphy. "Might just as well get used to it," he said. "We will be using it a lot."

The steamy hot shower took all the stress of the day, and to have a woman who really loved him by his side, made Mike realize just how happy a man could be. "Susan, I love you more than a man has a right to love a woman, but I can't help it."

That started the tears from Susan, "Oh Mike, you big dumb Irishman."

Susan sobbed, "I've been in love with you ever since you stood between me and those hoods. I think love is how you feel about yourself when you are with the other person. When I'm with you I feel safe and warm inside because you love me. I can be bitchy or loving and it won't make any difference to you. In other words, I can be me 24/7."

"Susan," Mike responded, "I didn't realize that I was in love with you until you weren't with me. I felt empty and alone even though I had a house to go to. I said house, not home - there is a world of difference in the two. Yes, our first encounter was two people desperately seeking love and ending with a wild sexual encounter. I realized then that I could never go back to life the way it had been, I never even went to the house. Our secretary let me use her guest room and I told her all about you. Today I told my parents about divorcing Agnes and they weren't surprised. I told my best friend Hawk Bear Claw, and got things started, so here we are stuck with each other. It's only fair to warn you, if you haven't already figured it out, I'm a terrible flirt. But it never goes farther than that, with one beautiful exception."

"I think we flirted with each other" Susan answered, "and it worked out beautifully. Two lonely people found each other after years, and in my case tears, of searching. I love you Michael Murphy."

The way she expressed herself was so eloquent, and to Mike it was music to his ears. He had never heard love expressed so sincerely to him before. With those thoughts in their minds they drifted into a deep relaxed sleep.

Mike woke up first and dressed. Since he had not intended to stay overnight, he didn't have his shaving gear, toothbrush or comb. He brushed his hair back the best that he could. "I don't like what I see, but I can't do anything about it," he said to himself. He looked down on the sleeping Susan, realizing he had never felt this way about a woman. This was not just love. He wanted to hold her in his arms and protect her. If anyone harmed her in any way he would definitely pull the trigger and hope it was a military 45.

Susan stirred and propped herself up on an elbow. Looking at Mike with love in her eyes she said, "It isn't about sex is it." It was not a question it was a statement. "We must really be in love, not in heat."

"Susan, I haven't shaved, burshed my teeth, or combed my hair. This is the way I look every morning, so if you want to back out now I will understand. You, on the other hand, are beautiful even now, beauty comes from the inside out."

"Shut up you big dummy, and kiss me good morning. I promise now to love you for better or for worse. When the time comes I will say it in public and in church with my children watching. Where are we going to have breakfast?"

"We can have breakfast with Hawk, if we get going. He is one of the first people I want you to meet. We'll drop in at the office and you will meet Julie and Dad, then we'll take somebody's car to Mary's for breakfast, so get your cute butt in gear."

It was a 45-minute trip to the office. Mike didn't use the silent mode. He wanted people to notice the chopper. They got in about 7:45.

Julie was just getting out of her car; Murph Senior was already there. "Hello, Son," he said, "this must be the lady you hinted about."

"Dad, Julie, this is Susan Romaine; Walt Henderson's chief of everything. She is going to bring us up to date on the latest equipment and materials we use or will use should the need arise. We haven't eaten yet so can we borrow a car or truck to meet Hawk? We have some things to discuss and I'll explain the chopper and everything else when we get back."

"Take my car Son, and remember what I said when you first started driving."

"I know Pop, don't scratch the paint," Mike laughed.

"It has been a pleasure meeting you both," Susan remarked. "I'll see you later." She gave Julie a hug and kissed Murph Senior on the cheek.

Hawk was starting on his second cup of coffee when they arrived at Mary's. He was alone so they joined him. "You have to be Susan," Hawk commented, getting a good look at her. "I don't mean to stare, but you are very attractive. Don't look now, but every eye in the place is on you. Mike did his best to describe you and he knows some fancy words, but I was not prepared for what I see."

"Thank you, but you are being too kind," Susan responded. "We came for breakfast and I am hungry."

"Okay Hawk," Mike asked, "fill us in on the latest. I've got the chopper and that silent mode really works. I didn't use it coming in so it wouldn't tip any one off."

"I served the divorce papers late yesterday," Hawk reported. "She wasn't surprised, but she is definitely pissed off about the money. She wanted to know how you expected her to survive on such a paltry amount. She is figuring on taking you to court and breaking you, so watch your step. Now why did we put off surveillance? Does Susan have anything to do with it?"

"Yes she does," Mike answered. Turning to Susan he said, "Honey, I have reason to believe your ex-husband is around here working on some kind of drug deal. I probably should have told you earlier but I didn't. I'm sorry if you are uncomfortable with the situation, but you will be both protected by me and the chief."

"I'm not the least bit apprehensive," Susan replied. "I've seen you in action and I have a move or two of my own. What makes you think he is here?"

"I was going to ask the same thing," Hawk chimed in, "and what was the 'action' Susan was referring to?"

"When I was in here yesterday I heard the group at the round table talk about Ramon and what he is trying to set up. He has to hurry and get back to Cuba before the Feds find him. Susan told me her ex is a major player in drugs and his clout goes clear to the top in Cuba's politics, so I added up and think I have it figured correctly," Mike related.

"Just how do I fit in the picture?" Susan asked.

"We are going to get in the noisy chopper this early afternoon and head for Mt. Hood. Before we get there we will change course and come in over the river silently. We want you to use binoculars and see if you can identify anybody on the ground. We will be pretty high but with the high-resolution glasses you can read the paper from several thousand feet. If it is your ex we need to know. Susan, you mentioned a doctor you are in contact with in Cuba puts you in touch with your children. If your ex is here, we could use Walt's jet and get them out while Ramon is still here. Do you think the doctor will cooperate?"

"If you can accomplish that, Michael Murphy, you are stuck with me forever," Susan said. "You are my knight in blue jeans and cowboy boots. The action I was referring to, Hawk, happened in Galveston. Three thugs stopped us; one had a gun. Mike asked them to put the gun away and we would forget the whole thing. The one with the gun asked what would happen if he didn't put the gun away. Mike said, 'first I'll take the gun away from you and if your friends are still around disable them. Then if the gun is chocolate you will eat it; if it isn't I will stick it up your ass and pull the trigger.' Hawk, he did just that except pull the trigger; it was so quick you wouldn't believe it."

"What time do you want to go flying, Hawk?" Mike asked. "How about 2:30? That will give them time for lunch and to go about their business. Susan if it is your ex you may be in considerable danger. You are going to stand out like a glowing cigarette in the dark so be very careful."

Thank you for your concern and I will heed your advice," Susan answered. "I have an idea and a plan that I can test on you two and if it works, I will be fine, if not plan B goes into play. The pass code is, 'Angel One is Lizzy'. The correct response to affirm the plan must be 'Heaven'.

"We had a lot of excitement around here yesterday, Mike," the Chief spoke. "One of my officers found your pickup at the truck stop. Nobody seemed to know anything about it. We dusted it for prints but couldn't come up with anything so we put it in the impound lot where you can claim it. Also somebody took off, pardon the pun, with your pride and joy."

"You mean my Cub?" Mike querried. "Just how in the hell did that happen?"

"Your crew was getting it checked out in case you needed it," Hawk answered. "Julie called them in for a safety meeting and while they were all inside somebody got into her and fled the scene. The perpetrator must have been familiar with your place and knew just when to act. I don't think it was a coincidence, but we will find both the bird and perp you can be sure of that. I've got to patrol my city. I'll see you at 2:30. Susan, it has been a delight putting my feet under the same table as yours. If you see, hear, or need anything and Mike is not around, you call me. You will have the entire police force at your beck and call."

Mike and Susan went back to the office. Mike had bought a mixed box of Mary's rolls and donuts so they could have an impromptu introduction. Susan called Walt to tell him Mike was on board and the jet was being prepared.

Walt told Susan to stay where she was and get things up and running ASAP. He had visited Lizzie earlier and she was doing fine but would have to be hospitalized for several weeks.

"You stay right where you are. I'll take a commercial flight home and try to keep Henderson Manufacturing running. Tell Mike to get started on his new airport, because when the Gulf Stream is ready I want it there in Portland. Tell Mike, hello, and when you see Murph Sr. tell him hello from me too."

"Murph Sr. is here now; do you want to speak to him?"

"Yes I do. Put him on. Hello Mike. You have raised a fine young man and I congratulate you and your wife for the great job you've done. I unintentionally called him son a time or two, and he didn't object. I liked the way it fit, so I have more or less unofficially adopted him. I hope you don't mind."

"Walter," Mike Sr. said, "raising him was the easiest job I've ever had. Giving him to the Navy was the hardest. I'm back at work full time now and have never felt better. I'm going to run the electronics business and Michael will run Angel Flight from here until we get something better. Your Miss Romaine is quite a woman and knows her stuff. When you get a chance, come on over and bring your wife; we have plenty of room for you. I'll never forget our first encounter."

"Nor will I Murph," Walt interrupted. "You gave me a lesson I've never forgotten and it has served me well for many years. I never thanked you for it, so all I can say now is thanks. My wife and I will be calling on you in the near future; I would like you to use your clout with the necessary people, so we can build a 5500 to 6000 ft runway capable of handling a corporate jet. I want it first class, with an auxiliary generator in case a storm takes power lines down. We will be flying life-saving missions and have to be able to land. Blizzards are things we can't do anything about, but there is no excuse for not having lights. I'm sorry if I sounded like I was running things and stepping on toes. That's not my intention. This project is very important to me, so if I sound impatient please forgive me."

"Walter I've known you too long to take offense with anything you say," Mike Sr. remarked, "we will do all things possible and some impossible things to get this dream of yours running. So good talking to you. Bye."

"Julie", Mike Sr. called, "Miss Romaine will be moving her office here, so let's find her a desk, a chair and a phone so she will at least have a work station. Call that young carpenter that served in the Marine Corps and get him started building an office for her. I also need the name of the dirt mover and concrete man we use. They have always done quality work at a fair price so I see no need to ask for bids. Besides we are already late with the project. Boy, do I feel gooooood."

Julie and Susan were getting acquainted in Julie's office when Mike came in. "Are you two plotting against me?" he joked.

"No" Julie answered, "I was just telling her that I know all about Galveston. At the time, I had misgivings about it, but now that I've met her and looked into her eyes, I see she is completely nuts about you. I also told her you two could shack up at my place, but please do be quiet when you're not sleeping. We will fix up an office for her this afternoon."

"Julie," Mike said, "With Susan running Henderson Manufacturing, and helping me with Angel Flight, she needs a bigger office. Why not move her into my office? I'm seldom there anyway, and when this thing kicks into gear, I'll be around even less. We will have ample office space in the new terminal building, so if we can manage for a while under those conditions, we'll be fine."

"I've got no objections," Julie said. "How about you Susan?"

"None, I just don't want Julie to think she is playing second fiddle. I've been here less than eight hours, and already I'm putting someone out of an office and you all seem to be catering to me. I want to be part of a team effort, not the coach or general manager."

Hawk came in, "I brought your pickup out, you owe the city a $45 towing and a $35 impound fee. I'll take the check back with me. I think it's time to *aviate*."

Julie cut the check and handed it to Hawk. "Thank you Chief, for your quick response. Michael, it wasn't fifteen minutes after I called about your airplane that he came skidding in here."

"Just doing my job Ma'am, just doing my job," Hawk teased. Hawk and Susan got into the observation seats and Mike was, of course, the "driver." As planned, he made as much noise and dust as possible on lift-off. Mike set a course toward Mt. Hood but planned to divert long before the noise and downdraft from the chopper could cause an avalanche. Switching to silent mode, he headed for Hood River and then headed east climbing to 10,000 ft. Susan checked out the binoculars exclaiming, "I can read the license plates from up here. In fact you can see a lot of things from up here."

Mike gave Susan some landmarks for reference points so she would know where to look. "We'll make this pass just for fun and practice, then I"ll drop to 5,000 ft. If there is any activity, we will come back slow and noisy at 1,500 ft. That should get their curiosity and cause them to look up. Tell us if you spot Ramon. We are also taking pictures so I hope they are all smiling," Mike laughed.

"Oh my God," Susan cried," there's that Cuban bastard, the one in the hat and light suit, standing by the Hummer. I don't recognize anyone else. That broad he is talking to looks like she could bite spikes in two. She's got big tits and Ramon loves big tits. My guess is he is trying to get between her legs by promising her a cut of the business or a dealership; that's the way he operates. He has a hair trigger and an explosive temper, so if she doesn't come across he is apt to shoot her."

"Okay," Mike said. "Now we get down and dirty." He dropped to 1,500 ft., made a 180 degree turn, canceled the silent mode, cranked up the noise, and made a low, slow, noisy pass over his house. As expected, they all looked up, and some even waved.

Hawk laughed and commented, "We got quality pictures. We'll send them all an 8 by 10 matte finish photo to hang on their cell walls. Let's get out of here."

Mike climbed to 10,000 ft. and headed for Hood River. He engaged the silent mode, and retracing his earlier route, headed for the office. "Since you drove my pickup home, I'll drop you off at your office. See you in the morning at 10:30 for the shooting match."

"Mike," Susan questioned, "can you take me home after the shoot out? There are some things I need that I don't have, and I do want my car. This whole thing developed so quickly it caught me off guard. I only brought enough clothing for a week or so, but since Walt wants me here, I've got to move everything here. Don't expect me before Tuesday. I've got a lot of stuff to do."

"That's okay." Mike answered, "I would prefer you were not in the area until we get a rope on your ex. We'll leave right after lunch."

It was about closing time when they got back. Julie reminded them, "Supper will be at 6:30. Don't be late."

Mike Sr. was still at work so they went in to talk. "Mr. Murphy," Susan started.

"Whoa, stop right there, Susan. Yes, I am Mr. Murphy, but from what I gather from my son, and the very short time you and I have spent together, you are to be my daughter-in-law. I will be proud to have you carry the name Murphy, so call me Pops or Dad, but not Mr. Murphy, please. That will lessen the confusion when you call "Mike", okay? I've talked to my wife and she is very anxious to meet you. If you can come by later this evening, I can promise you the best applesauce cookies you have ever eaten."

"Okay, Pops it is... We will be over this evening. I can't remember the last time I've had an applesauce cookie. We have to go now. We both need to shower and change clothes. We'll see you later." Parting with a hug and a loving kiss, she took Mike by the hand and left.

In the truck she broke down and cried. "Oh Mike, I have never felt so loved by so many people in my life. I had never met any of them before today and they act as though they have known me all my life."

"That's just the way it is here. We are friendly folks. You could knock at any door, asking for help and be welcomed. They would give you all the help they could and then call someone else when they ran out of resources. They would never expect anything in return. Their reward is the good feeling inside."

"Michael, I can hardly wait to be a part of this town," Susan sniffed.

Mike helped Susan get her suitcases out of the truck and into what was to be their room for a while. While Mike was cleaning up, Susan was helping Julie with the last-minute details of supper. The two were having a very serious, secretive conversation when Mike came into the kitchen. Julie smiled at Susan and gave Mike a cup of coffee to nurse, while Susan went to clean up and change clothes.

"What did you two talk about?" Mike asked.

"Just girl talk," Julie responded, "nothing important, just girl talk. She is a fascinating woman, Michael. She is definitely the one for you and if you make a little noise tonight, I'll understand," she laughed.

"Dad wants Mom to meet Susan, so we will be a little late getting back tonight," Mike said, "We'll help you clean up the kitchen before we go, and that is not debatable. I'll wash, Susan will dry, and you will put away, the whole job will take fifteen minutes tops."

It was 7:30 when Mike's Dad took Susan by the hand and presented her to his wife. Winnie, "This is Susan Romaine."

Mrs. Murphy shook hands and a little coolly said, "Let's go into the den." Mike and Susan sat on the couch while the senior Murphys sat in their recliners. The conversation wasn't going anywhere until Murph Sr. said, "I promised Susan some of your applesauce cookies, Winnie. What would you like with yours, Susan?"

"A glass of cold milk please," Susan answered. "Nothing goes with cookies like cold milk."

"I'll have the same," Mike spoke up."

"Well then, it's milk all around," Winnie said, and went into the kitchen, followed by Susan. "I don't need any help," Mrs. Murphy said.

"I know, Mrs. Murphy," Susan responded. "It's obvious you don't approve of me and for that I'm sorry. Whether you believe me or not is up to you. Your son and I were thrown together by fate and I believe in fate. He saved me from being killed or raped, or both, at the risk of his own life. At that time we hardly even knew each other's name. I am truly in love with him and I believe he really loves me, so whether or not you approve of me, I have agreed to marry him. I know about Agnes, and probably more about her than you do because there are some things parents never know, only guess. Now let me carry the cookies, and you carry the milk. We will join the men, have some cookies, and Michael and I will leave. We have a busy day ahead of us tomorrow."

"Susan, put the tray down," Winnie said, tears streaming down her cheeks. "I want Michael to be happy more than anything else in the world. You stood up to me and made it clear that you want the same thing for him. You are definitely the one for him. I'm sorry I got off on the wrong foot. Please forgive me and call me Mom. You are the kind of daughter I've always wanted. Agnes was cold, and I could never get close to her. You are warm, sincere, and absolutely beautiful. Hug me, and let's have some cookies and milk."

"What took you so long in there?" Mike asked.

"We had a mess we had to clean up," Susan answered. "Oh my, Mom there aren't enough o's in gooooood to describe these cookies."

As they were leaving, Mike's mom said to Susan, "If he gives you any trouble let me know, I can still spank his butt."

"Indeed I will, Mom, indeed I will."

They let themselves quietly into Julie's, and slid between the sheets. A goodnight kiss led to quiet foreplay and wonderful, fulfilling lovemaking. Then they fell asleep in each other's arms. In their minds they had identical thoughts, 'That's the way love ought to be.'

CHAPTER 11

Mike heard Julie in the kitchen so he slipped on his jeans and shirt, and brushed his hair before plodding barefoot into the kitchen.

"Coffee is done. You two will have to wait on yourselves this morning. I've got a lot of things to do today, so I will see you later," Julie said.

"Don't fix supper for me tonight," Mike responded. "I'm flying Susan to Portland after lunch. I too, have a lot of things to do, so I have no idea when I'll be back. That was a neat diversion we pulled off when we got the plane. Did I see you give a thumb's up?"

"Yes, you did, and as soon as possible, let the crew know what came off and why," Julie said. "I lit into them hard and they felt terrible because they know how much you treasure that old plane. Gotta go, bye."

Susan was up and stirring when Mike took her a kick-in-the-butt cup of coffee. "That's to get your motor started," he grinned. "Mine's idling right now, but unless you get going it's apt to race out of control."

"We'll have plenty of time for that later on", Susan responded. "I need to go to the office before the shootout. While I'm in the shower would you fix me some toast?"

"One order of toast coming up--toasted, not just dried out," Mike answered.

Susan came into the kitchen with her empty coffee cup and laid a heart-thumping, good-morning kiss on Mike. "Last night was delicious," Susan purred.

She wore jeans with a rawhide rope for a belt. Her thin denim shirt had the top two buttons undone leaving just enough cleavage to arouse curiosity without revealing anything. The tail of the shirt was loosely tied at her waist. Her raven black hair was gathered in back by a turquoise and sterling silver concho. Long, dangling turquoise earrings and beaded moccasins completed the ensemble.

"There is no way you can be inconspicuous, Susan," Mike stated. "You take my breath away, and Hawk will run you in as a traffic hazard if you're turned loose on the streets. You will definitely turn heads."

When they got to work, Murph Sr. called Susan into his office and was beaming. "I don't know what you said to Winnie, but all she can talk about is you and how happy she is for Mike to have found you. She is a firm believer in fate and is sure the Man upstairs put you two together. She says it will be a marriage made in heaven."

"Pops, do I have a desk yet?" asked Susan. There are some things I will need to put away and I don't want to bother anyone with them."

"This will be your office, I'm moving into Mike's, and we've hired a carpenter to partition off some space for him. With your responsibilities you need more room and security. I can run things with the space I'll have and Mike won't be in his office much anyway. We'll get the moves done today so when you get back, your office will be ready. Here are the keys to the desk; the bottom right drawer is reinforced for extra security and, it's fireproof. Please be careful and get back as soon as you can." With a fatherly hug, he said, "I love you, Susan." As he turned back to his work, she didn't see the tear in his eye.

They had time to stop at Mary's before the shootout, but Mike pointed out the Hummer at the curb. He suggested it was not a good time to go in. Ramon might be in there.

"That's a damn good reason for me to go in," said Susan. "I want him to see me. He doesn't know where I live or work and has no way of finding out. I want to get him pissed off; then, maybe he will make a mistake and Hawk can nail him."

Mike noticed Hawk sitting in his regular vantage point so he found a spot and parked.

"This is going to be fun" Susan said. "I've been wanting to face him for a long time and now I've got some back-up."

All heads turned as they entered, and there sat Ramon at the round table with his hired hands. He was completely caught off guard by Susan's presence. His eyes widened and he glared at her with hate in his eyes. Hawk, sensing something was about to happen, unfastened the thong on his gun.

Susan walked up to Ramon and clearly stated, "I'm as surprised to see you, as you obviously are to see me, you drug-dealing son-of-a-bitch. You've crawled out from under your rock to come over here and push your trade. Did Daddy Castro send you or did you have a brain fart and figure out this move by yourself? By the way, how are my children? Why don't you tell your slimy friends why you keep them captive, when they want to be free and live here where we have food, medicine, and good schools. Here, there are opportunities to be something besides a drug dealer or whore, and you don't have to sell your soul or ass to get the necessities of life. You are so important and smart; give them the answers to those questions you bastard. Thank you, I feel so much better now, I'm not even hungry. Come Mr. ...er Murphy is it? Let's talk about the plumbing business."

Mike was as surprised as Ramon was at Susan's tirade. "Mr. Murphy I'm waiting. I have other calls to make. I can't stand here and wait for him to crawl back under his rock." With that, she walked out the door.

When Mike caught up to her he asked, "Do you think that was a wise thing to do?"

"Absolutely. I know him; I know how he thinks; I can read him like a cheap novel. He is stupid Mike, not just dumb; stupid. He has no education. He got where he is by murder and by politics. I was serious when I asked him if Castro planned this move, or if it was his own idea. He is probably livid and can only think of how to get back at me. He will not harm the children; that's a fact. They are with his mother and if he were to harm them, she would kill him on the spot and he knows it."

Hawk followed them into the Police Station. "Little lady, I think you got him pissed off."

"I intended to, Chief. Like I was telling Mike, I know him. He has been careful up until now. But now he is, as you said, pissed off. He can't chew gum and walk at the same time, and he is only thinking of getting to me. Right after the shootout, I'm going back to Portland and get things started so I can move back here. He will look high and low for me, but if I'm not here he can't find me. Oh, did Mike mention we are getting married as soon as possible? You are going to be stuck with me. Why don't you two show me some shooting," she said with a grin.

"We fire six rounds rapid fire. A perfect score is sixty, then we fire six rounds slow, at a silhouette with a five-inch bull's-eye. A perfect score is thirty. Here are your ear protectors and safety glasses," Hawk said, handing her a sealed plastic bag. "Ready on the left. Ready on the right. Ready on the firing line. Commence firing."

Hawk, although he carried a Colt Peace Maker 45 caliber while on duty, preferred a WWII German Luger. Mike used a 38 caliber Colt Python. They pulled their targets. At rapid fire; the score was Mike 54, Hawk 56. At slow fire; Mike 25, Hawk 24. "Close but no cigar," Hawk crowed, "I'll have a Rueben."

"Do you boys mind if I try?" Susan shyly asked.

"Go right ahead, little lady, Hawk answered, "Whose weapon do you want to use?"

"I have my own," she replied. Opening her handbag, she pulled out a chromed 38 caliber Baretta. At rapid fire she put all six rounds in the center for a perfect score, at slow fire she put the first four dead center, then shot the eyes out. Removing her safety equipment, she explained, "I didn't do this to show off, I have been shooting at Ramon every time I had a chance. Seeing him today just sharpened my senses and boy, do I feel good."

"Susan," Hawk said, "everybody is treated the same in this town. That means I need a spent round, the serial number, and your finger prints on file. Miss Johnson will take your weapon, and get the information and spent round."

"Chief," Susan said, "with all due respect to you, I have no problem with your requests, but I am very particular about my weapon. I am the only person who has ever fired it, so I will fire into the tank, and then she can get the serial number. After we are finished here, I would like to use your facilities to clean and oil it."

"Miss Susan, anybody who can shoot that good has a deep respect for the gun. I've been around guns for many years and never knew anybody, including myself who was as conscientious about caring for a weapon as you are. Anything you need, Miss Johnson will get for you. Mike and I will wait in my office."

Did you know anything about her skill, Mike?" Hawk asked. "Not a thing, Chief. She did mention that she had a trick or two. I wonder what the other one is," Mike answered

"I'm all cleaned, cleared, and checked out, and ready for the next round. A Rueben sounds good," Susan said. "I like kraut with a pork roast."

Mary's was just starting to fill for the lunch trade when the three of them entered. Ramon wasn't there, but a couple of his henchmen, and the broad with the big tits were sitting in a booth. Susan walked up to her and said, "Be careful of Ramon. He wants to get in your pants and he doesn't take rejection at all. I say this not vindictively or with malice toward you. None of you has caused me any problems and I would like to keep it that way. I might look like a 120-pound weakling, but I can handle any one of you, and I don't need the Police Chief to back me up. I say again, Miss, if Ramon is rejected he will kill you. His philosophy is, if not me, then nobody. Have a good day."

What was that all about?" Hawk asked Susan.

"Just another burr under his saddle. If she rejects him, she will be on guard. Those henchmen will fear for their lives if they displease him, and may take off, leaving him with a recruiting problem. In the business they're in, if you are an asshole of a boss, word spreads like wildfire," Susan commented, adding "he probably doesn't have any mules he can trust in Cuba and is here to recruit some new blood."

"You seem to know a lot about him," the Chief said.

"I was married to the bastard and watched him promote himself by murder and intimidation. Hell, he can't even read, so whatever Castro or any official tells him, is Gospel to him. He is the laughing stock of Cuba. Castro tolerates him for the drug money. If he stopped bringing it in, someone would find him in a cane field with a gunshot in the back of the head. Castro does know how to play hard ball."

Ramon's crew were talking among themselves with an occasional glance in Susan's direction. As they were leaving, they came to where Hawk, Susan, and Mike were sitting. The woman spoke to Susan, "Honey, I don't know you and you don't know me, but woman-to-woman, thanks for the information. I'm in no position to leave, and I'm not sure I would if I could, but I can assure you that you are in no danger from me. However, Ramon is a different matter."

"I'm leaving for New York right after we finish lunch," Susan offered. "I'll be hard to find there. Good luck to you."

The younger and cleaner of the two men said, "Senora, thank you for telling us about Ramon. When the others came back from lunch they told us what you said, and most of us are leaving tonight. This lady is going to keep Ramon busy so we can get away. Gracias."

"Well Susan," Hawk said, "it appears you derailed his train. He will try to put it back on its tracks but it will take a while. He will have to start in square one again. I've got policing to do and you have a plane to catch. That reminds me, Mike, you might look for your Cub in Klamath Falls. I got a report that there is one that looks like yours in the back of a shed. Bye now."

When Mike and Susan got to the office Susan said, "I won't be but a minute or two, why don't you get the chopper ready? I really need to get back." She went to her office and put a black leather bag in the bottom right-hand drawer and locked it. Checking to make sure it was locked, she located Murph for a hug and a kiss. "See you later, Pops. Bye, Julie. Everything working as planned?"

"Better than planned. See you later," Julie responded.

Mike lifted off and climbed to 5,000 ft., following the Columbia River and setting down in Troutdale at Beaver Air. He wanted an update on the refurbishing and some kind of estimate on when it would be ready.

'The engines are in transit as we speak. They should be here Monday at the latest. We are working 24/7 to get this done," Mr. Jensen reported.

"Mr. Jensen," Mike interrupted. "Speedy work is fine, but not at the cost of quality. If this bird is going to save lives it has to be safe. When you have completed the work and it is ready for me to pickup a patient, I want you to imagine that patient is your own five-year-old daughter. If you would put her on board, sign off on the job, if not, do it over. Do we understand each other?"

"Yes, Mr. Murphy, we understand each other perfectly," Jensen answered.

"Susan, there are some things that have popped up that we need to talk about. This needs to be soon - like right now," Mike stated.

"If you don't have a tight shedule you could stay over, and I could cook dinner for the two of us. I really can cook and I would love to cook dinner for the man I love," Susan answered.

"How can I refuse an offer like that?" Mike chuckled.

CHAPTER12

Meanwhile, back in The Dalles, Hawk got on his radio and reported a Ford pick-up with California plates. "A big-titted female and two Latino males heading towards Mike Murphy's. Detain the Latinos and bring them in for questioning. Treat them with respect, that is an order. Let the female drive the truck to her destination. I repeat; treat them with respect."

The patrol car, with two frightened men inside, got to the station thirty minutes later. The restraints were removed and Hawk indicated seats, so they sat down. "Before we start is there anything you want --- bathroom, soda, coffee, water, anything? I want everybody out of here except these two gentlmen, and this conversation never happened. Am I understood? Good, now get out and shut the door."

Turning his attention to the Latinos, he asked, "Do you understand English?"

The grittier of the two said, "Yes, sir, we were both born in LA and went to high school but couldn't afford college. We put on this act whenever it is beneficial. We have no criminal record, in fact, this is the first time either of us have even been in a police station."

Hawk was grinning from ear to ear. "I pride myself in being a good judge of character and I believe you. "You should try acting for a career, you are very good at it," he said. Do you really want to get away from Ramon?"

"Yes sir," they answered simultaneously. "Which of you owns the truck?"

"I do," the spokesman said.

"I need both your names," Hawk continued. "I am going to send an officer and a tow truck to retrieve your truck with the story that you both have outstanding warrants. The officer will bring back as many of your personal belongings as they can. Meanwhile, if you want to clean up and shave, we can accomodate you. You will have to wear prison clothes while you are in here to keep up appearances. I suggest you wait until early morning before you escape. You will have a better chance of getting away. If I find out you've pulled a scam on me you will be found, and I am the one who gets first bite of the apple. There won't be much left for the rest. I'm giving you a break, so don't screw it up. Go back to LA and find legitimate jobs or you won't live to thirty."

"Thank you, sir. We have learned a valuable lesson, and will find money for college or trade school. Our names are Thomas and Jesus Rocha. I am Thomas, and Jesus is my little brother. Our mother will be very glad to see us. We haven't been home in a long time and our father died four years ago. We will go home and help Mom."

"I think I would like to be a policeman like you some day," Jesus spoke up. "You are not like the cops we see on TV."

"If you decide to pursue that as a career I would be pleased to write a letter of recommendation for you, and when you graduate you can have a job here," Hawk told them. "Get cleaned up and rest, you will have a long day tomorrow and a short night tonight. There will be $100 dollars in the glove box and a full tank of fuel. Don't let me down. Good-bye and good luck. I've got crooks to catch."

CHAPTER 13

Susan stopped at the market to get groceries for dinner. She found a pair of nice steaks so she picked those up and decided to add, tossed salad, baked potates, garlic bread, coffee, and to top it off with Spumonti and Sangria. "You can do the steaks on the patio or I can do them in the broiler," she told Mike.

"I'll do them on the patio. How do you like yours cooked?" Mike asked. "I like mine pink in the middle."

"So do I," Susan responded.

"Two steaks, medium rare coming up," Mike called from the patio. "I could get used to this very easily. I can't ever remember an evening like this -- steaks on the grill; a calm, beautiful woman, and fine wine to top it all off. I could die a happy man right now." "I'm in total agreement, but don't even think about dying,"

Susan said. "What are the things we need to discuss?"

"I want to protect myself from a vengeful wife. Agnes is not the quiet person I thought she was. I don't know what triggered the turnaround - maybe the drugs or the thought of making a lot of money dealing - but something hit her button and turned her on. I am going to transfer all my assets to Susan Romaine, and sell my share of Murphy Electronics and Engineering to you for a dollar. I'm going to work fulltime at Angel Flight at zero salary, only expenses. I will have no income and no assets, and she can have the house. I don't want it anyway. When this all plays out, we - that's you and me - are going to find a small ranch where your kids can

run and play. They will have to have horses and a farm dog. We
need a cat for rat and mouse patrol, maybe more than one cat, and
a garden for fresh tomatoes. That's just for starters; we will expand
later. I have a plan for getting your childrern out of Cuba. We have
to wait until the jet is finished, which will be a week or more, so we
must keep Ramon here at least that long. In the meantime, contact
your doctor friend and alert him we may be flying an Angel Flight
and would need his help. More information as it becomes available.
One more thing in regard to your children. If the opportunity
comes, I want to adopt them so at least everybody in the house
will have the same last name. You and I will discuss discipline with
them so they will know who is in charge. I don't believe corporal
punishment ever does any good. There are other ways that work
better."

Tears of happiness and joy fell in abundance from Susan's eyes.
"Michael do you realize what you just said?" Susan asked. "You have
a plan for getting my children out of Cuba, you want to adopt them,
and make a real home for us with a yard and pets and a garden. My
heart is overflowing with love and emotions I didn't know I had.
You are willing to do this for me whom you've known less than
two weeks. When are you going to drop the shoe? Nobody is that
generous, even for sex. All I want to know is, why?"

"Sweetheart, I've looked into your eyes and into your soul.
You are the genuine article. What I see is what I want. I've wanted
children of my own, but Agnes was not responsive to the idea and
I'm not sure that I'm not sterile. You came into my life, and as I
told you, it was mostly lust, but I did have genuine feelings for you
and then the lovemaking was indescribable. We weren't screwing;
we were expressing love in the most intimate way. I realize now, I
fell in love with you then and there. Be prepared for the children
to be spoiled by my folks. The cookie jar will always be full, with
plenty of cold milk and lemonade in the fridge. Not a lot of soda
drinks but a lot of ice cream and very limited amounts of junk food.
Maybe sometimes we will watch TV as a family. The only answer
I can think of is, I am totally in love with you and all I want to do
is make your life easier and happier. There it is, take it or leave it."

"The song, "It Had to Be You", goes through my mind every time I think of you, I've wandered around, and finally found, someone who can make me feel glad". Susan sang. "Let's get the dishes done and turn in. I'm tired and we have a lot to do."

Mike joined Susan in the shower. "Conserve water he said, shower with a friend." They dried each other being careful to hit the right spots and slid between the sheets for some quiet pleasure.

After an early breakfast Susan drove Mike to Troutdale and the chopper. A warm, I love you and miss you already kiss, and Mike was on his way home, and Susan to Henderson Manufacturing.

He put the chopper away after refueling and checking the oil etc. He wanted it ready at a moment's notice. That was the way he was with all modes of transportation. Ready to go at all times. He checked with Julie before going to see his Dad.

"Are you working too hard Pops?" he asked. "You are putting in some long hours and Mom and I worry about you."

"Son, work - if you can call doing something you like, work - is the best therapy. I sleep better than I have in years, I've always got something to do so I'm never bored and don't have time to be depressed. My pulse rate is normal; my blood pressure is usually 145 over 70. The doctor said I'm in better health and physical shape than I was ten years ago. In fact, his words were 'whatever you are doing keep it up.' At your Mother's insistence I saw Doc yesterday afternoon."

CHAPTER 14

That afternoon, at the office, Mike had an idea. "Julie," Mike called, "I would like to take you to dinner tonight at that new high-toned supper club. What do you say?"

"What woman could refuse an invitation like that from one of the best-looking men in the country? Of course I want to go. Shall we dress up?"

"If Hawk got all my clothes from the house, yes indeed. Let's go home. I've got some things to run past you." As they sat at the kitchen table, Mike told Julie about transferring his assets so Agnes couldn't take him to the cleaners.

"Are you sure you're not setting yourself up for somebody else to clean you out?" Julie cautioned.

"I realize the risk is there, but I feel very comfortable with my decision," Mike answered. "I'm going to go through the stuff Hawk retrieved and see how gussied up we can get. You do get gussied up on occasion, don't you Julie?"

"Not very often, but I do have a clean dress somewhere I can wear. You go see what you've got so we can look like a fashionable pair. I've got to shower and put up my hair no matter how we dress," Julie responded.

Hawk had managed to get all of his clothes. He dug through until he found his dinner jacket and pants. The phone rang; it was Hawk. "Thanks for retrieving my stuff, old friend," Mike said.

"No thanks necessary. The reason for the call is to tell you we also got your Lincoln. I'm bringing it by and one of my patrolmen will bring me back. I see you found your plaything."

"Yes I did, and on the way back I took an aerial view of the house. There was only an out-of-state, late-model sedan in the yard and no pickups or activity," Mike reported. "Gotta go; thanks, I owe you one, a big one."

Julie was out of the shower. Mike told her about his dinner jacket and the Lincoln. "We are really going to dress and turn a few heads. We'll leave about seven if that will give you enough time to get ready."

"It's a little past six now so I'll have plenty of time. Now where in the hell is that clean dress?"

Mike showered, shaved and lounged in his robe while polishing his shoes, giving them a Marine Corps spit shine. He was dressed and ready at 7:20 when Julie knocked on his door.

"I'm ready when you are," she announced.

Mike opened his door and gasped. Julie was an attractive woman, but tonight she was a breath taker. Her dark brown hair was up in back, held by a jeweled tiara. Her form-fitting, salmon-colored, floor-length gown was slit up the side, accented by diamond earrings and a single diamond necklace.

"Julie," Mike almost whispering, said, "You are radiant. Every man in the place is going to envy me, and every woman is going to be jealous and will watch her man like a hawk."

The black Lincoln was Mike's one extravagance. He kept it garaged and waxed. He said, "I don't gussie up very often, but when I do, I think black is the only color for a luxury car. Of course, nobody's going to see the car because of your radiance."

"You keep talking like that and you'll need to lock your bedroom door," Julie joked.

"If I hadn't met Susan, you would have to keep your door locked," Mike answered. "Let's go break some hearts and have a fun evening"

The kid at the valet parking almost fell down he was so focused on Julie. When the maitre de escorted them to their table, he did it with a flourish. He presented his arm to Julie and she knew just what to do. He pulled the chair out for her, and then helped her get comfortable, and with a slight bow said, "Enjoy your dinner."

As predicted, all eyes were on them. Julie spoke quietly to Mike, "They don't know about the divorce, so you know what they're thinking. Let's really have some fun with them." She reached across the table, took Mike's hand, stared dreamily into his eyes, and mouthed a kiss. Mike kissed her hand and they continued their flirting until the waiter brought their salads and rolls, followed shortly by the lobster. Mike ordered wine to follow dinner. The orchestra was playing soft big-band music and they danced. It took a turn or two around the floor before they got in sync, but after that they seemed to float like they had danced together for years.

As they were waltzing, Mike spotted Ramon, Agnes, and the big-titted woman. Agnes hadn't seen much of Julie and never like this, so she didn't know who she was. Mike could feel the venomous looks from Agnes. Ramon was licking his lips watching Julie, and the big-titted blonde seemed noncommittal, just slopping down a beer. He called Julie's attention to the trio and she just snuggled up to Mike and gazed dreamily into his eyes. "Julie," he whispered, "I think you are trying to seduce me. If I were the cheating kind you could be successful."

"I know honey," Julie answered," it's nice to know I've still got it, and if I ever find the right man again, I'll use it. Here comes Ramon; I think he is going to cut in, what shall I do?"

"I'll handle it." The 5-ft 3-inch, 175- pound Cuban, tapped Mike on the shoulder.

With his bad breath and Spanish accent, Ramon asked, "May I have a dance with the beautiful lady, senor?"

"I'm sorry sir, but my fiancée is very allergic to grease. Dancing with you would make her so ill that when we get home tonight there would be no lovemaking. That would make me very angry, thereby ruining what has started out to be one of the best nights of my life. You can ask your skinny dinner partner how no sex affects me. If you are getting any screwing from her I'd be very surprised because she is practically a virgin; I seldom got any, and when I did it wasn't any good. Masturbating was better than her. Now if you want to take this discussion outside, just say the word. If not, get out of my face -- you're breath smells like a sewer."

Ramon went back to his table enraged. He gave his dates an animated account of what had happened, and the venom in Agnes was almost visible. Big Tits laughed, gave Mike a subtle thumb's up, and downed another brew. They left, with Ramon glaring at Mike and Julie.

Julie spoke up, "That takes some balls, Michael. You had better be on guard because he is not going to let this stand."

"I will be careful. I stepped between you two because he does not accept rejection. You didn't reject him; I did, but you had best be on guard yourself until Hawk and I put him away. That piece of crap is Susan's ex. If you think I laid some crap on him, you should have seen and heard her."

"I've had about all the excitement I can stand for today. Let's take some strawberry pie home and sit in the kitchen," Julie said. "The coffee maker is ready. I'll punch it on and by the time we get dressed for bed it'll be done. Mike, I've had a wonderful evening. I haven't danced in years, and you were so patient with me. After we got in sync, I noticed we were being watched and admired. Are we engaged? You referred to me as your fiancée," she laughed. "I know it was for effect, but I admit I got a thrill out of it, and if you ask, I'll say yes."

"Julie, I'm in love with Susan. I have always admired you and consider you more than a friend, and it will always be that way."

CHAPTER 15

Mike woke up to the smell of coffee brewing, and bacon frying, and the sound of Julie singing.

"Good morning, Sunshine," she said, as he headed for the bathroom.

"You are in a good mood this morning. Is there anything I can do around here to help with my rent?" Mike asked.

"The grass needs cutting, the yard needs weeding, and my garage door needs some fixing. Other than that, I can't think of a thing," Julie answered. "I'm still reveling in last night. I guess I need to get out more, but where do I meet decent men? Definitely not in a bar. If you go to a single's club, all you have are guys who only want sex. If you don't put out the first night, you never hear from them again. I'll settle for one night like last night, once in a while, over a one-night stand. How do you want your eggs, and how many today?"

"Three, scrambled with onion and cheese, please," Mike answered. "Is there a sports team you follow? You might go to a few home games, and maybe a road game or two, and sit with the crowd that supports and roots for them. Get excited, be part of the home-field advantage. That is a very good place to meet men. They are not there to get laid. They are there to watch the game, and if they meet some lady watching the game, you have something in common. Pick a sport you like and understand. Read up on stars of the game, but most of all be honest with yourself. Start out to enjoy the game and be honestly enthusiastic about it. Going to the game will get you out where men are. There will be some assholes there, too. Assholes are everywhere. When you meet someone and it looks like he might be a keeper, be sure you know what you are talking about in regard to the sport. Nothing will turn a man off faster than some airhead who doesn't know the difference between a home run and a field goal, pretending she is having a good time.

"I don't know how long it will take to get my chores done. I want to check with Hawk sometime today and find a garage for the Lincoln, so if you have a schedule for today, don't let me mess it up."

"I generally do laundry, housekeeping and marketing on Saturdays and skip lunch and have pizza for supper. So nothing you have going is going to bother me," Julie responded.

"How about if I cook burgers on the grill tonight? You can take care of chips or a salad, and ice tea. Later we could go for a shake." Mike suggested.

"No shake," Julie countered, "I'll pick up a melon and some grapes instead. We'll eat at 6:30."

"Sounds like a plan to me," Mike agreed. "See you for supper."

By the time Mike had finished his chores it was almost 1:00 p.m., so he went to Mary's to talk to Hawk. He was sitting alone in his usual spot and waved to Mike, nodding in the direction of the back corner booth. Mike looked where Hawk indicated, and there sat Ramon with two men Mike didn't recognize. They had probably come in the out-of-state sedan. It appeared they were in charge; Ramon was nodding yes and saying "si" a lot. The two men were dressed in expensive tailored suits to conceal the guns they wore. The tailoring job was good, but not perfect. If you really looked, you could detect a bulge that didn't belong.

Mike had sat down when Ramon and his friends approached. Ramon opened his mouth to speak, when Mike interrupted him, "I know I pissed you off last night, but I have no regrets about that. In fact, my fiancée was turned on by it. We didn't get to sleep until late, and she was singing like a canary this morning. So I should thank you. That being said, I will warn you in front of this man (indicating Hawk) and your two associates. If my fiancée or the lady

I was with Thursday - who did a pretty good job of pissing you off herself - are in anyway hurt; I will hunt you down, shove your big Military .45 up your ass and pull the trigger. What were you going to say Ramon? By the way, your breath still smells like a sewer. Try a mouthwash or brush your teeth or both, and do it often. It won't make you less offensive, but your breath would smell better. That in itself would improve your love life; nobody likes to kiss a sewer."

Ramon stood in disbelief. He had come to town like a very important man running a business empire, then in three days most of his hired hands had quit. He had also been humiliated in public by an ex-wife; and then again at dinner in front of people in the supper club and the two women he was with by this nobody. Today, again this nobody was humiliating him in front of not only people in the cafe, but also in front of two professional thugs. This nobody also humiliated three of his only remaining men. It was only a little past 1:30 p.m., and it had already not been a good day, thought Ramon, as he and his recruiters left the cafe.

"What was that all about?" asked Hawk. "And your 'fiancée?' What the hell is going on? Mike, my friend, you have made another enemy, or maybe three. What are you trying to do to me?"

"Just trying to help Chief, just trying to help. Susan told me a lot about Ramon. He has no education and believes he is cock of the walk in Cuba when, in fact, he is no more than a gopher. He thinks he has clout clear up to Castro himself because his orders come from the Capitol. Castro wouldn't know him if he lit his cigar. Right now Ramon is so mad he can't think of anything but how to get back at me, so he is going to start making mistakes. He carries a big gun, but he has to have somebody else pull the trigger. They execute by electrocution and he is terrified of the thought, so he is very careful to keep his hands clean. All of his hired guns have left except those two, and I think they will have second thoughts about staying around with Ramon's bankroll giving out. Without putting yourself in jeopardy of any kind, can you keep him around for a week or two? The jet won't be ready until then, and if he is still here Susan and I have a good chance to get her kids out of Cuba."

"It shouldn't be too hard. As of now he has just been a pain in the ass, which is not against the law. That's fortunate for some people. Carrying a concealed weapon is legal, so I don't have positive proof of anything to charge him with. If what you just told me is true, his time is running out. Look who's coming through the door."

Mike turned to see Ramon's last two hoods coming toward them. He and Hawk sprung to their feet and got in a defensive position. Hawk had already drawn his piece and said, "STOP right where you are." They did, and voluntarily raised their hands.

"Sir", the one on the left spoke, "My name is Jose Garcia, and this is, don't laugh please, Jesse James. We came to surrender our weapons and tell you we are going back to San Diego. Your friend here spotted our guns, so if you like, you can take them. Now, can we lower our hands and sit down?"

"Yes, but sit at that table. I'm 95% sure you are being truthful, but that other 5% has gotten people killed. I want to know why you are doing this."

"Sir", Jesse answered, "we are small-time operators, and at this time there are no wants or warrants out for us, so we felt safe in coming to you. Ramon got in touch with us through a round-about way and promised a big score, so we jumped at the chance. We asked him about the law up here, and he said all they had was some hick Indian with no backup. We were okay with that until earlier today. I called Galveston and talked to a fiend who has contacts in the Police Department. She told me the story about some Navy flyboy taking out three armed thugs by himself and only using his hands. It was the talk of the department, and when she told us about the gun in the ass, I knew we weren't going to get involved. If you check, you will note our guns are not loaded. We are going back to find another line of work, construction maybe. Something outdoors with benefits. We have been in jail and it sucks."

Hawk said, "I'm getting soft in my old age. The Sheriff of San Diego County and I are somewhat related. If you want to stop by the office, I will write a letter to him and ask him to help you find a job. You haven't had a run in with him have you? I'll tell him I want to help him get crime off the street. He is tough, but fair, and will bend to help you, but if he feels the bending and is starting to break, you best give your soul to God because your ass will be his. While you are in the office, I want you to make a statement much the same as you just told me, and anything you can tell me about Ramon's plans would be helpful and confidential. We know he is up to no good but what and when, we don't know."

Mike got up to leave, and shook hands with Jose and Jesse, "Good luck, gentlemen. Remember, the harder you work, the luckier you get. Hawk, you've got policing to do and I've got chores to do. See you later."

He was about to the door when his attorney, Ross Dillon, came in. "Just the man I need," Mike exclaimed. "I want to divest myself of all assets except the house. I want to transfer them to Susan Romaine. I would like it done yesterday, but that would cause you to commit perjury yourself and I won't be a party to it. How fast can you get it done?"

"My golf partner canceled, so we can get started right after I have some pie and coffee. Would you care to join me?"

"No, thank you. I've just had coffee with the Police Chief, but you take your time and enjoy. If I bought your pie and coffee, that would legally be a retainer, wouldn't it? I don't expect you to work for pie and coffee, but to pay $500 for pie and coffee would cause some eyebrows to raise."

You make good sense, Mr. Murphy. Pie and coffee will be just fine as a retainer," the lawyer agreed.

In the attorney's office, Mike explained why he wanted to do what he was planning. "I don't think Agnes would be vindictive, but there is a strange crowd hanging around her. We, the Police Chief and I, are certain drugs are, or at least were, being dealt there but some recent events have seriously altered the situation. I want to be fair with her, so I will leave alimony for you and her attorney to work out."

"That will be fine, Mr. Murphy. If you will fill out these forms and sign them in front of a witness, your assets are protected. Miss Romaine will have some forms to fill out and sign, also. How can I get in touch with her?"

"Could you fax the forms to her?" Mike asked.

"Yes, but the signature can't be faxed; it must be original. Do you have her fax number?"

"It's 971-534-2724. She will be here this week and deliver the forms in person. I'll run up to the Police Station and have Hawk or somebody witness my signature and be right back."

Mike returned five minutes later.

Ross looked everything over and offered his hand, saying; "You are now protected, and as soon as Miss Romaine shows up with the proper documents, I'll file it with the necessary agencies. The transfer will be immediate and there will be taxes due."

"I understand sir," Mike answered. "Thank you for getting this done so quickly. I knew it should have been done earlier, but it slipped my mind. If you hadn't walked in when you did, it still wouldn't be done. Good-bye."

CHAPTER 16

Mike got back to Julie's in time to cart groceries in for her and help her put them away. He called Susan to tell her about the incoming fax. "It's important that we get this done quickly, so business is taken care of. I love you and miss you terribly. We have derailed Ramon's plans for the moment and Hawk is going to let him alone for now. As soon as the jet is ready we are going to get your children. Get in touch with your doctor friend and have him ready to move at that end. We can give him 24 hours notice when we want them at the air terminal. My plan is quick and simple, a little risky, but I think I can have the US Navy as a backup if necessary."

"Okay, sweetheart, I miss you too. I've never had problems sleeping alone, but now I know what being alone really feels like. It's not the lovemaking; it's the fact I don't have you to cuddle up next to for protection. I may not make it back Monday; there are a lot of loose ends to tie up, but I'll get there as quickly as I can. I've got an appointment in ten minutes so I have to hang up. I love you, Michael."

Burgers hot off the grill, with onion, dill pickle slices, lettuce, mustard on a real bun toasted on the grill is about as good as it gets. Top that off with cold sun tea, chips and a salad of melon, grapes, strawberries, apples, pineapple, blended together with orange juice and you have a meal fit for a king or queen. Add to this, the aroma of an Oregon spring, with the fruit trees blossoming and promising their sweet fruit later, the sweet perfume of the pine forests wafting on a gentle breeze, and the silence that comes at the end of a busy day. To make it absolutely perfect would be sharing it with Susan, Mike was thinking to himself.

"Your mind was going 100 miles an hour," Julie said.

"No", Mike said, "I was just thinking how nice this has been and hope we can do it often. I'm tired and I'm going to bed. We can do dishes in the morning; then I'm going to spend the day with Mom and Dad. Would you like to join me? You would not be in the way and Mom would like a female to talk to. As a bribe, I promise some homemade applesauce cookies."

"With an offer like that how can I refuse?" Julie responded. "What time are we going to leave?"

"Around ten. They are early risers and will be ready to take a milk and cookie break about the time we get there," Mike answered. "Let's take the leftover fruit salad with us."

CHAPTER 17

It had rained during the night. The smell of freshly cut grass, combined with the aroma of an Oregon morning filled the nostrils and made one glad God gave him one more day on earth. Mike was up first and punched on the coffee. By the time he had showered, it was done and Julie was stirring in her room. He poured her a cup, knocked on her door, and announced, "Your coffee, Madam. If you would take it please, would you like breakfast in bed?"

"Susan better appreciate you, or I will try my best to steal you from her. I would love breakfast in bed," Julie answered.

"What would you like to order, Madam?" Mike teased.

"Two eggs basted, wheat toast, toasted not dried, butter on the side, two sausage patties, hash browns, orange juice and coffee."

Mike prepared her tray, and then spotted a bright red rose in her garden. He snipped the rose and put it in a bud vase on her tray. Carrying the tray he knocked on her door, "Your breakfast Madam!" he announced.

"Come in Jeeves," she teased. Julie had combed her hair, applied a little makeup and was wearing a white silk bed jacket. When she saw the tray and the rose, she cried in joy. "I feel like a queen," she said.

"There has never been a more beautiful, or deserving queen, anywhere at anytime in history," Mike said softly.

A leisurely breakfast on the patio suited Mike just fine. It gave him time to think and plan his moves. Julie was enjoying her privacy and pampering. Watching the Sunday morning shows was one of her favorite parts of the weekend, and to be waited on, and to watch TV while lying in bed was delicious, but all good things must end. The show was over, and all there was to watch was a televangelist saying...and if his listeners didn't send him several million dollars, the Lord was going to call him home. "People fall for that," mused Julie. "The Lord is going to call everybody home in His own time no matter how much money you have."

Mike washed, and Julie dried and put away the dishes from last night and breakfast, and left a clean kitchen. "Cooking is a lot easier if you don't have to start by washing dishes and pots and pans," Julie admitted.

They swung by the office on the way to Mike's folks. There was a door open on the big shed that housed, among other things, the Piper Cub. "Damn," Mike swore. "I was sure I closed and locked that on Friday." He went inside, but didn't see anything suspicious or out of place. Then he made a quick check of the Cub, which appeared to be okay. He made a mental note to run it out and double check everything in the morning. The floor was damp where the rain had blown in, so the door must have been open all night. "Strange," he said to himself.

They got to the Murphy's in time for break, and fruit salad was just right. "I'm so glad you came," Winnie said to Julie. "I haven't had a chance to thank you for all you've done for us while Mike was in the hospital. He said the business ran as good as if he was there, and the way you help Michael learn the ropes is far more than you are expected to do."

"I don't have a family," Julie said, "and when I started here I felt like it was home. In my mind, you are my family. I only did what needed to be done and I was in the best position to do it."

Mike and his dad were deep in discussion about the new airport and terminal building and how they should add a building for offices.

"With Murphy and Son Electronics and Engineering and Angel Flight, we need more space and room for expansion, which will mean more office help and computers. In business or anything else, you grow or die; you can't stand still," Murph Sr. explained. "You are going to stay for dinner, aren't you?"

"We hadn't thought about it, but what do you think, Julie?" Mike asked.

"Only if I can help," Julie answered.

"That will be fine," Winnie said. "You can set the table. Everything is in the sideboard-tablecloth, napkins, dishes, everything."

"You don't have to get formal for me, Mrs. Murphy," Julie answered.

"I'm not; we have a friend, Howard Morrison, who lost his wife a little over a year ago. He has two sons who are away in college. Weekends are very lonely, so we have him over as often as we can without being solicitous. He has a real estate and insurance business that keeps him occupied during the week; the weekends are hard on him. My cookie jar is about empty. Why don't you and I go to the kitchen and have girl talk, while Michael and his father talk about their airport? Dinner is in the oven and all that's left is to heat the rolls. One more thing, you are family, call me anything but Mrs. Murphy."

"So how is the airport coming, Dad? I've been preoccupied with my own problems and I haven't taken the time to consult with you."

"The last of the concrete for the runway was poured Friday. The footings for the buildings will be poured tomorrow, and construction will start late this week or next Monday. Donavan Brothers Construction has the general contract. I didn't bid the electrical or mechanical, so there won't be any favoritism," Mike Sr. answered.

"I think we should have an emergency generator," Mike said. "If the power is knocked out and we have a bird in the air, we have to be able to land it. There will have to be a transition switch so we don't push power into the grid and electrocute someone. A mechanical timer would be nice in case we have a bird scheduled in at 2:00 a.m. The generator would kick in and the lights would go on without someone needing to stay around and maybe falling asleep.

If the power comes back on, the switch kicks off and everything is normal; if the power is still off, the lights go on and the bird lands safely."

"Great thinking, son, I'll put that in the specs right now," Murph said. "Walt is furnishing as much of the material as he can at cost, and is arm twisting other companies to do the same. We will have a first-class facility at a bargain-basement price."

"Mike, Michael," Winnie announced, "Howard is here." Howard Morrison stood an even 6ft in his socks and a solid 190lbs, with slightly wavy black hair, perfect teeth, a warm friendly smile, a permanently cocked left eyebrow, and a firm handshake that indicated strength without showing off.

Murph went to greet him and introduced him to Michael, saying, "Howard, this is my son and business partner, Mike. And this is our secretary and the real brains of the outfit. Julie Robertson, Howard Morrison."

"As soon as the rolls are done we can eat," Winnie announced. "Julie, if you would put the veggies in serving bowls, I'll finish the gravy and put the roast on a platter. Then we can sit down."

It wasn't planned, but Howard from force of habit pulled the chair out for Julie and helped her adjust to a comfortable position. Dinner conversation was light and exploratory. Since Mike, Julie, and Howard were strangers to each other there was a natural curiosity about each other. Winnie and Murph just sat and listened attentively, interjecting only when it was appropriate. They had somehow communicated to each other - let's let the young folks talk while we sit back and listen.

Dinner ended with a generous slab of Winnie's fresh peach pie with a dollop of French vanilla ice cream and coffee.

"Mom," Julie said, surprising herself with how natural it sounded, and lighting up Winnie's face with a pleasing smile. "I haven't had such a dinner in my entire life. All I can say is thank you, and if you don't mind, I would like to thank someone else." Holding hands on both sides, the others joined, and she said, "Gracious Father, I thank You for all Your blessings and Your grace. I thank You for the love that surrounds this table, and ask

Your blessing on each and everyone here and those whom we are thinking of. Amen."

Silence filled the room until Winnie spoke, "Julie, you are as dear to me as any daughter could be. When you called me Mom, I thought my heart would burst. And your prayer was unexpected and appreciated by each of us, and no doubt heard by the One to whom you directed it. Now if I don't shut up and do the dishes I'm going to come apart right before your eyes. Julie, I love you."

"I love you too, Mom," Julie responded. "I'll wash, you dry, and we will put away while the men talk."

"Howard," Mike said, "I'm looking for a small ranch, 25 acres, more or less. Do you know of any reasonably close and affordable?"

"As a matter of fact, I do, "Howard responded." I have not seen it myself, but the people responsible were in my office on Wednesday. It belonged to their parents who were killed in an automobile accident near Hood River. A drunk ran a stop sign and broad-sided them, then a semi hit them head on. Of course, the drunk wasn't hurt and neither was the trucker. The drunk was on a suspended license for operating a motor vehicle while intoxicated, and the DA is tired of people who think it's okay to drive drunk. He is charging him with motor vehicle homicide, operating without a license, and anything else he can pin on him and will try to have him put away for 30 years. The children live back east and have no desire to own property here. The house sits on about 50 acres, is 15 years old, custom built for them by one of the better homebuilders in the area, with 3 bedrooms, den with wood-burning fireplace, 1&1/2 baths, double garage, no basement, and is in pretty good shape. The kids took everything they wanted and left the rest, including furniture. They are asking $150,000 and if you don't buy it, I will. Possession is immediate on completion of credit report. I can get you a very good rate of interest on a mortgage if you are interested."

"I am definitely interested and would like to see it," Mike responded. "When can we look at it?"

"I don't know for sure what my appointments are this week. Call me or stop by the office tomorrow, and we will set something up," Howard answered.

It was getting close to dark when Howard excused himself. "It was a most delightful day, Winnie, and a delicious dinner as always. Julie and Mike, so glad to have met you both. I'll hear from you tomorrow. Good night."

"We need to go too, Mom and Dad. Howard seems to be a solid person, knowledgeable about many things" Mike commented.

"And a real gentleman," Julie chimed in. "I'm glad you asked me to come with you. Your mother is so sweet and loving. You and your parents have spoiled me completely rotten these past few days; it will take me a while to get back to normal. Did I hear you and Howard talking bout a ranch?"

"Yes, you did Julie," Mike answered. "Susan and I need a place of our own, and we are going to get her children out of Cuba. Kids need a place to run and have pets and chores. The place Howard described sounds promising. I'm going to look at it as soon as he has a place for me in his appointment book."

At a little past 8 a.m. the next morning, a candy-apple red sports car convertible came to a skidding stop in front of the office. It was piloted by a buxom gum-chewing blonde with a definite southern drawl. She was wearing a very short, red skirt and a white ruffled blouse, off the shoulders and cut low enough to draw much attention.

"Hi, sweetie - you handsome dog," she said to Mike. "You must be Mike. Susan told me all about you, but she never said how cute you were. Where can I find Miss Julie?"

Mike escorted her to Julie's office, gave her a puzzled look, shrugged his shoulders, and went out to call Howard. Blondie presented a letter to Julie that read:

This is Barbra Dahl. She may seem like an airhead but, don't sell her short. She is a top-notch secretary that I've known and worked with since I came to Henderson Manufacturing. Around here the guys refer to her as Barbie Doll, for obvious reasons. I explained to her as best I could what her duties and responsibilities were and the pecking order. She is a terrible flirt and at times seems a little horny, but overall she's an excellent secretary. I would consider it a personal favor if you would take her under your wing and get her off on the right foot. She has my office and desk keys and the forms for the attorney, Mr. Dillon. Would you see that he gets them? See you soon, Susan.

"Well, is it Miss or Mrs., whatever shall I call you?" Julie asked. "Where do you want to start?"

"It's Miss, and you can call me Barbra, like Striesand. I want to meet everybody so they will know who and what I am. Let's start with Pops, then down the pecking order."

On the way down the hall to Murph Sr.'s office, they encountered Mike.

"Mike," Julie said, "Susan is going to be delayed in getting back, so she sent Miss Dahl to fill in for her. Barbra, meet the senior Mr. Murphy."

In a low, sultry voice, dripping with honey, she purred, "Oh, honey, I'm so glad Susan couldn't make it back on schedule. You are as cute as your son and more to my liking."

Murph being straight-laced, but not wanting to be rude, thanked her, grabbed some blueprints, retreated to his office, and shut the door. He did not see the faint smile on Julie's face.

CHAPTER 18

Mike called Howard for an appointment and was told, "My 9:00 o'clock cancelled and I have nothing until 1:00 p.m., so anytime in between will be fine."

"How about right now, Howard?" Mike responded.

"That's fine with me," Howard answered, "I'll wait and we can go in my car."

"I'm on my way," Mike answered. "Julie, I'm going to meet Howard and look at the ranch."

Mike thought it best to stay as much out of Barbra's way as possible, and he did have things to do, like find where to park his Lincoln. "Julie, I've got some errands to run, I've got my cell, so call if you need me. Supper at 6:30 as usual?"

"I don't know what we're having, maybe something from the deli, "Julie answered.

The ranch was off the old highway west of town, about 20 miles. It lay between the mountains and the Columbia River. "Fifty acres, more or less," Howard commented, "with a nine-acre pond full of pan fish, and when the river runs high, an occasional sturgeon will find its way into it. Salmon use the creek that connects the pond to the river as a route to the pond. The house is a brick, ranch-style, with three bedrooms, two bathrooms, a family room with wood-burning fireplace, and formal dining room. There is a ranch style kitchen, efficient, and room for a table large enough to accommodate six people comfortably. Back among the aspens and pine trees, is a barn with stalls for six horses and a tack room. An old saddle is still there on its rack. A few fence posts are still standing, giving silent testimony to the good times of the past. The house is just as it was when the former occupants left. The heirs want nothing, only to rid themselves of the property and spend what money they will gain from the sale."

"You could move in today, with only your personal effects and groceries," Howard said.

"Considerate it sold," Mike stated.

"I'll arrange for the financing and give you a call when the paperwork is all done. What name do you want on the deed"? Howard asked.

"To make it perfectly legal make the deed to Susan Joy Romaine," Mike answered. "I'll explain later."

"Julia is a very handsome woman," Howard remarked on their way back to town. "Has she ever been married and is she seeing anyone?"

"The answer to both questions is no" Mike replied.

As he stepped out of Howard's car, Mike shook hands and said, "This is a contract."

"I know about your "contracts" and it's fine with me," Howard said. "Talk to you later."

Mike spent the rest of the morning tinkering with his antique Piper Cub, until there was nothing left to do but fire it up and bore holes in the sky. He flew over his house and noticed a couple of different vehicles. A newer pickup was in the driveway behind the Hummer. An older van was in the yard, the garage door was open, and he could see Agnes' mini-van. Ramon and the blonde were having an obviously heated discussion. They were waving their arms and shaking their fists at each other like two boxers - each wanting the other to throw the first punch, but hoping it never came.

Mt. Hood was in all its splendor and the snow bunnies in their bikinis were lying against their propped-up skis, getting red and drawing attention to their young tender bodies. He dipped his wings and revved the motor in salute and they waved back. 'It's too bad,' he thought to himself, 'that youth is wasted on the young. I wonder what Susan's children will think about all this beauty.' Making a slow banking turn, he went over the dam at Bonneville and headed up river towards home.

Construction had already started on the new airport. The grading and filling were going exceptionally well. "I'll have to tell the contractor how pleased we are at the speed things are going". The footings for the combination airport terminal and office space for "Angel Flight" and "Mike Murphy and Son Electronics and Engineering" were almost ready to pour.

"Damn, we forgot a hangar and maintenance facilities for the jet. That bird is the reason for all this. We had a community brain fart."

He was about to touch down when something caught his eye.

He powered up, and went around to look. There was a set of tire tracks that led up to the back of the shed that housed; among other things, his plane. The tracks cut off from a seldom-used back road and looked fairly fresh. The weeds and grass hadn't dried out yet. The rain had helped them stand up to the abuse of the tires.

After a successful landing, he put the Cub in its place in the shed, chocked the wheels, refueled, checked the oil, and put the sleeve over the Pitot tube. Grabbing a flashlight from his toolbox, he went outside to investigate. He couldn't tell from what he saw as to whether they had been made by a car or truck. He would definitely tell Hawk what he did know about them however.

When he got back to the office, Barbra was sitting at Susan's desk. When she heard Mike come in, she spun around. She had no underwear on and two things were obvious. She was not a blonde and she wanted Mike to notice.

"Honey," she purred. "Where have you been? I missed you. Julie had already booked you for supper before I had a chance, so why don't you come over to the hotel for some dessert?"

"Sorry, Miss. I have a busy evening planned. I'm going to see some friends I haven't seen in five years, and besides, I am a one-woman man and Susan is my woman. I never did partake of, or believe in, one-night stands."

"I wasn't thinking one-night stand," Barbra purred. "I thought you could move in with me as long as I'm here, and Julie could have her privacy. I get so lonesome at night, especially when I don't know anybody to talk to. You are the only man close to my age, and Susan has told me so much about you, I feel I've known you for years. Besides, it wouldn't be a commitment."

"Barbra, I'm trying to be polite because you are a friend of Susan's, or so she thinks," Mike stated. "I am totally committed to Susan. Yes, we barely knew each other when we made that commitment, but I had never felt like that before. Love is not entirely how you feel about the other person; it's also how you feel about yourself when you are with that person. What kind of person would try to seduce a friend's fiancée? By the way, what is the natural color of your hair? I can see it's not blonde."

"Mike sweetie," Barbra cooed, "I am, among other things, persistent. The invitation and the gate are always open for you. Later, honey."

Mike found his dad and said, "I've got to stay away from here, that woman is in heat and she just showed me she is not a natural blonde. We forgot plans for maintenance facilities and a hangar for the jet or jets. I can work on that, and finding a qualified mechanic. That should keep me out of the office a lot. I'm leaving now. Is there anything I should know or do? You've got my cell number. If you need me call. Good night."

"See you for supper, Julie," he announced going out the door. He drove to Mary's for a cup of coffee to soothe his jangled nerves. He had hoped to see Hawk and report what he had seen at the office, but Hawk wasn't there and his car wasn't at the cop shop so he must be crime fighting..

He moved to a booth with a phone, and called Henderson Manufacturing and asked for Susan. "I'm sorry, she is out of the office and can't be reached," he was told.

"This is Mike Murphy. Could you transfer me to Walt Henderson please?"

"Walter Henderson here, may I help you?"

"Walt, this is Mike, I've been trying to reach Susan, but I'm being told she can't be reached. Is she okay?"

"Yes, Mike, she is perfectly okay. She is on a special assignment for the company. It is not dangerous, but it is hush-hush," Walt answered.

"If you talk to her, please ask her to call me," Mike said. "The person she sent to fill in for her is driving me nuts."

"You must mean Barbie Doll," Walt chuckled. "She is totally different than Susan, but I can't fault her work and that's the main reason she's there. Susan is supposed to check in with me later today and I'll have her call you. How are things progressing with Angel Flight?"

"The jet should be ready at the end of next week. When is Lizzie going home?" Mike asked.

"Late next week, which might just work perfectly for a maiden trip for Angel Flight," Walt responded.

"I hope so. The grading for the new runways will be finished this week. They will start the ironwork Monday, and start pouring the concrete later in the week. The footings for the buildings are ready, so things are going ahead as fast as possible. The general contractor is getting a lot of work done in a short period of time. I've never seen anything like it. We will use him on our larger contracts," Mike reported. "Good talking to you Walt, I'm anxious to see you."

"The feeling is mutual son," Walt answered. "I talked to your dad and he sounds twenty years younger. Getting back in the harness was the best therapy for him. He was concerned about the cost of the project, and I told him he had a blank check. Angel Flight will be a not-for-profit company and we will apply for tax-exempt status. Once that is granted, I'll lean on some of my cronies that need to give some of their money to us or Uncle Sam. We'll need to work like hell to stay nonprofit, because there are millions of dollars out there waiting for a worthy cause. I can't think of a more worthy cause than helping to save a child in any way we can. I thank God for my resources that enable me to do this, and I'll convince others to do the same. It seems the more I give to causes like this, the more I have to give. What goes around comes around.

I didn't mean to preach, but you hit my favorite nerve. Take care Mike, I love you."

Mike felt the emotion in Walt's voice. Walt is putting his heart and soul as well as his money into Angel Flight, Mike thought to himself. *If I don't give 100% of myself, I would be letting him down and I sure don't want to do that. It's strange, a few days ago I left home feeling sorry for myself, and in an hour and a half I was able to help someone who needed what I had to offer. I helped save a child's life, met the woman I had been searching for, met a man who is as close to me as my father, and even calls me son, and now he and I are building a not-for-profit company to help children of mainly, financially disadvantaged parents, but not excluding anyone. If we can help, we will help. I haven't had time to feel sorry for myself since. It is amazing how God knows just where you ought to be, even though you had other plans.*

As promised, supper was at 6:30 - barbequed ribs, potato salad, and cole slaw from the deli. Mike and Julie rinsed the dishes and stacked them to do in the morning. The 10 p.m. news was just over when the phone rang. Julie picked it up and held it out to Mike.

"It's for you," she said, "a woman."

"I'm not going over there for dessert or anything else," he said loudly, about to lose his patience. He didn't see the wry smile on Julie's face. "Hello," he shouted into the phone.

"Hello sweetheart. Walt told me you called and you were worried about me."

"It's Susan," he reported to Julie. "Where were you not going for dessert or anything else?" Susan asked.

"Your friend, Barbie Doll has been hitting on me from the very beginning. If you don't already know, she is not a natural blonde. She didn't tell me, she let me see for myself. She invited me over for dessert tonight. I thought it was her on the phone; that's why I shouted. I have to stay as far away from her as possible. I trust myself but not her. I've asked Julie and Dad to make sure she and I are never alone together. When are you coming home? I miss you and the more I'm around her, the more I miss you."

"I think I can wrap this up by the end of next week. Walt tells me the Angel Flight will be ready by then and Lizzie will be able to come home. We can have a reunion and maiden flight all in one. I love you, Michael Murphy; I really do, but didn't know just how much until this week. I will explain later and I will call when I get a chance. This assignment is very important to me, and of course that affects you too. It is not dangerous in any way but very secret. I've got to hang up now. Give Pops my love and tell Julie to keep Barbie Doll away from my man or she will answer to me. You have never seen me in action, but it's not a pretty sight. Good night, sweetheart."

"Good night darling, I love you too." Mike hung up the phone, breathed a big sigh of relief, and said to Julie, "I needed that; boy, did I ever need that. I won't be in the office much for reasons you are aware of, but you can get me on the cell or by radio if I'm in the Cub. I've been around the block once or twice, but I have never encountered a woman like Barbra. She is not a natural blonde and she made certain I could see for myself. To have a woman do that is not a turn on; it's repulsive. She is so hot if you put an egg between her legs it would be hard-boiled in less than five minutes. I'm going to have breakfast with Hawk, so don't scramble me any basted eggs. A kick-in-the-butt cup of coffee will suffice. Good night, Julie."

"Good night, Mike. The coffee will be ready when you are. Supper at 6:30 as usual. Bring something home we can snack on before we go to bed. We are all out of your Mom's cookies," Julie responded.

CHAPTER 19

Hawk was alone in his usual place the next morning when Mike arrived.

"So what's new on the crime front Chief?" Mike queried.

"Still investigating and keeping Mr. Romaine under surveillance. What's new with you?" Hawk answered.

Mike said, "Sunday, I drove by the office on the way to the folks. I found the shed door open, so I checked inside. Everything seemed in order so I locked the door and went on my way. Yesterday, I had to leave the office because of some pressure I was under, so I got in the Cub and just toured. I flew over the house and noticed some strange cars. Ramon and the big blonde were having an animated discussion. More to the point, there was a set of tracks from the old county road up to the back of the shed. They were still visible because the rain kept the weeds and grass fresh. I couldn't tell if it was a car or truck or anything from the tread marks. I protected them in hopes you or one of your detectives could read sign better than this paleface."

Hawk took notes and said he would personally look into it. Mike told him to watch out for the hot blonde. "She wants to get laid and she has selected me to be the one. She is not a natural blonde. I didn't have to guess; she showed me. I don't know if she will hit on you or not; this is just a friendly warning. I'm going now to find an architect and get some plans drawn for a maintenance facility for Angel Flight."

"There is sure a lot of activity out there," Hawk commented. "Just what are you building?"

"We are building a first-class airport with runways capable of handling jets. There will be a terminal building, with a restaurant and coffee shop that will give people in the area another choice for eating out - maybe ethnic, like Chinese or Mexican. This town is at a standstill and facilities that can handle jets - especially corporate jets-will encourage industry. That will bring jobs, new houses, and increase the tax base, which helps to hold property taxes down. We are asking Washington DC to get on board. If they do, they will fund 95% of the cost, Oregon 3%, and we will pay the rest. The beauty of this is, that the government money is not tax dollars; it's from landing fees from airports nationwide," Mike continued. "With a terminal, we can encourage small carriers to put us on a regular schedule, probably one in the A.M.. and one in the P.M.; nevertheless, it's a start. We will move our offices into a new building on site to help the city grow. I won't let the city or the business Pop has busted his ass to make successful, die. My phone's ringing, Hawk, excuse me. Hello, this is Mike."

"Mike," this is Julie. "The shed door was open again, and I checked it myself before I left last night and it was locked. Somebody has been in the office. Nothing seems to be missing, but there are doors open that are normally locked. What should I do?"

"Don't touch anything," Mike cautioned. "You, Pop, and Barbra get out, lock the door and wait for Hawk, who is already in his patrol car with siren blaring, heading your way. Keep me posted. I'm going to find an architect. See you for supper. Bye."

"William Howland and Associates, Architects and Engineers, had an office in town, so Mike called for an appointment. The girl who answered said, "Paul Anderson is the only one in, would you like to speak with him?"

"Yes, I would," Mike answered. "Can I ask who's calling?"

"Yes you can. Go ahead and ask," Mike responded. "What are you, some kind of wise guy?" she shouted.

"No, you asked if you could ask who's calling. I said yes you can ask, so go ahead and ask," Mike answered.

"I've had enough of your bullshit," she said and hung up.

Well, Mike thought to himself, *If he is in, I'll just go over and see him and see what kind of airhead she is. Even hot pants Barbie Doll, would be preferred over her.*" It was a main-floor office with a conference room and two ample offices. The secretary, or whatever she was supposed to be, looked to be 16 or 17. The hair on one side was blonde, the other half red. She had three nose rings, a pierced tongue and lower lip with matching jewels. She wore a low-cut blouse, ragged denim shorts, and flip-flops that showed her black painted toenails.

"Can I help you?" she asked.

"I would like to see Mr. Anderson." "Ya got an appointment?" she asked.

"No, I don't," Mike answered. He wondered how long it would take before one of them would get angry.

"Well, ya gotta have an appointment. We ain't gonna let just anybody walk in off the street without an appointment and take up our associates' valuable time," she retorted.

"Miss," Mike said calmly. "I spoke to you on the phone a few minutes ago and you hung up on me saying you had enough of my bullshit. Now it's my turn. You are, without a doubt, the poorest excuse for a secretary I have ever seen. Your costume is more for trick or treating than for office attire. You got pissed off on the phone when I answered your question and I said, yes you can; go ahead and ask... When you say 'can' it means 'am I able to?' The correct and universal way is to say 'may I' which is asking for permission. I don't have any idea how you got this job, but your attitude and attire disgust me. When you talk to my college roommate, Bill Howland, tell him Mike Murphy stopped by. Since I didn't have an appointment with the gentleman asleep in his office, I'm taking my million-dollar project elsewhere. Good day."

Mike got in his pickup and found a shady spot to park. He called Portland Information and got Howland's phone number and was soon talking to his old friend. "You've got a real problem back here, Bill. You would be money ahead to close this office temporarily. I say temporarily because this town is about to sprout, which is the reason I went to your office today. Walt Henderson and I are starting a new air service. We are going to fly critically injured or sick children to wherever they need to go at no charge. He is forming a not-for-profit corporation and those with means can get a tax break and do some real good. Our problem is this; in our excitement to bring our airport to first-class level, we forgot about a maintenance and hangar facility for our jets. At the present time we have only one jet. It's a Gulf Stream, and any others will be similar. We need plans last week. Can you help us?"

"I'm sure I can Mike," Bill answered. "We did Beaver Air five years ago and it sounds like you need about the same thing. We still have all the drawings on file. If you could meet me there, we can look their place over. Maybe with a little change here and there, we'll have what you need."

"Bill, Beaver Air is refurbishing our jet as we speak. Can you get away tomorrow morning?" Mike asked.

"Hell Mike, I'm the boss, I can get away anytime. How does 9:30 sound?" Bill responded.

It seems to be coming together pretty well, Mike thought to himself. *I'll call Julie and ask her to find someone to make room in the shed for my Lincoln. I can drive that out early and be gone before hot pants, Barbie Doll gets to work and time it so she will be gone when I get back. I'd better get to work."*

He took old highway 30 to Chenoweth and talked to the general contractor's superintendent. The new school would be finished in time for the fall classes. "Mr. Murphy, your people are far and away the best I've seen in their field. I think I will use you almost exclusively. They are ahead of schedule and under budget. Where did you find them?" the super asked.

"They are all around you. We take ordinary craftsmen; give them an incentive to do better. They know we will accept nothing less than the best they can do. That doesn't mean they have to do better than everybody else; it means they have to give us their best. In return, we insure the married hands for one million dollars. Their wives are the beneficiaries. The single employees are at half that amount and their parents are the beneficiaries. We also give full medical and hospitalization coverage, two weeks paid vacation, plus sick or family time and bonuses. If we feel someone is taking advantage of us, we turn it over to the committee, which is comprised of senior employees. They have a come-to-Jesus meeting with him or her and they make the decision. Usually, that meeting is the first and last warning. If the employee continues in errant ways he is fired on the spot, paid to the minute, escorted off the premises, and will never be hired again. We don't have much turnover. In fact, it has been four or five years since we had one quit and that was because his mother-in-law was dying a slow and painful death in Ohio. When it's all over, he can and probably will come back and his job will be waiting for him. My father struggled and busted his ass to give me every opportunity to do what I wanted. I chose Navy flying. Dad always said that if he ever had employees, they would not have to worry about insurance. He has been successful without unions because his benefits are better than the unions, and all done with a handshake contract. If and when you want to do business with us, we will sit down without lawyers, come to terms, and shake on it. That's the way it will be and there is no debate. You will be dealing with a hardheaded Irishman and his son. What is your name sir?"

"Harrigan, Sir, Patrick Harrigan. There will be no problems three Irishmen can't work out. It's been a pleasure talking, or should I say listening to you," he laughed. "Good Day to you sir. I've got to get back to work."

Mike got to Julie's just after 5 o'clock, made coffee, and was watching the news when she got home. "What's new at the office?" he asked.

"Hawk dusted the place for finger prints. He found a lot of them, so he took ours to eliminate us from the list of suspects," Julie reported. "He thinks the tire tracks were left by a Hummer, but couldn't read the tread markings. There is nice spot for your car in the shed and we found a tarp to cover it and keep the bird poop off. Barbra showed no interest in Hawk, so it has to be you she is after. I asked her to lighten up; she didn't take it very well but we will see."

"I'm going to drive the Lincoln out in the morning before Barbra gets to work. I talked to my friend, Bill Howland, and we are going to meet at Beaver Air. He did Beaver Air five years ago and from what I told him he thinks the same plans with a change here and there would work for us. If they do work, we gained about 30 days. I will ride home with you if that's okay."

"That will be fine with me, but wouldn't you rather ride in a red sports car?' Julie joked.

"Only if you were driving. I don't want to go anywhere near Barbie Doll," Mike said. "Seriously. Let me treat you to dinner at Reynaldo's Hideaway. I feel like some good Latin food."

CHAPTER 20

Wednesday morning started off as planned. Mike put the Lincoln in its spot, covered it with the tarp, and was in the air by 7:30. He arrived at Troutdale with time to check the refurbishing of Walt's jet before the meeting with Bill Howland. "Good morning, Mr. Jensen," he said, "I'm to meet Mr. Howland here at 9:30. I would like an update on the progress on the Angel jet."

"You're just in time, Mr. Murphy, I was about to call you. I believe you and I are going to be seeing each other fairly often, so if you don't mind, I would like to be on a first-name basis. You call me Vic and I'll call you Mike or Michael, which do you prefer?"

"Mike is fine with me, Vic," Mike answered. "Now back to business."

"Everything is going smoothly. The Rolls Royce engines you wanted are installed. We made some factory-approved adjustments and additions. You won't be able to outrun an F15, but he won't suck the wind from you going past. The medical equipment is being installed. When that is complete we will put it in the paint shop, which is the next to last step. The final step is to see if we can get it off the ground, check the performance of the engines, and get it back down without breaking anything. If everything goes according to plan, and I see no reason for it not to, you can have it a week from Thursday, any time after 3:00 p.m.," Vic advised.

"Sounds super, Vic, especially the extra speed. There will be times when every second counts, and the extra juice might very well be the difference. On our initial flight we had a strong tail wind, which helped a lot but we still lost her. A Medic refused to let her go and somehow brought her back. We will be going to Galveston in Angel One to bring her home," Mike explained. "Excuse me, Vic, I think I see Mr. Howland coming this way now."

"Good morning gentlemen," Mr. Howland said in greeting. "I see you two have met."

"Vic is refurbishing Walt Henderson's jet, turning it into a medical ambulance so we can fly critical children to the proper Shrine Medical Center. We need a facility where we can service our aircraft onsite, much like this one," Mike explained. "Vic, Bill tells me he built this facility for you without any input or feedback, just, to use an old phrase, by the seat of his pants. Is that true?"

"Every word, Mike," Vic answered. "And I wouldn't change one thing."

"Bill, what do you need from me to get this show on the road?" Mike asked.

"How many offices and what size? Will there be an executive-type office?" Bill answered. "Excuse us, Vic, thanks for your endorsement. Mike and I are going to work on his project so we'll go to the coffee shop and finish our discussion there."

"I'll see you a week from Thursday, Vic," Mike chimed in.

In the coffee shop, Mike and Bill Howland put together the specs for Angel One. "We'll need one executive office. That will be for the general manager of the entire operation - Angel Flight and Mike Murphy and Son, two smaller offices - one for Angel Flight, one for Mike Murphy and Son. Also, cubicles for a staff of secretaries and an office for an office manager and a comptroller. Have I forgotten anything, Bill?" Mike asked.

"I can't think of anything. I thought you were a fairly small company doing electronics but these specs are for a larger company. What's the story Mike?" Bill asked.

"Bill you know as well as I, you can't stand still. You go forward and grow or go backward and die. We are not about to die. When you started you had yourself, a secretary and a receptionist. You hired associates as the need arose; now you have a branch office back home and are looking to open another some place. You have been moving ahead since the day you hung out your shingle. We are no different. Do you know of a contractor who could get this done quickly without sacrificing quality?" Mike queried.

"There is one I can think of," Bill answered. "He is building a new school in Chenoweth. The last time I checked he was on schedule and could probably start fairly soon. You will not find any one who can start tomorrow. Phillip Higgins, Inc. is the one I am referring to. His office is in Hood River. Get in touch with them. They did this facility and you heard what Vic said."

"I talked to his superintendent yesterday," Mike said. "An Irishman named Harrigan, a real character. I'm going to drop in at Hood River on the way back and see if we can get together. I think that Irisher and I can work together. Get on those prints and plans. You have a deal, and here is my hand on it. I've got to go. It's been great seeing you and don't forget what I said about your branch back home."

"I won't forget what you said, but you didn't ask how much your project will cost. And how about a contract?" Bill protested.

"I gave you my hand, that's all the contract anyone ever gets from us. It's been good enough for over 20 years. As far as the cost is concerned, you have been in business for several years and are growing. That tells me you are not screwing your clients and I don't anticipate being the first one. Anytime you want your money, send us a statement and we'll cut you a check. Remember you are dealing with a stubborn Irishman. Do we have a deal?" Mike asked.

"We definitely have a deal, Mike. Forgive me; I'm not used to straight-forward people. I haven't personally closed a deal in several years because I got tired of dealing with their lawyers. It seems if you don't have everything in triplicate and notarized, you are apt to be sued, so I let my associates close deals. I have insurance to protect my butt and theirs, so I don't lose much sleep worrying about it. It has been so good to see you. I'd forgotten just what good friends we are. I will be over personally to close the office and I would like you to go with me. Also I am going to personally handle your project. It will get me out of the rat race, and we can rekindle what we once had," Bill said.

"Why not bring your wife when you come? It's not going to be all business, we can socialize. Mom and Pop would love to have you stay with them. I've told them about the dumb things we did at State, so they know more about you probably than your wife does. Did you marry that tall, gorgeous redhead with thick, kissable lips or did you let her get away?" Mike asked.

"I married her and we have two daughters and two sons," Bill answered. "How about you and Aggie?"

"I've just recently left her. I won't go into details, but I give you my solemn oath there was not another woman involved. There is now, and I have never been so happy with life," Mike responded. "Please come and bring Marge; I gotta go, bye."

He dropped in at Hood River just past 2 p.m. He looked up their number and punched it up. A smiling female voice on the other end, responded, "Higgins Inc. How can I help you?"

'This is Michael Murphy, of Mike Murphy and Son. I just left William Howland. He is doing a project for me and recommended your company as the one best suited to my needs. I don't mean to be flippant, but I need to talk to somebody in your company. I flew in and I don't have an appointment. Is there any way you can think of that would make it possible to have a face to face today?"

She giggled and said, "Gee whiz, Mr. Murphy, the only way I can think of is to come out to the airport, pick you up and bring you to the office. When you are finished, I'd let you buy me a cup of coffee at the airport diner. Do you think that would work?"

Mike laughed, "I'll be the dumb Irishman waiting out front reading a paper," he said.

"Saints' preserve us," she said, "another one."

Twenty minutes later, a pickup with Higgins Inc. on the side, pulled up with an auburn-haired driver that looked to be about Mike's age. "Margaret Kelly," she said. "If you're Michael Murphy hop in; if not get the hell out of my way, I've got places to go and people to see. I can't be wasting my time on the likes of you." All of this with a smile on her face and twinkle in her eye.

She wore sage-green tailored slacks and matching blouse, simple gold earrings in her pierced ears, sensible shoes, and a plain wrist watch. She was a construction company secretary and knew her job. Mike had no doubt about that.

The office was on the ground floor of an old hotel that had been converted to offices. Margaret ushered him into the office of a man in his 50's, and introduced him as Mr. Higgins.

"Michael Murphy Mr. Higgins," Mike said extending his hand. "I have a problem that I explained to William Howland. He said your company would be the first one he would contact in a similar situation, so here I am."

"Just what is this problem you have that Bill said I could fix?" Higgins asked.

"We are building a new airport for our current business and another one we are starting. In our exuberance, we neglected to provide maintenance facilities for our upcoming fleet of corporate jets. We need it done yesterday, but know it's not going to happen. All we want is someone to say they will do their best to get it done in as short a time as possible. We will accept only the best you can do. We will not sacrifice quality of product for speed or price," Mike explained.

Margaret stuck her head in the door and announced, "Pat's here, Shall I have him wait?"

"No, send him in," Higgins ordered.

Pat turned out to be Patrick Harrigan. "Good afternoon, Mike," Pat said.

"Back at you, doubled," Mike responded.

"I take it you two know each other," Higgins stated.

After a successful meeting, Margaret was driving Mike to the airport and quizzing him about problems with unions. "It seems we have to be so careful to make sure no union rules are being broken. On one job, the iron workers walked off because a carpenter bent a re-rod out of his way so he could get through. How do you avoid those pitfalls, Mike?"

"We provide better benefits than the unions and pay more than union scale. We are more a family-type company and all we expect is, as I told Phil, the best you can do and we accept no less. Each employee gets a bonus at the end of the year, besides being paid for the days between Christmas and New Years. My dad and I draw a good salary and we make no apologies for it, but compared to what I've seen other executives draw, we are way down below their scale. I don't know how I could spend all the money some of those people draw as wages. How much is enough? Here we are, and I insist on buying you a cup of coffee," he added.

"There was no question about the coffee," Margaret joked, "but now I want a piece of raisin cream pie. They bake their own pies here onsite and they are delicious."

"Margaret, you are an attractive lady who seems to know what you want. I see no evidence of a wedding ring. Why?" Mike asked.

"I'm a free spirit, Michael Murphy," Margaret said, "and I'll have no one who wants to own me. Too many married women are no more than unpaid whores. She does the cooking and cleaning, laundry, marketing, has babies, raises them, and satisfies her horny husband who seldom, if ever, even thinks about her as a person. A whore satisfies a horny man, gets paid well for maybe 30 minutes of his pleasure, and doesn't have to cook or clean for him. He's got a wife at home to do that for him. I'll have no part of that. When I marry, the man will be the man I want, not one I'm going to change after the wedding. We will work and play together and make the marriage into what we both want, not what other folks think a marriage should be."

"Margaret," Mike said, "you will make some lucky man a wonderful wife, and I wish you all the best."

"Thank you, Michael. When I find that man you say will be so lucky, he will get lucky after the wedding, not before. I hope he and I can learn together," Margaret commented.

"Listen to the voice of experience," Mike offered. "Communication is the secret ingredient of any successful venture with two people, and marriage is not a venture. It's an adventure; there is always something new to discover. A marriage is like everything else; it either goes and grows or stagnates and dies. It's up to both of you to make it grow. One can't do it alone because it then becomes one-sided. That's what happened to me; don't let it happen to you."

CHAPTER 21

Mike touched down a little past 5 p.m. and most everyone had left for the day. He put his airplane in the shed after refueling and checking the oil so it would be ready to go at a moment's notice. Barbra came out of the office carelessly waving a gun. "Honey," she said in her soft southern drawl, "I was looking for some papers Susan said she had in her desk. I opened the drawer and found this cute little pistol," pointing it at Mike.

He screamed, "Don't ever point a gun - even one you think may be a toy gun - at anything or anybody you don't want to kill." She raised the gun, pointed it skyward, and pulled the trigger, and the gun went off. "You stupid broad, you could have just as easily killed me as you blew a hole in the sky. Starting now, I'm going to teach you gun safety. You heard number one; never point a gun at anything or anybody you don't want to kill. The next is; always assume the gun is loaded. If you abide by those two rules you greatly reduce the risk of accidentally shooting someone. Since you chose to fire it, you get to clean and oil it."

"Okay, honey, I'm sorry I shot the sky," Barbra said, in her pouty, feel-sorry-for-me voice. "I'm real glad I didn't shoot you. I'll clean the gun in the morning. I've got a headache."

"Bull shit," Mike answered. "I'll bet if I said I was coming over to your place for dessert, your headache would go away. So pretend I'm coming over and get your ass back in the office, and I'll tell you what to do. Make no mistake; you are going to clean the gun. I'm going to tell you how, and tomorrow morning we are going to the police station and have a shooting match with the Chief. I'll pick you up here at ten. You will be out of your office until at least two, so adjust your schedule accordingly, and don't argue. This is not a debatable issue."

"Mike honey, you are so darling when you are upset. Your nostrils flare and your beautiful eyes widen. I surely do just melt when I look at you. Let's go into the office and clean this little ol' gun. Gracious sake, I believe my headache is almost gone," Barbra said in her most seductive and sultry voice.

Julie stood watching the whole thing in amused silence. *"Poor Mike,"* she said to herself, *"He is in for such a rude wakening."* "Mike." She called to him as she walked out to her car, "I've got to be going, Barbra can bring you home. Can't you, dear?"

"Oh yes, Julie, it will be my pleasure to bring Mike home," Barbra answered.

"I'm referring to my home, Barbra, not yours," Julie stated. "Oh, dear me, my little ol' heart was just pounding in anticipation, and you had to go and spoil it. I'll see he doesn't miss supper and I'll see you in the morning," Barbra pouted.

When she finished the cleaning, Mike noted the gun wasn't as clean as Susan had it, but he didn't want to be trapped with Barbra any longer.

"Sugar," she said, "there's nobody here but us two, and I have needs, so why don't we use the couch in your Daddy's office."

"I don't know how to make it any clearer, Barbra," Mike stated. "You are a very attractive woman and could probably show me some horizontal dancing moves I've never heard of, much less used, but I am not going to fall into that furry trap you have set between your legs. I've told you time and time again, I'm a one-woman man, and Susan is my woman. All you want is sex, not love, and there is a world of difference between the two. I want love, not sex. This is something I probably shouldn't tell you, but maybe it will help you understand. Susan and I have laid in bed, cuddled, kissed and gone to sleep in each other's arms. We have also had the best lovemaking in the history of man. We call it loving - you want a screwing - and there is a big difference. I hope we have closed the book on that subject for good, because I have a lot to get done in a short time, and fending you off continually is taking its toll on my work."

"All right Mike, honey," Barbra said, "I'm convinced you are a lost cause and I promise to lighten up. I'm still going to flirt because that's my nature, but I'm not going to throw myself at you. After all, a girl can only stand so much rejection. Will you give me a forgiving hug? I promise that I will not make any unwanted moves."

"Barbra, nothing would please me more than to be able to hug you as a sweet friend. I miss being able to hug Susan, so you would be an acceptable substitute, but we won't let it go any further," Mike whispered. After a warm and sincere friendly hug, with no sensual overtones they turned off the light, locked the office, and left.

The ride to Julie's was pleasant. Soft music was playing, allowing each to be lost in thought.

"Here we are," Mike stated. "If you have jeans, you might think about wearing them tomorrow. The pistol range is not the fanciest place in town, and you will get gun powder on your hands and clothing." A quick kiss on the cheek and he was out of the car before she could react. "Good night, dear friend," he said. "See you in the morning."

"Well, it's about time you showed up," Julie teased. "You just have time to wash up before supper. Tell me about your day while we eat."

"It has been an eventful day, Julie. The Angel jet will be ready Thursday afternoon about three. I met with Bill Howland, the architect that did Beaver Air, and we can use most of those specs on our project. He told me about a contractor in Hood River that had done Beaver Air, so I stopped to see him. It turns out he is the general contractor on the school in Chenoweth. We are doing the electronics there. I was explaining our situation to him when his superintendent from Chenoweth came in. I had talked to him yesterday. He is an Irishman named Harrigan. He's bringing graders Monday and will start without the final plans. Bill Howland is going to work with the contractor, Higgins Construction, and last, but far from least, Barbra and I had it out and reached an understanding. In fact, we had a hugging session before we left and it was just that - two friends giving each other friendly hugs. I think things are going to sail along pretty smoothly from now on."

CHAPTER 22

"I'm going to teach you how to baste an egg this morning, Julie," Mike teased. "Scrambled is fine but it doesn't' have any character. A basted egg lies there and tempts you with its big, beautiful, yellow eye, sometimes half closed in a sly wink, then when you eat it, it slowly oozes down your chin in a sensual waltz. A scrambled egg just lies there and waits for salt, pepper, and catsup, nothing else. It just lies there, and says, 'let's get going, we've got a lot to do today'."

"Are you sure you want to teach Barbra how to shoot?" Julie asked. "She just may shoot you, out of frustration. The way you treat her with more than cold indifference, and the way you talk to her is terrible. If she wasn't so hot for you, she would be in tears most of the time. But I guess that's between you two."

"I'm pretty sure we closed the book on that yesterday evening. Anyway, today is a new day and I'll play the hand I'm dealt. She will be out of the office most of the day today. Is there anything that Barbra has to do that's urgent?" Mike asked.

"Nothing that I know about," Julie answered. "She is a first-rate secretary. I can't believe how much she gets done when you aren't around to get her motor running. I've been in this type of work longer than I want to admit and I can't hold a candle to her. I swear, she could be gone for a week or more and be all caught up the second day back on the job. It won't hurt a thing if she is gone all day."

Mike got to the office just as his Dad drove in. "Hi Pop," he said. "I need to fill you in on my success yesterday." He explained everything to a beaming father.

When he finished, Murph said, "Son, I am so proud of you. The way you handle this business is as good as anybody could do. You should handle Barbra as well. She is just a young girl looking for the right man and thinks you are the one."

"We settled that issue yesterday, Dad. I haven't seen her yet, but we are going to shoot with Hawk in a little while. We'll see if our little talk held or if I need to do it again. Higgins Construction will be rolling in Monday to start grading, so things are moving forward. I'm short on Mom's cookies. I'll see you Sunday. It's time to go shoot. See you later."

"Hey Barbie Doll," Mike said, "Are you ready to do some shooting or would you prefer to shoot holes in the sky?"

"My, you are in a good mood this morning, Mike," she answered. "I would like to learn to shoot and pretend I'm shooting somebody that is giving me trouble, and I'm ready. Shall I drive, or do you want to?"

"I'll be a passenger," Mike replied. "I like riding in your ragtop. Don't forget your gun."

Hawk was waiting, and when Barbra entered with Mike, he asked why she was there. After Mike explained, Hawk said to Barbra, "Okay but we have to take your fingerprints for our records. We treat everybody the same."

When they got to the pistol range, Barbra suggested that Hawk and Mike shoot first and said , "you can both he'p poor li'l ole me."

The shoot off ended like it did most of the time - the win was by five points. "All right Barbra, let's see where we need to start," Hawk offered. "Carefully remove the gun from its case and pull the slide back until it clicks and locks into place. Remove the clip and check your ammo."

"Is that the same as bullets, Chief, honey?" Barbra asked.

"Yes, Barbra, it is the same as bullets," Hawk answered. "Now replace the clip and release the slide, being careful to point down range, because you now have a loaded gun in your hand. Now do what you think you should do, and then we'll start making corrections. Make sure you are pointing it toward the target, holding the gun in both hands, aim, and squeeze the trigger. Forget all those John Wayne and Clint Eastwood movies where they draw and shoot from the hip. That only happens in the movies. It's hard enough to hit your target when you have time to aim."

Barbra took a stance, raised the gun, and fired. "Well, you hit the wall," Hawk commented. "Now that you know what to expect, take careful aim and squeeze off three rounds, taking time to aim between each round."

"Not too bad, at least you put one round on the target. It wouldn't be a life-threatening injury but he would be pretty pissed off and his wife or girlfriend would not be pleased if they wanted kids because his baby-making tool would be gone," Hawk laughed. "Now squeeze off the rest of the clip slowly, and always aim between rounds. Speed is important, but accuracy is the most important. When you pull down on a person armed with a gun, you must put them down before they put you down. You aim to kill - that's what they are doing."

Barbra emptied the clip and Hawk pulled the target up so she could see. "Pull the slide back until it clicks and locks, release the clip, and remove it." He handed her a box of shells. "Now reload," he said, and put the first two in the clip so she could see how it was done. "I don't think you are squeezing the trigger," Hawk commented... "I think you are pulling it and closing your eyes. Just concentrate on squeezing and keeping your eyes open. Pretend you are romantically and gently squeezing Mike's hand and try to see the bullet come out. Empty the clip at your own speed, taking aim before each round."

"Gracious sakes alive, that is a lot for poor li'l ole me to remember all at once. I will pretend I'm squeezing Mike - that part is easy - but the loud noise makes me jump. But I will try, I really will," Barbra promised.

The first two rounds went astray, but she settled down and had a much better grouping. "Much better," Hawk said. "There are two that would be terminal and one that would put him in intensive care with a pretty grim prognosis. Let's take your fingerprints for the record and a spent round for a ballistics comparison. Mike and I will wait for you in my office."

"She was a good student, Mike, and really tried. I noticed she was very steady, not shaky, and did begin squeezing off rounds. It wouldn't take much to make her an excellent marksman."

Barbra came out of the ladies room drying her hands. "You were right Mike, Sugar. That gunpowder is all over me and my clothes. I should have worn a bandana; it's even in my hair. Do we eat lunch now? Shooting made me hungry," she remarked.

"It is lunchtime, Barbra," Hawk answered, "and I would like to buy your lunch. May I?"

"How can a girl refuse an offer like that from such an important and handsome gentleman? I would be pleased to accept your invitation." Looking at Mike, she continued, "Some men are too concerned about themselves to even think about anyone else's feelings."

They sat in Hawk's usual spot, and soon after they were seated, Ramon and two Latino-looking men sat at a table close by and began talking Spanish in low tones, all the while glancing at Barbra and her escorts.

Barbra leaned over the table and whispered, "Do either of you two speak Spanish?" Getting a negative response, she sat a little while, then slowly getting up, she looked at the Chief and Mike, and whispered, "prepare to back me up." She sauntered over to Ramon's table and in perfect Spanish told them that the three of them together didn't have the balls or guts or anything else to carry out what they were planning. She invited any one of the three to stand up to her as she took a martial arts defensive stance.

Ramon was livid. She looked at him and said, "you first you greasy bastard." To everyone's surprise, he stood up and made an advance on Barbra. Before anyone could react she kicked him on the left side of the face and just as quickly on the right, followed by one to the jewels and finally to the chin. Ramon's eyes opened wide, and then closed as he fell unconscious on the floor.

Barbra wasn't even breathing hard. Turning to the other two, she said, "Next." Nobody moved. She said to Ramon's companions, "Get out and take your garbage with you but don't forget to pay for your lunch and be sure you leave a nice tip.

"Mercy sakes alive," she said, glancing at the pair of stunned men and waitress at her table, "I don't know whatever possessed li'l ole me to do such a thing. I believe I'll have a hamburger deluxe, fries, a large milk, sweet tea if you have it, and pecan pie. The Chief is buying."

"Where did you learn those moves?" Mike asked.

Barbra (Susan disguised for some time) leaned over the table and whispered very low. "Do not react when I tell you this. The best place to hide is in plain sight, and Lizzy is Angel One. Those three were going to kill you two and then play with me before they killed me too. I had heard that said before, but Mike stepped in and took care of the situation. I don't believe I could have disarmed that hood in Galveston, so I had been hesitant. I was about to give it a try when Mike stepped up to the plate. I would like to keep up this charade for as long as possible, and if I had you fooled, Mike sugar," she said in her sensuous southern drawl, "I figure I can fool anybody."

"Hawk," she continued, "that is not my gun. Mine pulls slightly left; I don't know how to aim this one. Mine has a soft easy trigger pull; this one is a man's gun. The trigger is stiff and pulls hard, and when you check ballistics you will see the difference. I think someone - and we are pretty sure who it is - is trying to set me up. When it happens, let's go along with it until he hangs himself."

"You should go to Hollywood; you are a great actress," Mike remarked. "I'm sorry I said those unkind things to you. Can you forgive me?"

"Of course I forgive you. You stood up to all the pressure I put on you including that disgusting display of the - pardon me, Hawk - furry trap I had set between my legs." Susan answered. "I don't want to go back to the office; I want to shower and clean up.

Would you take Mike honey back to the office for li'l ole me, please, Chief?" she continued.

"Would I dare refuse to honor a request from a lady that can fire four or more rounds from a Beretta, and then shoot the eyes out? On top of that, she can put a grown man down unconscious and incapacitated in less than two minutes and not break a sweat. Me refuse? I don't think so," Hawk answered.

"Where have you been staying?" Mike asked.

"All I'll tell you is that there is an endless supply of applesauce cookies," Susan answered, "and if we are going to continue this charade, I should stay there until this is over. I didn't intend to blow my cover, but when I discovered this piece of crap had been substituted for my gun, I had to at least expose the gun. Then when I heard Ramon plotting to have you killed and me raped, I decided to do what I've been wanting and training to do for a long time. I really enjoyed that. The best part was the kick in the nuts. That was a textbook move. He didn't need the last one, but I was on a roll, so what the hell."

"I think you and I should go to dinner tonight. I should show off my new girlfriend," Mike stated. "We'll do it right - dinner jacket, flowers, the whole nine yards. We will be seen in public as an item, causing tongues to wag. The notice for divorce has been published and for me to be seen in public with two different women should give people some new dirt to play in. I'll pick you up at seven, okay?" Mike asked.

"Okay," Susan answered, "don't be late."

"I can tell when I'm not needed," Hawk joked. "I'll let you two alone to make your plans. Susan, if you ever think you would like to join the Police Force I'd hire you in a minute. The only thing you would need is to be more aggressive."

"Thanks Chief, when we get settled here I will volunteer to teach martial arts to your department," Susan remarked.

"I will see that program goes past the City Council," the Chief said. "I've witnessed what a person trained in martial arts can do," he added. "And the department could use the additional weapon. Thank you." He turned to Mike and said, "Come on Mike, the lady has to get ready for her date tonight and I have to check on Ramon and his friends."

When Mike got back to the office he told both Julie and his dad about Barbra being Susan. In unison they said, "We know."

"Who else knew?" Mike asked.

"Nobody else knew, just Murph, your mom, and I," Julie answered. "It was hard to keep a straight face when she was hitting on you. You proved to her you were a one-woman man, and she was your woman."

"Susan and I are going out to dinner this evening, and since it's so hard to cook for one why don't you join us?" Mike suggested. "It will be a gussied-up affair - dinner jacket, flowers, and the whole nine yards. The gossips have seen the notice about the divorce, so if I am seen with two beauties it will give them some new dirt. Susan and I will check into the Hampton House for tonight. I don't think we can be quiet while we're not sleeping. Barbra will be back to work tomorrow, but will be late."

"I don't want to be a fifth wheel and cool your reunion," Julie offered.

"Don't flatter yourself, Julie," Mike teased. "A blizzard couldn't cool our reunion. We'll leave at 7:00." He called Susan to tell her about Julie joining them. "I told Julie we were going to check into the Hampton House for tonight because we couldn't be quiet when we weren't sleeping, and that Barbra would be back in the morning but would be late."

"Why Mike, sugar, what a wonderful plan," Susan said. "I'll pack a suitcase with clothes for tonight and for work tomorrow. You and Julie can pick me up there, then in the morning I'll check out. My car will be there, and I'll just go to work like normal, but I will be feeling a lot better. I wasn't lying when I said a woman has needs. I didn't until you came along. When I was hitting on you I hoped you would take the bait, but prayed you wouldn't. I told you before, you were the answer to my prayers. I'll see you at 7:00. I love you Michael Murphy."

"I love Susan Romaine and Barbra Dahl, but I love Susan Romaine most of all," Mike responded.

"Oh Mike, sugar, you make my li'l ole heart just go pitty pat when you talk like that," Susan said in her most seductive voice and southern drawL "Now I have to take a cold shower before I can do anything else. Later! Bye."

CHAPTER 23

Mike called Susan from the car to tell her he and Julie were waiting out in front. Susan came out soon in her best Barbie Doll attire; very short red skirt, and white blouse with a v-neck almost to the waist. With her ample breasts, she drew a lot of leers from the men in the lobby. Gaudy, costume jewelry - bracelet, necklace and earrings and 4-inch heels completed her costume. If one didn't know better, you would think she was a hooker working the convention of car dealers being held there.

At the dinner club, Susan continued the Barbie Doll impression. When the valet opened the door for her, she exited in a most unladylike manner. With her very short skirt and long legs, it would have been almost impossible not to. Julie, in her lemon-colored, long, silk sheath slit up the side was very ladylike and offered her hand for assistance. The valet was too busy imagining what he was doing with Barbie, so Mike took Julie's hand.

While the three of them were waiting for the maitre d', Susan was scanning the room. She quietly said to Mike and Julie, "over to your left, halfway down, sit the three Musketeers; Ramon, Agnes, and the blonde. Do you think she is a real blonde, Mike, honey?" Susan teased.

The maitre d' approached, cleared his throat and in a quiet voice, said to Mike while looking at Susan, "I'm sorry, sir, but we prefer not to serve her kind."

Before Mike could say anything, Susan in her best Barbra Dahl sensual southern drawl, speaking almost in a whisper said, "You mean that a poor li'l working girl can't have dinner with her date and friend, but you would serve that greasy drug dealer and his date and friend? I don't know, honey, but that seems like discrimination." Grabbing Mike by the arm, she said, "Come on sugar, let's blow this dump."

The maitre d' responded, "Please Miss, I don't want a scene, just follow me please." When they got to the table Mike helped Julie, leaving the maitre d' no choice but to help Susan.

As he left, she called, "Thanks, sugar, I'll tell all my friends what a nice place you got here."

Mike saw Howard Morrison being seated. He seemed to be alone. "Excuse me ladies, I just got an idea, so play along." He walked over to Howard and asked if he was waiting for someone. When Howard responded in the negative he said, "I am in an embarrassing position. You remember Julie? We met you at the folks."

"Yes, of course I do, a very attractive lady," Howard answered. "How can I help you?"

"The gaudy-looking woman with us is making it uncomfortable for Julie. If you wouldn't object, it would be a big relief to her if she could join you. She doesn't know you are here, so if you would rather not, no feelings would be hurt," Mike answered.

"It would be my pleasure to have her join me. I don't like to eat alone and cooking for myself gets old, so once in a while I come out here to be in a crowd. Please bring her over," Howard said.

Mike retreated to his table and whispered to Julie, "Howard Morrison is here and he is eating alone. This is not a setup. Would you like to join him for dinner? Barbie Doll and I have some catching up to do, if you don't mind."

"I've just been dumped for some bimbo," Julie said, winking at Susan. "Get your catching up done so you can concentrate on business. I'll see you in the morning."

Julie took Mike's arm and he paraded her to Howard's table. With her lemon-colored silk sheath, slit on one side, ending midway between the knee and hip, silver shoes with 3-inch heels, diamond earrings and necklace to match, she was, to say the least, striking. Howard gasped when he saw her. "Julia," he said, "You look absolutely beautiful I'll see she gets home okay. Is that all right with you, Julia?" Howard was obviously enamored with Julie to the point where he could hardly speak.

"That would be fine, Howard. Thank you," Julie responded. Mike thought he detected a little hint of excitement in Julie.

"Who knows?" he mused to himself. *"That could turn into something."*

Back at his table with Barbie Doll, he noticed she was sitting where Ramon could get full view as she crossed and uncrossed her legs. "Don't worry, sweetheart, I've got underwear on. He just thinks he is going to see something. Little does he realize he has seen it before and didn't appreciate it."

"Susan, please stop talking like that; you are degrading yourself," Mike said. "I'll take care of him myself and enjoy every minute. Why should you have all the fun? Now, if you want to act like a whore do it with me now, but not too aggressively. We have to eat and dance first to put on a good show. You've got Ramon really excited; you can tell from here. I don't know where he is going to get relief. Agnes sure won't help him, and I think Blondie is a lesbian. He will have to rape Agnes or do himself. From experience, I'm telling you, doing himself is the best option."

"Michael honey, I think you just might have a career as a matchmaker," Susan whispered. "Julie and Howard have not taken their eyes off each other since she sat down, and he is so attentive to her. When she had to go powder her nose, he stood up, helped her with her chair, and watched every move. When she got back, he pulled her chair out for her and helped her get comfortable. I would say that man is interested."

Mike explained, "Howard lost his wife a year ago and with nobody home he's very lonely. Julie and I went to have cookies and milk with Mom and Dad and Mom insisted he stay for dinner. Howard was also a guest so that's how we met. That reminds me; Howard is in real estate and has a property that sounds like something we should look at. I have an appointment with him to go look at it, and I'd like you to come too. I've not seen it but it sounds like a good place to raise children."

Ramon had gone to the men's room, and when he came out he came directly to Mike and Susan. "Senor, you have run all of my men away, and this poota humiliated me, injured me, and beat me. For that I'm going to kill you both, but not before I enjoy her most luscious body. Do you understand? I'm going to tie you up and force you to watch what I do to her, and then I will kill you both." "Unless you've got more in your tank than you've shown up to now, you are writing a check with your mouth that will come back stamped, insufficient funds," Mike responded. "So crawl back under your rock and play with yourself some more to relieve your tension. Get out of our way. We are going to dance. Come Miss, whatever your name is, or would you like to dance with sewer breath?"

"No mister, I can't stand grease. All I want is to take you to my hotel room and make sure you get your money's worth. I don't give change."

If looks could kill, there would have been two dead people where Mike and Susan stood. Ramon was positively livid. His breath was coming in short gasps, and he was sweating profusely. He stammered something neither Mike nor Susan understood, and all but ran to his table. He was ranting and raving, throwing his arms up in the air, gesturing at his tormentors while Agnes sat stone-faced and Blondie just smiled. Ramon definitely had had better days. The three of them left hurriedly.

Meanwhile Howard and Julie tried out the dance floor. After a few turns around the floor they got into rhythm and glided like they had been together for years - a most impressive display of ballroom grace.

"Mike honey," Susan suggested, "Why don't we try a dance or two to make it look good and then leave. Julie and Howard aren't aware of anyone else in the world." During their token dance, Mike whispered, "Barbie Doll, I'll take you back to the table so I can double check with Howard to be sure we have our signals straight. Then we can leave."

Howard assured Mike he would take "Julia" home, so Mike and Barbie Doll left.

Once in the confines and privacy of their room, their emotions roared into action. At the conclusion of an oh-how-I've-missed-not-being-able-to-do-this embrace, they sat on the couch.

"Let's take our time and not rush like two horny teenagers, even though I must admit I am as excited as I've ever been." They started with kissing and petting and slowly built the fire into a roaring crescendo that ended in unison.

"Michael," Susan moaned, "you have filled every nook and cranny of what I imagined love should be like. I don't mean just the sex, incredible as it is. It's the mental part of love that most couples miss out on. I've heard many women complain about her man satisfying himself and then rolling over to sleep, while she is just getting started. I don't know how we manage to be in step all the way every time, but it is wonderful the way it works. To make sure we don't forget how, let's shower and practice some more"

"I think that's an excellent idea, sweetheart," Mike answered. We need to practice because it will be at least Thursday before we can get another session in." After showering and another practice session, they fell asleep wrapped in each other's arms.

When Mike got to the office the next morning, Julie was there humming to herself and flitting around like a Jennie wren. "You are in good spirits today, Julie,"

"It was a wonderful evening, Mike. We danced the last dance, then he brought me home. I didn't want to give him any false hopes, but I don't think he had any intention of GOING ANY FARTHER. We sat in the car and just talked until almost three a.m. He never tried to kiss me or anything. Thank you Mike for getting us together. He asked if I liked sports. I told him I had just seen the movie, *"Pride of the Yankees,'* and that I would like to know more about the game and the other all stars like Babe Ruth and Ty Cobb. He asked if I would go to a home game with him, and naturally I said yes, so we are going to the season opener, - whatever that is - Sunday afternoon."

CHAPTER 24

"Where you been sugar?" Barbie asked when she saw Mike.

"I had to change into more suitable attire for work," he answered. A dinner jacket would have been too formal. You are in an extremely good mood this morning, Barbra."

"I got lucky last night and got rid of all my frustration," she answered. "We did get that Cuban bastard pissed off, didn't we? He can only think of one thing now, so hunt him down. He likes to be the hunter. He feels he is superior to the one he is hunting. His huge ego will be his downfall. You are my insurance policy, Michael. Don't let it lapse."

"I've got a paid-up contract, no danger of it lapsing," Mike assured her. "I'm going to be out most of the day, but I will be meeting Hawk for lunch. If you can get away about 1 p.m., we'll be at Mary's."

"Okay sugar, I'll be there," Susan replied.

Mike sought out his Dad and found him in the shed looking at the lock on the door. "Somehow someone is getting in here anytime they want," he reported. "While you're in town, stop by Ace Hardware and get one of those new-fangled locks that don't use keys. It's a combination lock that you can change any time you want. It probably won't stop them, but it will slow them down and complicate their lives a little.

"Son," he continued, "I've known Julie for some time and I have never seen her like this. What's going on?"

"Julie, Susan and I went to Hernando's last evening," Mike related. "Pop, you can't believe how beautiful Julie is until you see her as she says, all gussied up. Ramon and his female companions were there too. I was wondering how I could stave off a confrontation between he and Susan when Howard came in. I escorted Julie to his table and the rest is history. They were oblivious to everything else. They danced the last dance, he took her home, and they sat in the car and talked until 3 a.m. I look for good things to happen with those two. God knows they need some good things to happen. Susan was playing her Barbie Doll role to the hilt. She looked right at Ramon and carelessly crossed and uncrossed her legs. He was so worked up you could see it from across the room. He went to the men's room, then came directly to our table and made threats. He was making an ass of himself, so we just helped him out. He and his girlfriends stormed out. He was so mad, I thought he might have a heart attack. I'll get the lock and send it back with Susan or Barbie, whichever. See you later, Pop."

Mike went into town and stopped at Ace Hardware to get the lock for his Dad. Howard was there getting keys made for a property he owned as a rental. "I always change locks on rental property. You never know how many keys the former tenant had made or who has them," he said in passing. "Mike, I want to thank you for bringing Julia to my table. I had a delightful evening, the best I've had since my wife passed. When I looked at my watch and saw it was almost 3 a.m. I couldn't believe it. The hours just flew by. We are going to the home opener this Sunday. There will be some Hall of Famers there and I'm sure she can get some autographs. She told me she knew a little about the game but wanted to learn more, so I naturally volunteered to teach her; but you never know."

"I'm glad you and Julie hit it off so well. She needs to have a life. I'll see you Monday at 9:30 a.m."

CHAPTER 25

Harland Grading, the dirt mover on the runway system was finishing up and moving the big equipment to their next job when Mike arrived. "Good job, Mr. Harland. We appreciate the fast job you did. We seldom, if ever, have to rush, but this is really a life-or-death project. From this facility we will be flying critical children to hospitals and burn centers all over the country. We have patients now that we are putting on commercial flights. It is not an ideal situation but we have to do what we have to do. Our aircraft will have state-of-the-art equipment and a registered nurse, specially trained in this kind of operation. We are doing all we can to help these kids but it still leaves one wishing there was more we could do, so we pray a lot. It really hurts when the answer is no."

"How much do you charge people for this, Mr. Murphy?" Harland asked.

"Nothing, Mr. Harland. These people have enough to worry about with their child's life in danger. They don't need the worry of how to pay. We are color blind, as well as not being able to see any reason to turn some one down. If the people have the means, they are encouraged to support the program, but we never send a bill," Mike explained. "And please call me Mike."

"Mike, it has been a pleasure to work for you. You will be hearing from us, and please call me Jake," Harland responded.

It was time to meet Hawk and Barbie Doll for lunch so he went to Mary's. Susan and Hawk were already there. "Sorry I'm late," Mike apologized.

"What's new on the crime front Chief?" Mike asked, ignoring Barbie.

"Nothing new, I haven't seen hide nor hair of Ramon or those two you scared off.

When you leave the office starting now, and until further notice, wipe everything down. Wear gloves so you don't leave your prints. If someone is getting in, any prints left behind would be theirs. I will send them to the FBI lab in Quantico. They have one of the most complete set of fingerprint files in the world. If the prints are on file, they can identify the owner. One of my officers was at Hernando's last night. He said you put on quite a display for Ramon. It got Ramon so worked up you could see it across the room. The officer didn't hear what you two said to Ramon but he was plenty pissed off. Watch your back Mike, and you too, Susan or Barbie whichever you prefer," the Chief answered.

"As long as that bastard is walking around here, I'm Barbie or Barbra, whichever you prefer at the time, Chief honey," she replied.

In almost a whisper Mike said to Barbie, "Call your doctor friend. I have a PLAN THAT WILLL INVOLVE HIM, but will in no way put him in jeopardy. It may happen next Saturday or Sunday. We won't be able to give him a lot of front time, so here's what he needs to do: Start taking the children to the airport, so they are familiar with it and the people get used to seeing them explore, like kids do. We are going to have mechanical trouble and be forced to land and will need a doctor to check our patient. While the doctor is examining our patient, the children will stroll down to the end of the runway. I'll sit so the tower can't see the door being opened. When they question me as to the delay, I'll explain that we are having trouble securing the door. All this time, your children are running for the plane. You will be in the door so they will know it's okay. Once on board, strap them and yourself in, and we are out of there. I will alert Gitmo that we have rescued two American citizens and Castro might be pissed. I wouldn't want them to engage in a firefight-just let me get started. We come into Miami under the radar-it's an Angel Flight. Who's going to question us? We fuel up, bust ass for someplace in the Midwest, set down, go to a hotel, and let you get reacquainted with your children. I'll take a backseat while you do. If Lizzie and Walt are okay with it, we will stay a day to rest. The whole thing depends on Lizzie's condition and Walt's approval. What do you think?" Mike asked.

"I'll say this Mike," Hawk answered. "It is going to take a lot of balls to pull it off, and for a paleface you have big balls. That sounds like something my Shoshone forefathers would pull on the Cheyenne." In Shoshone Hawk said, "Great spirit, grant this brave the wisdom he needs to successfully finish ths coup. As he soars with the wings of eagles, bring him safely to his teepee with the woman he loves and her children. Thank you for gifts of courage, wisdom, and friends. May we go in peace."

The lunch crowd was totally silent. The Chief had never before revealed any kind of religion. Mike spoke up, "Hawk dear friend, I don't know what you said in your native tongue, but it touched my soul. I know you well enough to know if you were giving me hell everybody in town would know exactly what you said. I'm sure it was a sincere prayer and I thank you. If you believe in blood brothers, I would be honored to be your blood brother. It is something you take seriously and I know you must think and pray about it. There is a ritual that must be followed and I'm willing to take any test required. I have no brothers or sisters. I feel you are as close to me as any natual-born brother could be. I seldom say this to a man except to my father - I love you, Hawk. Your joys are my joys, your troubles are my troubles, and your enemies are my enemies."

"Oh Mike, sugar, that was the sweetest thing I ever did hear," Barbie chimed in. "It even made me cry, and Hawk, I too felt what you said, in mumbo jumbo language. I'm not making fun of it; it's just that I'm not as good with words as some people - especially Mike honey and you. My gracious, I'll bet if you set that to music it would go to the top of the charts overnight. Well, I have to get back to the office. I've got some important phone calls to make.

Bye, Chief. See you later, sugar. You know where I'm staying, but tonight I just may be a working girl."

"I hope she's careful with her working-girl routine. There are a lot of car dealers and salesmen with lots of money and big expense accounts over there, without their wives to rein them in. It could be a bad situation." Hawk continued, "About blood brothers, as you said, we Shoshone still practice it. You won't believe this, but we still have a tribal council, and they must approve it. You would not only be my brother, you would be Shoshone and have a Shoshone name. I would like to have you as my brother because, like you, I have no real one. I will present this to the council at the next meeting. We meet each full moon. I have to go and catch some bad guys. Be careful my friend, and soon to be my brother. I love you too."

CHAPTER 26

The power company had set the poles and was running a 7500kv line to the mechanical room in the terminal building. Mike found the electrical contractor's superintendent and asked about the generator. "We need to order it now, "Mike said. "Do you think diesel power is better than gasoline? Would diesel be harder to start in cold weather? Don't forget the transfer switch. We've got 7500kv to block."

"I think the diesel power is best," the super said. "The generator and the fuel will be in a heated building so starting is no problem and we will install an ether can that fires automatically. I've seen semis start in twenty-below weather with that ether can. We are ready for the transfer switch when it gets here. To give you an answer to your next question, if the generator and transfer switch were here now we would finish Wednesday."

"If those items are here Monday, then what?" Mike asked. "Wednesday," the super replied.

"I'll make the call on my cell phone right now," Mike said. "I just spoke to the manufacturer and they are going to load the items today and get a team of drivers to get it here so it will be waiting for you Monday. Walt Henderson has got some clout."

Paper work and reports filled the rest of the day, and by 5:15 Mike was ready to call it quits. "Supper at six," Julie reminded him.

"I'll be there for supper but not for breakfast. I'm going to look over the car dealers' convention this evening and see what I can pick up. I'll get my chores done tomorrow," Mike answered, "and since you have plans for Sunday, I'll find a room at the Hampton House. So I'll see you Monday."

"Be careful what you pick up at the show," Barbie commented. "You wouldn't want to pick up anything you can't share with someone you love."

"I will be extremely careful about that," Mike said.

Susan, acting in her disguise as a hooker plays out the following scene to ensure her reputation (false) for future encounters, if necessary.

Barbie drew a lot of attention as she slinked through the lobby. A salesman with too much alcohol and too few brains grabbed her by the arm with an invitation to go to his room with him for some horizontal dancing with no music. "Sugar," she whispered in his ear in her most sensuous voice, "for $500 I can give you something you can't get from your wife. What's your room number? You go ahead and get ready, leave the door unlocked, and I"ll be right up. Can I have my money now?"

"I've changed my mind lady. Go find some other sucker," the salesman said. "I don't need the aggravation."

"Hey sweetheart," Barbie replied, "you propositioned me. I didn't hustle you. I don't fool with children; I like a man that knows what he is doing so we both enjoy it." Spotting Mike coming in, she continued, "Like that handsome man coming in the door." Leaving the salesman standing with his mouth open she went up to Mike and laid a kiss on him that would fire the furnace in a dead man. "Play along," she whispered. "There is a lot more that I can show you. Your room or mine?"

"I can't get a room. They're all full because of a convention or something," Mike answered.

"Sugar, if you pay for the room we can use mine," Barbie said. Then looking at the dumbfounded salesman she said, "See you later junior, and in the meantime why not just let your meat loaf."

In the privacy of their room, Susan explained what had happened in the lobby. "What would you have done if he had come up with the $500?" Mike asked.

"I would have used my fingernails and laid some deep, hurting scratches on his neck and face and back and anyplace else I could. Then I would have given him his money back. I wouldn't have gotten screwed and neither would he. Let him explain to his wife how he got scratched," Susan answered.

"Let's shower and get ready for bed and watch TV. We've got this entire weekend to ourselves. Let's not burn ourselves out the first night," Mike suggested.

"That sounds good to me," Susan responded. "I'll shower first and order some coffee. I've got some of your Mom's cookies to go with."

"Order some ice cream too," Mike suggested.

While Susan was showering, Mike called Walt to update him on Angel Flight. "The bird will be ready to leave its nest Thursday," he said, "I thought I would sign it out and do some checking of my own. We can make a leisurely flight to Galveston on Friday. How is Lizzy? I've got a plan to get Susan's children out of Cuba that I will talk to you about when I see you. The plan will work and I will need Lizzy to play a part in it. She will not be in any danger, but I don't want to cause any adverse reaction to her surgery."

"The new airport facilities are coming along nicely," Mike continued. "With the good weather we've had and the contractors knowing how important this project is, they are putting in one or two hours overtime and donating it to Angel Flight and we are running ahead of schedule. Your project has really caught on. Most restaurants and all the bars have jars with an angel on them and the money keeps coming. The bank has set up an angel account, the school kids are doing car washes, slave auctions, bake sales, anything they can think of to raise money. They are taking a personal interest in this because it's for kids, and might be them or their brother or sister who may be in need of an angel flight. With their enthusiasm, they're making the adults dig a little deeper. I never even dreamed it would catch on like this. When everything is complete, we could have an open house with hotdogs, chips and soda, and let them see what they bought into. I'll contact a network TV station and have them tape the operation, including the specialized equipment. They can run it on their news show and the whole country will see what a small town in Oregon has accomplished with hard work and dedication. I might even try to get the Blue Angles to do something. The town deserves recognition. With your permission, I would like to use a photo of Lizzy as our logo. After all, she is actually the one who started this whole thing. I've given you a lot to think about. I'm going to let you ponder, while Susan and I chow down on some homemade applesauce cookies and ice cream.

"Bring a bunch of those cookies with you Friday," Walt ordered. "If your plan to rescue Susan's children poses no threat to Lizzy, go ahead. She is doing fine and is anxious to come home and her grandparents are just as anxious. Since Lizzy's surgery, her grandmother has worked her way out of depression and is feeling much better. Life is good. Give Susan our love. I'm looking forward to seeing you two on Friday. Bye."

"I'm done in the shower, sweets," Susan called. "What flavor?"

"What flavor what?" Mike asked.

"Ice cream," Susan answered. "You suggested ice cream to go with our treat."

"Oh, yes I did," Mike admitted. "I must have had a brain fart. I think peppermint stick would go good."

"Peppermint stick it is," Susan answered.

They had a very pleasant and relaxing evening. Coffee, ice cream and homemade goodies shared with the one you love. Walt was right. "Life is good."

CHAPTER 27

"You've got Julie's chores today, and I have some things to do, so why not have breakfast and meet here when we're done. Then we'll go from there?" Susan offered the next morning.

"Sounds like a plan," Mike agreed.

"I don't feel like getting dressed yet. Can we have room service bring up our breakfast?" Susan pleaded.

"Why not?" Mike agreed.

After breakfast and a see-you-later-kiss, Mike was out the door. Susan dressed in her Barbie Doll uniform and attitude, and went to the lobby looking for the salesman from the night before. He was standing with several others. She walked up to him, "Sugar, I'm so sorry about last night, I don't know what caused me to act that way and I would like to make it up to you. I just found out that bastard I was married to is going to let me have custody of my children. I have to give up this life and be a mother. I need one of those cute mini-vans with the sliding doors and all. I have an almost new candy-apple red convertible that matches my current lifestyle, but that is going to be behind me. Do you have what I am looking for? I'll pay cash, and I have all the papers on my convertible."

"I may have just what you are looking for downtown; Miss?"

"Barbra Dahl. Call me Barbie Doll - everybody else does - and I have no idea why. What's your name, Sugar?"

"Jason, Jason Mason, Barbie. Would you like to see it now?"

"If you mean the mini-van, yes. If you had other ideas, I told you that was history," Barbie snapped.

"I meant the car, Ma'am. The office is open all weekend because of the convention, and we can get you in it yet today, especially since you have cash. We won't have to wait for bank approval," Jason responded. "Where is your car? Do you want me to drive?"

"Out front on the left. Yes, you drive," Barbie answered. "That's your car there, isn't it?" Jason said, indicating a shiny red sporty convertible.

"My goodness, Sugar, how did you ever guess which one was mine?" Barbie asked.

"You told me you had an almost new, red convertible, but even if you hadn't told me I think I would have been able to figure it out. I don't mean to offend you, but that car has your profession and lifestyle written all over it," Jason answered.

"Honey, you didn't offend me at all," Barbie said. "I am what I am. There's no denying that, but I do hope to change my image. Could you show me something that says, "mother-of-two" instead of this, that says 'fast-car, fast-woman?"

"Ma'am, I think I have just what you are looking for at our downtown lot. Shall we go?" Jason asked.

"Let's do it honey, I'm getting excited already; about the car, not that you don't excite me, but that part of me is over and I don't have anything you could take home except this: You are married and have a wife that loves you; don't take a chance on losing her over a quick piece of tail with someone who doesn't care what happens to you after she has let you do your thing, and she's collected her money. You'll go home feeling guilty, and when you and your wife start that most beautiful and fulfilling part of marriage, you are going to think about that whore you paid $100 or more for ten minutes of playing and less than five seconds of euphoria. You put your pants on and she gets dressed and goes to find another $100 sucker. With your wife, you may play for ten minutes more or less for the same euphoria, but when that part is over you lie there in each other's arms and fall asleep. When you wake up she's still there. If she's not lying beside you she is probably in the kitchen making coffee for you. The man you saw me with is the man I'm going to marry. What you see is a facade. I am a one-man woman and he is my man. Now where is my new car?"

"Ma'am I will take that home and I thank you for it. I think that purple mini-van next to the white pickup says mother-of-two, don't you agree?" Jason offered.

"I believe you are exactly right. It does say mother-of-two," Barbie said. "I have a lot of things I have to get done today. How soon can I take possession?"

The paperwork will take an hour or so, but I'm sure it will be ready by noon. No, I promise you it will be ready at noon if we can strike a deal," Jason said.

"Jason," Barbie said, "I will be living here. The man I'm going to marry lives here as well as his parents and secretary. What I am saying is, we influence a lot of people, and I'm trying to blackmail you. You didn't screw me last night because I wouldn't let you. Now you have the opportunity, but if you do, it will be the only time. The ball is in your court. I'll be back at noon."

Jason went into the office, and after thinking about everything she had said, wrote an offer. He took it into the manager, who studied it carefully, and said, "You realize you cut your commission out. Was it worth that much?"

"Boss," Jason said, "That much and more, and that car needs to be detailed, the paper work finished, everything ready when she gets back at noon. This is not a debate."

"Just who in the hell do you think you're talking to?" the manager roared.

"I'm talking to a man who was made manager because he couldn't make a living selling cars. If your father didn't own the business, you would be washing dishes at Mary's. That's who I'm talking to," Jason answered.

Everyone in the place heard the discussion, including people interested in buying new automobiles.

"Okay, wise guy, pick up your check. You're fired," the manager said.

"Don't do it Jason," A distinguished gray-haired gentleman said. "You are and have been one of our best salesmen - not the best every month but never further down the line than second, except last March. That's when you should have stayed home and got some rest, but you didn't and you finished third. That's dedication. You move into my son's office. You are now the sales manager and what you say, I will back up"

"Charlie, you will take orders from him or go wash dishes some place. I put you in that office at your mother's insistence and when you go crying to her, I'll catch hell for it for a while, but she will eventually get over it. It's way past time you started earning your paycheck. You live off a percentage of each sale and don't do a damn thing to warrant it. Clear your desk out and take your porno magazines with you. Get out, go home and come back Monday with a work attitude or don't come back.

"Why do I feel so good? I just put my son on the unemployed list and I feel good about it. Jason, you're the man in charge. See what everybody wants for lunch, and have it delivered. Boy do I feel good."

Barbie was on time and went looking for Jason. Finding him in the manager's office was a surprise. "Sugar, you never told me you were so important," she said.

"I wasn't, and it's all because of you." Jason then explained what had happened.

"Here is the cash, where do I sign and how much do I owe?" Barbie asked. Jason showed her the offer. "That's not enough, Jason. You can't provide for your family doing business like that. I noticed you don't have my name filled in. Here is my driver's license to prove who I am, and the car will be registered in that name. I told you what you saw was a façade, and it is for a reason. My ex-husband is in the area and wants to kill me. I've changed my appearance and have met him face-to-face and he doesn't recognize me. So just type the correct name in and remember, you are the only one who knows. If you haven't started a college fund for your children, take this and start one. Now let's get some tongues to wagging, and have a God-loves-you-and-so-do-I hug. I promise you, Jason, you will hear from us." As she got to the door, she turned and said, "Bye sugar, I love you."

Jason sat down at his desk. *What a woman!* he thought to himself.

Ivan Kozak, the owner came in. "What was that all about Jason? Did I make a mistake promoting you? Explain yourself." "It's a long story, sir, and I will start at the beginning. Last night I had too much to drink and she prevented me from making a fool of myself and possibly ruining my marriage. What you see is a facade. She's not really a prostitute. Anyway, this morning she asked if I had a mini-van that said mother-of-two to replace that sporty red ragtop, that says fast-car, fast-woman. She talked some sense into my head and then told me she will be living here, and they have a lot of friends that trust their judgment. I figured that what I had learned from her was worth my commission. I also promised her the van would be ready at noon and told Charlie it was not a debate. That's when you came in. Here is the unbelievable part. When it was time to settle up, she looked at the offer, and said it wasn't enough and gave me $1500 cash to start a college fund for the kids. The hugging was a God-loves-you-and-so-do-I hug, just to start tongues wagging. I see it worked."

"Jason, my boy," Ivan said. "If this is any indication as to how we are going to do business, every car dealer in the country is going to want you for their manager. You bring me their best offer and I will meet it, plus. Have I told you how good I feel?"

"Yes, Mr. Kozak, several times," Jason answered. "After lunch, I would like to talk to you about how to improve our image and increase sales. I have some radical ideas I've thought about very carefully, based on what I overhear on the street, in the supermarkets, even in church during the coffee hour, wherever people just visit."

"Jason," Ivan said. "I'm having chicken for lunch, you bring whatever you're having in and let's talk now. What are your ideas?"

"Mr. Kozak," Jason began, "we sell more cars than anybody else in the county and that's a fact. Our problem is in the service department. It's referred to on the street as Kozak's whorehouse, because you are going to get screwed. When a customer brings his car in for service, the service salesman often doesn't know the difference between a wheel cover and a radiator cap. These salesmen have their names embroidered on their shop coat; they carry a clipboard, and give the appearance that they know all there is to know about automobiles, then tell the flunkies standing around to vacuum out the car and get it washed. That's the foreplay, the screwing comes later. It's a computerized world now. The days when a mechanic with a pair of pliers and screwdriver could fix any car are over. The person who greets the customer should be the best mechanic in the house. By asking the right questions he could determine where to start looking and tell the customer if that clink, squeak, or thump has the potential to be serious, or something minor that could be corrected in a few minutes. We would guarantee our work for 90 days or 10,000 miles, which ever comes first. We would charge book rate, and if the job is not done properly, the mechanic would do it over for no charge. If the mechanic is no longer here, the dealership will pick up the tab and most important, we will not take advantage of anybody, especially women, because of their lack of knowledge. Our waiting room should have complimentary coffee or tea, and a limit of two cans of soda. It should have windows to allow the customer to see who is working on their car and what they are doing. The way we operate now, the car disappears. When it comes out later, all cleaned and vacuumed out, it looks great but too many times the work they paid for wasn't done because it wasn't necessary, but the customer has no way of knowing. I would like to work for a dealership that means it when they say, 'You, the customers, are the reason we are here, and we pledge to treat you fairly. We are not the cheapest but we are the best. We guarantee it and put it in writing.' That's just for starters sir, I have other ideas I'm working on that I will present to you at a later date."

"Jason my boy, I can see I need to get out and press the flesh. I had no idea that our reputation was in the dumpster," Ivan responded. "I've spent 25 years building a business and no time trying to build a reputation. I thought one would take care of the other, but I know now I've been wrong. Do you have any ideas on how to turn this thing around?"

"Yes sir, I do," Jason answered. "We must completely change the service department's attitude, and I would start with a meeting of all service personnel. Close the service department for half a day, preferably Monday morning. Serve pancakes, eggs, sausage, coffee, milk, and juice at 8 a.m. Start your meeting at 9 a.m. Before the meeting, spend time in the service department observing. You are looking for the person you want to represent you - honest, intelligent, and the best mechanic in the house. All this is top secret. You will call this candidate into your office and explain to him what you want and give him full authority to implement the changes, with the assurance that you are backing him up all the way. To have that much responsibility thrown at you is a decision that you don't make on the spot. Give him two or three days to make up his mind. If he accepts, the meeting would be held the next Monday morning. If he doesn't want the responsibility, ask him who he thinks would be the best person in or out of the dealership. Either way, his job would not be in jeopardy. He is to tell no one. At the meeting, you will introduce the new manager of the entire service department which includes parts, lube, and tires. Every employee in every department will answer to him. The days of Kozak's whorehouse are over as of right now. Anyone who can't live by the new rules is free to pick up their check and tools and leave. I'm only laying out one rule, to which there is no exception or debate. If you do a poor job on a customer's car; when they bring it back and they will because we, that means you, guarantee that job for 90 days or 10,000 miles, whichever comes first; you will fix it right. You got paid for the first job; you will not get paid to do it over. Then, you turn the meeting over to the new manager then promptly leave to reinforce that he and his staff is in charge"

"Son," Ivan said, "you've laid out a plan that can't help but succeed, if it is monitored so it doesn't get out of control. Find someone else to be sales manager. My wife has been on my back for years to lighten up, so you are second in command. I've needed a general manager for a long time and you are it. There will be a formal announcement with pictures in the paper. I'll announce it over the PA system, then go play a little golf. It's been at least five years since I hit that last ball, but I think that is about to change too. Have I told you how good I feel? Here are the keys to everything. I may not be back for a few days. You are in charge."

Ivan made the announcement, which caught everyone off guard, and then left.

Jason went to the PA and said, "I've had all the excitement I can stand today. Let's go home. It's 2:15; your pay stops at 6:00. See you all Monday, and we will start turning this dealership around. I don't know where my office will be, but with or without an office, I am available."

CHAPTER 28

Late that afternoon, a woman with a black attaché case, came into the hotel lobby. She had dark red hair in a bun, with a rhinestone clip holding it in place. Her tailored, knee-length coat-dress was in very dark-gray serge with pinstripes, covered a white blouse with V-neck, showing off a string of black pearls that matched those in her earrings. Black, horn-rimmed glasses and black 3-inch heels finished the ensemble. A striking woman, who drew a lot of attention. Paying it no mind, she asked the gaping desk clerk in a soft, almost sensuous voice to please ring Michael Murphy's room.

"Hello," Mike answered.

"Mr. Murphy," she said in a low, sultry voice, "this is Rhonda Le'Hundt, from Henderson Manufacturing. I realize it is late on a Saturday, but Mr. Henderson was adamant I see you and show you the very latest in electronics that he thought you could use in your joint venture. It won't take but a few minutes. I thought we might talk over dinner. I'm staying over, but I won't talk business on Sunday."

"I'm waiting for someone now," Mike said.

"You could leave them a note, and they would be welcome to join us BUT WE WILL PROBABLY be done before they arrive."

"Okay," Mike agreed. "I'll change my shirt and clean up some and be right down. How will I recognize you?"

"I'm sitting in the lobby facing the front desk, and I have dark red hair," Rhonda said.

Jason came into the lobby and couldn't help but notice Rhonda. She gave him a come-on smile and recrossed her long legs. That brought a reaction.

He walked up to her and said, "Lady, you are a beautiful woman and yesterday I would have accepted your invitation and been all over you like a gorilla. But today, a lady came into my life and has forever changed it. She made me realize what I would lose by yielding to those urges. She also bought a car, and to make a long story short, because of her, instead of being a salesman I am now general manager. If I ever see her again, I want to thank her and give her a big I-love-you hug."

"Jason, don't let on that you know me, but you can hug me if you like. I'm so pleased the way things worked out for you." The timing of the hug, followed by a kiss was perfect. Mike had just stepped out of the elevator and saw the whole thing.

Jason recognized Mike from last night, so he straightened his tie, cleared his throat, and speaking softly said, "I'll see you later, sugar."

"You must be Rhonda," Mike said coolly.

"Yes, I am, and you must be Michael," Rhonda responded. "Let's go into the dining room where I can show you the sell sheets. Mr. Henderson thought you would be real interested in some of our remote switches. Until you get a permanent operator, you can turn your airport lights on from as far away as fifty miles, just by pushing this button. And we have a wide range of new things I would be glad to show you at a later date."

"You need to talk to Dad about the rest of your products. He's running the show now," Mike answered, looking at his watch.

"Is the party you're waiting for late, sir?" Rhonda asked. "It is almost nine, could we order dinner now?"

"I'm sorry, Rhonda, but I'm not hungry. I'm worried," Mike said. "Her ex-husband is in the area, and has promised to kill her, after he rapes her and forces me to watch the whole thing."

"Mike, I want to tell you two things that can't go out of this room, and then, I'm going to ask you for one thing in return. Okay?" Rhonda asked.

"Okay," Mike agreed. "Lay it on me."

"First, Lizzy is Angel One. Second, the best place to hide is in plain sight. Will you please order dinner? I'm starved. Barbie Doll ran off with a trucker with a really big rig, and we will probably never see her again. Rhonda Le'Hundt will take over her position starting Monday. Monday we are going with Howard to look at a piece of property he thinks we might be interested in."

Rhonda noticed Jason sitting with a group of men, probably salesmen. She excused herself and went to his table. "Excuse me gentlemen, but I need to borrow this young man for a while," indicating Jason. She escorted him back to where Mike was seated. "Michael Murphy, this is Jason Mason, the new general manager of Kozak's Autos," she stated.

"I've heard of Kozak's whorehouse," Mike sneered.

"That's why I brought him over," Rhonda said. "He sold Barbie a car at such a good price, it caused a ruckus with the sales manager. Jason promised Barbie it would be ready at noon, and was barking out orders when the sales manager asked who he thought he was talking to. By the way, he knows who I am and why. You finish the story Jason."

Jason related his entire saga, from sales manager to general manager, in the course of a few hours. "We are changing our policies and past business practices, as of yesterday," he said. When you or anyone else brings a vehicle in for service, the job including parts, is guaranteed for 90 days or 10,000 miles, whichever comes first. If the work was unsatisfactory, we will provide you with a vehicle at no cost, until yours is ready to roll. Since you paid to have it fixed once and the mechanic was paid for doing it right, we don't expect you to pay for it again and we are certainly not going to pay the mechanic again. I believe that should help improve our image, and as the lady said, it was all because of Barbra Dahl. It is a pleasure meeting you sir, and I hope we can do business."

"We will do business, Jason" Mike said, "and please keep our secret."

"Tomorrow is Sunday. Let's bore holes in the sky and fly down to Klamath Falls," Mike said. "I want to talk to the owner of that chopper we used, and see if he would sell it. We could make good use of it with our jobs spread all over two states."

"That sounds like a pleasant way to spend a Sunday. Could we meander a little? I've only seen the view from a jet at 400mph or more."

"We sure can. We've got all day to get there ,and if it gets dark on us coming home, we can divert to Hood River or Troutdale," Mike said. "Let's try to get in the air by seven."

CHAPTER 29

When they got to the office the next morning, Rhonda said, "While you are doing your pre-flight, I'll put the fact sheets I showed you last evening in my desk drawer."

Mike noted the new lock on the shed door was still locked, but had the appearance of being tampered with when Rhonda called. "The door is unlocked and I know damned well I locked and checked it Friday."

"Just use your key and lock it back up," Mike said. "I'll call Hawk and tell him. He can get a key from Julie or meet her out here. I'll leave the pickup right where it sits so we won't disturb anything that might be a clue or evidence."

Mike called Hawk from the phone in the shed, and reported what they had found. "When you finish, the spare key for the pickp is hanging on a hook under my hard hat. If you would put the truck in the shed, I would appreciate it. I'm going to try and buy that chopper we used. I'll talk to you in the morning. Sorry to have to call you at home."

"I'll get out there as soon as I can, but in the meantime, I'll dispatch an officer to secure the place," Hawk answered. "Crime doesn't take weekends off. Why should we?"

The flight plan was to meander around, set down and fuel up in Eugene, meander around and set down in Klamath Falls. Mike taxied up to the fuel station there and asked, "Is the owner of the chopper around?"

"That would be Red Kely," the fuel jockey said. "You will find him in the coffee shop. He has no family and spends almost all of his time here. He won't work on Sunday and he comes out here to watch the jets. You won't have any trouble spotting him."

Rhonda led the way, with Mike trailing a little behind. She paused and removed her sunglasses. "I'll bet that man at the counter with flaming red hair is who we are looking for," she said.

Mike approached the redhead and asked, "Are you Red Kely?" The answer came in as thick an Irish brogue as anyone ever heard. "Of course I am, and who would be wantin' to know?" he answered.

"I'm Mike Murphy, sir, and this is Rhonda Le'Hundt," Mike stated. "I flew your chopper last week to help our Police Chief gather some information on a drug operation. My father and I have an electronics business. We install cable TV networks and hook up and maintain TV in the classroom. With our business spread over two states and expanding, I thought your chopper would come in very handy and we would like to buy it. Is it for sale?"

"I'm sorry sir, but no, she is not for sale. As much as I would like to help a man with ties to the old sod, I have a sentimental attachment to it. I bought it as junk, restored it to its original condition, then learned to fly it. As time and money allows, I upgrade it with all the bells and whistles. There is not a faster or quieter chopper, as you found out, in the country. When I got her she was a dog, so I've renamed her, The Old Dog. I just can't let her go."

"You said you restored her," Mike questioned. "Do you have a FAA ticket for repairs?"

"I have a ticket that says I'm qualified to rebuild, repair and maintain any aircraft engine or air frame," Red answered.

"Would you consider moving to our place?" Mike asked. "And why would I want to do that?" Red asked.

"We are building a first-class facility. We will need a base operator later. But right now we need a mechanic to maintain our jet. We are starting a service to fly critically ill children to the nearest facility for the treatment they need. At present we only have one jet. It's a Gulf Stream that is being outfitted for that purpose as we speak," Mike answered.

"And how much are you going to charge these little darlin's parents for your service?" Red demanded to know.

"Nothing. We feel the parents have enough worries about their child, so why should we add more. Red, I was a Navy pilot, I trained to kill, and I was top-gun. I flew with the Blue Angels. I was able to help a child get to a hospital for a heart transplant. She died, but the medic was able to bring her back. Out of that experience, and a series of divine interventions, Angel Flight was born," Mike answered. "That's the kind of flying I want to do."

"I would like to be a part of that myself," Red answered. "I won't sell the Old Dog but you're welcome to use it anytime, and if you are offering me a job, I'll take it. I forgot to mention, I also have a flight instructor's ticket. When do I start? It will take me a week or two to untie the bindings here and get moved."

"Your pay starts next Monday. When you are ready to move your furniture, let us know. We will have a truck with pads and dollies and two men to load, transport, and unload. You just bring the chopper," Mike stated. "Here is my hand on it. We haven't talked wages but I think two Irishmen can work things out. My hand is all the contract there is. If you require more than that, it's been a pleasure meeting you."

"A hand between two Irishmen is stronger than any contract," Red said. "Here's mine. I'll be reporting for duty as soon as possible."

"Let's eat lunch here and meander back," Rhonda suggested. "That's fine with me," Mke answered. "We'll have to re-fuel in Eugene, and do a little less meandering to get back before dark." The setting sun on Mt. Hood created a breathtaking sight as they passed over it from the southwest. It was late afternoon when Mike taxied up to the shed. He and Rhonda sat quietly, each with their own thoughts about the day's events. "Let's put this bird to bed and get ready for tomorrow," Mike said.

"This has been such a wonderful day. I'll be so glad when this bullshit is over and we can just go on living," Rhonda said. "I'm anxious to hear what the Chief found. There's no doubt in my mind who is responsible, but unless there's solid evidence against him, that Cuban bastard can just walk around free as a bird."

"Hawk knows Ramon is here illegally and could bust him for that, but we want to put him away for good," Mike said.

"Enough about that, let's talk about us," Rhonda suggested. "What are our long-range plans? Am I going to be able to stay at home and enjoy our children, or am I going to have to work?"

"I want you to do what you want to do. If you want to stay home with the children, and that's what I think you should do, please do it. You and your children have to get reacquainted, and you are bringing a stranger into their lives. There are a lot of adjustments that will have to be made by all of us. I've never been a father, so that's new - especially when the children are almost grown. As far as money is concerned," Mike continued, "we can do okay on what the electronics company pays me. We won't be millionaires but we will be rich. We will have love, health, and all those other things that money can't buy. Yes, we will be very wealthy."

"What about discipline? Whose responsibility is it?"

"That will be established as soon as the four of us can sit down and talk about it," Mike answered. "I don't believe in corporal punishment, except for lying and sassing. The children have to know we are on the same page, and they don't play one against the other."

"On another subject, "said Mike, "while I was following you this morning I couldn't help but notice what a beautiful butt you have. I don't know what to call you, Susan, Barbra, or Rhonda. You are all gorgeous, and I'm in love with all three, but it will be nice to settle down to one."

"Call me whatever you feel comfortable with at the time," Rhonda said. "But don't you ever refer to me as your old lady. It's digusting, degrading, and shows a total lack of respect. Let's get back to our rooms, freshen up, and have a pizza delivered. We can watch TV and relax, a fitting end to a great day."

"Order a large, of any kind," Mike said. "I'll stop and get some cola to wash it down with, unless you would prefer something else?"

"Cola is fine with me. I'll order a large combo. Why do I always have to do the ordering? Don't you know how?" Rhonda teased.

"You have such a sensuous voice. The delivery guys hurry to see the party attached to it, so we get faster service," Mike countered.

CHAPTER 30

The next morning, Mike introduced Rhonda Le'Hundt to Julie and his dad with no mention of who she was.

She will be out of the office this morning," Mike stated. "I want a woman's perspective on the house I'm going to look at and she has agreed to help me. When we get back, Miss Le'Hundt, Julie will fill you in on your responsibilities and you will do as she says. Do you have any questions?"

"No sir, Mr Murphy. You have made everthing perfectly clear," Rhonda said tearfully realizing that Mike had to pretend he didn't recognize her as his beloved Susan. "If I'm to help you with your decision on the house and get back here in time to get anything done, we had better get going," she added icily as she went outside.

"Where did she come from and what happened to Barbra Dahl?" Julie asked.

"It's a long story. I'll fill you in tonight. Supper at 6:30?" Mike asked.

"Supper at 6:30," Julie answered. "Don't be late."

"I had to treat you as I did this morning out of necessity," Mike explained. "There is only one other person who knows who you really are besides ourselves and that is Jason. It is getting serious around here. Ramon hasn't been seen for several days and even though the best place to hide is in plain sight, I don't want to push the envelope."

"I was sure you had a good reason, but when you want to come down hard you really know how," Rhonda answered. "I'll have to file that away for future reference. Now stop the truck and give me a kiss. We have been so busy worrying about Ramon and working we forgot to take time for us, so get ready for Thursday night."

"I'm as anxious for Thursday in Troutdale, as you are," Mike responded.

Mike pulled to the side of the road so they could do a little huggin' and kissin'. "We had better stop now," Mike insisted, "or we will be very late for our appointment with Howard. Hold those thoughts for Thursday."

Howard was waiting for them in his office.

"I'm Rhonda Le'Hundt, Mr. Morrison - a friend of Susan's," she said as she extended her hand. "Mr. Murphy asked me to help him by looking at the house from a woman's perspective, since Susan couldn't be here herself due to some personal problems. She has trusted my judgment in the past, and there is no reason she wouldn't now. We are as close as sisters. Shall we go? I have a lot of work waiting for me at Murphy Electronics."

"The property is about fifteen miles from town, but I think when you see it you will forget the commute," Howard said. "You will have privacy, which you can't have in an urban area. You will have your own little world. There is a deep well that has been tested every year for the last twenty years. The state says this is the purest water in the state and has tested that way from the beginning. The heating and air conditioning system is only two years old. It is a well-to-well, electric heat pump system, backed by a propane furnace. The house is well insulated so with our naturally mild weather, utilities will be no problem. Here we are, your own little world."

Mike and Rhonda both gasped at the beauty and obvious serenity.

"Mr. Murphy," Rhonda offered, "if Susan doesn't like this place, will you marry me? I could live out here, knocked up and barefooted, and be as happy as a lark. And when you get home from work, supper will be waiting with a fresh pot of coffee. After supper we can watch the boats go up and down the river."

"Howard," Mike said, "it seems I have no choice but to buy this place. Yes, Miss Le'Hundt, if Susan doesn't like this place, I will gladly marry you. I don't know about knocked up and barefooted, but supper and fresh coffee waiting is an offer I would find hard to resist. Howard, here is my hand on the deal, draw up the necessary documents for my signature, and I would like possession as soon as possible."

"Mike you have just bought yourself a piece of heaven. I envy you, and wish you the very best," Howard stated. "The papers will be ready for your signature tomorrow after lunch. I will need some earnest money; it's the law."

"I'll have a cashier's check with me when I sign," Mike said. "I would like to see inside. Would you mind if Miss Le'Hundt and I came back this evening, when we don't have a deadline to meet?" "I see no problem with that. After all, you offered your hand on the deal and I know your reputation. Here are the keys."

"How are we going to sneak away this evening, Michael?" Rhonda asked on the way to the office after leaving Howard.

"You will call Julie's, and tell her you have to see me and set things straight. You are not used to being treated like I treated you this morning, and unless we can work things out, you are going back to Portland," Mike instructed. "I will come over, and we will take your new car and drive out to our place and look inside. I'll bring a good flashlight, in case darkness catches up to us. I don't think anyone has caught on to who you are."

"Call your doctor friend," Mike continued, "and tell him we will be there Sunday at 11 a.m. We will ask for a doctor to help with our patient who is having breathing problems. While he is attending to our patient, the children will act like all curious children, and walk to the end of the runway looking for bugs or flowers or anything curious children look for. When they are in place, the doctor will exit the aircraft. We will taxi to take-off position, and I will advise the tower I have a light on that indicates the door isn't closed, and I am going to exit and see if

I can fix it. As soon as the door opens, you step out with me so your children can see you. I'll get back in the driver's seat and as soon as you are all on board, I'll advise the tower that the door is properly closed and locked. You and Walt make sure everybody is buckled in, including yourselves. With everyone on board, I kick the bird in the butt, and we are out of there. The worst thing that could happen is the guards get suspicious and try to stop the children. I don't think they will shoot, and active children are hard to corral, so have them run to the airplane, no matter where it is. I am not leaving without them. Once in the air, after twelve minutes, we will be in Florida. Castro's best take that long to tie their boots, and we have support, if we need it, at Gitmo. Here we are back at the office, time for me to act like a bad ass. Just don't forget, I am in love with you."

"Back at you Michael," Rhonda responded.

Mike left to see Hawk to catch up on the latest news, and to hear what he had uncovered at the office.

"Not much news, old pal, but I did pick up quite a few prints, and we took a casting of tread prints. We sent them to the FBI lab in Quantico," Hawk reported. "We should have the results back in a few days. 'Where is Susan or Barbie Doll?'"

"According to what I hear," Mike answered, "she traded her sports car in on a mini-van and took up with some trucker with a big rig, but I'm sure she will show up. She has no use for Ramon and, as long as he is up and about she will be bugging him every chance she gets. Speaking of Ramon, what's the latest on him?"

"Nobody has seen him or Aggie since your last run in with him," Hawk answered. The blonde bomber is around now and then. She is not causing any trouble, just arousing curiosity. The feeling in the department is that she is a bull dyke," he added. "Nothing concrete, just a hunch."

"I've got to go, Chief. We got another new hand to train. Her name is, Rhonda Le'Hundt tall, well-put-together redhead," Mike said.

At the new airport, Pat Harrigan was barking out orders and waving his arms like a naval signalman to the cat skinners and grader operators. They must have known what he meant, because the job seemed to be running smoothly. At the pace they were going the hangar and other facilities would be ready in about six weeks, which wasn't bad for the late start and temporarily working with no plans or specs. Phil Higgins had a first-rate crew, no doubt about it.

"Patrick," Mike said, "you are indeed a man of your word. You said you would be here today and here you are."

"Actually I got here yesterday afternoon with my flagman. We shot some elevations and put up some flags so the skinners could start as soon as they got their machines unloaded," Pat stated. "Phil wants this to be the start of a new method of doing business for him. You made an impression on him and he is trying to model his company after yours, and the crew is really excited about it, especially the insurance. The union has been trying to organize us for several years and Phil has been doing his best to prevent it. I think when they come around this time, they are going to be escorted out with, 'don't come back until you can beat what we have.' I've got to get to work. Thanks for everything."

CHAPTER 31

Mike got to Julie's as the coffee finished. She poured two cups and said, "Sit down and tell me what is going on. Where did Rhonda come from and what has happened between you and Susan? I thought you two really loved each other or were you both just in heat?"

"This is top secret, Julie. No one is to know," Mike stated. "Barbie Doll traded her red sports car off on a dark-purple mini van. The last I heard she took up with some trucker with a really big rig and we probably never will hear from her again. Do you follow me? A dark, almost purple, mini-van?" he repeated, grinning.

"I thought there was something kind of familiar about Rhonda," Julie answered, smiling. "She is really sly, and I might add, a very good actress. What did you think of the house?"

"Julie, if I were to plan and specify what I wanted for a home, it would be exactly what I saw today. I bought it without looking inside. Rhonda is going to call me to come over and set things straight or say she is going back to Portland. It's only a ruse. We are going to check out the inside, so I'm not sure what time I'll be back, if at all. Darkness might catch up with us and we may have to spend the night. But leave the light on anyway. I'll set the table, you dish it up, and tell me about your Sunday with Howard, who by the way, refers to you as Julia."

"Michael, I thought you were the perfect date until Howard came along," Julie explained. Her eyes almost closed in rapture thinking about Howard and their first date. As you know, we went to the season opener, a baseball game. How you can find romance at a baseball game I don't know, but it was romantic. After the game, we had pizza and beer at Vito's. Then he brought me home. We had coffee and talked baseball. He really loves the game and played in the PCL. That's the Pacific Coast League, for you, uninformed ones. He bought two season tickets. Anyway, we watched the news, he left at 10:45, and was a perfect gentleman all day. Damn."

The phone rang, breaking the spell. Julie answered and handed it to Mike saying, "There is a pissed-off, weepy broad that wants to talk to you."

"Hello," Mike answered, "what can I do for you? It's late, can't it wait until morning? I'm sorry you feel that way, I'll be over as soon as I get the dishes stacked. Good-bye."

"You aren't such a bad actor yourself," Julie commented.

The sun was just dropping behind Mt. Hood, when they drove up to the house. The furniture was still there and the electricity was on, so they had water but no lights because the bulbs were gone. Rhonda found some candles and asked Mike to see if he could raise the garage door manually and put the car away. "I want to spend the night here," she said, "and listen to the sounds, and I don't want to wait for Thursday night in Troutdale."

"Put a light in the window. I'll put the car away and be right back," Mike stated. "We will have to get up fairly early to get back in time to clean up for the work day." he added.

Rhonda had placed a candle on the chest of drawers, after making sure there was no danger of fire. Fully satisfied, they lay together in the soft glow of the candlelight.

"I'm going to get used to this real easy, Mike honey," Rhonda spoke. "I'm not sure I want light bulbs in our room. The candlelight is so romantic, not that we need any help feeling romantic now, but after 20 or 30 years we may need a little help."

"I won't have any trouble at all," Mike answered. "After all I've got three beautiful passionately-aggressive women already after my body, and who knows who is also lying in the wings for her turn. I do prefer the soft glow of the candle. You are incredibly beautiful in good light; the candlelight just enhances what you already have." Looking around, Mike added, "I am used to this already, I'm going to get the utilities put in our name and have all the appliances checked over. We have moved in."

"I won't have time to do much here, like cleaning out cupboards and washing windows while I'm hiding out," Rhonda said.

"I don't expect you to do all that. I will find someone to do the work while you supervise," Mike responded. "I want you to have some energy at bedtime. Let's lie here and listen to the sounds of nature," he added.

Somewhere in the nearby mountains, a cougar screamed. In a tree by the house, an owl asked the eternal question, WHO? The majestic Columbia River made gurgling music as it rushed to the Pacific Ocean. This was the lullaby that sang the loving couple to sleep, and one they would always remember. This was the first night in their home, a night to remember.

It was a cold shower in the morning that brought both to full alert. They dressed in a hurry and had breakfast at the Hampton House. Mike went to Julie's to get a hot shower and shave. A cold shower only wakes you up or cools you down, depending on the need. It doesn't do a thing to make you feel clean.

Before he left, he packed as many of his clothes as he could into a couple of suitcases, plus his shaving gear, and put them in the pickup. He was going home. What a wonderful word--"home." It means love lives there, a "house" is where people live. There is a big difference between the two, and too often people forget.

CHAPTER 32

The generator and transfer switch was delivered on time as promised. The electricians were wiring them in, the power company had their lines in, and things were going well. Mike found the superintendent and asked "When will we have lights?"

"I said Wednesday, and I'm sure we are on target to be finished. We will have all the wiring done, and switch plates and outlet covers installed today. Tomorrow we test, and retest so we are sure everything works like it's supposed to," the super stated. "The transfer switch is working fine, but I'm not comfortable with it. I would feel better if it was replaced."

"I will order a replacement today," Mike said. "In the meantime we'll go with the one in place. As soon as the replacement comes in, I'll call you and you can install the new one."

"I'll feel a whole lot better when it's replaced." It's probably nothing, but something about it is bugging me. I called another super who came over and checked it out, and he found nothing wrong. I will install the replacement for nothing, but I do want it replaced."

"You will be paid for your time, plus travel," Mike said. "I will take it up with the manufacturer. He stands behind his product, just as we stand behind our work. We don't work for nothing and neither should you. When you sign off on the punch list, take it to Julie and she will cut your check. Thanks for doing a first-class job and in a very short time."

Mike went to see his banker to see what his line of credit was. He explained he had just bought a home and would need earnest money to close the deal.

"You do own another property, don't you sir? Are there any encumbrances on it?" the banker asked.

"No, sir, it is free and clear, but my wife and I are getting a divorce and it will be a part of the property settlement," Mike answered.

"I can give you a credit line of $100,000 at 6.5%. That should suffice until you arrange for a mortgage." the banker said.

"Fine," Mike agreed. "Get the papers ready and I'll be back after lunch to sign them."

"But, sir, these things take time. It will take a week or more to do all the paperwork and get employment verification and a credit check."

"I don't understand," Mike said. "Not one minute ago you offered me a credit line of $100,000 at 6.5%; now you have to get approval. May I use your phone please?"

"Of course," the shylock said, thinking to himself that he's almost hooked another sucker.

Mike dialed Walt's direct number.

"Walt, this is Mike. I need a favor, but first I want you to know we are on schedule with the airport. We will be leaving for Galveston this Friday at nine, as planned. Now the favor; I'm putting you on the speaker phone, so this banker can hear both sides. Susan and I bought a home and I need some earnest money. I've been offered a credit line of $100,000 at 6.5% but he says he needs a week or so to check credit and employment. Can you help?"

"Mike, I will send a certified check for half a mil by courier, now. Where do you want it sent? Congratulations on everything."

"Send it to Morrison Real Estate, Wasco, Oregon. I'll tell Howard it's on the way, and thanks." Mike responded.

"No thanks necessary, son. You and Susan are as close to my heart as any children could be," Walt answered. "Looking forward to Friday. Tell the shylock sitting there to kiss your Irish ass as you leave."

"You already told him." Mike laughed.

Mike hung up the phone, thanked the banker for its use, and laid $5 on his desk. "For the use of the phone," he said and stood to leave.

Shylock, seeing a sucker spit out the hook, was stumbling and stammering for words to save face and get part of the half mil in his bank. "Sir, there has been a terrible misunderstanding and I apologize for it."

"There has been a mistake for sure and you made it," Mike responded angrily. "You thought I was some rube that just fell off the turnip truck. My father and I are Mike Murphy and Son Electronics and Engineering. If you would get off your ass and see what is going on outside your little cage you would learn that there is a class A airport facility being built that will help bring more business to our town, which means more people to buy homes. They will also need a bank, but if you intend to screw them like you tried to screw me, you are inviting someone to open another bank with people who have feelings for other people, not for the dollar. My father and I do over a million dollars a year business on the shake of a hand. That takes about 10 seconds, not a week or more. We use this bank for our business, but I am going to move our business to one of the banks in The Dalles. Don't bother to show me the way out. I found my way in and I can find my way out."

Shylock just stood there shaking in anger. *"Just who the hell does he think he is talking to me that way?" He said to himself, "There are a lot more fish in the sea and if one slips off the hook now and then, there is another to take the bait."*

Mike went to Howard's office to inform him of the check that was coming. "You figure what would be an appropriate amount for earnest money, and when the check gets here, I'll endorse it over to you. You take your commission plus the earnest money and give me a cashier's check for the rest. I'm not going to use the bank here. Shylock and I had a come-to-Jesus meeting. If you could find a lender who would give me a good rate I would appreciate it. We are moving in today. I'm going to get the utilities put in our name, and have Chip and Dale check all appliances, the heating and AC system, water heater, everything they can think of, including the garage door opener. I want everything in good working order ASAP. Is that okay with you?"

"I see nothing wrong with that. You certainly have the resources to back you up. Have you spoken to Julia lately?" he continued. "I have never enjoyed a baseball game as much as I enjoyed Sunday's. Don't misunderstand, my late wife and I had a great marriage and I miss her. Julia fills that empty spot in my heart and I look forward to seeing more of her. She is a lovely lady and very charming. The time just flew by. I confess I was getting excited, so I left before I might have made a fool of myself and destroyed any possibility of ever seeing her again. Has she ever been married? As attractive as she is, I would have thought someone would have picked the sweetest fruit off the tree by now."

"She has never been married," Mike answered. "She was engaged and had a wedding date set when she came across him in bed with another woman. His excuse was, 'I couldn't wait any longer. I'm a man and a man has needs that a woman doesn't have or understand.' Julie has never let a man get close to her until now. I'll tell you this in strictest confidence, she is very interested in you, and I believe she was also excited. The ball is in your court, Howard. Gook luck."

CHAPTER 33

Mike drove out to his new home and stowed his gear. He took the time to really look the ranch over. There was a barn back in the trees that was in good shape. A paint job and general cosmetics would be all that would be necessary to put it in tip-top condition. A wide alleyway ran down to the barn. One side of the barn had box stalls for six horses plus a tack room with pegs for reins, harness, halters, quirts and other tack items. The other side was a workshop with an anvil and the remnant of a forge. A ladder led to the loft that had a hay fork for putting up loose hay, and a trap door to drop hay into the mangers in each stall. The builder of this place loved horses, that was obvious. A few fence posts were still standing, giving mute testimony to the past glory. A week of hard work cutting weeds and grass and putting up fence would ensure that Susan's children could have their horses safely contained. Further back in the trees was a ten-acre pond fed by springs and melting snow from the mountains, with a stream gurgling over the lava rocks to the Columbia River. There were no doubt fish in the pond and perhaps in season, a salmon or two.

"What a place to start a new life," Mike said to himself. "Father God, Brother Jesus, I thank You for Your grace. Forgive my sins and help me to be worthy of the blessings You have bestowed upon me. Bless Susan and her children and help me to rescue them. You have blessed me with the resources to do it. Watch over us as we start our life together, and with Your blessing we can accomplish

anything. There is so much to thank You for, so I will just say Thank You. Amen."

Driving back to town, Mike realized he was hungry and he stopped at Mary's. Mike found Hawk in his usual spot and joined him. The Chief was usually upbeat, but something was bothering him. "Whatever your load is dear friend, please let me pick up one end," Mike said.

"Okay Mike, you have always been there to help when I needed it," Hawk said. "But today I don't need the help; Little Faun needs it. Bear Claw is bored just sitting around with nothing to do, and he has started drinking. It hasn't got a hold on him yet, but it won't be long before it does."

"Hawk, you are not going to believe this, but I do have an answer," Mike stated. "Susan and I have just bought a ranch out on the Rowena Road. It needs someone to clean it up and do some cosmetics on it - mainly weed cutting, grass cutting, wooden fence building. I would like to hire both Little Faun and Bear Claw to do the work. If they like, I would give them housing out there in return for their help around the ranch. Little Faun could teach Susan's daughter the way of the Indian, and Bear Claw could teach them how to ride and take care of animals. Do you think they would be interested?"

"Mike," Hawk said, "that is exactly what they need. You said your ranch is on Rowena Road. Is it a mixed red-brick three-bedroom house with double garage, a barn, and pond - 50 acres more or less?"

"Yes indeed. How did you know?" Mike asked

"Since the previous owners died, we have been keeping an eye on the place. We missed last night because one of my patrolmen had a brain fart and forgot," Hawk answered.

"Not to worry Chief, everything is okay. I stayed out there last night and I am moving in today with Rhonda," Mike grinned.

"Who the hell is Rhonda, and what happened between you and Susan?" Hawk demanded.

"It will all come out in good time Chief," Mike asserted. "This is all necessary. Don't worry about Susan and me. Nothing has changed between us. Have your folks take a look; if they are interested let me know. They could start tomorrow if they wanted to. There is more work out there than meets the eye It's kind of like trying to polish a turd; the more you polish, the more it needs polishing. I'm not offering this as a charitable thing. We really need the help. Little Faun and Bear Claw will earn their pay."

"Thank you Mike. Like I said, you are always there when I need you," Hawk said. "They do not want charity; they are very proud."

"I'll have one of our construction trailers moved out for them to use until we can build a decent house for them." Mike asserted. "I'm going to be busier than a one-legged man at a butt-kicking contest for the next few days, but I will see you Thursday for our shootout. Rhonda will probably want to compete. See you then, Chief."

CHAPTER 34

Chip and Dale were finishing up on a small remodeling job, and said they would get out to the ranch Friday morning. Mike went back to Julie's and got the rest of his stuff and moved it into the ranch house. He called Rhonda and told her what he had done and asked where the rest of her things were.

"They are in a storage building on old 30 east of town," she reported. "Come by and get the key and move my things in. I can get the rest from the hotel on my way home. I talked to Dr. Graza. He will have Carlos and Maria ready when we get there. I'm so excited about seeing them I can hardly stand it. I've got a lot of work to do. Love you, see you at home. Bye."

Mike gathered Rhonda's belongings and hung them in the closet in the master bedroom. He replaced the missing light bulbs and then turned the thermostat up on the water heater and heard it click, then the burner came on. "Hooray," he said to himself, "hot shower tonight." The stove was electric and seemed to work okay, but there wasn't anything to cook. He turned the fridge on and it worked, but had been off and shut up so long there was an odor about it. "We will replace it with a family-sized one, and also we need a new range," he thought aloud.

While the water was getting hot, Mike went up the road to a mom-and-pop grocery store and got a pair of steaks, a bag of charcoal, fixings for a salad, spuds for baking, a bottle of Sangria, dish soap, foil to wrap the spuds in, and hand soap. "I'm Mike

Murphy," he introduced himself. "We just bought the ranch on Rowena Road," he said to the quizzical grocer.

"This is our first day there, so we have nothing to start housekeeping with. I need a cooler and some ice; the fridge smells bad. We will replace it. We will be out of town on business from Thursday until sometime next week. It's a flexible schedule. We will be doing business with you folks. We have two growing children, and they will put a lot of groceries away. I don't like supermarkets. They are cheaper but less personal. I'm a people person. I like to know who I'm doing business with, and if they have a problem I want to help. There will be an Indian couple moving out to the ranch to help us. I don't know what their diet is, but I expect you to accommodate them with courtesy and respect. She understands money, so will fill her shopping cart and pay for everthing at one time. I want you to check me out, so you will know if I can be trusted. My father and I have built a very successful business on the shake of the hand for a contract. That's the way it is; if you want to do business with us it must be on those terms.

"Mr Murphy, I'm Bernard Ivan Bubb. This establishment is called B.I. Bubb's and I will shake your hand right now. Whatever you need, if we don't have it or can't get it, you really don't need it," he laughed. "We look forward to your business and friendship."

"Thank you Bernie," Mike said. "I have to get home and start cooking."

Mike took the broiler rack from the range. He found some lava rock to enclose the charcoal, and then laid the broiler rack on it. He washed up some plates and found some wine glasses that he washed and placed in the ice chest to cool. He washed the spuds and wrapped them in foil and put them on the broiler rack to cook. He set the table with a candle for light. When Rhonda got home, everything was ready.

She broke into tears, and sobbed, "If you think this is going to get you anywhere, you're right. I have never in my life been treated like this. You big Irish sweetheart, you are as hard as granite on the outside, but marshmallow-soft on the inside, and I fall in love with you again every day. It seems you do all you can to make things go easy for me, except that butt chewing you gave me on Monday. Even though I knew it was not sincere, it did hurt my feelings and those were real tears. Before we sit down to dinner, I want a welcome-home-I-love-you kiss, but don't get carried away. I don't want our dinner to get cold."

After dinner they sat out on the patio enjoying their wine. The charcoal was still putting out some heat that felt good. "I can't promise you a homecoming like this every night, but if I could, I would," Mike said. "I get so much pleasure out of trying to spoil you, because you accept my clumsy efforts graciously. These are words to a song I remember that expresses how I feel: I love you more today than yesterday but not as much as tomorrow."

"Not to break the mood," he continued, "but we have hot water so we can shower tonight. We need to get a family-sized fridge and replace the range. We can do that tomorrow. The grocer up the road has good quality meat and produce, and we should patronize him as much as possible. Chip and Dale will be here Friday morning to make sure everything works. The utilities are in our name, so we are home owners. I think Little Faun and Bear Claw are going to move out here and help us with the chores. Hawk said Bear Claw was starting to drink out of pure boredom, and Little Faun was worried about him. I told Hawk it wasn't charity; we really need the help. You are going to be a mother to your children and a wife to me, in that order. You won't have time for many domestic chores except for learning how to bake applesauce cookies."

"Why sugar," Rhonda said in her Barbie Doll, sensuous, southern drawl, "just listening to what you did today makes me so tired, I think we should go to bed right now. Don't you? That wine has given me such a warm feeling. We can do the dishes in the morning."

It was one of those honeymoon nights, that a couple never forgets and can never duplicate. They fell asleep fulfilled and exhausted. They never heard the owl or the cougar or the airhorn ON THE TOWBOAT as it guided its empty barges downstream to be loaded for a return trip.

"What a glorious morning," Rhonda commented. "I thought I saw a coffee pot when we were looking around Monday. You shower and shave while I scrounge up some fixin's. We definitely need an automatic coffee maker. Let's shop for the range and fridge first thing this morning and get that out of the way, plus a coffee maker and toaster oven. The pots and pans that are here will suffice for now."

"Good plan," Mike agreed. When he finished his toiletries and stepped into the kitchen, he heard the click of the old chrome percolator, indicating the coffee was ready. It was also deliciously strong, a real kick in the butt and heart starter. He leisurely savored the first cup and was on his second when Rhonda seated herself with a cup.

"I'm already used to this, sweetheart," Mike said. "The only thing better than going to sleep with you is waking up with you beside me. The coffee is delicious and you are beautiful and I am in love with you. Life is good and God is great, all the time. What more could a man ask for?"

"If you are going to keep talking like that we will never leave the house, and we've got a full plate for the next few days. Kiss me good morning, finish your coffee, and let's get going. I'll meet you at Home Furnishing," Rhonda said.

The owner, Sol Katz, listened to what Mike and Rhonda wanted, then led them to the appliance department. "With a family of four, including two growing children, I would recommend an ice maker plus ice and water in the door. Cold water on demand encourages them to drink more water, which we all should do. Also look for milk and orange juice storage.

"At my house," Sol continued, "we have a limited supply of sodas. A six-pack lasts our two boys over a week, but they go through milk and orange juice by the gallons, which is a good trade off. Unless you buy large quantities of meat or fish or are a sportsman, I would not worry about the freezer space. There is enough capacity for a gallon or two of ice cream and whatever you are going to hold over for a short time. A refrigerator is like my store; I keep the merchandise fresh by turning my inventory. If I doesn't sell, get rid of it - even at a loss and put fresh stuff in its place.

"For your range, you want it easy to clean, so little spills are cleaned up before they are burnt into the grate. Your children will want to cook if their mishaps are easily taken care of. That's my sales pitch. The price on the tag is delivered and installed and not debatable. If you bought the entire inventory or one waste basket the prices are firm. I don't put a ridiculously high price on, and let you, I hate this expression, - Jew me down so you think you really got a bargain when it was more than what I would have sold it for in the first place. Everything you see is in stock and can be delivered within two working days or less. For an additional fee of $10 each, we will haul your old appliance away. You don't need me to tell you what you want, so look around. I'll be at my desk in the showroom when you decide."

"He makes buying appliances simple if you listen to what he says," Mike commented. "It never occurred to me to plan for quantities of milk and juice or how unimportant a freezer usually is. And the part about ice water on demand really struck a nerve. When I'm at Mary's they put the pitcher of ice water on my table and I usually empty it, but other than that I don't drink a quart of water a week. Let's get that big one with the icemaker. It looks like it can hold enough of everything for a family of four to last a few days, and that simple range with the burner control on top looks good."

"Do we really need that big a fridge? We pass a grocery store almost everyday, and like the man said, 'Keep it fresh',"

"You are probably right," Mike responded. "Let's ask Sol what he would do in our situation. He knows his business and is honest. Let's let him decide."

"Mr. Katz," Rhonda said, "Mike and I are in a quandary about the correct size refrigerator we really need, so we decided to let you make the decision for us. If you were in our position, knowing what you know, which one would you deliver? Mr. Morrison has a key to the house and will let your people in. We will be out of town beginning tomorrow until sometime next week. We did decide on that simple 36 inch white range with the burner controls on top.

Here is my hand on the deal. Mr. Morrison is acting as our agent and will cut you a check when you ask for the key."

"You mean when we return the key?" Sol questioned.

"No, I mean when you ask for the key," Rhonda stated. "You took my hand on the deal which makes it a binding contract. You have been in business for some time and you are honest. This town is not big enough for a crooked businessman to survive in. The Indians used to say you can only scalp a person once. You obviously haven't counted coups. Good day sir. Come, Michael," she said. "We still have things to do."

Outside, Rhonda said, "You get things ready for tomorrow, and I'll wind things up at the office. There is no sense getting a lot of groceries until the new fridge is installed, but you could pick up a toaster oven and coffee maker. Get a bag of bagels and cream cheese and fresh coffee and filters. I'll do supper tonight. Supper at 6:30, just like at Julie's. See you then sweetheart."

Mike called on Howard to get the finances straightened out. He left him $5,000 to cover any charges Chip and Dale would have, plus the appliances. He then remembered he had no walking-around money, so he took another $5,000 and went to the bank to get travelers' checks. Shylock saw him coming and rushed out to open the door for him.

"Mr. Murphy," he said. "I'm so happy you have changed your mind about my bank. I can offer you a 30-year fixed-rate mortgage at 2.5% with no early-pay-off penalty and $100 closing costs."

"That sounds like a spectacular deal, sir. Is that something anyone can get, or is it especially for me?" Mike asked.

"We couldn't offer that to everybody, sir. I made that offer just for you," the banker said.

"What you are saying then is that since you are losing money on me, you are going to stick John Q. Public with the cost by raising his interest rates, early-pay-penalty and closing costs. I only came in here to get some travelers' checks, but I have changed my mind. I will wait until I get to a bank that doesn't have a slime ball like you in the front office. In fact, I think this town needs an honest bank," Mike continued. "I'm going to see about forming a co-op with Howard Morrison, B.I. Bubb, Sol Katz, and any others who are sick of you, and either open one of our own or buy you out. Think about it you chiseling weasel, I can still find my way out."

Mike was steaming mad when he left the bank so decided to take a coffee break at Mary's. Hawk was in his usual spot and waved Mike to join him. "You look a lot better today than you did the last time I saw you. What happened, did you hit the lottery?" Mike asked.

"No nothing like that. Besides all that money would just cause more trouble than it's worth," Hawk responded. "Everybody I know who doesn't have any ambition would all of a sudden be my best friend and want a hand out. Lawyers would be crawling out from under their rocks to help me protect my assets and the list goes on and on. The reason I feel so damn good is sitting across from me sipping coffee. I spoke to Little Faun and Bear Claw about you needing help. They were a little concerned about it being charity - you know how proud they are. Bear asked where this ranch was and when I told him on Rowena Road, he told Faun to start packing. It seems he fishes and camps there often. He knows the place and knows what needs to be done. He said not to worry about moving a construction trailer in for awhile. They can get by on their own until it gets real cold. My friend, I watched fifteen years disappear from those two. They acted like twenty-year olds and when Faun said, 'don't you have someplace to go?' I didn't know where I was going, but I knew where they were going by the gleam in their eyes. You stirred the ashes into a fire Mike, and for that, the three of us, Faun, Bear, and I, thank you. They will move out there Friday so tell me who and what they can expect. Let me buy the coffee."

"I'll have keys made so they can get into the house," Mike said. "I would like Little Faun to really clean house, including laundry. We have messed up the sheets, so they need to be washed. I guess the best way to explain what we want is to have her treat it like it was her own. Chip and Dale will be there Friday so make sure they check the washer and dryer. If they need to be replaced, see Sol Katz. Tell him who they are for, he knows what we will need and take care of it. Bear Claw can get the weeds and grass cut and restore the fences. The children are going to have horses so we have to fence them in. Also ask him to find a suitable place for a vegetable garden. It's too late for this year, but we can get it ready for next. Any machinery he needs we can get from Murphy and Son. Most important of all, make sure they enjoy themselves. That's all I can think of, but if they see something that I've missed - fix it, paint it, or throw it away. They are wise and don't need me or anyone else to tell them what to do."

"Hawk, my friend," Mike continued, "you have no idea what a burden you have lifted from my shoulders."

"It's a simple case of one hand washing the other," Hawk answered. "And after all, we are brothers. The council okayed it and the ceremony will be the full moon in June, which on our paleface brothers' calendar is the eleventh. I am proud to be your brother. In our culture, this is serious. We are brothers as much as if we had the same parents. Little Faun and Bear Claw will spoil your children rotten, but they will not be spoiled brats. They are also excited about having grandchildren and I will be an uncle. See what you started when you asked about being blood brothers?"

"Like most ignorant palefaces, I had no idea it was such a serious matter. Now I am even more anxious for the ceremony," Mike answered, "but being brothers isn't going to cut you any slack tomorrow. I feel like I can't miss, so give it your best shot. You're going to need it," he teased. "Thanks for the coffee. I'll get the tip."

CHAPTER 35

Mike drove to the new airport. What he observed brought a big smile to his face and a thrill to his heart. The runways were finished, including the striping, the marker lights were complete, landing lights were on, and the electrical contractor was just completing his punch list. Angel Flight was about to get underway.

The remote for starting the emergency generator was ready for a test. Mike volunteered to test it. He went to the shed and rolled out the Cub. He climbed to 7,000 ft. and flew in a big circle. When he was between five to seven miles out, at an altitude of 7,000 ft, he punched the button and all the lights came on. *"It works just like it should,"* he said to himself.

Coming in he flew over Aggie's house and noted no activity.

Her car was nowhere in sight, the Hummer was in the yard behind the house and the rental car Ramon was using was in the driveway. He also noticed the yard was overgrown with weeds. That was not normal. Aggie took pride in her yard and gardens but they had not been taken care of in weeks. There was something radically wrong there, and he'd have Hawk check it out. He put the Cub in the shed after refueling and checking the oil. He locked the door and double checked it before heading for home.

On the way, he stopped at Frank's Hardware and bought a toaster oven and coffee maker. He asked Frank, "What do you think about our bank?"

"It's the only bank in town so we are stuck with it. Sometimes I think he sticks it to us, but what are we going to do?" Frank answered. "Like I said, it's the only bank in town."

"I just had it out with him and we are moving our accounts out of town until we figure out an alternative" Mike stated. "We are building a class A airport with the hopes of bringing new business to town. There is space available for offices, a coffee shop and fine restaurant. If we could form a co-op with the other businessmen in town, and either buy the existing bank or start our own, would you be interested?"

"I'd move out of there in a heartbeat, if there was an alternative," Frank answered. "What I would prefer is to start our own. If the business community moved their accounts, the populace would follow suit and he would be forced to sell. We would be in the driver's seat."

"That's kind of what I had in mind," Mike responded. "If you would talk up the idea to the other businessmen in town and get their input, I would appreciate it. I don't want to dump this in your lap, but at the present time I need 28-hour days to stay even. My secretary will be at your disposal for letter writing. You know who the business leaders are. If we can get them on board it will fly, without their support it's an uphill struggle. I'm out of town for a few days, but I will touch base with you when I get back. Thanks Frank."

Mike stopped at Bubb's and got bagels, cream cheese, coffee filters, and coffee. He asked B.I. the same questions about the bank, and got much the same answers. He said, "You can count on my support, and I'll talk to my customers also. Thanks for the news, and for shopping with us."

When Mike got home, Rhonda was already there. "I stopped at the deli," she said, "and got chicken and slaw. The coffee's done and we can eat anytime."

"How about now?" Mike answered. "We need to talk about what my role will be in regard to Carlos and Maria. I've never been a father, so I will have to learn as I go."

"We will both have a problem with that," Rhonda said. "I'm a mother but haven't been a parent in a long time. I think the best solution to the problem is to take it slow and talk things over with the children. If we let them know there is problem, they can help us both by giving us feedback. If they realize they are part of the problem, they can also help by being part of the solution. I intend to spoil them rotten, but they will not be brats. Children should be spoiled, but they should understand discipline. There is a world of difference between a spoiled child and an undisciplined brat."

"I will not stand between you and your children," Mike said. "I don't believe in corporal punishment. There are other ways to enforce behavior. All I can do is try to remember what my father did and do the same things. The difference is, he is the only father I've ever had, and your children will not know me at all so there are serious adjustments to be made on all sides. I really want to be a dad to Carlos and Maria. Most any male can be a father, but it takes a real man to be a dad. My father was a great dad and I want to be like him."

"As long as we remember we love each other and are also in love," Rhonda replied, "things will work out, maybe not instantly but over time. I promise I will not override your decisions without first privately discussing it with you. We can't let them play one of us against the other. Now let's talk about a family home. Do you have any ideas?"

"As a matter of fact I do. I think this living room should be the family room with big-screen TV and DVD, and a good stereo system because I like to listen to classical music. If the children want to listen to their type of music they can each have a stereo with headphones. The family room should be the computer room so we can monitor what they are doing. Not spying - monitoring. Their bedrooms are for sleeping and school work. I would like a sit-down-at-the-kitchen-table dinner every night, whether we are here or not. When we're gone, Faun and Bear Claw will eat with them. That will help give continuity to their lives. Education is very important. When they get home from school, they can do whatever they want after their chores are done. After dinner, if they have homework or reports to do, they will go to their rooms and get it done. If they don't have any schoolwork, they will help clear the table. Bedtime is 10 p.m. on school days. That's bedtime - not getting ready for bedtime. They can each have a TV in their room, but we will block out the garbage and encourage them to watch with us as a family. And while I'm on the subject of family, we need a good popcorn popper. This is going to be a home, not a house. A home is where love lives. Love seldom even visits a house. Let the furniture wear out from use, not from dusting, and let the grass wear out under the swings. Grass will grow back but you can never replace the laughter from the swings. I guess I've said about all I've got to say on the matter so now I'll listen to you."

"It's obvious you had a great childhood by the things you have stressed as important," Rhonda remarked. "I can't think of anything I would change. You are going to be a wonderful dad to the children because it's important to you and you want to be. You could have walked away when you learned I had children, but you didn't. You even asked if you could adopt them. I am so in love with you, I feel my heart will burst, and when you talk about our family I want to cry. Ramon was only a sperm donor, never anything more, and definitely not a dad. I'm sure it will only take a short time for the children to love and respect you. You have my okay to ask them about adoption and explain what it means. Do you realize it's after 11 o'clock? If you want to make love to Rhonda Le'Hundt, this is your last chance. Susan will be back tomorrow."

"With no disrespect, Rhonda," Mike stated, "I'm going to wait for Susan. Barbie Doll was an experience, and you could not be more opposite. You both were satisfying, but I fell hopelessly in love with Susan, and I have missed her terribly so I'm going to wait for her. We can go to bed and cuddle but no lovemaking; not 'til Susan returns."

They lay silently in the candlelight listening to the river, the owls, and the cougar - thinking about the next few days and hoping it all would go well.

CHAPTER 36

The new coffee maker worked perfectly, going on at 6 a.m. They awoke with the aroma of fresh-brewed coffee filling their nostrils. After a heart-starting cup they did their toiletries and had a bagel with cream cheese. They tidied up the kitchen and went to meet Hawk for the shootout.

Hawk was waiting in his office and Mike introduced Rhonda Le'Hundt. "If you have no objection, she would like to shoot with us," Mike said.

"I have no objections, Mike," the chief said. "Don't you know any women who don't like guns?"

"I've never thought about it, Hawk," Mike answered. "Aggie hated them, and until I met Susan, I never knew many women well enough or long enough to find out."

"Are you two going to talk all day or shoot?" Rhonda demanded. "I have more important things to do than stand around listening to you two ratchet jaw about other women and how they feel about guns."

"Okay, Rhonda, let's go shoot. Do you want to shoot first or see how we do it?" Hawk asked.

"I'll watch, then shoot," Rhonda answered.

As usual it was a close match, with Mike just edging out a win.

Good shooting, Mike," Hawk congratulated. "Okay Rhonda, do your thing."

"Can I use that target of the man in a suit?" Rhonda questioned.

"It's okay by me," Hawk said. Mike nodded his approval.

In six rounds she put one in each button on the target's three-button vest, one in each eye, and the last right between the eyes. Hawk stood stunned.

Rhonda broke the silence. "Hawk, Lizzie is Angel One and the best place to hide is in plain sight. This is my gun. I checked before we got here. Where that piece of shit Barbie Doll had came from, I don't know. I do know somebody else has fired mine before today. Whoever it was tried to clean it but there is a spot almost everybody overlooks and it wasn't touched. You said yourself you didn't know anyone that took care of a gun like I do. I was showing off for you today. Barbie Doll and Rhonda Le'Hundt are going away and Susan is coming back. Michael and I are leaving, right after I buy our lunch. We will be out of town for a few days on business but will be in touch when we get back."

Mike stowed the baggage in the Cub and went into the office for last-minute details. "Julie, he said, "There's a redheaded Irishman named Kely, who goes on Angel Flight's payroll starting Monday. He will be dropping by in the chopper. Rhonda has disappeared but Susan is back. If Frank from the hardware store calls and asks you to type some letters for him, please accommodate him. We are going into the banking business and he is going to help get things started. Hire someone to help in the office, because I can see you are getting overwhelmed with work and Susan will be tied up with other things. Get all the help you need; you be the judge. You are now the office manager with a 10% raise. Susan and I are out of town until sometime next week on Angel Flight business. Howard is really interested in you, so enjoy his attention because he is sincere. We have to go. Ready Susan?"

"I was just talking to Pops," Susan said. "He was very glad to see the real me instead of those substitutes, but understood the reason for the deception."

The Cub whined, then started. Mike let it warm up completely. "I'll give you your first and very important flying lesson right now," he said. "You never take to the air with a cold engine. You start it up and let it idle until the temperature gauge is up. Also check oil pressure. Once you are in the air and the engine quits, you are a glider pilot with few options so you make certain everything is okay before committing yourself. The engine is warmed up, the oil pressure is normal, we have a full load of fuel; now let's see if I can get us off the ground. We line up on the runway, push the throttle wide open. We are moving, the tail comes up, we've reached flying speed, a little back on the stick to get the nose up, and we're off. Ease the stick back to neutral to maintain a gentle climbing attitude. If I held the stick back, we would have looped if the Cub was built for it, but since it wasn't we probably would have crashed. I'm going to ask Red to teach you to fly if you want to learn. I can't imagine why anyone would not want to learn, but that is the difference in people. Some like to drive race cars, others like bike races; neither of those has any appeal for me. I want to be able to fly anything that's airworthy. I packed that remote for starting the generator. I tried it out yesterday and it really works slick. I punched the button and the lights came on as advertised. There's Bridal Veil falls on your left, Troutdale just ahead."

They found Jenkins in his office. "You're just in time," he said. "I have a last-minute favor to ask and it may sound silly but it is very important." Mike interrupted. "I need to fake engine trouble, so if you could install a smoker on the port-side engine that I could turn on from the cockpit, it would be worth your while. We won't be leaving until midmorning."

"I'll put a man on it right now," Jenkins said. "And there will be no charge."

"Mr. Jenkins, I appreciate the offer but I must decline," Mike said. "My reasoning is this; if something goes wrong and it doesn't work I can't come back to you because it cost me nothing. On the other hand, if I pay and it doesn't work you are obligated to repair, refund, or replace. In this case it would be a refund because we are only going to need it once. Do you understand where I'm coming from?"

"Yes, Mr. Murphy, I do," Jennkins answered. "Would you like to see your bird?"

"Yes indeed we would," Susan answered.

They followed Jenkins to the hangar and there she stood: Gleaming white with blue Medivac insignia. And on the vertical stabilizer and over the door and on each wing was a beautiful, curly-haired blonde Angel.

"Michael, when Walt sees this he is going to come apart," Susan said. "He is very good at hiding his feelings unless it's something he really cares about and believe me he really cares about Angel Flight and you. After all had it not been for you, Lizzie would be dead and maybe Mrs. Henderson too. You turned everything around. Mr. Henderson is much better, and you gave him a new project. I can hardly wait to see his face."

"Mr. Jenkins, I don't know when I'll be able to retrieve my Cub, so if you could put it in a corner someplace where it will be out of the way I would appreciate it," Mike said. "My father bought that for me for my sixteenth birthday present. It was a pile of parts on a trailer when I got it, but the parts were all there so I rebuilt it, took flying lessons in it, and learned to love flying. It is a part of me, so please take care of her."

"It will be my pleasure to do so, and there will be no debate on this. It is on the house."

"Well if that's all, we will call the Mariott and they will send a courtesy car to pick us up," Mike stated. "We will see you in the morning."

They registered as Mr. and Mrs. Mike Murphy representing Angel Flight. When they got into the privacy of their room they sat on the couch holding hands and letting the tensions of the past few weeks drain away.

"It's too early for dinner,' Mike said. "Let's take a dip in the pool. I saw a sporting goods store up in the next block. We can get swimsuits, which we should have anyway, and I need the exercise."

"That's a good idea," Susan agreed.

Mike had no trouble finding a swimsuit for himself, but Susan was looking for a one-piece suit in her size. All they had in one- piece suits were for big ladies. She finally settled on a two-piece that left something to the imagination.

They changed into their swimwear in their room. "Honey," Mike said, "If you went outside with that suit on you would be arrested as a traffic hazard. Every woman would be jealous and every man, unless he is blind or dead, would fantasize about you and envy me. You are that gorgeous."

"I just happened to remember. I can't go into the pool. The chlorine would react with the dye in my hair and maybe turn it green or some other weird color. I'll sit by the pool and get some rays while you swim."

Mike was enjoying the water. The temperature was just right for a refreshing swim. He heard a commotion in Susan's direction so he went to investigate. Some young, well-built, college-age man who obviously thought he was God's gift to women, was giving Susan a hard time. He was insinuating that what he had every WOMAN HE WANTED AND she could have it too. Susan was on her feet and the stud was salivating in anticipation.

"You in trouble honey?" Mike called out.

"It's nothing I haven't handled before," she replied. Turning to the stud, she asked, "Can you swim?"

"A little," he said. "I don't come to the pool to swim; I come to pick up women."

"Well, you better practice swimming," Susan said, "because your pick-up technique sucks." With that and a martial arts kick to the jaw, the stud was in the water. "Now before you say anything you will regret, by law I must inform you my fists are registered as lethal weapons, and I suggest you take a cold shower before my husband steps in and kicks the shit out of you. He only has Marine Corps training so he's not as gentle as I am. Consider yourself very lucky and go buy a lottery ticket."

Back in their room, Mike remarked. "You are incredible. You can out shoot anyone I've ever known or even heard about, a martial arts expert, beautiful, and sensational in the sack."

"I thank you for the compliments" Susan said, "except for the last. The first two I do solo; the last takes two. Let's shower and dress, go have some lobster and wine, and then come back and sweat up the sheets.

"That sounds like a plan to me," Mike said. "especially the part about sweating up the sheets. Let's call Walt and see if he and his wife could join us for dinner. The least we can do is let him know we are in town. We can still sweat the sheets later."

"Wonderful thought," Susan replied. "I'll make the call while you're in the shower. He and his wife will be here about six," Susan announced as Mike stepped out of the shower. "And he insists on treating us to dinner. I told him we didn't have any fancy clothes. He said where we are going has the best lobster on the west coast and is less than informal. A clean shirt is as formal as it gets, but the management runs a tight ship so there are no incidents. The floor is littered with peanut shells, which adds to the atmosphere. "Sounds like a place the "fleet" would like, only they also like to kick butt; especially with jar heads," Mike said.

Mike and Susan were waiting in the lobby when the Hendersons arrived. After a brief introduction they got into Walt's van.

"Would you like to see your new bird?" Mike asked.

"Yes, I would Mike, and I think Margaret would too. Right, honey?" Walt addressed his wife.

"Yes, Walter is so excited about you and the mercy flights," Mrs. Henderson said. "He tells everyone what you did for Lizzie and what you two are cooking up and has no trouble doing some arm twisting to raise money. Not only for now but to commit down the road. He has always loved new projects and this is very near and dear to both of us."

At Beaver Air, they were met by Jenkins who had stayed to oversee the installation of the smoker.

When the Hendersons saw the jet it was all oohs and aahs, until they saw the Angel Logo; then holding hands and embracing each other, they let the tears flow, which were contagious.

Regaining her composure, Margaret said, "Walter and I have been doing some serious thinking regarding Elizabeth. She is all the family we have, with the exception of you two. When Walter and I are gone, she will naturally inherit most of our assets. We would like you two to assume responsibility for her care until she reaches maturity in the event that something happens to us."

"Are you sure you want us to be her guardians?" Mike asked. "You hardly know me. You know Susan, but nothing about me."

"Son," Walt said, "I've known your father for more than twenty years and the nut falls close to the tree. I've seen you in action and I've watched you and Susan interact. If we were to draw up a list of all we are looking for, you two are the perfect fit. Yes, we are sure."

"There is one stipulation and it is not debatable," Mike asserted. "There will be no monetary consideration. We will do it because we love you and Elizabeth, not for financial gain."

"Now that that's settled, let's go eat lobster," Margaret said. "I haven't felt this good since before our daughter was killed. Walter told me you had a magic spell about you that makes one feel better and he is correct. I might even have a little wine tonight. You two have an infectious glow about you that shows you really are in love."

"I've got to tell you two," Mike spoke up, "this beautiful woman is as tough a person as I've ever known. The Chief of police and I have a weekly shootout. We fire six rounds slow fire at a target with a four inch circle where the heart is, and six rounds rapid fire and we are damned proud of ourselves. She puts all six rounds in a three-inch circle, then to top it off, three in the same three-inch circle, one in each eye and the last round right between the eyes. This morning she shot the buttons off a three-button vest and one in each eye and one in between. She is also an expert in the martial arts. This afternoon at the pool she stood flat-footed and kicked a 6ft 2 in., 250 lb. guy in the jaw and dumped him in the pool. Walt, if I hadn't stepped in in Galveston and rescued those thugs she might have really hurt them. We are on the same page and in love. Look out world, here we come!"

The lobster bar was all it was advertised to be - raucous, with peanut shells two inches deep on the floor. It was a working-man's establishment - a lot of hard hats and a few clean shirts. It was a friendly place, the kind of place with people you would seek out if you needed help. You would state your case to the bartender, who would announce your needs to the patrons, who would see that you were okay, buy you a drink, and send you on your way. No meeting with the board, studying your problem, referring it to committee, and coming back next week.

Mike noticed a well-dressed couple at the next table. The woman had never been in this place before or in any place like it. She thought it was beneath her standards. She studied the menu and said to the waitress, "I'm so hungry for lamb. Do you serve lamb?"

"Lady," the waitress said. "We serve anybody who walks in the door,"

"What I meant was," the snob continued, "I didn't see it on the menu, and I was wondering if you served it."

"Madam, this is a lobster bar. If it ain't on the menu, we ain't got it. Do you go to a Honda dealer when you buy a Cadillac?" the exasperated waitress demanded. "Wakeup to reality. How much lobster do you want? I don't have time to wait for some airhead to make up her mind. I've got other customers waiting. If you want me fired, my name is Jean Adkins. Charlie, help these people find the door and bus this table. Hi, Walt darling, where have you and Margaret been and how is Lizzie getting along?"

"We are going to get her tomorrow," Walt explained. "Jean, this is my pilot and his soon-to-be wife; Michael Murphy and Susan Romaine. Mike and I have just started a service dedicated to transporting critically ill or crippled children to a hospital that specializes in their need, and there is no charge for the service. It is a not-for-profit corporation and a great place to donate funds to cut your taxes. We call it Angel Flight. Mike is the angel that literally dropped out of the sky and saved Elizabeth's life."

"Mike, your money is no good in here," Jean said. "I own this place. That's why I could talk to Miss Goody Two Shoes the way I did."

Susan interrupted, "Miss Goody Two Shoes has returned with a couple of goons. Can I handle the problem for you, please?"

"Let her do it, Jean," Walt said.

The goons were coming straight for Jean when Susan stood up and got between them and Jean and in a firm, steady voice said, "Stop right where you are. You are not welcome here, so do yourselves a favor and leave before you get hurt."

"And who are you going to call? The Marines?" the greasy one sneered.

"No, I take care of the little problems like you myself," Susan mocked. "My husband there was a Marine. He handles big problems; I handle the small ones. Now, I'm going to ask you to leave or prepare for the surprise of your life. I have an idea. Let's make this interesting. I'll cover any bet anyone wants to bet. I will whip both of these goons here and now by myself. Jean will hold the money and I'll give you ten minutes to put up or shut up and get out."

Greasy sneered and said, while waving a fist full of money, "We got three grand. Lady, let's see yours."

"Darling," Susan cooed, "would you get into my bag and get just three thousand dollars out of my coin purse? Leave the rest of the money there in case someone else wants to bet." Handing her money to Jean, she said to the goons, "Your ten minutes are up and you are still here, so do you want it one at a time, or are you going to double up on me?"

The waiters and waitresses and the customers had cleared a circle and were eager to see what was going to happen.

Susan said tauntingly, "Don't turn away or you will miss the whole show."

Grease said, "We got other things to do so we're going to double up and get it done quick."

"Are you both going to come from the front or does one of you want to try from the rear? I'll wait for you to make up your so-called minds and get in position."

"We're both coming from the front," Grease announced. "We want to see the fear in your face."

The goons came slowly at Susan. She just stood there, taunting. "It's still not too late to change your minds." Then she said, "Now you've stepped over the line and it's too late." The point of her size 6 shoes with 4-inch heels, caught Grease in the jewels, a quick right jab and his partner's nose disappeared into a bloody mess.

Before Grease could recover, a chop to the nape of the neck and he was down and out. His partner on his knees said, "Lady, I've had enough."

Susan turned to Jean and said, "I think a 2-pound lobster would be about right, don't you?"

"Such a sweet innocent little girl," Mrs. Henderson teased. "If I hadn't seen it I would not believe it."

Jean approached with a sack of money, mostly twenties but a lot of C notes. "What do I do with this?" she asked "It's rightfully yours."

"Just give me my three thousand and donate the rest to Angel Flight. I think Walt has a bank account for that purpose, don't you?" Susan asked.

"Indeed I do and it is growing bigger by the minute," he answered.

"I'm going to have signs made and have fish bowls placed for donations," Jean said. "I'm also going to put your story on the menus. Most people have never heard of such a thing and will support it. I'm going to challenge the "Lobster Pot" to a contest to see which of us raises the most money in a thirty-day period. The loser has to work at the winner's place and the winner has the dinner of his choice anywhere on the west coast. These are the places people come to have fun, a good dinner and, on occasion, entertainment. Any time you want to quell a disturbance for me you go right ahead. It was like watching a ballet and my customers will long remember this night. Your dinners are up. I'll be right back with them."

"This has been a very interesting evening to say the least," Walt remarked.

"I would say more entertaining and informative," Mrs. Henderson said. "I meet our - shall we say - 'adopted' son for the first time. I get out of the house, and feel great for the first time in weeks, have a marvelous dinner at our favorite bistro and see a demonstration of martial arts. No, I think it was more informative and entertaining," Mrs. Henderson insisted.

"Whatever," Walt said. "What time are we leaving tomorrow?" he asked.

"I would like to be in the air by 9 a.m.," Mike answered. "Are you up for some excitement Walt?"

"I'm up for anything, Mike," Walt stated.

Jean came up to the table and quietly said, "I hope I'm not going to be in trouble for telling you this. There is an arrest warrant issued for a Susan Romaine for the murder of Agnes Murphy. It just hit the news."

"Thanks for letting us know," Mike said. "I know positively she didn't do it and I'm sure I know who did. The Police Chief is sure who did it, and is only following orders from the D.A. It's time for us to leave anyway. We have an important business trip scheduled for the next few days. Susan is innocent and the Chief and I will prove it."

"I'll tell you the whole story on the trip tomorrow," Susan stated.

"I would like to hear it too," Mrs. Henderson said. "Is there room for me on the plane?"

"There is plenty of room" Mike assured her. "Walt doesn't do anything halfway. When he bought an executive jet, he bought top of the line."

"I thought you were afraid of flying, honey," Walt said.

"I am, but if Lizzie's not afraid, I will let her comfort me," Margaret answered. "I'll pack for a week and see you in the morning."

Mike called Hawk at home. "We just heard the news. You and I both know who did it and we can prove Susan's innocence. We are not running. We are on a rescue mission and will surrender Susan when we get back, probably Tuesday. I'll call you every day and you know how to reach me."

"This has been a full day for you honey," Mike said to Susan. "Yes it has," she answered. "That sneaky bastard. He took my gun, and if Agnes has been shot, you can bet it was my gun that did it. That can be the only way to tie me to the crime. Then he put my gun back in the drawer. I'm sorry, honey, I was only thinking of me.

Are you alright?" You said the love wasn't there, but you at least cared about her."

"Yes, I cared," he answered. "I hope she didn't suffer. Now I also have a reason to confront him. Can I have him first?"

"Yes, you can have him first, but I get to shove the gun up his ass and pull the trigger," Susan laughed. "I think we need to slip between the sheets for some mutual consolation."

"If what I think is going to happen happens, that's a term I've never heard used," Mike teased.

They consoled each other for the better part of an hour and fell asleep completely exhausted from consolation.

CHAPTER 37

By 9 a.m., the Hendersons were on board with their luggage stowed away. Mike made his walk-around inspection, and determined that his aircraft was airworthy. He had the weather report and had filed his flight plan. The APU was up and running, and the passengers had been properly briefed on procedure in case of emergency.

"We have clear skies and fine weather all the way. We will set down in Salt Lake City for a pit stop and to walk around," Mike announced. "Sitting too long is not good so we can stretch our legs. Now let's see if I can get this thing in the air."

Mike signaled the ground crew that he was starting the portsside engine. The Rolls Royce whined, the turbines spinning faster and faster, then started. Its twin brother on the starboard side followed suit. All the instruments were reading like they should, so he called Ground Central for taxi clearance. Given clearance, he taxied to the runway and made a final check before calling the tower for take off.

"Okay, Angel Flight. You are cleared for take off," the tower reported.

"Roger, tower," Mike acknowledged.

Easing the engines to full power, they were soon at speed, so Mike eased back on the yoke and brought the nose up and they were airborne.

"Angel Flight, calling Departure Control. Do you have me on your scope?"

"Yes, we do, but at the speed you show on our radar, Central Control will take over shortly," they answered.

At 20,000 ft., Mike switched off the fasten seat belt sign and invited Walt to sit in the co-pilot's seat.

"I'd better sit with Margaret," he said.

"Margaret," Mike said, "I know this is your first plane ride so I will try to explain what is happening as we go along. You will hear a thump or hiss or some other noises. Don't worry, it's just a valve opening or closing. If you feel you're getting sick, Susan will get you a barf bag. There is a restroom behind you on the left or port side. That's everything I know about flying. Susan are you going to help me fly this thing?"

"No, you're on your own. I'm going to sit back here and tell the Hendersons what is going on," she answered moving back to be with Walt and Margaret.

"With my hair the color it is, if I hadn't been with Michael you would have passed me by."

"You're right," Walt replied. "When I first spotted Mike, I wondered who the hell you were and what had happened to Susan."

"Among her other talents, she is a very good actress," Mike said. "Do your Barbie Doll act honey. Just imagine a blonde in a very short red skirt, low cut blouse, in a candy-apple red sports car convertible."

"Hi sugar," she purred to Walt, in her southern drawl. "My you are a fine looking man. Is there anything I have you that would like to see or touch? For the right price it can be arranged."

Walt and his wife were laughing so hard they didn't even realize they were 20,000 ft above the ground!

"Oh my," Margaret said, "I've used my imagination and pictured you as Mike described. It's no wonder you drove Ramon crazy."

"Then with my red hair, I was Rhonda Le'Hundt," Susan continued. "I met Michael in the hotel dining room and pitched the new line of products and he bought a remote control for the new generator. He didn't know me, so I had to tell him who I was.

I learned one important thing about him. As Barbie Doll, I tried my best to seduce him but he never even came close to taking the bait. He is loyal and true to his word."

"I'm going to fly over Crater Lake," Mike said. "If you've never seen it from the air, you've never really seen the beauty of it. The water is as pure a blue as you'll ever see. I'll descend, and do a low circle so you can get a good view of it. New England has it's beauty, but without the snowcapped peaks of Mount Hood, Mount Adams, and the others, it doesn't quite measure up. Of course that's an Oregonian speaking. Someone from New Hampshire or Vermont would argue that without the reds, yellows, oranges and the blends of color, we fall short. I've seen both, but the clincher for me was the difference in winter weather. Ours are much milder. We'll also go over Salt Lake and make a pit stop. We need to walk around for our legs' sake, then it's about three and a half hours to Galveston."

"Roger Angel Flight 1, Follow UPS heavy."

"Roger Tower, acknowledged Follow UPS heavy." "Tower to Angel Flight."

"Go ahead tower."

"Your logo indicates you are a Medivac. Is that true?"

"Roger Tower. This is our maiden voyage. We are going to pick up a patient."

"There was a house fire last night," the tower said. "And a seven- year-old boy has third-degree burns on his hands, arms, and face that he got saving his mother and little sister. If we can get him to Houston they can do wonders for him. What would you charge to fly him to Houston? They have started a fund for him. His mother is widowed and works two jobs to keep them together."

"Tell the hospital to get him ready for transport and get him here. We have an experienced nurse on board and state-of-the-art equipment. There is no charge to the patient or family. They already have enough to worry about, so we don't want them to worry about transportation. We exist on public donations. Make sure his mother and sister are with him. We don't separate families, especially in time of stress. Where do you want me to park this thing?"

"Southwest gate 3." The manager has heard this and wants to know where to send donations and if you use JP4?"

"First National Bank of Portland, Oregon, Angel Flight. We are a registered not-for-profit corporation and all donations are tax-deductible. Yes JP4 would be fine. We're making a pit stop here, but can be rolling in thirty minutes or less."

They got out of the plane and were welcomed into the terminal with applause and cheers. The local TV reporter was there, along with the newspaper asking questions.

Walt held up his hands for silence. "This is team number one of what we hope will be followed by many other teams. This is my pilot and his wife, the Murphy's. I am Walter Henderson and my wife Margaret is the lady with the beautiful smile. We thank you for this fine and unexpected reception. Remember when the world knows about Angel Flight, you witnessed its maiden voyage. Now if you will excuse me, I must find the men's room."

Susan had changed into her nurse whites and Mike changed into his captain uniform. They were a striking couple and drew looks of admiration. Susan grabbed Mike's arm and drew close saying, "This is really exciting isn't it?"

"It really is and this is what I want to do."

After taking off from Salt Lake with their new passengers; Betty Walker, her daughter Missy, and Jack, the burn victim who had saved his mom and sister, Walt soon discovered that the family had lost everything in the fire. "Mrs. Walker, do you have family to help you in Salt Lake? Or would you consider moving?"

"Sir," she said, "the only family I have is in this airplane. I would move in a heartbeat for the right opportunity, but with no skills what can I hope for?"

"Mrs. Walker, you have exactly the skills my wife and I are looking for," Walt answered. We are on the way to pick up our 5-year old granddaughter whose parents were killed by a drunk driver. You obviously have excellent parenting skills. My wife could use some help around the house, so this is what I'm offering. Before I go any futher, your decision will not change this in any way. My wife and I will set up a trust fund for your children's education

- a full ride, no strings, so that he can be a little boy and not a workaholic. I'm giving him an allowance to stay home and be a big brother. We have a big house. It's too big for just us. You and your children can move into our house. You will have your own living quarters with TV, a bath and a half. In exchange you will practice your parenting skills on our granddaughter and help my wife with the housework. The salary we'll work out later. When Jack is able to travel, you call me and I'll arrange transportation for you and your family. I want you to see what you might be buying into before you make your final decision. In the meantime, here is some cash to get you through for a while. How much is there I don't know and I don't want to know. Here is my card. If you need anything and don't call me, I would really be hurt because my wife and I care about you. Please don't say anything. Let me have my moment of glory."

"Would anyone like coffee or a sandwich," Susan asked. "Maybe I should look and see what we have before I offer something we don't have. Missy can I get you something?"

A frightened little voice said, "May I please have a glass of water?"

Margaret came back to where Missy was seated, and said "Missy, I have a granddaughter just your age. She is in the hospital where the doctors fixed her heart."

"How did it get broken?" Missy asked innocently.

"Some bad man was drunk and ran into their car and her mommy and daddy died," Margaret explained tearfully. "And that's how her heart got broken. It broke Walter's and mine too, but we didn't have to go to the hospital and get ours fixed because we were stronger than Lizzie. We fixed ours ourselves. I miss Lizzie so much. Would you come sit on my lap like Lizzie does and let me sing to you?"

Missy looked at her mother and Mrs. Walker said, "Go ahead honey, it's all right. This is new to her. She has no grandparents," Betty directed to Margaret.

"Well, she does now, if you let us. I absolutely guarantee she will be spoiled." Margaret stated.

"I think our family is growing, Susan," Mike said, "and I like it. Betty and her family blend in nicely."

"It's like I said earlier, it's destiny," said Susan. "We ask for God's help, and are so upset that our prayers aren't answered, that we forget we may be the answer to someone else's prayer. He answers every prayer with yes, no, or maybe later, but we only accept yes for an answer. If you want to see God's handiwork look at the front row. Margaret, Missy and Walt are nestled together asleep with the most peaceful and beautiful smiles you will ever see."

CHAPTER 38

"Angel Flight do you copy?" came from Mike's radio. "Roger, mystery voice, I copy. Who and where are you?"

"I'm in your blind spot, 3000 ft above. Lieutenant Commander Scott Walter, VMF 312, MAG 33, attached to 3rd Marine Division."

"You always were the sneaky one, Scotty. I'm the only one you couldn't sneak up on until today, but I wasn't playing top gun today."

"Murph, what are you doing flying ambulances?"

"Doing what I like to do, prolonging lives instead of shortening them."

"Explain it to me Mike."

Mike explained the whole thing to Scotty and said, "When your tour is over, I've got a spot for you."

"It really sounds good Murph. I'll be knocking on your door soon."

"Before we break off Scotty, what is our air speed? We just got this out of the shop this morning and I think my air speed indicator is off. It reads almost 5 and I've still got more juice."

"There is nothing wrong with your speed meter, Murph. It's right on."

"Do you remember our private channel?" Mike asked. "See you there in a short-short, Scotty out."

Scotty resumed his conversation on the private channel. "Did you make the trip, Murph? What can I do for you?"

"Do I know anyone at Gitmo or in the Caribbean near Castroville?"

"Tex Ford is at Gitmo. What do you need?"

"Hopefully, nothing. I'm going to rescue two minor children for their mother. Land and takeoff under radar can happen in 10 or 15 minutes, depending on how alert his military is."

"I'll pass the word. When is this incursion going to take place?"

"This Sunday afternoon about 16:30. Thanks for any help Scotty, Murph out."

"Houston air traffic. This is Angel Flight. We have a patient for the burn center. He is not critical but we would like priority clearance."

"You are cleared to William Hobby, Angel Flight. Use runway 4 left. The ambulance is waiting at Southwest gate 3. I'm switching you to their tower control. Houston Air Traffic out."

"We've been listening and have you 5 by 5. You are early. A navy pilot called us and said you would be early. That's why we are ready. What do you have under the hood?"

"As far as I know, stock Rolls Royce RB211-524L. Beaver Air in Troutdale, Oregon installed them. The mechanic said he could juice them up some, and I guess he did. I'm going to try to land this thing, so I'll be busy. Thanks tower. Angel Flight Out."

Mike rolled to a stop and the Medics were inside and getting Jack into the ambulance, almost before the door was fully open. Betty and Missy got into the ambulance with Jack and left with the siren wailing its mournful song.

"I want to go to the hospital where they've taken Jack," Margaret said. "Betty needs mothering and I need to be a mother. She will never replace our daughter in our hearts but she takes up a lot of the emptiness left by her death."

"Let's all go," Susan suggested. "She is alone, in a strange place and she needs family, and damn it, I'm going to try and be a sister to her."

They found her in the waiting room, Missy curled up sleeping in a chair. Walt and Mike hung back, while the women did the womanly things. Margaret took the chair next to Betty and put her arm around her shoulder.

"Betty, honey," she said, "I need to be a mother. Since my only child was killed, there has been a vacancy in our hearts for Walter and me." He doesn't show it, but he really wants to be a father. We believe in destiny. You had probably been praying for help for Jack and something told us to stop in Salt Lake. Who put those things together, if not God himself? I want to mother you."

"And I want to be your sister," Susan spoke up. "I've never had one to share secrets with and all those other things sisters do."

That did it, the dam burst and tears flowed from Betty like she had never wept before.

"Why are you all doing this for me?" she asked. "You know nothing about me."

"We do it because we're selfish," Mike said, "It's a rush we get by giving, whether it's money or changing a tire, anything that we can do. You said we don't know anything about you. We know all we need to know. You are one of God's creations who needs help. What more do we need to know?"

"Can I get in on this?" Walt asked.

"Why not?" Margaret responded. "Nothing's ever stopped you before," she teased.

"I just called the Holiday Inn and gave them my card number. When you are ready to leave here tonight, they will send a car for you. All you have to do is sign the tickets for meals, and don't forget ice cream for Missy and you too, of course. When Jack is ready to travel, call me and I will personally see that transportation is available. There are no strings attached. If you want to accept our offer, that would be wonderful, and it is not charity. You will earn every dime. If you choose not to accept, it will be disappointing but won't change the education I promised. Please think about it before you make a decision. It's your life. I cannot or will not make the decision for you. It's been a long day and I need my rest. Let's check in someplace tonight and finish this tomorrow."

"That is a good idea, Boss," Mike said.

"Amen to that," Margaret and Susan chimed in.

They checked in to the Holiday Inn. Walt called the hospital where Lizzie was. They said they would bring her over to William Hobby field in the morning at 9 a.m.

Mike called Hawk as promised and listened to him attentively. "All I can say for sure is Susan's gun fired the shots and nobody has seen her since before the murder. I can only testify that the woman I knew as Barbra Dahl was, according to fingerprint analysis, Susan Romaine." Hawk continued, "We won't have any touble proving her innocence but we need to find whoever did it. Ramon Romaine is a person of interest, but we can't find him. Excuse me, I said can't, I should have said haven't found him. I've got trackers that can trail a snake through water, so he will be found. I told the D.A. what I know and that you were aware and not running, so thanks for letting me know where you are. Keep in touch."

Mike, Susan, and the Henderson's were ready for the chopper when it arrived with Lizzie. Angel Flight was fueled, Mike had made his walk-around, and Grandma and Grandpa were smothering Lizzie with kisses, when she spotted Mike.

"Gramma, do you believe in Angels?" Lizzie asked.

"That man," pointing to Mike, "is and angel." Pointing to Susan she said, "And she is too. When those other people stuck me with a needle and I went to sleep, that lady held me in her arms and we got on that man's back and he carried us to a place that had a tunnel with a bright light at the end. Gramma, it was so pretty. It had swings and dollies. A nice man who had a light coming from him looked at me and smiled. He said I was too early and should go back, so that lady took me back. I don't know where that man went, probably to bring somebody else to the tunnel. Anyway when I woke up. Grampa was beside my bed holding my hand."

"Buckle up everybody," Mike said. "We are going to burn holes in the sky."

"What a beautiful story, Lizzie," Walt said.

"It's no story Grampa, it happened, it really did. You believe me, don't you Gramma?"

"Yes Lizzie, I believe you," Margaret said. "Now we are going on an exciting adventure and you get to play-act. You still like to play-act don't you?"

"Oh yes, that's the funnest thing to do there is. You can be whatever you want to be. I like to play-act that I am a Princess with a big castle, with lots of cookies to have with my tea, when my maid brings it to me. Then sometimes I'm a Gramma like you, and rock and kiss my dollies like you do me. Play-acting is really fun. What am I going to play-act?"

"I'll tell you what we are really going to do and you tell me what you want to be. That lady - indicating Susan - has two children that some bad people are keeping away from her, so we are going to rescue them like Princes do in the fairy tales, only these bad men have guns. We are going to pretend we have trouble with our airplane and a sick little girl on board. We are going to ask for a doctor to come and look at our patient. While he is doing that, the children will pretend they are looking for bugs or something, way down where we landed. Then we will get the engine fixed and the doctor will get off and we will go where the children are, because we have to take off from the same place we landed. When we get down there, the children will run to the airplane and we will fly away."

"Grandma, I could play-act the sick little girl. I could do that real good and fool everyone."

"That's a fine idea Lizzie. You be the sick little girl and I will be the worried Gramma. Won't that be fun?" Margaret said, "I hope I can be as good at play-acting as you are. When we get home we will practice a lot."

Mike turned in a flight plan from Houston to Miami. Over New Orleans, he set his course for Havana and descended to 5000 feet. "Central Control to Angel Flight, do you read me?"

"Here's where we start our show," Mike stated. "Lizzie, you get on the gurney and Susan will tuck you in and fasten your straps so you won't fall out. Margaret put on your worried Grandmother act."

"It's no act Michael," she answered.

"Susan you sit up here and be ready to talk to Havana. They will, no doubt, expect English but when you talk in Spanish to them they may let their guard down just enough to let this thing work," Mike ordered.

"May day, May day, Air Traffic Control, this is Angel Flight. We are heading for Miami. Our instruments are not functioning. We have no compass. We don't know if our radio is working or not because we can't hear anything. We have smoke coming from our port engine. We have a five-year old girl strapped to a gurney. In words of one syllable, HELP," Mike screamed.

"Air Traffic Control. This is Captain Tex Ford, US Navy. I have spotted an aircraft with smoke coming from its port engine below me and heading southeast. The nearest place he can land is Havana. I can lead him there but Fidel won't want me too close. What do you want me to do?"

"If you can get his attention, lead him to Havana. Castro may be an asshole but I don't think they would shoot the plane down, especially under the circumstances. I will contact their approach center and advise. Thanks for any help. Air traffic out."

"Angel Flight. If you copy, Scotty called me about your flying ambulance and also told me about your secret address. I'm going to drop you a line as soon as I get back to the base. Let me know if you get it. Tex Ford, out."

Mike punched up his address. "I got your card Tex. Thanks," Mike answered.

"I don't have enough fuel to hang around very long," Tex stated. "There are enough of your buddies within a stone's throw to bail you out of a jam, if the need arises. We will monitor this address. See you later."

Tex dropped down and flew wingtip to wingtip, then gave a thumbs up and executing a perfect Imalman was gone.

"Havana Tower calling Angel Flight."

"This is your academy award opportunity, Susan. You can't hear them, so tell them what our problems are and what we need, especially the doctor. We've gone over this many times. It's show time everybody," Mike announced.

The runway was a little rough because of lack of maintenance. The fire trucks were standing by and as soon as Mike put the plane on the ground he reversed the thrusters, braked to a stop and shut down the smoking engine. As they were taxiing to the terminal, Susan gasped.

"Oh Mike there they are. My children. I can hardly wait to hold them."

At the terminal, Mike got out and stopped the firemen from spraying foam on the engine.

"Let me look and see if I can find what caused the problem. He asked if they had a 15mm end wrench he could use. Handing it back to the mechanic he said an oil line was not tightened, but it was okay now. Getting back into the cockpit he got on the radio. "Angel Flight to ground control. Do you copy?"

"Si, Senor. We hear you fine. Can you hear us okay?" Ground Control answered.

Walt came up and strapped himself into the co-pilot's seat. Susan says, "The children are in position behind that marker light, and the doctor is just leaving."

"This is going to be quick," Mike said. "Susan come up here and thank them for their help and courtesy. If we can ever help them in any way, just call Angel Flight. Then get back and stand by to take on passengers."

The twin rolls Royce engines screamed into life and Mike taxied to the runway.

The message delivered, she stood by the door. Mike stopped in position to block the view of the marker from the tower. The door was open and Maria and Carlos were running for the plane.

Mike told Ground Control that light indicated the door was not secure, but he had it repaired and was ready for takeoff.

The children were on board and strapped in.

"You are cleared for takeoff at your pleasure senor. Senora Romaine, you are even more beautiful than when I last saw you. Ramon is somewhere in the USA and when he finds out you have the children he will be very angry so be very careful. Those in the drug business have many eyes and ears and he will find you. Good luck. This is Tomas Rocha."

"Tomas," Susan answered, "We know where he is and he knows where I am. I had a chance to use my martial arts on him. The pilot of this plane and I are going to be married as soon as possible so we are going to close the book on Ramon, once and for all. Thanks for your help, Tomas. God bless you."

"He already has and continues to do so. Tomas out."

"That was a dear friend from my past that warned me about Ramon. I was young, naïve and I thought in love, so I paid no attention to him nor took his advice. As it turned out, he was right and I was wrong," Susan lamented.

"Central Control. This is angel Flight. Do you copy?" Mike called.

"Angel Flight. This is Central Control. We read you loud and clear. What is your status, are you still in an emergency situation?"

"Negative Central. We put down in Havana and corrected our problems, which were minor. A loose oil line and the cable to the radio was just stuck on, not screwed together like it should have been. I will discuss these minor problems with the responsible parties when I get back. A doctor came aboard while we were in Havana and said our patient was okay to go home.

Do we need to clear customs?"

"Negative, Murph. The entire US Navy has called, including the Admiral himself and vouched for you. Where do you want to divert to?"

"It's been an exciting few hours. Clear us to Tampa." "Roger Angel Flight. You are clear to Tampa."

Mike taxied to Buccaneer Sky Harbor. Susan was busily getting everybody ready to unload.

Margaret said, "Susan. I can do this, not as efficiently as you can, but I can do this. Go see to your children."

"Thank you Margaret."

In a matter of seconds, mother and children were hugging, kissing, crying, and laughing all at once in joyful reunion. As Mike walked past he said, "Take all the time you need. We are going to stay here a day or two to catch our breath."

"Michael, this is Carlos and Maria. Children, this is Michael Murphy. He is the one who planned this rescue. This is Mrs. Henderson and her husband Walter, and their granddaughter, Elizabeth. I work for Mr. Henderson. He owned this airplane but gave it to Michael so he could help children by taking them wherever they had to go for the help they need. I want you to know and respect all of these people. They all risked everything, even Lizzie, to rescue you. And one more thing, Mr. Murphy and I are going to be married and if you want to, he would like to adopt you. That is what you will decide. No one else is going to make that decision for you. You will live with us and Michael will treat you like you were his own children."

"No no no!" Carlos screamed in terror. "Poppa beats us and his friends try to do bad things to Maria, but grandmamma stops them."

"I promise you no one will ever beat you or try to do bad things to Maria," Mike said. Your lives have now been changed, for the better I'm sure, but it will take a while for you to trust me. I have never been a poppa so you will have to teach me how to be a good poppa. Susan, find a place with a pool. The kids need to play. I'm going to see to the bird and meet you in the waiting room."

Mike found the station manager and told him to fill the tanks with JP4 and do whatever needed to be done so it would be airworthy.

He joined the rest of his party in the waiting room. "We're staying at Friendship Inn. They have a big pool and all kinds of things for children," Susan said, "and their courtesy bus is on the way."

CHAPTER 39

At the motel, Mike registered as Michael and Susan Murphy. "We want connecting rooms," Mike said. "You and the children take one room and I'll take the other and leave the connecting door unlocked. The children will figure out soon enough what a couple in love do in bed. I want them to respect you. If they see you and me in bed together they may get the wrong impression and I'm going to have an uphill battle as it is gaining their respect. When we get home we can explain to them what we expect of them and ask what they expect from us. It will be easier to talk to them at home than it is in a motel."

Walt and Margaret thought it would be good if the children bonded with each other so Maria and Carlos would have an Anglo friend. "There is a variation in ages but that might work to an advantage. Carlos has already established his position as big brother and protector of Maria; if he were to bond with Lizzie, he would assume the same position with her," Margaret suggested. "He would have responsibilities and that would help him mature."

"I think that's a great idea Margaret," Susan commented. "My children have only the clothes they are wearing so we have to go shopping. You want to spend some quality time with Lizzie. I'll pick up a swimsuit for her and you three can relax and enjoy each other. Michael and I are going to be parents. We will take the children shopping with us and then get some supper - whatever they want."

Carlos and Maria had never seen so many things to buy and they wanted one of almost everything. Susan explained that there would be other days to shop. It wouldn't be necessary to buy everything now. "You may each have one thing. Choose something you've always wanted. After we finish shopping we are going to get supper. What would you like?"

"Pizza," was the answer. "Godfather's Pizza," Carlos repeated. "Have you eaten it before?" Mike asked.

"No, senor Murphy. We only saw it on television and it sounded very good and fun. Then I would like to have a hot dog. Are they really dogs senor?" Carlos asked.

"No, Carlos. They are not dogs. In some places people do eat dogs and cats. In this country, people who come from places that eat dogs, eat them here. It's part of their culture and though we may not like it, they are free to practice their beliefs and culture unless it violates our laws. Human sacrifice is practiced in a few parts of the world, and it does not violate their law but here we call it murder and that is against the law. You may call me Senor Murphy, if you like, but most people, especially my friends, call me Mike. So when you think of me as a friend you can call me Mike."

My mother calls you Michael, why is that Senor?" Carlos asked.

"I really don't know Carlos. You'll have to ask your mother about that."

Maria chose a soft teddy bear. Carlos said, "I would like a baseball glove but what good is it with no ball or bat?"

"Carlos, your mother didn't tell you that I once flew with the Blue Angels. As a result I have received many honors and gifts. I have wondered many times what to do with things after they've hung on the wall or been on display. You've helped me solve a problem. I have an autographed Hank Aaron bat that is now yours, and I also have a lot of baseballs given me and signed by Pete Rose, Ozzie Smith, and a lot of others. They are also yours. All I ask of you is to take care of them. When you are finished playing with them for the day, put them away. I'm going to shake your hand on this. And when I shake hands on a deal, it's a promise. I will also promise that you will not be beaten and no one is going to do bad things to Maria or Lizzie. Do we shake on that?"

"Si, Senor Murphy. We shake hands on that," Carlos answered, extending his hand, "Can we go eat pizza now?"

"As soon as your mother and sister finish trying on swimsuits."

"We picked out each other's swimsuit," Susan announced. "It was so much fun. We will do a lot of shopping, after all, isn't that what women do?"

Carlos showed Susan his new ball glove, "Look Mama. It's brand new. I've never had one that somebody else hadn't worn out and thrown away. And Mike is going to give me his Hank Aaron bat and some balls that have been signed by guys like Pete Rose, Ozzie Smith and even Roberto Clemente. Can we go to Godfather's now? I've been thinking about pizza so bad I can almost taste it."

"What kind of pizza do you want, Maria?" Susan asked.

"I don't know. I've never had any so I don't know," Maria answered, her lips trembling.

"Hey sweetheart," Mike said, "don't cry. This is a fun night and we don't cry on a fun night. We apologize for not realizing you are in a new world and are confused, so let's dry your tears and start over.

"Mike," Carlos said. "Can I have pepperoni and mushrooms?"
"Absolutely. Will a medium size be enough?"

"Maybe, but if I want more, I can have more, right?" Carlos answered, again extending his hand to Mike.

"Right," Mike answered and shook Carlos' hand.

"It's your turn Maria. If you like sausage, you could try it. If you don't like it, you don't have to eat it, and nobody's going to spank you," Mike said.

"Shake his hand Maria," Carlos said. "That makes it true. Mike and I shook hands two times already."

Maria hesitated then shyly extended her hand to Mike. He tenderly took her hand, gave it a gentle shake and softly said, "It's a deal."

Susan noticed Mike's eyes tearing up. She squeezed his hand under the table and gave him a look that said more about how she felt about him and how she felt about herself than any words could adequately express.

Mike, choking back tears, said to Carlos, "I don't know if you realized that you called me Mike two times already. Does that mean we are friends or was it a slip of the tongue?"

"Oh, it was no slip of the tongue, it just felt right and we are friends. Shake."

"Thank you Carlos. I want to shake on the deal. After that I think we need a warm hug. It's a man thing to do. It's not sissy. If you watch baseball you see players hug each other and you wouldn't call them sissies."

Carlos didn't hesitate. He hugged Mike as though he had wanted a hug for years and never got one.

Susan watched her son and the man she loved bond right before her eyes. It was to be a life-long bond.

Maria said, "Momma told me how much she loved you. She said I wouldn't understand what love really is until I get older. Carlos and I were scared when Doctor Garcia told us we were going to run away, but I feel all warm and fuzzy inside now. Can I have a hug?"

With those words, she was in Mike's arms hugging him and threw in a kiss or two. That broke the dam. Maria and Carlos ate pizza and wondered why Susan and Mike were crying.

The Henderson's and Lizzie were ready for bed when Susan, Mike, and the children got back. It's been a long exciting day and us old folks don't have the stamina to keep up with you," Walt said. "We want to check with Lizzie's doctor to be sure it's all right for her to swim. We don't need any more heart operations. You two enjoy your family and we'll see you sometime tomorrow."

"Now that I think about it, it has been a very long day, but a day I will never forget," Susan said opening the door to her room. "Carlos, Maria. I don't know what your bedtime habits were, but beginning now, you will take a bath or shower and brush your teeth every night before you go to bed. In the morning, you will put on clean clothes, put your dirty ones in a pile until we get a hamper to put them in, eat breakfast, brush your teeth, and comb your hair before you go outside. Any questions? Maria, you go first.

Remember there is a man in the room so you undress and put your pajamas on in the bathroom. If you need help, call me."

"Carlos, you are the man of the house. You will watch over your sister and anybody she is playing with. If you need help call Michael, or me."

"Momma, why do you call Mike, Michael? He said his friends call him Mike, aren't you his friend?"

"His name is Michael. His other name, Mike, sounds so harsh I just can't call him that. He is so tender and loving and when I address him as Michael, I'm saying I love you.

"Are you going to sleep with him tonight?" Grandma Romaine said if you really loved someone you should sleep together. I think you and Mike really love each other, so if I am the man of the house, I say it's okay. I'll watch over Maria tonight."

"You have grown up so much, so fast, Carlos. It's hard to believe you are only 12 years old. I'll wait for you to bathe and brush your teeth. Then we will say our prayers. I'll tuck you in before I go to bed."

Susan held Maria tightly in her arms trying to get her fill of all she had missed condensed into this one overdue moment. Carlos came out of the shower with shining teeth and a big smile. "Momma, I had hot water and soap, and a clean wash cloth. The towel was big and soft. I really feel clean."

With Carlos on one side, Maria on the other, and Susan's arms AROUND BOTH, MIKE, WHO HAD been in his room, joined them on their knees next to Carlos. "Father God, Brother Christ, we thank You for bringing us together safely. Bless all the people who helped. Thank You for Lizzie and her grandparents. We don't dare to try naming everyone we want You to bless because in our human imperfections we would forget someone, so I close with, thank You for Your grace. Amen."

In unison Carlos, Maria and Susan said, "Thank You for Michael, Amen."

"Good night you three," Mike said.

"Just two Mike." Carlos said. "Momma is to sleep with you because you love each other."

"I'll explain later," Susan said following Mike through the door.

"Don't forget to brush your teeth, take a shower or bath, and shut the door," Carlos said.

"Okay Susan, explain,"

"I told Carlos he was the man of the house for now, and he was to watch over Maria and her playmates. He asked why I addressed you as Michael, not Mike, and things just went on from there. My little boy is suddenly a little man. The way things are going, adoption is definitely going to happen and they will both ask you if you would. Sweetheart, my heart can't stand much more love. I have dreamt of this day every day since I left Cuba, but I could not imagine I would find the man of my dreams who would make it all happen. At the same time, I need you and I want you now. We can shower later."

All the held-back desires and emotions were unleashed in a display of unbridled love.

"Let's shower together, Michael. We haven't done it in a while and I am more than ready for the consequences."

Susan got in the shower first to adjust the temperature to her liking. Mike liked it very hot. Susan preferred it a little hotter than lukewarm.

Mike joined her and after lathering each other and rinsing off, the games began. He kissed her beautiful breasts softly licking her nipples. Susan was moaning and stroking Mike. He picked her up and she wrapped her legs around his waist and let go a satisfied moan as he slid inside. They finished what they started, where they started it.

"I'm ready to sleep now," Susan said. "So let's clean up and get to bed."

They fell into bed exhausted from all the day's activities and were soon asleep.

CHAPTER 40

The phone rang at 7 a.m. Walt was on the other end sounding excited. "Do not turn on the TV. Tell Susan to make sure her children can't see the news. I'm in the coffee shop. Get your butt down here and I"ll explain."

Mike dressed in a hurry and conveyed to Susan what Walt had said. "I'm going to get more details and fill you in. It must be about yesterday."

"There is nothing for us to get nervous about. Our emergency landing in Cuba made the network news. The thing the children should not see is the reported story on the kidnapping of one of Cuba's drug dealers. Ramon Romaine's children were with Dr. Garcia at the airport when he was called to advise the crew of the medical airplane that was forced to land in Havana. He said the patient would be okay if they got her to a care facility before too long. While the doctor left the children unattended, someone whisked them away. The tower operator, Tomas Rocha, was watching the medical airplane and said he saw two men in suits grab the two children and speed away in a black Cadillac. I hope the networks got a good shot of Angel Flight. We can use the publicity. I've got to shave and get my family some breakfast."

"Speaking of family, how's it going so far?"

"It will be wonderful to have them out of Cuba! Those kids have been abused and if it hadn't been for Grandma Romaine Maria would have been molested or worse. We had pizza last night and bonded. Carlos and I shook hands on a couple of deals and I went from Senor Murphy to Mike and got a hug I'll always remember. Maria added a kiss to her hug. If this is what being a father feels like, I'm loving it."

"Mike, you are being a dad. Most any adult male can father a child. It takes a special kind of person to be a Dad. You will never be their father but you will always be their dad. Ramon will always be their father but never be their dad. Dads are more important than fathers. Fortunately most children have both as you did, and there are some who have neither. Those are the ones who usually die a violent death or end up in prison, or both. You are a good son and you already are a good dad. Keep up the good work."

"Thanks for the advice and lesson, Walt."

"You're welcome, son. Your father and I are very proud of you."

Susan was up and dressed and her children were watching cartoons on TV. Susan had the remote in her hand, ready to shut it off at the least hint of breaking news.

"I'm going to shave and go to breakfast. Anybody who wants to go with me better be dressed and have their hair combed."

He heard the TV click off and a flurry of activity from the next room as the children hurried to get ready. Susan came into where Mike stood shaving, her eyes aglow with adoration for her knight in shining armor. Taking him in her arms she planted a combination good-morning-I-love-you, and wasn't-last-night-wonderful, thank-you kiss full on his lips.

"Darling, the children are so happy to be away from Ramon and his thugs. Carlos told me in Cuba he slept sitting in a chair so he could watch for danger. He told me last night he was going to go to bed and not worry about their safety because his friend Mike promised that no one would ever beat them or try to do bad things to Maria. He said, 'we shook hands on it, Momma, and that made it real.' Then he asked if it would be all right if he loved you? Mike Murphy you are one hell of a man and I can't imagine who could be a better role model for my son than you," Susan said through tears of joy. "Finish shaving and let's get the kids fed."

"Okay, but I have to start over," Mike laughed. "I forgot where I was, and besides you've got my shaving cream all over your face." Mike presented himself to his newly acquired family and announced, "This is the first day of the rest of our lives, and I can hardly wait to get started. Carlos and Maria, I want you to know I fell in love with you both as soon as I saw you, just as I fell in love with your mother, the first time I saw her. I don't know how to be a dad so I need you to teach me. If I am doing something wrong, tell me, because I will tell you if you are doing something I think is wrong. We can have your mother be the umpire and help us make the right call. I don't want you to be afraid of me. All I ask is for you to tell me the truth no matter what. You will never be spanked or beaten. There are other ways to discipline that are more effective. I think it would be a good habit to start the day with a good-morning-hug and say, I love you, and mean it."

As Carlos approached with his hand extended, Mike knelt down to greet him. They shook hands and Carlos said, "I love you Poppa."

Through tears of pure joy, Mike said, "Thank you children. Someday when you are older you may feel this kind of joy. I don't believe many people have the good fortune to be brought face to face with what is really important in life. The love of a family is something you get by giving love. You can't buy it, no matter how much money you have. It is one of God's gifts. Susan, I thank you for your love and the opportunity to be a part of your children's lives. As I said, it is a gift that can't be bought, only freely given. Let's go to breakfast before I make a bigger fool of myself."

"Michael, I never realized how terrified they were or so starved for what you have given them," In her best Barbie Doll impression, she continued, "Mercy sakes, my heart just goes pitty-pat just thinking of you. I do believe it's about to burst. Please, can I have my good morning hug?"

"How can I refuse such an offer?"

The Henderson's and Lizzie had just been seated when Mike and his family got to the coffee shop and they joined them to chat about yesterday and what to do today.

"The doctor said Lizzie could go swimming. We just watch the incision for any signs of leaks, so I thought I would take her after lunch." Margaret said.

"There is a ballgame this afternoon," Walt said. "I've never had the opportunity to enjoy a game with a son and since you are as close to a son as I've ever had, would you and your son like to go?"

"Si, Grampa Walt," Carlos said. "I would like very much to see a real ballgame. Poppa bought me a new fielder's glove and gave me his signed Hank Aaron bat, and baseballs signed by Pete Rose, Ozzie Smith, and a whole lot of other Major League players. I like baseball."

"Okay we men will do the guy things and you girls do the girl things like shopping and hairdos," Mike said. "Are you going back to your natural hair color?" he asked Susan. "I loved you with black hair, as a blonde, and as you are now. I was just curious."

"I'm going back to natural black," Susan answered. "The children remember me with black hair and that's the way it's going to be. What time shall we rendevous for dinner?"

"The children need to get on a regular schedule ASAP. I think six-thirty is a good time for dinner, what do the Henderson's think?" Mike said.

"Six-thirty is fine with us," Walt answered. "I'm going up to do my morning chores and rent a car. We might as well see the sights while we're here. I'll meet you at the front desk in thirty minutes."

"Let's go check on the bird," Mike suggested. "There shouldn't be any problems, but you never know."

Mike noted the jet had not been moved since he parked it Sunday. Locating the service manager, he asked why it was still parked where he left it, and if were they finished servicing it.

"We haven't serviced it yet sir," the manager answered. "The boss said there was no hurry, that it was just some millionaire's toy, so let him wait. When I told him about the Medivac Logo, he just shrugged his shoulders and said, 'so what?'"

Mike was livid. "Where can I find him?"

"Probably in the bar. His latest squeeze works there."

Mike returned to the car, told Walt that there was a minor problem and that he and Carlos should come back in an hour and pick him up at the main terminal at Delta's entrance.

Returning to the service manager, Mike asked the name of his boss and what he looked like.

"His name is Charlie Beltz. Greasy dark hair, sweaty shirt, needs a bath, and has bad breath."

"He should be real easy to find."

Entering the bar, he spotted Charlie perched on a barstool, a drink in front of him talking to a redheaded barmaid about 20 pounds overweight. Most of her excess was in a set of breasts that ran Dolly Parton a close race. Throwing caution to the winds, he sat next to Charlie and started hitting on the redhead. "Hey gorgeous, what does it take to touch those beauties? I'll bet you've been asked that many times."

"You are the first gentleman to ask. The rest of the pigs just grab. I've got a 30-minute break coming and you are welcome to help me pass the time."

"Red, if you will give me a rain check, I'll redeem it as soon as possible. I need to find someone to refuel my toy. That's what I call my jet."

Charlie stood up and said, "That's the business I'm in - servicing private airplanes and jets are my specialty."

"If your personal appearance is any indication of the quality of your work, I'm not interested. Your appearance tells me your facilities are dirty, run down, and instead of tending to business, you are in the bar trying to get in Red's pants. She doesn't need you, there is already an asshole in her pants and she doesn't need two. Please take no offense Red. You can do a lot better than this scumbag."

"No offense taken, handsome. Charlie get lost. I can hardly wait for you to redeem your rain check."

"I didn't mean to lead you on Red. I was trying to get under Charlie's hide. I have a beautiful wife and family and I'm not going to jeopardize that for a split second of ecstasy."

Following Charlie to Buccaneer Sky Harbor, Mike confronted him. "What is your excuse for not giving Angel Flight priority? Someone's life is at risk and every second's delay can make the difference between life and death. You are not fit to chock wheels, and I am gong to do my best to see that you are unemployed. I will be in contact with the CEO of Sky Harbor and let him know what a piece of crap you are and how you are demeaning Sky Harbor's good name."

Mike pulled the chocks, climbed aboard, and started the portside engine. He got the Tampa ground control and explained his dilemma. "Do you have facilities there to service private aircraft? This is a Medivac unit and needs to be ready to go at a moment's notice."

"Taxi to Delta gate 4. They will serve as your ground crew while you are here. I want to talk to you later today," ground control said.

"Thanks, I'll call you about 1 p.m."

The guys played 18 holes of miniature golf. Carlos did very well, winning seven holes. They rode around taking in the sights, then went to the ballpark. They got box seats on the third base dugout. Mike excused himself to call the Tampa ground control.

"My name is Fred, Angel Flight. There's a family here from Portland, Oregon who spent their last dime to get their son to the hospital here. The company the dad worked for was supposed to loan them money to get home, but for some reason it never came through. He was upset and called to find out what happened. One word led to another and they fired him. We've set up collection boxes around and have some money, but not near enough to pay your rate. Can you help?"

"Absolutely, we can help. That is the reason we are in business. It will not cost them anything. We are a not-for-profit corporation so all donations are tax deductible. Give them the money you have collected; they need a break. Talk to your people about our organization and spread the word. Make checks payable to Angel Flight, Care of First National Bank of Portland, Oregon. Have them ready to leave at 9 a.m. tomorrow."

The teams were warming up and Carlos was beaming. "Oh, Poppa, this is so much fun. I really like baseball. Do we have baseball at home?"

"Yes, we do, son. A friend of mine has season tickets and you will probably get a chance to use one of them sometime." It was a close game. The lead changed several times before the home team squeezed out the winning run home. The highlight of the game came in the last of the sixth when a foul ball headed right for Walt. Carlos stood up with his new glove and snatched it before it hit Walt. The crowd roared, the batter called time and came over to give Carlos a high five and went back to the plate and sent the next offering deep into the left field bleachers.

After the game, Carlos and Mike went to find the hitter to ask him to sign the ball.

"What's your name, son?"

Without any hesitation he answered, "Carlos Murphy, sir. This is my dad, Mike, and my Grandpa Henderson."

On the way back to meet the girls, Mike told Walt about their passengers. "They need a break, Walt. Let's see what we can do to help."

"We'll see what abilities he has and maybe one of us can find a job for him."

The ladies had been swimming, then went to a salon and had manicures and hairdos. Susan's hair was back to its natural black and she had bought an extension so it appeared to be long.

"Momma, Momma," Carlos said. "Dad and I had so much fun with Grandpa Walt. We played little golf and I beat both of them. Then we went to the ballgame and I caught a foul ball and the people yelled and the batter gave me a high five. It was the funnest day ever. Dad says a friend of his has season tickets and I might get to use one."

Susan hugged her son and asked, "Do you know you have called Michael dad several times?"

"Yes I know, Momma. He is my dad, not my poppa. My poppa beat me. My dad loves me and we do things together. Sometimes we just talk or just sit, but they are always happy times."

Maria came to show her manicured nails and new do.

Mike smiled and admired the manicure and hairdo. "You are as beautiful as your mother, Maria. How about a hug?"

Maria, hearing what Carlos said about poppa and dad, climbed into Mike's arms, wrapped her arms around his neck, and whispered, "I love you, Dad."

"Love at first sight sure saves a lot of time doesn't it, Susan?" "And money too. No need for expensive gifts, although they would still be well received."

"Carlos didn't mention getting the ball players' autograph. When the player asked his name he didn't hesitate, 'Carlos Murphy, sir. This is my dad, Mike, and Grandpa Henderson.' It blew me away."

"We will have a family on board tomorrow. They are down on their luck and need a ride to Portland. We will be leaving at 9 a.m.," Mike stated.

Mike rolled out of bed at 6 a.m. and gave Susan a good-morning kiss. "I've got to get a weather report and file a flight plan and do all those other incidentals, so I'm leaving now. If the rest of you get to the terminal by 8:30 we can leave on schedule. Go to Delta's gate 4."

"You are a handsome dog in your airplane driver's suit," Susan said sleepily.

CHAPTER 41

The weather at Kansas City was rain, with the possibility of tornados. Omaha was clear; the temperature would be in the mid-70's. Portland, scattered clouds but no threat of storms. Tampa to Omaha to Portland 3000 miles, more or less.

Mike went to settle for the fuel and servicing but was told, "Delta will service you at any place they serve." It's a small tax write-off for them but they want to help."

Mike finished his preflight walk-around and had the APU up and running when the Henderson's, Susan, Carlos and Maria arrived. They had just been seated when a young man in coveralls with a Delta logo over his pocket, came from the terminal, leading a couple with a boy who looked about Carlos' age with his arm in a sling. He had been cutting firewood when the chain saw somehow bucked and tore muscle tissue, nerves, and almost cut his arm off. The doctors had done all that was humanly possible to repair the damage. "The rest is in the hands of the Head Surgeon," he said, pointing upward.

Mike welcomed them aboard and introduced everybody, Susan made sure the seat belts were fastened and instructed them on how to use the oxygen masks. Susan went up front and took the co-pilot's seat.

"Well Captain, honey, sweetheart, darling, love of my life," she purred.

"Let's go home."

"Yes dear. Let's take our family home," Mike agreed. The passengers were Bob and Lois Koch and their son Bob, Jr.

"Don't call me Junior," he admonished. "Call me Rob."

Susan had arranged for the boys to sit together. Maria and Lizzie sat side by side. Lois Koch sat with Margaret, and Bob and Walt sat together.

The time came when Mike switched off the seat belt sign and Susan went back to see to their needs.

"Mr Koch, what kind of work do you do?" Walt asked.

"I was installing cable TV until I got fired, and please call me Bob. The owner of the company I was working for has a lot of clout in the area and told me he would see to it that I never get a job in Portland."

"If you had the chance to go back to work for them would you do it?"

"Yes, but only because I need the job. We are trying to get by on my salary so Lois can be home when Rob gets out of school. We would like to have another child, but it's tough enough as it is, without one more mouth to feed. Lois is real disappointed that things are the way they are, and the cost of getting Rob to Tampa took most of the savings we had. I would like to thank the people responsible for this plane ride. I understand there is no charge. How can they do it, Mr. Henderson?"

"It's a long story Bob, and I will be more than happy to tell it to you. There was this CEO with more money than he could spend in two lifetimes. His only child, a daughter, was killed by a drunken driver leaving her four-and-a-half-year-old daughter an orphan, so her grandparents took the little girl to raise. The granddaughter developed a serious heart problem and the nearest hospital that could perform the surgery was in Galveston. The CEO had a big corporate jet and pilot and was all set to go when the pilot showed up drunk. Grandpa went nuts screaming, hollering, and swearing when this retired Navy pilot steps in and offers his help. He was certified up to and including 747's so grandpa's jet was just a toy to him.

We got to Galveston, the surgery was successful, and the pilot said that all his jet training was to kill or destroy, and that to help preserve life was the kind of flying he wanted to do. On that trip to Galveston we built Angel Flight. That little blonde girl we dubbed Angel One, since she was our first passenger. We decided to be a not-for-profit corporation and fly any child, anywhere, at no cost. If the people have the means we encourage them to kick in whatever they thought it was worth. I'm the CEO of Henderson Manufacturing and I'm having the time of my life selling corporation executives on donating to Angel Flight instead of to those politicians in Washington. That's the story in a nutshell. The pilot up front is the one who flew me to Galveston and the lady with him was the nurse on board."

"To say thanks seems hardly enough,"

"Mike and I are selfish, Bob. Remember the time you saw somebody in need of help of some kind and you stepped up to the plate and gave it your all? Do you remember how it felt?"

Bob thought about it for a minute, and broke out in a big smile. "Yes, sir, I do. It made me feel - I don't know how to describe it - but it was better than great."

"That's why we do it, Bob. Jesus said, 'As you do it to the least of these my brothers you do it unto me.' I believe I know what company you were working for and the owner needs an attitude adjustment. I am one of the best attitude adjusters in the country. Don't worry about finding a job. I know of a company that installs cable TV, mainly in schools, and I will talk to them personally. You may have to move 90 miles or so, but I can assure you it would be well worth it. I'll go sit with my wife, and send your wife up here, so you can talk over what I said."

"Please fasten your seat belts," Susan announced. "We will be landing in Omaha in a few minutes. The temperature is 74 degrees, winds are calm. We will be refueling and we must exit the airplane. We will be on the ground for an hour. You may walk around, use the restrooms, do whatever you want. Please don't wander too far away. If you will tell me what you want to eat for lunch, I'll order it and we can eat leisurely in the air. We are about two and a half hours from Troutdale-Portland, the weather is typical Pacific Northwest weather."

Mike greased the Gulf Stream jet onto the runway with his classic smooth landing - no bump, just the scream of protest from the tires as they awoke from a sound sleep, to an instant 135 miles per hour. Mike taxied to Sky Harbor where the ground crew was waiting. The fuel truck was on the way, the wheels were chocked, and an attendant waited at the door to offer any assistance. "This is the way it's supposed to be," Mike commented to Walt.

"Mike, Bob Koch is in a bind. The company he worked for has told him not to bother looking for work in the Portland area. They are just barely getting by on what he makes but are willing to sacrifice so that Lois can be home when Rob is. The fare to Tampa wiped out their savings and they are really down in the dumps. I think we can help."

"What can we do, Walt? Or more to the point, what can he do?"

"He installs cable TV and has eight years experience. I mentioned I knew of a company that hires good people and would speak to them on his behalf. I'd hire him myself and find something for him to do, but he has a trade and it would be a waste of talent to have him driving a forklift or some other job."

"You've sold me Walt, I'll have Susan bring him up front and give him a pre-employment interview."

"Thanks son. You won't be sorry."

Mike went into the office of Sky Harbor to settle up. "You folks do a terrific job. Do you have the phone numer of your corporate office? I need to talk to them about their Tampa Terminal."

A neatly dressed, gray-haired gentleman stepped from an office. "Perhaps I can help you. I'm Gordon Sweetman, president of Sky Harbor International. What about our Tampa Terminal?"

Mike explained his experience there and Gordon listened attentively.

"Mr. Murphy, if you would fill out one of our customer satisfaction survey forms and list all the things you told me and sign it, I will personally take action."

"I'll be happy to."

"You have my hand on it."

Mike grinned, shook hands and said, "You're my kind of man, Gordon. We just made a deal. My father and I do not sign contracts. A handshake has served us well for many years, besides saving us a bunch of money on attorney fees."

"Forget the survey form. I believe what you told me to be true and action will be taken as soon as I can get there."

Carlos and Rob were looking at the assortment of airplanes Sky Harbor had for hire, when a security guard said, "You look like that kid the Cubans are looking for. What's your name, kid?"

"Carl Murphy. What's yours?" "You've got a fresh mouth, kid."

"I'm sorry, sir. It's just that I've been asked that question all day." Spotting Mike, he called out. "Dad! Would you tell this man who I am? He thinks I'm some Cuban kid they're looking for."

Mike came over and showed the guard his ID. "I'm Michael Murphy, sir, and this is my son. Is there a problem ?"

"I still think he looks like that Cuban kid and he has a fresh mouth. All I did was ask his name and he smarted off."

"Okay, son, tell me exactly what happened." Turning to the guard, Mike added, "My son does not lie and I will believe what he says. Go ahead, son, and don't leave anything out."

"Robbie and I were just looking at the airplanes, not touching anything, when this man says I look like some kid the Cubans are looking for and asks my name. I said, 'Carl Murphy. What's yours?' Then I called you.

"Is that the way it happened, sir?"

"Yeah, that's the way it went down. You see what I mean about a fresh mouth?"

"Frankly I don't see any fresh mouth attitude. He wanted to know who was asking the questions. And speaking of fresh mouths, your breath is terrible. Don't breathe on any flowers or you will kill them. Come on son. Let's go home."

Bob had taken the co-pilot's seat and Susan was visiting with Lois.

"Walt was telling me about your situation and I think we can help," Mike said. "Besides burning holes in the sky, I am partners with my father in an electronic contracting business. We do all the electrical work on a job, and have contracts for cable TV installations for most of the school districts in Oregon and Washington. Those we don't have contracts with we are working on. If you are interested in working for us, we can always use a good worker. All we ask is that you give us the best job you can. There is always someone faster or stronger or maybe smarter. We only ask you for your best and will not accept anything less."

"I've heard of your company and my old boss used to cuss you out for beating him on so many bids. I am definitely interested. Mr. Henderson said we may have to move East a ways. We have nothing to hold us in Portland. Rob's grandparents live in Detroit. I enlisted into the Army. I learned cable splicing and was discharged in Portland. I met Lois and the rest is history. I've never been back to Detroit and have no desire to return. Our folks visit once or twice a year. Lois and I are ready for a change, if the change is for the better. I can only offer you a good day's work every day. I'm not the best or the fastest but I am steady. I haven't missed a day of work since the day Rob was born, and that is the only day I've ever missed. I don't smoke, I enjoy a beer on occasion, and that's about all I can say. I want the job if you are offering it to me," Bob continued. "Lois and I discussed moving and decided we have always started at the bottom and worked up and this would be no different."

"Welcome aboard, Bob. Here is what you get for your honest days work. Beginning on day one, you are insured for $1,000,000 full coverage on health care for your family, including dental and glasses. Rob is guaranteed a college education at Oregon State or the University of Oregon; two weeks paid vacation each year, and if you need time off, call in so we can cover your job. You don't need a doctor's report; your word is sufficient. If there is an indication that you are taking advantage of the benefit package, the committee (our senior employees) will have a heart-to-heart talk with you. We are a nonunion shop. Our pay scale is higher than the union's and our benefit package is not matched anywhere."

"Where do I sign and when do I start."

"You don't sign anything, anywhere, and you start the day you show up for work," Mike said, extending his hand.

Bob gripped Mikes's hand firmly and said, "Thank you."

"That handshake binds the deal Bob. That's the way Dad and I do business. When you are all packed and ready to move, we will send a truck for you. You are now part of the family, and we take care of each other. When you need help, don't be afraid to ask. We are all like you - human beings that need to give as well as receive. Go back and tell Lois and send Susan up here, please."

Susan sat in the co-pilot's seat as usual. Mike told her to fasten the seat belt. She gave him a curious look but did what he asked.

"You are about to get your first flying lesson, honey. Take hold of the yoke like I am. Everything you do with this airplane you do gently, but firmly. Put your feet on the rudder pedals and imagine there is a very fresh egg between your foot and the pedal and you don't want to scramble the egg. Do you feel comfortable? I don't mean not nervous - I mean you don't feel over extended or anything like that?"

"No, I feel fine - nervous and excited. You make it look so easy, and I've always wanted to learn to fly."

"I'm putting you in control. Leave the controls in neutral, that's where they are now. I've got permission from central control to climb to 21,000 feet. Here is what you are going to do. Wait until I finish explaining, then I'll walk you through it. You will add a little power by pushing those throttles ahead just a tad, then ease back on the yoke to bring the nose up, and return to neutral. Watch the altimeter - that's this gauge here - when you approach 21,000, push the yoke forward to bring the nose down. When the bubble is level, return to neutral, and ease back on the power. Whenever you're ready. Remember, gently but firmly. If I feel something is wrong, I'll say, 'let me have it.' Just take your hands off the yoke, and I'll do the rest."

The combination of a good student and excellent teacher paid off. Leveling off was a challenge but other than that everything went smoothly.

"Flying is pretty simple. It's the gauges and regulations you have to know that are difficult. It just takes practice, like driving a car. You have to react without thinking, to avoid an accident. The more you practice, the tighter the bond between you and your airplane. You know what it will do, so things become automatic. You will notice a plasticized card over the sunscreen. One side is a pre-takeoff checklist which you read out loud and check each item on the list, so that you won't forget something. I saw a film from WWII where a pilot took off from an aircraft carrier with his wings folded. He got airborne but as soon as he tried to turn, he lost what lift he had and ended up swimming. He thought he was too smart to need a checklist. On the other side is a landing checklist. You do the same thing with that. Those two items are absolute. When it's just you and I on board, you'll do more practicing so that you can relieve me on a long trip. Portland-Troutdale on the horizon. Fasten your seat belts please," Mike announced.

Another of Mike's classic landings and they were taxiing to Beaver Air. "Fill with JP4 and make ready to roll. Wheels up in one hour," Mike ordered. Seeking out Jensen, he reported how satisfied he and Walt were with the preformance of the aircraft and how well the smoker worked. Beaver Air took the Koch's home.

Walt's car had been parked at Beaver Air while they were gone. Mike, Susan and the children walked with the three of them to their car and Margaret commented, "It has been an exciting and rewarding four days, Thank you Michael for being so loving and caring." Lizzie gave both Mike and Susan a hug and said good-bye to Maria and Carlos.

Walt, embracing both Mike and Susan, said, "You are both as dear to Margaret and me as our own daughter. Tell your dad we will see him soon and we expect a wedding invitaion."

"I never had a real wedding and I want one," Susan said. "Not a white wedding dress and all that, I just want a church wedding and I would like you and Margaret to stand in as my parents. That means you have to walk me down the aisle and give me away. Would you do that?"

With tears streaming from their eyes, the Hendersons agreed. Saying good-bye to Maria and Carlos with a hug and kiss, they left.

"You are ready to roll," Beaver Air announced.

Mike settled up for fuel and service, made his walk-around and climbed aboard. Carlos and Maria were strapped in; Susan was in the co-pilot's seat. "Do you want to start down the checklist, honey?"

Susan answered eagerly, "Yes I do. I want to start the engines and everything. Do you think I could taxi to the runway?"

"Sure you can. You steer with the brakes. Remember, gently but firmly."

"Checklist is complete. Starting port engine. Starting starboard engine. All lights are green, all gauges reading normal. I guess we're ready to go home."

"Ground control this is Angel Flight. We are ready to roll and request taxi clearance."

"Roger Angel One. Fall in behind UPS. Thank you. Ground Control."

"Push the throttles ahead a little to get us moving. When you want to turn left, apply light pressure to the left rudder pedal. It is now a brake pedal and when you want to turn right, use the right pedal and when you want to stop use both - firmly, but gently."

Susan taxied to the runway. UPS took off.

"Angel One, this is the tower. As soon as this United clears, you are cleared to go."

Half an hour later, Mike landed at the home base of Angel Flight and taxied to the yet-to-be-completed hangar. Letting go a big sigh, he said, "I love this job, but it is so good to be home. It sounds and feels so different now that I have a family. I now realize I never had a home before, only a house. Susan, I love you so much. You are the most important person in the world to me and just the thought of what my life is now compared to what it was brings tears to my eyes. I have never been happier."

CHAPTER 42

Red Kely was chocking the wheels, the fuel truck was standing by. "'Tis good ta see ya, Michael me boy, and you too Susan. The young Lad and Lassie must be yours. A fine-looking pair they are. Anything in particular I should be attending to?"

"It's good to see you Red; there is a smoker in the port engine I want removed, other that that, everything is okay."

"Red," Susan said, "these are our children, Carlos and Maria." Carlos offered his hand, and said, "Pleased to meet you, sir." Maria curtsied and said, "You have red hair," which brought a smile and laugh from Red. "Indeed I do," he said. "A gift from my dear mother, God rest her soul."

Hawk was standing in the background waiting for an opportunity to speak to Susan and Mike.

Julie and Mike, Sr. drove up in Julie's new minivan. Hugs and kisses all around. Susan spotted Hawk and motioned for him to join in. "Everybody," Susan said, "these are our children, Maria and Carlos."

"These people are part of your new family, children," Susan said. "They will help you when you need it and protect you from harm." Indicating each one, she started with Murph. "That's your Grandpa Murphy, next to him is your Aunt Julia, you've already met Red, and that man with the badge is Hawk. He is the police chief and our very good friend."

"Julie, will you see to the children? I'm sure they need to use the bathroom. Michael and I have some business with the Chief."

"Yes, of course I will and I just happen to have some fresh-this-morning applesauce cookies."

"You go with Aunt Julie," Susan said to Carlos and Maria. "Your dad and I have to go with the Chief, but we will back and take you home."

"This is only a formality," Hawk stated. "I have to arrest you, and book you on suspicion of murder. The DA knows you are innocent and is not going to bring you to trial. We hope the smokescreen will make Ramon careless and show himself. He is damn good at hiding but I've got the best tracker in the country, so when I get tired of waiting we'll go get him. Meanwhile, he can live the life of the hunted, always looking over his shoulder. The paperwork is finished. You're released on your own recognizance. Little Faun and Bear Claw have taken years off their lives. Thank you my, brother."

No handshake here. Only a manly hug would do.

The trip to the ranch was twenty minutes of questions. "Why is that mountain white? Are there any grizzly bears? Why did you have to go with Hawk? When will we see Grandma Murphy?"

Mike parked on the driveway to make it easier to unload. There wasn't a lot to unload but he wanted the kids to breathe fresh mountain air as soon as possible. Carlos walked around sniffing the pines and balsam and then he saw a teepee with smoke coming from it.

"Dad," he shouted excitedly, "Indians! There are Indians down there. Are they going to scalp us?"

"I don't think so. Let's go ask!" "Aren't you afraid Dad?"

"No, son, the only thing I'm afraid of is snakes."

"I'm not afraid of snakes, Dad, so if you see one call me and I'll take care of it for you."

"We have rattlesnakes here, son, and they are poisonous."

"I read about them, Dad. They make a noise so you know they are there. That way you can escape before they bite you. They are more afraid of you than you are of them."

Bear Claw stepped from his teepee in buckskins, moccasins, and headband with an eagle feather sticking out.

Carlos raised his hand in peace and said, "How."

Bear Claw returned the peace sign and asked, "What does little brave want?"

"Are you going to scalp us?"

"It is the custom of my people to scalp only an enemy. Are you my enemy?"

"No, sir, I come in peace."

"In that case my young friend, you have nothing to fear from me. My son is the Police Chief you call, Hawk. My wife, Little Faun, is up at the house helping get you settled in. Would you like to see your ponies?"

"Dad, can we go see the ponies please?

"I want to see them too son. Let's follow Bear Claw."

Bear Claw led them to the barn and lit a lantern. Carlos and Mike gasped at what they saw. Four beautiful pintos standing fourteen hands tall; two mares and two geldings.

"These belong to you now, little brave. They are green broke and I will help you finish them. I raised their dams from birth until I had to put them down and waited for the day I could pass them on to someone like you. Your dad and my son are going to be made brothers by blood at a Pow Wow at the next full moon. That means I will also be your grandfather and Little Faun will be your grandmother. We will pick an Indian name for you and your sister."

"Bear Claw," Mike said. "He is not afraid of snakes, poisonous or not, and I have witnessed his courage in other ways. How about Brave Little Man. Would that be all right?"

"That name fits him. Do you like it Carlos?"

"Yes, I like it a lot but I want to be called Carl when I'm not Brave Little Man. Is that okay, Dad?" "Carl it is son, starting right now."

"We will name you Brave Little Man at the Pow Wow. We will find a name for Maria and name her at the same time."

"We had better get to the house or Susan will think you did scalp us," Mike laughed.

"Momma, Momma," Carl shouted excitedly, "I've got four ponies like the Indians ride, - black and white spotted, and some brown. I think they are called Pintos. Anyway that Indian is Hawk's dad and he gave them to me, didn't he Dad?"

"That is right Susan; Bear Claw said they were his. They are only green broke and he is going to help Carl finish them."

"They are going to name me Brave Little Man, at the Pow Wow when Dad and Hawk are made brothers by blood. He will be my grandpa and his wife, Little Faun, will be my grandma. Where are she and Maria? Oh, and he wants to find an Indian name for Maria and I am Carl, not Carlos."

"My, my," Susan said proudly. "All that happened in such a short time."

"Maria is here with me," Little Faun said, standing in the doorway. "I am Little Faun, Carl. My husband is so pleased to be able to pass those ponies to you. Horses were a very important part of our culture. We didn't have money so if you had many ponies you were considered wealthy and powerful. Those ponies are direct descendants of those his father had and they mean a lot to him. Our son, Hawk, told his father he couldn't take care of them properly so asked Bear Claw to wait until the right person came along. You are the right person, Brave Little Man. Maria is such a pretty girl; we should name her Rose Petal. What do you think Carl?"

"I think that is a good name for her, and we should call her Marie or Mary, when she is not Rose Petal."

"I like Marie better," Maria stated, peeking from the kitchen. "Enough excitement for the day" Susan said. "I'll show you where your rooms are and the towels, wash cloths and soap so you can get ready for bed."

"Momma," Marie said, "I'm hungry and we didn't have much lunch."

"We've got ice cream in the freezer. You can have a dish of ice cream and some oreos and milk before you go to bed. Tomorrow we have to buy you some clothes and see about school and what furniture we need. It will be several days before we are all settled in. I'm sorry Little Faun; I didn't mean to be rude. There is no excuse for it; please forgive me."

"Susan, in the past few weeks your life has been completely turned around. It's no wonder that you forget things you would normally not. I barely know you personally, but I love you with all my heart. You do not need to apologize to me. Remember I will soon be your mother-in-law," she joked, "so let's start off on the right foot."

"That's a great idea. What shall I call you?"

"Why not call me Faun? And call my husband Bear, or call us Mom and Dad, whatever you are comfortable with."

Faun sat with Susan and the children and had ice cream with them. Mike was on the phone with the funeral director, making arrangements for Aggie's service.

"Carl, Marie, when Mike and I have to go on an Angel Flight, Faun and Bear are going to take care of you. Is that all right?"

"I'll be busy with my ponies," Carl said.

"I'll help Grandma Faun, and she can teach me some Indian things," Marie answered. "Can we sleep in the teepee?"

"Whatever Grandma says. She is in charge."

"We have so much to do in the next few days," Susan said, "Faun will be taking care of you a lot. We have to arrange for a wedding and you two children are going to be a part of it. Michael is marrying you as well as me. We have to have a nice suit for you Carl, and a pretty dress for Marie. I'm not going to get a white wedding gown. I'll get a long, lacy, lemon-colored, formal...I'd like Michael to wear his Navy uniform if he can. Off to bed with you two. A goodnight kiss for Grandma and me and Dad. Brush your teeth and say your prayers."

Faun was on her way to the teepee, the children were asleep, and Susan and Mike had some quiet time alone. Susan poured each of them a cup of fresh coffee and sat back waiting for Mike to speak.

"I didn't hate or dislike Aggie. She didn't deserve to die the way she did. I have no emotions except that she was one of God's creations and I loved her for that. It took me a long time to figure that out, and that brings us to here and now. Susan I have never been happier in my life than right now. Before you, I had no purpose in life. It was the same thing day after day. Now, with you and the children I have responsibilities, a reason to get up and challenge the day.

John Miers is the funeral director I talked to earlier this evening. He suggested a closed casket or cremation because of the condition of her body. We will have a memorial service Saturday morning. Whether you go or not is up to you. I don't think I will need emotional support. Mom and Dad will be there and her garden club and church friends."

"I'm not going. Those people already have me branded as a home wrecker and probably always will, so I'm not going to flaunt myself in front of them. Did you overhear what I said about wedding plans?"

"Yes, I did and I'm going to wear my dress whites with all the braids and medals. I kind of snuck into town, so I would like the citizenry to know where I was for ten years. Not to flaunt it but to help raise the level of appreciation for all our service men and women. What date have you picked?

"I thought the Saturday before Labor Day would be good. That gives anyone from out of town some traveling time."

"That suits me fine; I'll get my uniform from Mom's and make sure it still fits. I may have added a pound or two in civilian life so I'll have time to trim down to size. I know she is anxious to meet her grandchildren so I'll suggest a cookout for tomorrow evening. It's been a long day; let's hit the sack."

The stress of the day caught up with them and they fell asleep almost immediately. The windows were open, letting the cool mountain breeze waft into the house carrying a light aroma of Bear's fire. The river played its melody as it cruised to the Pacific Ocean. The quiet night was shattered by the scream of their neighborly cougar, followed by a frightened little girl climbing into bed between Susan and Mike. The activity awoke both of them. Since they had been asleep and hadn't heard the cougar, they couldn't understand why she was frightened. The cougar screamed a second time and Marie snuggled up to Mike for protection.

"Can I sleep here please?"

"Yes you can sleep with us tonight, but if you snore and keep me awake I'll have to put you back in your own bed," Mike teased. "That scream is a cougar. Some people call them mountain lions. It is looking for food. If you were in its territory, you might be in danger but as long as you stay away you will be safe."

"Oh Daddy, I don't snore. You snore. I heard you last night. Carlos - I mean - Carl and I heard you and laughed."

"She's right, sweetheart. I find it comforting to know my hero and protector is by my side, and it doesn't keep me awake. If it did, I would use my secret weapon to wear you out so you would be too tired to snore."

"What secret weapon, Momma? Will you show me?" "Children when you get older and really love someone and are married or going to get married, if you haven't already learned the secret, I'll tell you what it is. Now, go to sleep."

CHAPTER 43

After breakfast, Susan said, "Michael and I have a lot of things to get done in town. Do you want to go with us or stay home?"

"I have to start breaking my ponies, so we can all go riding," Carl answered.

"I want to stay home and play with Grandma Faun," Marie said,

"Carl," Susan said, "you take your sister with you when you do your chores and tell Faun where Michael and I are. We will be home late this afternoon and maybe have a picnic at Grandma and Grandpa Murphy's for supper."

Mike went past Mary's looking for the Chief, but it was early for him, so they went to see Howard and close the deal on the ranch. "It's good to see you two," Howard said. "I got you a mortgage at 4.6%, 30 years, no early payoff penalty. I put Susan as Susan Murphy on the papers. That's how she will have to sign. I took the liberty of acting as your agent on your other property. I will appraise it and get back to you, in case you want to put it on the market."

"That's fine with me Howard. I'm going to sell it. I'm sure you have people who do clean-ups to get property in the best saleable condition. I don't have time to fool with it now. I'll put the ball in your hands. That reminds me, my son loves baseball. I told him I had a friend who had season tickets and he might get a chance to use one. I would appreciate it if you would ask him to go to a game or two with you. I'll send the money or mail you a check."

"Why don't you and your family join Julia and I Saturday night? We are two games out of first place and playing the leader in a three-game series starting Saturday."

"What do you think Susan?" Mike asked. "Do you like baseball?"

"I know very little about it, but if our son is interested I should learn."

"Julia can help you a lot," Howard said. "She has become very knowledgable about the game. She knows the rules and is pretty adept at stealing signs and passing them to our coaches. That might explain why we have such a successful home-field record. Julia has stirred up emotions I haven't felt in a long time. She is a wonderful person. I feel so good when I'm with her, like I'm a complete person again."

"She confided in me that you are too much of a gentleman," Mike reported. "You've stirred up some emotions she has never had, so let your conscience be your guide."

"You get the tickets and we'll get dinner before the game and the junk food during the game," Mike suggested. "We'll meet you at Mary's, Saturday about five."

The next item on the agenda was to settle up with Miers' Funeral Home for Aggie's burial.

"I only want a decent urn, nothing flashy. She was not a flashy person. I'm sure she is at peace in the arms of Jesus. Thank you, John for your work and advice. I was at a total loss as to what to do. A person never thinks about these things until they happen; then you are at the mercy of funeral directors. I feel very comfortable about everything. Thanks again."

"Hawk ought to be at Mary's now. Let's go check in with him," Mike suggested.

"Hey, you two love birds," Hawk greeted them, "what's going on at the ranch?"

"Your folks and our children have bonded already. I had no idea how starved they were for a family," Susan said. "Your father gave Carl the ponies. I hope that is okay with you."

"It's better than okay with me. I was afraid I would be forced to take them and I don't have the time to finish them and breed the mares. Dad loves those ponies and to have someone like your son to turn them over to is an answer to a prayer. Pop still is a believer in signs. When I helped him move them out there, he said he had a vision that the ranch was where the ponies should be and that a young boy would be the one to finish breaking them. He sang a Shoshone song all the way out there and never stopped until the ponies had been fed, watered, and put away. Are you two going to be ready to shoot Thursday?"

"I'm not going to shoot," Susan said. "I've got a lot of shopping to do for Marie and Carl. They both need complete wardrobes - underwear, socks, shoes, everything. And I need to get them enrolled in school. What's my status, Chief?"

"Unofficially all charges against you have been dropped - but until we can prove Ramon did it, the case is still open. One of the prints that I got from your desk is a match for him. It looks like he put his hand on your desk when he reached down to open the drawer and switched guns. I got the the prints from under the lip. He didn't think to wipe that part of the desk off. We are 99% sure he did it, but we only have circumstantial evidence. The DA wants to prosecute but isn't sure he can get a conviction. If he is tried and acquitted and we later find the evidence we needed to convict, we can't bring him back and retry because of double jeopardy. He is eelier than we thought or lucky, but we will get him.

"See you later Chief," Susan said. "Let's get the truck so you can get your running around done and I'll have the van for mine."

"Good idea," Mike responded.

CHAPTER 44

Julie had hired some one to help in the office. The workload was steadily increasing to the point where she felt more help was necessary to prevent mistakes caused by rushing. The new clerk was a 40 year-old plus, matronly lady. She had experience in office work but knew nothing about the new age of computers and fax machines. Julie assured her she could and would learn and not to worry about her job performance.

"All we ask is that you give us the best you can do every day. Speed and efficiency will come with practice and experience," Julie told her.

"This is Vondra Cauldwell, Vonny for short, Mike," Julie announced. "Vonny, this is Mike, the son of Mike Murphy Electronics and Engineering and Son."

"Vonny, it's a pleasure to meet you. Welcome aboard. I won't be spending much time in the office. I'm the field man, so I travel a lot. Did Julie explain the benefit package to you? Do you have any questions about anything?"

"I don't quite understand the benefits. They sound so generous there must be a mistake."

"The simplest way to explain them is like this," Mike answered. "You are not just an employee, you are part of the family. We take care of our family in every way possible. We provide you with life insurance, medical including dental and eyeglasses. We expect you to take a vacation or at least time off to recharge your batteries.

When you have to take some time off for any good reason, call Julie so she can cover for you. Susan will be around some to help out and explain anything Julie and I have missed. One more thing, we are a family so if you need anything done around the house, like a light switch that doesn't work or a stopped-up drain, even a new roof, tell Julie or me or Dad or Susan. It will cost you a cup of coffee and some cookies for the labor. Any large project like a roof, we buy less than wholesale. I've got to see Pop."

"Well, son, how are things at the ranch?"

"Everything is going great Dad. Hawk's dad gave up his prized ponies to Carl. If it wouldn't interfere with any plans you have, we would like to have a cookout at your place this evening. Carl and Marie are anxious to meet Grandma Murphy. We'll bring the meat, probably hot dogs, or brauts and hamburger and buns. I hired a cable installer named Robert Koch. He has experience and that chicken-shit outfit fired him. The same outfit that we beat out and that spreads rumors about us. He will be showing up anytime, ready and anxious to go to work. Are you back at your pre-heart attack work level? If so, stop and take it easy. We've got a lot going on and you are needed here, not in the hospital."

"I'll call your mom and let her know. Now get out of here so I can get some work done."

"Have you met the new lass in the office?" Red greeted Mike. "She is a looker and just enough meat on the bones. I don't like skinny ones. I'm thinking of asking her to join me for corned beef and cabbage on St. Patty's day. The hangar is done, the tools are all here and put away. We are open for business. Angel is ready. I'd like to bring the dog home ASAP. I loaded my truck and drove up here with my stuff. The dog has got just odds and ends that need to be sorted and saved or thrown away."

"You are a true Irishman Red Kely," Mike laughed. "You can go from one subject to another without taking a breath. Yes I've met Vonny, and you're right, she is a looker. We can get the dog the first thing tomorrow morning. We'll put the Cub and the chopper in the hangar, out of the weather. I have a hunch that you are going to be busy all at once, with no warning, so before you get overwhelmed, run an ad or call someone you know that would be good at the job you are hiring them for. I don't care about gender or race, I want good, dependable and qualified people. It's my butt up there and I'm depending on you to protect it. This is your operation, Red. You are in complete control."

"I thank ya for your confidence, Michael Murphy. I won't let ya down."

The terminal building was in its last phase. Floor covering, painting, electrical and plumbing fixtures were being installed. The new office building was coming along nicely and would be finished in three to four weeks. An addition to the office building was just getting started. It would house the new bank. The replacement transfer switch hadn't arrived yet but the one installed was working fine.

Mike drove up to Aggie's house to look around. The place was a mess. Empty beer cans and liquor bottles were thrown where they were emptied. The yard was overgrown with weeds. Her prized rose bush had been run over, time and time again. Mike could not bring himself to go inside. Her last days on earth must have been a nightmare, he thought to himself. How in the hell could this have happened? She is now at peace for the first time in years. A lot of her misery was caused by her own jealousy and insecurity, but she still didn't deserve to die like this. "Ramon," Mike said out loud, "If you can hear me, pray that the police catch you before I do. If I catch you, you will want to die but I won't let you. I will start by taking my vice grips and peel the hide from your baby-making equipment and then I will put you on a dry log with your scrotum stapled down. I'll give you a rusty straight razor, surround you with bales of straw, set them on fire, walk away, and never look back. It would be for Aggie, Susan, and the way you treated your children."

Mike had never been so enraged. The thought of the torture Aggie must have endured was beyond comprehension. He was sure he would have felt the same if the victim had been a stranger.

"I think a glass of cold milk and some fresh applesauce cookies would make me feel better and I know just where to get them," he said to himself His Mom met him at the door with the loving hug and kiss that only mothers can deliver.

"It's so good to see you Michael." She was already pouring a glass of milk and getting the cookie jar down. "Your father just called and said we're having a cookout tonight."

"The kids are anxious to see Grandma Murphy, and what better way than a picnic. There lives have been totally turned around and they have adapted to their new lifestyle quickly. They both call me dad and show genuine signs of affection for me. I have never been happier or felt such a purpose for living until they came on the scene. I feel Susan was the answer to your prayers. She and the children fill all the vacancies I've had in my heart for years. Aggie's memorial service is Saturday morning. You are not obligated to be there, it's your decision. I don't need any back up. I'll be fine. We'll be here about six."

On the way home Mike stopped at Bubb's and asked him how the plans for the new bank were coming.

"Every merchant or businessman I've talked to is in favor and pledged to support it. You are the talk of the town the way you have stirred the business community into action. There's even talk of you running for mayor, and that really stirred things up. Would you accept the nomination and serve if elected?"

"Yes, I would, but we would have to have a fair and honest council if we are going to correct past mistakes. Not a rubber stamp council. A council that can look at both sides of an issue, debate it, reach a compromise, and support the decision. We must encourage the citizens to attend council meetings to learn the facts and when they hear the rumors at Mary's they can give the local chapter of CAVE (Citizens Against Virtually Everything) the facts. We are having a cookout tonight so I need hamburgers, brauts, franks, chips, two gallons of milk, a gallon of OJ, a bag of ice, and a six-pack of soda. That's all I can think of for now. Thanks for your help with the bank. Keep pushing it."

Susan had just gotten home when Mike arrived and they helped each other unload. Carl and Marie were with Faun and Bear. Everything was put away, the picnic basket was packed, and the soda was on ice in the cooler. Mike loaded the picnic in the van. They were ready to go to Grandma and Grandpa Murphy's house.

"Let's have a glass of iced tea and just sit and enjoy the day's events," Susan said. "What a nice way to wind down the day."

The cookout was the first ever for Marie and Carl. It was also the first time ever for Grandma Murphy to be a grandma and it was hard to tell who was enjoying it more, grandma and grandpa or Marie and Carl. Mike and Susan just sat back and watched. There had never been that much laughter and happiness in the Murphy's backyard.

"Let the grass wear out," Murph said. "It'll grow back but these moments can only be happy memories, that's why I put your old swing back up. If you can still remember how to play, you can join Carl and me in a game of croquet."

"Why don't we all play?" Susan suggested. "Can I just swing, Gramma?" Marie pleaded.

"Of course you can honey," Winnie said. "Just be careful you don't get hurt."

The children were asleep almost as soon as the car started for the trip back to the ranch.

"Michael darling, I have never been happier in my life. I have a man that loves me just for me. I have my children who at last can play and be children, thanks to the man I love. The children have a loving father and grandparents who are going to compete to see who can spoil them the most. I have a real home where there is peace and quiet."

Then Susan began to cry. "I could not even imagine peace and happiness like this. I worked hard so I wouldn't have time to think about how much I missed my children. I would like to stay home with them and not work so much."

"You should stay home and be a mother. I will need you on Angel Flight. I don't think I could trust anyone else to do the job you do, and with you, the overnights are sensational. Those overnights can be our vacations. We will take vacations with the children. I think Disneyland will be first on the list, unless you HAVE ANOTHER IDEA."

Carl woke up and groggily went into his room and prepared for bed. Mike carried Marie into her room where Susan helped her with her pajamas.

"I have to brush my teeth Momma," she said. "Didn't we have fun today? I've got to kiss Daddy goodnight."

In the quiet solitude of their room, the two people who were so in love did what people in love do. They gave to each other all the emotion they had. As they lay in each other's arms Susan said, "I could hardly be quiet. We had better get an overnight soon or the children are going to wonder what's going on in here. Carl will start asking questions and Daddy is going to have to answer them. I'll talk to Marie when the time comes. In the meantime, you had better start preparing your speech. You can use his ponies as an illustration maybe. I'm just as green about these lessons as you are."

"Carl needs a boy to play with. I hope the Koch's move out here soon," Mike mused. "Carl and their son seemed to hit it off well and they would be good for each other. If the family was interested in Aggie's house I would make them a good deal on it."

"If you're not sleepy or tired honey, we could exercise again," Susan teased.

"Are you needy or greedy?"

"I don't honestly know. I'm so in love with you, I can't seem to get enough of you and yet each time is totally fulfilling, leaving nothing to be desired.

Mike kissed her on her heaving breasts, causing the ripe nipples to rise to attention. As he entered, Susan let go a low moan of delight.

"Oh darling," she said, "you push all the right buttons at all the right times."

The cougar screamed, the river gurgled, but the lovers were sound asleep and heard nothing.

CHAPTER 45

Mike woke up at 7 a.m. He smelled coffee and heard Susan singing softly in the kitchen.

"Good morning sweetheart," he said, "You are in good spirits this morning.

"And why wouldn't I be? You are a magnificent lover. My children are asleep under our roof and it is a beautiful day in spite of the rain. How do you want your eggs?"

"Basted soft, please. That's a lot of bother isn't it?"

"You're worth the bother Michael. You can't keep up the pace you set last night on bagels and juice. You need eggs and bacon or sausage."

"I'm staying home and will bake cookies with my daughter for the second time in her life. She was too young to remember the first time. I'm going to try to make this one a happy memory. I'm going to call Walt and ask if he could train a replacement for me. I'm going to be a wife, mother, and Angel Flight nurse. I won't have time to do my job at Henderson Company."

"If I don't shoot well today it will be your fault, but I can't tell Hawk why I was off the mark."

"You were right on target last night sweetheart and that's the one that counts," Susan stated. "The furniture I got yesterday will be delivered this morning about ten. Super at six. Don't be late."

Red was waiting in front of the hangar. The Cub was idling and ready to go.

"Do you mind if I fly the dog back?" Mike asked. "I forgot that this is the day Hawk and I have our shootout."

"And why should I mind? I can sit up in God's sky, talk to the Man in private, and confess my sins. This little rain we're having is His way of washing the world and reminding us who is in control. No, Michael I don't mind a bit. You fly the Old Dog and me and the Cub will just saunter back to base."

"As I've said before, Red, you are a true Irishman. The way you have with words is almost musical. When you have someone to talk to the flight isn't as long as it is when you are alone. I never tire of Mount Hood. She is always beautiful with her white cape."

The last leg of the flight was as uneventful as the first leg. Mike set the Cub down with a Murphy classical landing.

"Michael me lad, I've been around airplanes all of my life and I have never seen one who was such a part of the machine as you are. You love to fly and it shows in the expression on your face when you are in the air, and the way your machine reacts to your control. I'll help you get the dog started and see you at the base."

The dog whined, sputtered, and came alive. With a thumbs up, Red taxied the Cub to the runway and left. Red kept the dog in tip-top shape and it wasn't long before Mike was on the way home. He pushed the engine for maximum speed, "to blow the cobs out," he would later tell Red. He passed Red about ten minutes later and cut back on the speed a little. He had time to spare as he circled Mount Hood, being careful with his altitude. He didn't want to start an avalanche. Her crest was above the clouds and with full sun and no polution to veil her beauty, she was a spectacular sight.

Using his onboard navigation system and his own common sense he was soon on the ground at the base. The fuel truck drove up. The driver had hair the color of Red's. He stood 6ft 9in., was so thin he had only one side, and a very obvious Adam's apple.

"Good morning sir," he said. "You must be Mr. Mike Murphy. My Uncle Red sings your praises to anyone who will listen and to some that don't want to hear but he has a very persuasive way about him. My name is Yale Yocom. I help Uncle Red whenever I can. I want to be a jet mechanic. He said if your business grows like you think it will, he'll need help so I volunteered to fill in while he's gone this morning. I wasn't doing nothin' anyway, so here I am."

"If you're blood kin of Red Kely, you have to be okay. When Red gets here, have him take you to the office and see Vonny. She will get the required paperwork processed. Red will work out a pay scale. This maintenance facility is his department. You will answer only to him. Make sure he orders work uniforms for you. I've got to go but I'll be back later."

"It's just you and me Hawk. Susan has decided to be a housewife and mother as much as possible. Have you seen or heard anything about Ramon?"

"Not a word or a sound, but I'm sure he is still around. The Meth problem is still here, but seems to be slacking off. I've got some of my Shoshone trackers deputized and they are literally sniffing the Meth labs out. Let's go shoot. I feel like a big lunch today.

Hawk was his usual calm sure shooter, but Mike was almost perfect, beating the chief by five points.

"Still feel like a big lunch?" Mike grinned. "Susan must have been coaching you."

"I can honestly say she never even mentioned shooting until last night, when she told me she wasn't going to shoot. I'm suddenly very hungry myself," Mike continued, "but I'm not going to eat a big lunch. Susan is having supper at six and I want to do justice to it. It sure feels good to finally beat you. Not just edge you out, but beat you."

"Don't get too used to the feeling. We shoot again next week remember?"

"I don't know what the reason for my success was."

"As soon as you squeezed off your first round I knew I was in trouble. I've never seen you so at ease and relaxed. If you keep that up, I'm in big trouble on the pistol range."

They sat at Hawk's usual spot talking about this and that, but doing more listening to the surrounding conversations than talking to each other. A lady in the next booth was telling her companion that she was going to start using her clothes dryer because someone had been stealing things from her clothes line - mostly underwear but also her son's Notre Dame sweat shirt.

At the round table, sat five Latinos. They kept looking at Hawk and finally got up and approached.

"Senor," the spokesman said, "we are working for Senor Salisbury. Here are our green cards. We have heard about your troubles with others of our kind and drugs. We don't do drugs.

We came here to make money to support our families. The drug dealers make all of us look bad and we want to help you in any way we can to catch them."

"What are your names?" Hawk asked.

"I am Luis Sanchez, that is my brother Juan. Over there, are our cousins, Rudy and Reynaldo Jimenez."

"Here is a picture of Ramon Romaine," Hawk said, showing the wanted poster. "If you see him, call my office day or night. Do not try to apprehend him. He has a vicious temper and has already killed one person we know of. I thank you for coming to me. As long as you obey the law you will not be bothered by my department and you are free to go anywhere you like. If anyone causes you trouble, don't try to settle it yourself. That would cause you more trouble. Let my department handle it. I promise the guilty party will pay, no matter who he or she is. We welcome good people to our town and hope you can bring your families here. We have just started to grow and there will be good jobs for good workers. Mary! The city is buying these gentlement their lunch." "I believe you just recruited some emergency help, Hawk.

Thanks for lunch."

CHAPTER 46

Red was in a playful mood. He had just come from getting Yale on the payroll and in a burst of bravado, asked Vonny if she would like to go to a movie with him and she said yes.

"'Tis sure the luck of the Irish. She likes the same kind of movies I do and she invited me to help her finish off the corned beef and cabbage she had left over. My nephew has a job, I've got a date. 'Tis indeed a glorious day. I don't suppose talking to the Man upstairs had anything to do with my good fortune, but you can be sure the Devil had nothin' to do with it."

"Did the weather bother you on the way back?" Mike asked. "No, I found the river and followed her till I spotted the bridge and turned right."

"There's some fella up there at the office saying you hired him as a cable installer and is real anxious to go to work."

"That would be Bob Koch. I'd better go greet him. I want to talk to him anyway. Order some work uniforms for you and Yale - eight sets each. This is the only order I'll give. A clean uniform every day, a beard or moustache is okay, but otherwise clean shaven and a neat haircut. Have Angel Flight in big letters on the back of the uniforms, with your name over the pocket and an Angel on the pocket."

Bob was filling out the necessary papers and greeted Mike with a big smile.

"I thank you for the job, sir, and I won't let you down."

"The only person we sometimes say sir to is my dad. I'm Mike. When you finish the paperwork, I'll introduce you to him, and then I need to talk to you. I think you might like what I'm going to say."

Ten minutes later, they were in Murph's office.

"Dad, this is Bob Koch. He has experience in cable installation. I told you about him Tuesday."

"Yes you did, son. I'm Mike, but to make it less confusing they call me Murph. It's good to have you aboard. And you're just in time. We just contracted with the State of Washington to upgrade and service the cable TV for every school in the state. If you know of anyone you would trust to join our company, give them a call. I need at least four qualified techs now. I don't mean to be rude, but I've got to get to work."

"Let's grab a soda and go sit where we can talk," Mike said. "On a bench in the shade. I want you to be perfectly honest with me. I'm going to ask you some personal questions and no one will hear the answers but me. Are you in a tight financial bind?"

"Yes, I am, Mike. Robbie's arm took all of our savings and getting fired really hurt," Bob answered. "Lois and Robbie are staying with friends until I get enough money ahead to bring them over here. Our furniture is stored in a garage. Yes, Mike, I'm in a bind."

"Would your furniture fit in that van over there?" Mike asked, pointing to a Mack with a 24ft box.

"With room to spare."

"Tomorrow morning, you and Bill Webb are going to Portland to get your furniture. I'm going to fly the chopper over for Lois and Robbie. Beaver Air will pick them up wherever they are staying, and take them to Troutdale where I can load them up and bring them here."

"What happens when we get here? Where will we stay? We're broke."

"As long as you've got family and friends you're not broke I have a house for you to move into and if you and Lois like it, I will sell it to you for what I paid for it fifteen years ago. You can live there rent-free for a year, only paying for utilities and I will split the cost of insurance and taxes. It will need some cosmetics and maybe some cleaning, which I will take care of. I'm not doing anything you wouldn't do if our situations were reversed. Follow me, and we'll get you checked into a motel and arrange for some food for you."

Bob checked in at the Super 8, on Mike's credit card. They went to Mary's where Mike told them to run a tab and he would settle Saturday.

"You order what you want, not what is the cheapest; call Lois and let her know what is happening. You might be a family again tomorrow night."

"I don't know what to say. Thank you is not enough but that's all I've got."

"That's more than enough. See you in the morning."

CHAPTER 47

Mike drove into the garage at 5:45 - just enough time to clean up for supper. He closed the garage door and stepped into the kitchen. He had never experienced what happened next. Marie came running from her room and jumped into his arms, smothering him with kisses. "I love you Daddy, and I miss you when you're gone."

Carl wasn't far behind but was unsure what his response should be. Mike, sensing his dilemma, knelt down to his level and hugged his son.

"Did you have a good day?"

"Them ponies are sure fun. Grandpa Bear said that I should work with each one until one starts to follow me, or comes up to me without being called. He said that is bonding and that one would be my horse."

He put Marie down and turned to see Susan with tears in her eyes. "Michael those children have been starved all their lives for what you give so freely and naturally. You are not their father but you are their dad, and they really love you. For the last hour they've been asking, "When is Daddy coming home?" Coffee is ready, supper in five minutes. Do I get a hug or anything?"

"I'm sorry sweetheart. I was so overwhelmed by my greeting, I had a complete brain fart. This is also a new experience for me. Coming home to a family, smelling dinner, coffee waiting, and a woman I love. How can anyone improve on that? Let me kiss your sweaty face. I love you Susan."

"A kiss on my sweaty face is okay for now but I expect you to make up for it later. Drink your coffee while I finish supper."

As Susan refilled Mike's cup, she announced. "Supper, kids. Make sure your hands are clean and your hair is combed."

When they were seated, Mike said, "Let's join hands and thank God for our blessings. Each one of us will thank Him for something. Susan will start, Carl will be next, then Marie, and I will finish. Don't be afraid to speak. Just tell God what you are thankful for today."

Susan started, "Heavenly Father, if I were to list all the things I am thankful for, we would be sitting here for hours. So I'll just say thank You for Your grace."

"Thank You God, for my ponies and Grandpa Bear," was Carl's prayer.

Marie said, "Thank You for a nice Daddy. I love him."

"Thank You for bringing these three into my life. There were times in the past when, I thought I was happy but those memories pale in the face of these. Amen."

Dinner was baked salmon that Bear had caught earlier in the day and dressed just in time for Susan to put it in the oven. A tossed green salad, home made biscuits, peas, and baked potatoes rounded out the meal, with apple strudel for dessert.

"With all your other assets, you can cook too," Mike teased. "Since your mother worked so hard preparing this wonderful dinner we are all going to help her. Marie you carry the dishes to the kitchen and put them on the counter beside the sink. Carl you carry the bowls and platter into the kitchen and put them beside the dishes. In the morning your mother and I will wash the dishes and you will carry the trash to the dumpster. These are your jobs. You will get an allowance because you are part of the family, not because you earned it doing your jobs. If you need extra money, I'll pay you for doing something extra. If you have any questions now is the time to ask."

"Daddy," Marie asked, "what's an allowance?"

"It's money you get because you are part of a family. It's yours to spend on anything you want without asking us for money. You must save 10% and give 10% to charity. That way you will learn to save to buy something you really want. The 10% you save goes into a piggy bank and can't be spent for anything. It is like a money machine. When you are older like your grandparents, it will start sending you money each month. The more you put into the machine now the more it will shell out when you are older."

"What is charity?" Carl asked.

"It's money or work or anything you give to someone who needs what you have but doesn't have the money to pay for it. The best part of giving is how good it makes you feel. I don't know how to explain it but you will find out for yourself. You should carry some of that money with you to give when you see the need. You can't out - give God. I'll tell you a true story that happened to me. When I was in the Navy, one of my shipmate's family members was trapped in a burning building and was rescued barely alive and needed blood. It was the rarest type, and my shipmate had the same type. He didn't have time to wait for the Red Cross to investigate to be sure the man needed money. I gave him all I had, something like $250. I was broke and my next payday was two weeks away. I shook hands with him and said a short prayer for he and his sister. When I got my mail later that day, there was a check in an envelope for $500. It was a refund from an overpayment from two years before. I didn't know about it or expect it. Like I said, you can't out - give God.

I'm bringing the Koch's down tomorrow so Carl can have a playmate. I think you will be good for each other. Robbie will need therapy on his arm and playing catch might be good for him."

"Dad," Carl said, "can I go with you tomorrow?"

"I'd love to have you with me Carl. If you have your chores done by 9 o'clock, you can go with me. Those ponies are your responsibility. You can't just pick up and go whenever you feel like it."

"I'll get up early and be done in plenty of time. Grandpa Bear said I was doing real good with the ponies and could maybe ride one next week."

The sound of broken dishes came from the kitchen, followed by a terrified scream from Marie. Mike scooped her up in his arms and asked, "Are you all right baby?"

Marie nodded yes, and Mike said, "That's the most important thing. You didn't drop them on purpose. It was an accident. You find the dust pan and brush and I'll help you clean up the mess. Now please don't cry, nobody's going to spank you."

Carl said Marie had dropped a plate while staying at Grandma Romaines' and poppa took off his belt and beat her with it. *"One more reason you best pray I don't find you before the police do, Ramon,"* Mike thought to himself.

The mess was cleaned up. Marie was smiling and gave Mike a hug saying, "Thank you for helping me. I love you Daddy, you are so nice to us."

Marie and Carl were anxious for Mike to see their new beds and clothes. Marie's room was lacy and pink with white ruffled curtains at the windows. Dolls and clowns were on the walls and bedspread. HER CLOTHES WITH NEATLY HUNG up in her closet or folded in her dresser. "Momma says I have to keep it neat."

Carl's room was baseball. The curtains were white terrycloth with ball fringe. Mike looked closely and noticed the balls were made to look like baseballs, with seams and an American league logo. A full sized picture of Orlando Cepeda was on his closet door. On the wall hung a bat rack with space for four bats, six balls and pegs for two gloves. One had Carl's new glove on it.

"Carl, I completely forgot to get the bats I promised you. I'll bring my old glove and we can play catch. Can I hang it on your bat rack?"

"Sure, Dad. When we go get Robbie, are we going in the jet?"

"No, we're going to take the Old Dog."

"What's the Old Dog?"

"It's an old chopper that Red Kely brought over with him. It belongs to him but we use it when needed, and pay for the fuel and maintenance. You'll meet Red in the morning. It's only 7 o'clock. What would you like to do besides watch TV? Is there a game we can all play?"

"I found a box of games in a closet," Susan announced. "I think Aggravation was in there. That's a fun game and Marie has as good a chance of winning as anyone, so let's play that until time to get ready for bed. Then we will have the rest of the pie with a dab of ice cream on it."

They played two games and were on the third, when time ran out. Marie won the first and was ahead in the third. Susan won the second.

"Well son," Mike said, "it looks like the game gods were smiling on the ladies tonight, but there will be other nights."

The pie and ice cream were gone, the children were in their beds, the house was quiet.

"Is this real or am I dreaming?" Susan said. "I thought this kind of day was only on TV sitcoms. How did you know what to do when Marie broke the dishes?"

"I used my heart and head. She was expecting a beating, which no child needs. She needed comforting and love. Since it was her accident she needed to help clean it up. If you learn to clean up your own mess at an early age, you are learning to be responsible for your actions. What did Walt say about your retirement?"

"He was not surprised. I do have a pleasant surprise for you from him. A company from New Jersey has offered him zillions of dollars for his business, most of it in cash, the rest in stock. He is working with attorneys and CPAs to get the best tax breaks possible. Except for Lizzie, we are the only family they have, so we are to be Lizzie's guardians if anything happens to them. He is putting several million in trust for Lizzie and you are the trustee. Several million goes to Angel Flight, which is tax deductable. An educational trust fund to help families put their children through school will get a few million. You are to be chairman of the scholarship committee. You will own the stock in the new company, plus he is outright giving me five million. He said I built the company and I deserved it. He and Margaret are going to do some traveling and do things they've wanted to do for years. They want to leave Lizzie with us while they are gone. Aside from that nothing exciting has happened."

"All this because I decided to fly to Troutdale for a cup of coffee and you seduced me."

"Now wait a minute. All I did was invite you in for a glass of wine to help me sleep. It was a mutual seduction and I did sleep better that night than I had in months or maybe even years. Let's go to bed after the news and I will really seduce you."

"Why wait for the news? When we see it it's already history. I'm going to shower and wash today's grime away and before I forget, that was a marvelous dinner. I really like coming home."

Mike was in the shower letting the hot water wash the grime and aches of the day away, when Susan came in and started washing his back. She handed him the wash cloth and said, "Your turn." Mike washed her back then down to her ankles and up to heaven's gate, back down the other leg, then up to her shoulder. Susan turned to face him. He started washing her breasts which were now heaving in ecstasy. Her nipples were fully extended, asking for attention. Mike responded by kissing and suckling on each one. His manhood fully extended, Susan offered herself and as he slowly slid in she let go a satisfying moan. Again they reached ecstasy in unison. They washed the love juices away, then rinsed and dried.

"We didn't make it to bed," Mike said. "Who seduced who?" "I'd say it was a draw," Susan responded. "I am so in love with you and so grateful to you for bringing so much happiness to my children. The fact that you are such a terrific lover - I can't help myself. To be honest, I think I seduced you."

"You bring out the beast in me sweetheart. I never felt so manly before I met you. Like I just said, you bring out the beast in me." He kissed her on the breast and slowly slid his hand down to heaven's gate and lightly massaged the sweet spot. Susan softly moaned and opened the gates and they did the horizontal dance with no music, again reaching ecstasy together. "I seduced you that time," Mike whispered. "I'd better have three eggs for breakfast."

"Would you like to try for four?" Susan teased. "Good night sweetheart," Mike said.

CHAPTER 48

Mike was up before Susan and was shaving when he heard her singing in the kitchen.

"Good morning honey," Susan said. "The coffee is done. How do you want your eggs this morning?"

"Scrambled with bacon, chopped onion and cheese." "One bacon, cheese, and onion omelet coming up."

Mike was on his second cup of coffee, when Carl come from his room, tucking in his shirttail.

"Can I have an egg and toast for breakfast, please?" "You're up pretty early son," Mike stated.

"I've gotta do my chores and ask Bear if the ponies would be okay if I didn't work with them today."

"You are so grown up for your age," Susan commented. "The way you have taken the responsibility for the ponies is a very grown up attitude and your Dad and I are proud of you."

"I love my ponies and Grandpa Bear and you and Dad. I don't want to do anything to make you not like me. I try real hard to be good and do what you say. Dad says if there's something I don't like, I can talk to him man-to-man even if I am only a boy."

Carl finished his breakfast and carried he and Mikes' plates and tableware to the kitchen.

"I'll be back when my chores are done," he shouted over his shoulder as he went out the door.

"I don't know what kind of magic you have, but my children are acting more like our children than I ever dreamed. Are you sure you don't have a flock of kids somewhere that nobody knows about? For a man who supposedly knows nothing about being a dad, you are doing a fantastic job. I'm a little jealous of the way Marie treats you. She immediately runs to you for consoling."

"I just do what feels natural. I've always had a soft spot for little girls and I'm very careful when I'm around them. I always make sure the parents see whatever I do, and I never touch them. Marie fills my heart to overflowing when she jumps into my arms and calls me Daddy. Her sperm donor best pray the authorities catch him before I do. I know I don't have the right to judge or exact penalty but I don't think I could restrain myself knowing what he put you through. If Carl continues in the way he is going he is going to be someone to reckon with in the future. He could be a doctor or a lawyer or anything he desires. The hardest day of my life will be when I walk Marie down the aisle and turn her over to someone else. The proudest day will be when Carl walks on stage and gets his degree. Here he comes now."

"Grandpa Bear said it was okay for me to be gone for a day. Ponies are smart" he said. "They remember what they learned. When they buck in the spring after they haven't been ridden for a while it's to get the kinks out and to say, "hello, let's play." Grandpa Bear sure is fun. Dad, can Robbie stay all night sometime? He can sleep in my bed and I'll sleep on the floor in my sleeping bag."

"It's fine with me, but you have to clear it with his mother."

On the way to the airport, Mike pointed out the lakes and streams where he used to hunt and fish and trap.

"I used to make quite a bit of money trapping. The market has changed and there are organized groups that want the use of real fur prohibited. You could still snare rabbits for their meat. Rabbit is very tasty. I've cooked it over an open fire on a spit made from green wood. The fire was very dry wood and there wasn't much of a smoke taste. Bear and Faun could teach you how to set a snare and clean and cook the rabbit. There's the Old Dog and there's Red," he added, pointing toward the hangar.

"Top o' the morning to ya, and the rest of the day for meself. And where are ye off to today, Michael me boy?"

"We're off to get Bob Koch's family and bring them here. I think they're going to move into the house my late wife and I own."

"I was by there yesterday. 'Tis a fine house but needs some work."

"If you and Yale could see to it being cleaned I would consider it a personal favor. Get all the help you need to clear out the furniture, dishes, everything except the fridge, stove, and washer and dryer. After you've all picked through it and taken what you want for yourselves, take what's left to the Salvation Army store. Howard Morrison was going to have a cleaning crew come in and clean the inside. I'll put you in charge of the whole operation. I don't expect Bob and the furniture until late this afternoon. I'll have Mrs. Koch here about 1:00 p.m. Anything you need, you get. We'll settle up when the job's finished."

"Consider it done. Yale! Get the big van. Today we're bed- buggers!"

Carl took his seat next to Mike and watched intently as Mike flipped switches and turned dials and knobs. Being a normal boy, he was full of questions and Mike patiently answered each one. The rotor blades spun slowly at first, then gained speed, and the dog sputtered into life. Mike let the chopper warm up and when she was ready and the gauges all read normal, he lifted off.

"Wow, Dad. This is really neat. Do you think I could learn to drive this?"

"Carl, one of the first and very important lessons of life is this. You can do anything you want to do if you want to do it bad enough and are willing to pay the price. The price is not always money. It could be long hours of training and practice. When you see figure skaters do jumps and spins, they make it look so easy, but they've spent hours and hours training and practicing. Most of them are still in school and they must get up at four or five in the morning, almost every day, to practice. Ozzie Smith spends hours practicing. I've spent many hours over many years learning to fly. Yes, Carl, you can learn to drive this thing and Red will teach you. You will have to be sixteen before you can get a license to fly by yourself, but if I am with you, you could fly anywhere."

"I want to learn to fly the jet, too. I want to be like you, Dad." "It makes me happy that you would like to be like me," Mike stated. "I want you to be the best Carl you can be. Don't be a copy of anyone. Be the individual you are. Be proud of being Carl Murphy. In everything you do, be sure that it was done the best that you can. When you are in school and your report card shows B's or C's , if that is the best you can do, then the way I look at it, it's as good as an A. Have respect for other people, treat them with dignity and kindness. Be the kind of person that others will say, I want to be like Carl."

"You called me Carl Murphy. Does that mean I am your son?"

"As far as I am concerned you are, but according to law until I adopt you, you are legally Carlos Romaine. You will register in school as Carl Murphy. You will claim the name, Carl Murphy. As soon as we can get the papers in order we will make it legal."

"Can we shake on that dad?"

"Here's my hand on it son. It's going to happen and nobody is going to stop it. There's where we're going, just ahead on the right."

"Would that be one o'clock Dad?" Carl asked. "That's right Carl, you are very smart."

Mike loaded Lois and Robbie and their luggage into the Old Dog. Carl and Robbie sat in the back while Lois sat next to Mike. "Is everybody strapped in?" Mike asked.

Carl helped Robbie then snapped his seat belt buckle. Mike secured Lois into her seat.

"Elevator going up," Mike announced.

He had switched on the silent mode so there was little noise. The Old Dog rose straight up as if it was in the Hand of God.

"Oh what a thrill," Lois said.

Robbie squealed, "Better than a carnival ride."

"I'm confused, Mike. Bob said you had a house we could move into, but he was so excited, I'm not sure of the facts."

"The house my late wife and I own is empty. I'm not going to bore you with the details. I think it would be adequate for your family. It is being cleaned out as I speak. Bob admitted to me about your financial bind, so this is what I offered. You pay utilities, we split insurance and taxes. If you decide to buy it you can have it for what we paid for it fifteen years ago."

"Why are you doing this for us? You hardly know us?"

"Remember in the Gospel according to Matthew it says,

'Whatever you do for the least of these my brothers, you do it also for me.' You were strangers who needed help and I took you in, just as you would if the roles were reversed. I thank God every day for His grace and His gift of resources that enables me to do things like this. But to be honest, I have a selfish motive. It makes me feel so good to do it. It's a high you can't get any other way and it is an addiction."

Lois was sitting in silence with her eyes closed. Mike could see tears trying to escape. She regained her composure, opened her eyes and said, "I was just thanking God for you. I haven't been in the praying mood since Robbie got hurt and everything seemed to be going against us. You have given us hope. Thank you."

"Lois, I want you to remember what God said to Jeremiah, 'For I know the plans I have for you, plans to prosper you and not to harm you. Plans to give you hope and a future.' God said it. I believe it, that's all there is to it."

"I've never seen Mount Hood so close," Lois commented. "She is beautiful".

"We'll make a slow low pass around the old girl so you can get a good look." Mike said. Completing the sightseeing, Mike set a course for The Dalles. "That's our destination on the horizon."

A short time later they set down in front of the house Mike had offered the Koch's. There were several cars in the driveway belonging to the cleaning crew. Lois followed Mike into the house and looked around. Robbie and Carl explored the bedrooms deciding which one would be Robbie's, then they went outside to just explore.

A jolly lady with a red bandana covering her graying hair came from the kitchen.

"I'm Hazel Miller. I am I charge of the cleaning crew. There was a red-headed Irishman here with a young lad and a van. He said we should pick through and take whatever we wanted except for the appliances. He has a way with words, he does. I'm Irish myself so we understood each other. We shampooed the carpets, washed the windows inside and out, scoured the tub and shower in the bathrooms and are just now finishing in the kitchen. I tried out the coffee maker and have a fresh pot ready. I saved some cups. Would you like some coffee?"

"Indeed I would," Mike said. "How about you Lois?" "Yes please."

"Hazel, this is Lois Koch. She and her family are going to live here, at least for awhile. Lois, take your time and walk through the house. We both know you would want some things changed, but in general I think it will be okay. I'm going to sit here and enjoy my coffee. For years I've been coming through that door wanting a cup of coffee. I would wait for Aggie to make it. Then drink it alone. I walk in the door and a perfect stranger in my house offers me a cup of fresh-brewed coffee. How ironic, he thought to himself. "Hazel, I'm being very sincere when I say, this is the best coffee I've ever had in this house."

Lois came in, poured herself a fresh cup, refilled Mike's cup and sat down.

"This is beautiful Mike, I'm sure Bob will agree, and we will buy it as soon as we can arrange financing."

Their conversation was interrupted by Carl shouting, "Dad! Come here. Look what I found in the field." Mike and Lois looked and saw Carl holding up by the neck, a 4 ft. timber rattler.

"What should I do with it?"

"Kill it. That's the first one I've ever seen up here. If I had my way, you could kill all snakes but they do more good than harm. Any you see near where people live, kill; the rest in their native habitat, let live. Can you kill it without getting bit?"

"Sure. It's easy. I saw a bolo knife in the garage. I'll hold him down with the hoe and cut his head off with the bolo. I'm going to save the rattles and show Grandpa Bear.

"You should have seen it, Mom. We were walking through that field and this rattler buzzed. Carl said, 'stop, don't move.' He found a stick and held it down. Then he reached down and picked it up by the neck. He wasn't scared or nothin'."

Carl dispatched the serpent and cut the rattles off. There were seven.

"Do you want to stay here and wait for Bob or go home with us and wait there?"

"After seeing that snake, I don't want to stay here alone. We'll go home with you."

Lois rode in front and the boys rode in the back of the pickup. "Sit down with your backs against the cab," Mike admonished Carl and Robbie.

Carl and Robbie ran down to show Bear the rattles. "You are a brave little man," Bear commented.

Carl took Robbie to see his ponies. When they stepped into the corral, the big gelding came trotting up to Carl and nuzzled him. "That's your personal pony," Bear said. "He probably won't let anyone but you ride him."

"When do you think I can ride him Grandpa?"

"I think now is all right, but you still have work to do. There is more to riding a horse than just sitting on one. You will communicate through the reins or your heels. You will not use spurs. You can lean and he will turn that way. Pull back on the reins and he'll stop. Loosen up on the reins and touch him in the ribs, and he starts. The more attention you give his ribs, the faster he goes. You learn to grip him with your knees so you two are working together."

"I think I'll wait till tomorrow after I get my chores done to try and ride him. I'm going to call him Scout. Yes, sir." Carl repeated rubbing Scout's nose. "Your name is Scout."

"Robbie," Carl continued. I'll have one broke for you too, so when you come out we can go riding. We can even go over to some of those lakes Dad showed me, and fish. Do you think your mom would let you stay overnight sometimes?"

"I don't know. I've never had a good friend before, so I never was asked."

Susan, Lois, and Marie came down to where Bear and Faun were camped. Susan introduced Lois to Bear and Faun.

"The boys are in the corral with Brave Little Man's ponies," Faun said. "Carl has bonded with a big gelding he named Scout." "I'm ashamed to say I've never seen the ponies," Susan said.

"Let's go take a look, Lois. Do horses bother you?"

"Heavens no. I was raised in a rural community and even though I never had one of my own, there was always a horse for me to ride. I entered barrel racing events at the fair but never won any ribbons. I had fun making those who finished ahead of me work harder for their points."

As they entered the corral, one of the mares raised her head, twitched her ears and cantered over to Lois, who immediately started talking softly to her. "You are a beautiful lady," she said. The mare nickered, as though she understood.

Carl watched all this in amazement. "Lois, she really likes you and I think you have bonded. I'll work with her next and you can ride her when you come out. If Robbie can come out and stay a day or two he can ride her and I'll ride Scout. What are you going to name her?"

"I wasn't prepared for this so I'll have to think about it. She will still be your pony, Carl. I'll claim her as mine, when I ride. I think Robbie will have a wonderful time out here with you and Bear and as long as it's okay with your Mother and Dad, and Bear and Faun don't mind, it's fine with me."

Bear said, "It would be a good thing for Brave Little Man to have someone close to his age to fish and camp with. Everybody should have a good friend, and these two have a friendship that is just starting to grow. It will grow strong and they may want to become brothers in blood as Mike and my son are going to do at our next council meeting. Soon they will think as one and be able to finish each other's sentence. I want to teach your young brave the ways of my people, like I'm teaching Brave Little Man."

"I would love to have Robbie spend some time with us," Susan said. "You and Bob are always welcome too. Except for Murph's secretary, Julie, you are the only woman I know in this town. Why don't we buddy up so we can each have someone to talk to who understands PMS?"

"I've always wanted to do volunteer work but never had the time," Lois commented. "I'm going to be a stay-at-home mom and have supper ready for Bob when he gets home from work. A real home-cooked meal. Not something picked up at a drive through. When you love someone it's not work to prepare meals. I can't thank you and Mike enough for your kindness and generosity. With Bob's new job we can breathe easier knowing we will have a steady income."

That night, after the two families and Bear and Faun had finished eating at the ranch, Bear stood up and stretched to his full 6 ft. He spread his arms, tipped his head back, closed his eyes and in his Shoshone language, began to chant, "Great Spirit, we gather here as my Eastern Brothers long ago gathered in peace and love to thank you for helping them survive another season of cold, and for the bountiful harvest that would help them survive another winter. I thank you for my new family of two fine sons and daughters, two energetic grandsons and a beautiful granddaughter. Grant them wisdom, strength, and health that they may sing your praises to their world."

Faun stood up and reached up to kiss her husband. With tears in her eyes she said, "Bear you speak so beautifully in our language, it always makes me cry. Are you going to teach our grandchildren to speak our tongue?"

"Yes, I intend to teach them all I know about our culture. I would not be a good grandparent if I didn't teach them things they won't learn in white man's school. Are you going to teach Marie the Shoshone ways?"

"Yes, I am. As she grows older she will learn how to weave and cure the hides that our grandsons will trap."

"I don't know what you said," commented Susan, "but I felt a sense of warmth and serenity as you spoke."

"You probably knew I was speaking to the Great Spirit. You felt Him answering my prayer."

"Carl, I've decided to call my pony, Beautiful Lady, if that's all right with you," Lois stated.

"That's okay with me. I'll call her, Beauty, because she reminds me of you and mom."

"I'll help with the dishes, then we have to go."

"You're not helping with the dishes," Susan stated. "You and Bob need to talk. Robbie can stay here as long as he wants or until you want him to come home. I'll be in about nine to help you get settled. Mike and I will do the dishes. You and Bob get to bed so that you will be fresh in the morning, "Susan added, winking at Lois, who returned her wink with a smile.

Marie dutifully carried the dishes to the kitchen. Carl and Robbie cleared the table of the rest of the dishes. Their chores done, the children went to their rooms to get ready for bed.

"Mrs. Murphy, I don't have any pajamas."

"You are close enough to Carl's size. I'll get you a pair of his, and some underwear. In the medicine cabinet there is a new toothbrush that will be yours.

Bear and Faun were ready to leave. Susan hugged them both. Much to her surpise, Bear returned the hug. "Thank you so much for coming," Susan said. "We will do this often and include Hawk and his wife. I didn't even think about him until we were finished eating. This just started out to be dinner with friends who didn't have a kitchen, and ended in a Thanksgiving dinner."

Bear and Faun left. Susan and Mike were deep in their own thoughts. Mike broke the silence. "Do you realize how much we have in common?" When we each married for the first time we were old enough, but not smart enough to know what love really is. Tonight is the first time I ever hosted a dinner party, and you used your fine china and crystal for the first time. We both have missed out on things that are important. We have a family that we both wanted and a circle of friends like we never had before. I would like to legitimize our relationship as soon as possible. Do it in secret first and then have your wedding like you want it, around Labor day. To us it would be a renewal of our vows, but to everybody else it would be our wedding day."

"I think that's a good idea. There's nothing standing in our way now, so it would be legal. I fell in love with you in Galveston. I've thought about that night many times since then, and said to myself that if it never went any further than that, I could never love another man. It wasn't the incredible sex; it was the way you treated me after and ever since. You seem to put my wants and needs in front of everything else. I wasn't used to that, but now you big Irish dummy, you've got me spoiled rotten and I love it."

"You're doing a pretty good job of spoiling me too. If I want coffee it's there - not I'll make a pot. It's not the coffee, it's the message it sends. It tells me welcome home. I love you, and as long as you brought it up, incredible love making any time. As far as spoiling you is concerned, I just want you to be happy. I say to myself, 'whatever Susan wants Susan gets.' You must be happy because I've never heard singing in the kitchen before."

The dishes were washed, dried, and put away.

It's a beautiful, full moon tonight," Susan said. "Let's sit outside and have a glass of wine."

"That would really put the cork in the bottle."

Mount Hood stood towering over all, like a Queen watching over her realm. The full moon bathed her snow-capped crest in light.

"She is a beautiful sight," Susan sighed, "but if you had no one to share the beauty with, why bother to give it more than a second glance?" The cougar screamed, the river gurgled its song on the way to the Pacific, and far off, a wolf howled it's mournful cry.

"God is in His Kingdom and all's right with the world," Mike said. "If only it were true. I'm so content and it's all because of you, Susan. Thank you."

They lay in each other's arms, with the moonlight streaming through their window. It was indeed a romantic setting and with the wine they had earlier, the inevitable happened.

CHAPTER 49

Agnes' memorial service was well attended. Mike was surprised at the number of friends she had. He was aware she belonged to several women's groups, like the Garden Club and was active in church. Few men were in attendance, and most of them were probably dragged there by their wives. Hawk was there but stood apart like he was looking for someone. Very few of the women came by to offer condolences and Mike felt that was only for show, and not heartfelt. The cleric presented the ashes to Mike without a word. Mike thought that if they knew the whole truth about the marriage, they might have felt differently, but he would never know.

Mike joined Hawk for coffee after the service.

"How are you holding up dear friend? What are you going to do with the ashes?"

"I'm holding up fine. I'm going to take Aggie's prize rose bush into the "Plantorium." They do wonders with damaged and distressed plants so I'll see if they can save it. I'll put the ashes in the ground when I replant it. I know that was one thing she really cared about. I feel she will be with it and can still help it grow. Bob Koch is moving into Aggie's house today. He is working for Dad. His wife, Lois, is a little skittish. If you or someone in the department could swing by and let them know you're watching the place, I'm sure she would feel a little more secure. Are you any closer to finding that bastard?"

"We know the area where he's hiding and we can pick him up most any time we want, but I want an iron-clad case before we do that. All we have is circumstantial evidence, even with the DNA. I don't want some sly lawyer getting him off. There are rumors that there is going to be a new bank in town. Do you know anything about that?"

"I've talked to Bubb and Howard Morrison about opening one that would deal fairly with everybody, and bend to help those who need a leg up, but that's all I know. I'll see Howard today and see where we stand."

"When you open your doors, the weasel will have to close his, because the people in this town are tired of being held hostage by him. I'm going to call on the Koch's right now."

"Thanks Hawk. I'll get the coffee. I've got a tab to settle with Mary."

"Mike, that was the happiest man I've seen in years. He had a quiet supper last night and looked kind of sad. This morning he came in with a very attractive lady he said was his wife, and smiled and joked. They both had three-egg omelets and the works, and left holding hands like a pair of newlyweds."

"They probably had a second honeymoon last night. Here's for the tab and here's $10 for taking care of them. I don't know if you are aware of the plans for our new airport or not. We would like to have a first-class restaurant out there. The new airport will have office space for rent or lease, a bank, and very soon some scheduled airlines. If you are interested let me know, or call Julie at my office. I'll wait a week before I advertise it. We will outfit it to your specs, including the tables and chairs and carpeting."

"I've been wanting to have more than a diner for a long time. How much would you charge?"

"I'm new at this, Mary. How does this sound? You have been in the food business long enough to be able to estimate what you can gross once the people in the area are aware of your business. We will take 15% of what you figure you will gross in a year. That is the top figure. When you reach full stride, 10% will do. We will help you with your advertising. We want this place to succeed, so will do all we can to help. Your lease will be locked in for five years, unless it needs to be lowered. That we would do instantly."

"I don't know how I could go wrong Mike. Here's my hand on it."

You've obviously heard of the way we do business, and here's mine. Put your plans and specs together ASAP. I'll have the architect that did our building get together with you as soon as you're ready unless you have someone in mind you'd feel more comfortable with."

"No, I think it would be better to use the same architect and contractor so things would go smoother. Thanks, Mike."

CHAPTER 50

Mike got to the Koch's just as the van was leaving. Carl, Robbie, Bob, Red and Yale were moving furniture around to suit Lois's taste. Susan was making the beds and hanging curtains. Lois handed Mike a cup of fresh coffee and said, "lunch in thirty minutes.".

Mike took his coffee outside and carefully dug up the rose bush. He put it in a bucket of composted, black dirt and watered it before placing it in the back of the truck. He walked around the yard sipping his coffee. Red and Yale must have worked well into dark to get the yard cleaned up like they did. "Aggie," he prayed, "I'm sorry things didn't work out for you the way you wanted. I know you are now at peace and I hope you forgive me for any hurt I caused you."

Lois announced lunch. "Sloppy Joes - make your own, chips, mustard, onions on the counter. Coffee in the pot, soda in the fridge."

"Lois, for someone who has been working as hard as you have today you don't seem a bit tired," Susan commented..

"Well, Bob and I talked until almost two o'clock this morning and we finished our conversation after breakfast. We haven't had a chance to visit like that in years." Lois smiled and winked at Susan. Bob just blushed.

"Can Robbie go to the game with us tonight, please?" Carl asked.

"Yes, but we would like him home tonight so we can start our new life in a new home as a family," Bob said.

They had front-row box seats on the third base site. They were early and the teams were still warming up.

"Hey Juan, Juan Marcos," Carl shouted excitedly.

The visiting short stop looked over and spotted Carl and waved.

"His family lived close to me in Cuba. When he came to visit his Momma, he would play catch with us. He is my friend."

After the teams had taken the field, Juan came over and shook hands with Carl, who introduced him to Robbie.

"Our bat boy is sick today. Would you two like to be our bat boys?"

Carl turned to Susan and Mike who both nodded approval.

In the stands behind first base sat a swarthy man with a beard and sun glasses. He wore a white, Panama hat and rumpled suit over a Notre Dame sweat shirt and was watching Carl and Juan with a great deal of interest.

Carl and Robbie were torn between rooting for the home team, or their friend Juan and his teammates. Juan went 2 for 4 with a stolen base and scored a run. His defensive play was flawless, making one spectacular play after another, and making them look easy. On a double play, he flipped to the second baseman, who was covering second without even looking. The crowd roared. They wanted their home team to win but they appreciated the talents of all players. Juan was picked best player of the game. He asked if he could give the medal to his friend, Carlos. "He inspired me to do my best." Carl went out to the mound and Juan knelt down to place the medal around his neck. He whispered to Carl, "Your Poppa was in the stands behind first. I know how you and Maria were treated by him and how you escaped. Tell Senora Romaine to be very careful. Ramon is a very evil man."

The crowd applauded Carl as he strode from the mound to where a proud mother and dad waited in the stands.

"Wasn't that neat, Carl? I've never been a bat boy before. Did I do okay?"

"You did good Robbie, real good."

"Thanks for taking me to the game," Robbie said as he exited the car. "See you later."

"Mom, Juan said Poppa was at the game tonight. Juan knew all about our escape. He said be very careful because Poppa is a very evil man."

"Thank you for telling us Carl," Mike responded. "We will be extra careful until this mess is all cleaned up."

"Would it be okay with you if we put bunk beds in your room so Robbie can have his own bed?" Susan asked.

"Sure, that would be neat. Maybe he could have some clothes out here too, then he could stay longer. What about Marie? She hasn't got anyone to play with."

"We'll find someone close by for her to play with," Susan responded. "You are such a good big brother. Not many boys would worry about a little sister like you do."

CHAPTER 51

Sunday morning arrived with the promise of being one of the ten perfect days of the year. Warm and dry with no wind. Mike's folks drove out after church. Winnie had not seen the ranch before and Murph hadn't seen it in several years. He used to fish in the pond.

"I'm so glad you found this place. When I used to fish here I hated to leave. It was so quiet and peaceful."

"Susan," Mike said, "Are you up to having a picnic cookout today? It's a beautiful day. I would like to have Hawk and his wife, Howard and Julie, Red and Yale, Vondra, the Koch's, Bear and Faun. Have I left anyone out?"

"No one I can think of. I definitely feel up to it. Make the calls. I'll get a grocery list ready. This is Sunday, Michael. Where are you going to get groceries today?"

"I'll call Bubb. I forgot about him. He could bring the stuff out with him and we need to talk about the bank."

Bubb was pleased to be invited and didn't feel patronized by being asked to bring the things they needed.

"We'll eat about 5 p.m., but come out as soon as you like," Mike told everybody.

He had just hung up after inviting Vondra when the phone rang. It was Walt.

"We're on our way to see you folks and need some directions. We decided to stay off the interstate and are on US-30. We are at the top of the loops. How do we get to you or your Dad's?"

"You are practically here now. Walk over and look down and to the East. The brick house with the barn is ours. At the foot of the loops there is a faded sign that says, Ferry. Turn left and you're here."

Winnie loved the house. "You've made a beautiful home from this house, dear. Michael is so happy he must glow in the dark. You will know the feeling when Carl gets married and his wife makes him happy. I'm so glad you asserted yourself at our first meeting. Now that Agnes is gone, what are your plans?"

"I've always wanted a real wedding in a church. I'm not going to wear a white wedding gown. I'm going to get a long dress. Michael is going to wear his dress whites. We are planning a Labor Day weekend for the ceremony. What I'm going to tell you now, is for your ears only and Pop's if you think he should know. Michael and I are going to get a legal marriage in Vegas as soon as we can. The Labor Day event will be a renewal of our vows but to everyone else it is a wedding. I don't mean to embarrass you, but Michael and I both feel we had our wedding and honeymoon in Galveston on our first meeting. How and why things happened the way they did, I don't know. I only know, after that night, I could never love anyone else. Michael actually apologized to me for his actions. He told me a little later he could not go back to what he left. He had decided the morning before he could not endure the insecurity and jealousy of Agnes and was leaving her. I'll testify he is a one-woman man. I tried to seduce him in the most provocative way and it just made him mad. Shall we join the others?"

Walt and Murph were getting reacquainted, Hawk and Bob Koch were getting to know each other, and Red was very attentive to Vonnie. Yale went fishing, the women gossiped, the men BS'ed and the children played. Hot dogs and hamburgers were consumed by the pounds. Soda disappeared by the gallon, coffee by the pot. Yes, indeed it was definitely one of the ten perfect days of the year.

Walt and Margaret were planning on staying over for a few days so Walt and Murph could get reacquainted and maybe do some fishing. Julie and Vonnie could run things for a few days, giving Murph a chance to get away and recharge his batteries.

Mike, Howard, and Bubb discussed the new bank. "Most every businessman I've talked to is eager for the new bank, Bubb reported. "I've got the same answers from those I've talked to," echoed Howard.

"We can round up enough assets to satisfy the Banking Commission in Salem. We need to form a corporation and get a charter," Howard stated.

"Do we want a State Charter or a Federal Charter?" Bubb asked. "Or does it make any difference?'

"I would vote for a State Charter," Mike sid. "Have you got any ideas on who is going to make up the corporation?"

Howard suggested, "We develop a Mission Statement. Publish it in the local paper and the Oregonian and announce a public meeting. Those interested enough to show up and ask questions should be given priority. The people will own the bank, the directors will oversee the operation, and answer to the corporation. We could call it The People's State Bank."

"What a great idea," Bubb commented. "How about this for a Mission Statement? Our mission is to provide our customers the best service possible, using the latest state of the art system and the highest interest rate possible on savings and low interest rates on loans. No matter what your needs are or your credit score is, our trained staff will listen and if there is any way possible to help you, we will."

"That sounds good to me Bubb," Mike said. "What do you think Howard?"

"It covers everything I can think of. Let's get this show on the road."

CHAPTER 52

The next morning, Mike had finished breakfast and was on his second cup of coffee when the phone rang.

"Is this Angel Flight?"

"Yes, it is. May I help you?"

"My daughter was hit by a drunk driver and is pretty well busted up. How much would you charge to fly her to L.A.?"

"Sir, we are a not-for-profit company and charge nothing for our service, no matter what your resources are. If you have the means, then a donation to Angel Flight would be appreciated. The important thing now is, where are you?"

"In an ambulance, about five miles west of Lyle heading east."

"Cross the river at The Dalles, go east two miles. We are on your right. Drive up to the hangar." After hanging up, Mike told Susan to prepare for an Angel Flight.

"We have to go now, Carl. Get dressed and go tell Faun we have to leave. We should be back late tonight or early tomorrow."

Susan was in her nurse's uniform and Mike dressed hurriedly in his flight captain's suit.

"You are a handsome dog in your airplane driver's suit," Susan commented.

"Flattery will get you anything you want. Why not have Murph invite Walt and Margaret to stay at the ranch and Margaret can watch Marie and Lizzie? Pop could set up his fifth wheeler for himself and Mom. Pop and Walt could fish. Hawk will bring my boat out, just in case they want to go after sturgeon, they can get out on the river. It would be almost like a vacation. Margaret and Mom could get to know each other better."

Mike got out of the pickup in front of the hangar, and Susan drove to the office to confer with Murph.

"How's my girl this morning? That was quite a shindig you put on yesterday. Winnie hasn't had that pleasant a day in too long a time. Thank you for it. It's no wonder my son is so in love with you. You are so lovable and considerate of others."

"You're embarrassing me, Pops. We have an Angel Flight and thought Walt and Margaret could move out to the ranch so Lizzie and Marie could spend more time together. Michael suggested you set up your fifth wheeler at the ranch, for you and Mom. It could be like a vacation."

"I'll do it, by golly, I"ll do it. Winnie needs to relax and I need to get away. Go do your Angel thing and I'll take care of Walt." With a fatherly hug and kiss he dismissed Susan and dialed Walt's motel.

The ambulance followed Susan to the hangar. Red had used the mule to roll the jet outside, where it stood, ready to go.

Susan helped the Medics get the patient onto the gurney and secure her. The medics had not experienced this type of service and watched Susan in amazement as she routinely went through the procedures necessary.

The APS was up and running. Mike made his walk-around inspection and boarded the aircraft. The medics left and Mike said, "Nurse, you may secure the aircraft for take off."

The patient was a teenage girl about 16-17 years old. Six feet tall with shoulder-length, golden blonde hair. Slender build, but not skinny. A basketball player, Mike mused to himself. The father introduced himself as Raymond Putnam.

"Welcome aboard Angel Flight." Mike announced, "The weather is a little turbulent between here and LA. We will fly west of it over the Pacific, until San Francisco, at which time we set a course directly for John Wayne Field. The temperature there is 85 degrees, winds are calm, humidity 25%. It will be a two-hour plus flight. Fasten your seat belt, please. If you need assistance or have questions, Susan will be happy to help."

Mike entered the cabin and shut the door.

"Nurse," he announced, "if your passengers are secure, could you come forward and help me with my paperwork?"

Susan took the co-pilot's seat and started down the checklist. "Checklist complete, sir," she announced. "Starting port engine. Port engine running, all gauges read normal. Starting starboard engine. Engine running, all gauges reading normal. Mr. Rolls and Mr. Royce are anxious to burn holes in the sky."

"Normally, at this time we would ask for taxi clearance, but today let's just get airborne. Susan, drive us to take-off position, remembering that you steer with your feet. Well done. Are you confident enough to try a take off?"

"If your hands are on the yoke too, I'll do it."

"That's fine with me. If I say, MINE - don't think, just let go. We don't have a tower to watch out for us, that means we have to watch out for ourselves. Before you turn onto the runway, look to see there's not a plane trying to land. Once you have committed yourself, ease the throttles ahead and get off the ground as soon as it's safely possible. Any questions?"

Susan thought carefully and said, "No. I think you have covered everything."

Checking in both directions and then again, she turned the jet onto the runway. She eased the throttles to the firewall. At 150 knots she eased back, got the nose up, and the rest of Angel One followed.

"That was picture-perfect, sweetheart. Do you want to continue or do you want me to take over?"

Doing her Barbie Doll impression she said, "Oh, sweetie pie, that was so exciting and my li'l ol' heart is just goin' pitty-pat. I don't think I could stand anymore of that kind of excitement. I could use a lot of your kind of excitement, though. When do you think you'll have time for me sugar?"

"If we didn't have passengers on board, I'd initiate you into the three-mile club right now."

"Whatever is the three-mile club sweetie?"

"It's members have all been made love to, at three miles high," Mike answered.

"How would you fly the plane and make love to me at the same time?"

"I'll show you at the first opportunity. Check the patient and have her Dad come up front. Before you go, I must tell you how much I love you and how much fun you are."

"Sugar, flattery will get you anything you want. You just made my li'l ol' heart go pitty-pat, pitty-pat again."

Mr. Putnam took the co-pilot's seat. "You wanted to see me?"

"Tell me about your daughter."

"Vanessa is the youngest of three children. She has a basketball scholarship at Oregon State. With two older brothers to teach her, she developed an outside shot. Give her time to setup a shot and you get at least two points. My youngest son, Gregory, is a senior at Oregon University. He wants to be a pharmacist. My oldest child is my son, Clarke. He has a successful craft store. He sells craft materials, like rattan for basket weaving or caning a chair. It's amazing what some people do for relaxation. My wife, Barbra Jean, is running our bookkeeping office. I also have an insurance agency."

"Are we going to loaf along like this, or go some place?" asked Susan as she entered the cockpit.

"Get your credit card out baby, I'm going to the wall. It might be wise to take your seat, sir. We'll continue our conversation when we're on the ground."

Putnam left and Susan shut the door behind him. "What's wrong Susan."

"She is very uncomfortable and the sedative they injected is either wearing off or she is allergic to it. I don't think it's critical, but the sooner we get her to the hospital the better her chances are."

Mike called traffic control and informed them of the situation.

"You are priority one to John Wayne. We have you on the screen and will clear the air for you. A Medivac chopper will be waiting at United Gate 1. Do you understand?"

"Roger, Air Traffic Control. Thanks for the help. Angel One out. Mike turned to Susan: "Go back and calm Mr. Putnam down."

Putnam came forward and retook the co-pilot's seat. After strapping himself in, he turned to Mike and demanded, "What's going on? Why did you go to full speed, and don't give me any garbage about shopping. I'm her father and I have a right to know the truth."

"You're absolutely right sir. The nurse is concerned about your daughter's discomfort. So far there is nothing serious but we want to get her to the hospital ASAP. Possibly, the sedation is wearing off or she is having an allergic reaction. The hospital chopper will be waiting for us and we have priority clearance. The hospital chopper has been alerted to our suspicions and will have a doctor and trained staff aboard. I would suggest you take your seat in the passenger area and follow the gurney to the chopper. I know you are concerned. The most helpful thing you can do is stay out of the way. I'm not being critical of you. I'm just trying to help you. I've been praying for your daughter since I first saw her, because I care. You have put your faith in me. Let's have faith in God. We pray, 'Thy will be done', so let's get out of His way and let Him help."

"I never have been a church-going man. I did ask God to help me and let it go at that. I see these Bible-thumping church- going people screw everyone they can and then go to church every Sunday and it turned me off of religion."

"I have a suggestion for you. While you are waiting for Vanessa's prognosis, pick up the Gideon Bible they have there. Turn to the book of Proverbs. There are thirty-one chapters in the book. Today is the 10th. Read chapter 10. Tomorrow read chapter 11 and so on. If you don't have one, get a study Bible and you and you wife start anywhere you want. Read the text, then take notes about what you read. The Old Testament is interesting history. You will find references to Jesus in Genesis and scattered throughout the Old Testament. The New Testament tells of Jesus' birth, death and resurrection, and the things He accomplished here on earth. It's not a fairy tale; it is the truth. The Bible says it, I believe it, and that's all there is to it. There is no debate. We'll be landing in about thirty minutes sir."

"Thank you for your frankness. I'm going to start tonight and try to keep at it. Nobody ever mentioned a simple method to get started reading the Bible. I thought you had to start in front and keep going until you read it through."

"It's not like a novel, although it has all the characteristics of one. You'll find murder, prostitution, wife stealing - all those things and more. The best thing you will learn is the hardest for most people to believe. You could lead a perfect life, never sin, and not get to heaven. Read Mathew, chapter 10, verses 16-22. You can't buy your way, or work your way. It's a gift by admitting to Jesus that you are a sinner, and ask for His forgiveness. I'm sorry. I didn't mean to preach."

"No need to apologize. I needed to hear that from somebody who wasn't going to pass the collection basket around."

"You won't hear it from those churches. They don't want to offend their congregations by calling them sinners. John Wayne just ahead."

Smoooooth as silk, Mike thought. No bumps, just the scream of the tires. The chopper was waiting as promised. Angel One had hardly stopped before the doctor and his staff were aboard taking vitals. Susan gave them her chart. The doctor complimented her on the neatness and detail of her report.

Handing it to his nurse, he said, "That's the way I want charts done. Neat, complete, and legible. This patient has an infection caused by some dirt or glass. The wound was not thoroughly cleaned before the dressing was applied. She will make a full and complete recovery, but will need extensive therapy. I want to talk with the pilot," he said to Susan. "If he has time, I should be out of surgery in an hour or two."

Mike stepped forth and took the doctor's hand, "I'm Mike Murphy, the pilot, and I have the time. My nurse and I will get Angel One ready for her next trip and come over when we finish, which would be about the same time you finish."

"Great. I'm Dr. Fischer. We'll talk later."

"Angel One. Do you read me?" came from the radio. "I read you loud and clear."

"We are going to escort you to Lone Star Air Park. They have the facilities you need to get back in service. What do you have under your hood? You really burnt a hole in the sky."

"All I know is I've got juiced up Rolls Royce engines. Beaver Air in Troutdale, Oregon, did a complete refurbishing from corporate jet to a Medivac."

A pickup with "Follow Me" beeped his horn.

Mike waved acknowledgment, he asked Susan, "start the port engine," which she did with expertise, and "follow that truck."

The Lone Star ground crew was waiting and as soon as Susan parked, the jet the crew chocked the wheels and started refueling.

Susan checked in with dispatch. "Nothing at the moment, but keep in touch," they said.

Mike and Susan used the restrooms and changed into street clothes. Mike wore jeans with a big buckle adorned with a Navy Tom Cat, a western-cut shirt, and his cowboy boots with the dogging heels. Over her black cowboy boots Susan wore jeans with a rawhide belt, loosely tied. Her jeans were to her waist and she really didn't need the belt. Her long-sleeved lemon-colored, silk shirt had pearl buttons and dangling, turquoise earrings accented her long, black hair tied with a rawhide strip with turquoise tips.

In the cab, on the way to the hospital Mike suggested, "Let's hop to Vegas tonight and get married."

"I like the married idea but hopping all that way turns me off, when we have a beautiful airplane we could use to fly there."

"Okay, okay, we'll fly and spend the night." "Now I'm really turned on," Susan purred.

The doctor and Putnam were in the waiting room when Susan and Mike arrived. "You make a striking couple," the doctor commented. "Tell me about Angel Flight."

Mike explained how and why it got started and how it got its name and logo.

"You haven't been in business very long but you have the attention of the medical community," Dr. Fischer said. "How can we help you?"

"The biggest need we have now is patients to fly," Susan said. "As our service gets busier, we will need aircraft and pilots."

"We can possibly recruit retired military pilots who would like to help preserve a life rather than kill," Mike responded. "That's what got me interested. I've been flying since I was sixteen. My Dad bought me an old Piper Cub. I rebuilt it and learned to fly in it. I went to Pensacola and learned to kill and destroy. I trained for that for ten years. I resigned my commission to help Pop in his business when he had his heart attack. One day, I was flying in my Cub and fate stepped in and I was able to get a 5-year-old to a hospital, where they operated on her heart. It felt so great to be able to do some good with my flying ability, I am hooked on it. If you could get your organization or people of means who could use a tax write-off to buy an aircraft, that would be a big help. As it is now, Angel One has no back up and when she is out of service, some child is apt to die because the family couldn't raise enough money for transportation. We do not charge anybody nor do we pry into their financial affairs. If they have the means to contribute, we encourage them to do so. It's all on their conscience."

Ray Putnam was listening intently. "Mr. Murphy, I'm not a man of great wealth. What you have given me today is priceless. Vanessa is going to make a full recovery. Had we not got here as quickly as we did, the infection could have spread and possibly been terminal. I started reading Proverbs like you suggested, and a light came on and I felt an inner warmth that I can't explain. When I get home I will cut you a check. How big, I don't know. I will spread the word about your company, and you in particular. You are a man to be admired and looked up to."

"Mr. Putnam, I thank you for your praise, but I'm only using my God-given talents to do his work."

"When you get time, write down the specs on the aircraft you need and how it should be outfitted," Dr. Fischer said. "Look for a pilot, because you have an airplane."

"Thank you Dr.," said Mike, shaking his hand. "Put your spec in there too. We just guessed what would be appropriate and it has worked out okay, but if we had feedback from doctors, we wouldn't be flying blind, so to speak."

"Okay, Mike. Then with a sly grin he said, "I understand from the grapevine that you and I just made a binding deal."

Trying hard to keep a straight face, Mike replied. "I had that in mind all along. We have to go now." With a big grin and a salute to the doctor, Mike and Susan left.

They saw Ray Putnam having coffee and joined him.

"Ray, don't give me any BS. Do you have enough money to get by on while you're here?"

"I'm a little short on cash right now, but I'll be okay."

"Here's some emergency money," Susan said. "I don't know how much is there, but when you are home with Vanessa and this is all in the past, send a check or give it to somebody who needs it. Come on Michael let's go to Vegas."

CHAPTER 53

They got to Vegas and called for the Sands' limo to pick them up. Once they were registered they asked the night manager where they could get a marriage license - a legitimate one that would stand up in court. They were directed to a small chapel a short walk down the strip. They went to their room and freshened up and then hand-in-hand strolled down the strip to the chapel. They were met by a middle-aged man and his wife. When Mike explained they wanted a real marriage, not a weekender, the parson smiled warmly and said, "We don't get many like you, but I can assure you this will be recognized in any court in the country."

The newlyweds strolled hand-in-hand back to the Sands.

"Let's watch people make fools of themselves for a while," Mike suggested so they watched the crap shooters and black jack. They turned to leave when an out-of-control drunk made a grab for Susan.

"Hey baby. How about dropping that rhinestone cowboy? Let me show you what a real man has under the hood."

Security was about to step in but Mike stepped in front of them. "That drunk is about to get a lesson he will remember the rest of his life. I will stand good for any damages he doesn't cover."

"Don't worry about that," security said. "He has a credit line here of half a mil. He loves to gamble."

"Hey, real man," Mike said to the drunk, "are you as tough as you want us to think you are?"

"No, I'm tougher than that," he spat back.

"I'll bet you $100,000 you can't whip me. In fact you won't even knock my brand new Stetson off."

Security was clearing space for a fight. The crowd was talking among themselves making bets with each other. A handsome gray-haired gentleman stepped into the center of the clearing. Holding his hand up for silence, he said, "I'm Al Cimono, the manager of the Sands. Will someone tell me what is going on?"

Mike stepped up to Mr. Cimono. "I'm Mike Murphy. My wife and I were watching your guests when this man grabbed at my wife and made some insulting remarks and I challenged him."

"Is that right security?"

"Yes boss. That's exactly what happened. Mr. Murphy said he would cover the damages Mr. Steele couldn't."

"Are all the bets down?" Mr. Cimono asked.

"No, they are not," Susan said. "Since I'm the cause of this I want a piece of the action. Mr. Steele, I'll bet you $50,000 you can't put me on my back. If you do I'm yours for a week." Turning to Mike she said, "Is that okay with you honey?"

"You know what you're doing and I'm not about to butt in on your business. Steele, do want me or her first?"

"You might be a little tougher than her so I'll do her first, then you."

"If all bets are down," Mr. Cimono said, "then let the games begin."

Susan stepped into the center of the clearing. Steele, on the edge, salivated over what he was going to have. He lunged; Susan sidestepped. He lunged again, Susan sidestepped and spanked him as he went past. Each time he made a pass she slipped away.

"Hey Sugar," she said. "I'm getting tired of this; are you? Let's put an end to it right now, okay?"

Steele nodded okay and straightened up. Susan walked toward him. He smiled, opened his arms to retrieve his prize, and got a size 6½ cowboy boot right in the family jewels. He bent over in pain and received the other boot square on the chin. Susan ripped off her belt, rolled Steele onto his stomach and tied both feet and one arm like a calf roper.

Mr. Cimono stepped into the clearing, looked at Steele, and raised Susan's hand. "I declare this match over and the winner is Susan Murphy. And furthermore since Mr. Steele is in no shape to continue, I declare Mike Murphy winner by default. My cashier will cut you a check from Steele's account for $150,000, which should close his account. Mr. Steele, check out time is 11 a.m. I expect you to leave by then and don't ever come back. Mike and Mrs. Murphy, your stay, including meals, is on the house. Thank you for giving me a reason to kick that pain in the ass out. Mike, did you have any idea that she was going to do what she did?"

"No, but I wasn't worried. She has more moves than anyone I've ever seen."

"What would you have done if he had put her on her back?" Al asked.

"Then he would have to have beaten me. I have earned a black belt in most of the martial arts besides being fleet champion in my weight class. I work out regularly and spar whenever possible. He wouldn't have been in shape to do anything for a month or better. I just got an idea I would like to share with you, if you have the time."

"Go have dinner and see me in my office about nine."

The word had obviously been passed around the Sands that this couple was to be given VIP status. They passed through Security with a nod and smile. One or two shook hands with Mike, and Susan drew applause from many.

Mr. Cimono greeted them personally and ushered them into his spacious office.

"You said you had an idea you wanted to share with me." "Vegas is called Sin City, as you are aware. I'm the general manager of Angel Flight. My mission is to transport critical patients to the nearest hospital that has the best facilities for their needs. We are a not-for-profit corporation and do not charge for the service. We hope that people with the means or assets will think enough of our efforts to contribute to our success. My idea is this, and please take no offense. The Sands has a reputation for providing any kind of entertainment that a customer wants to pay for. I stress, any kind of entertainment. That part of your reputation puts a cloud over the legitimate. "Not that prostitution is illegal in this state, and nothing is going to stop it. But it may keep a few families away from your club. We need aircraft. At the present time we only have Angel One and when she is out of service someone's child or wife or father may die because of the lack of an airplane. The initial cost of the type of aircraft we need exceeds four and a half million dollars. I don't have any idea what you gross a year or what your income taxes are, and it's none of my business. If you and your corporation could donate the aircraft it would be a pretty good tax write off, besides some positive publicity. I notice your family picture on your desk. A beautiful family, lovely wife, handsome son, and unless I miss my guess, that's Daddy's little girl. We have a son and daughter also so I can put myself in your shoes. Just supposing, and God forbid it ever happens, one of those three had to get to New York for lifesaving surgery. How much would you be willing to pay to get them there if there was no Angel Flight available? I would pay whatever it cost and Im sure you would too. But how about your dishwashers with the same problem? They would start making final arrangements. Wouldn't it be better for them if they could just call us instead of the funeral director?"

Al took a long pull on his cigar, looked up at the ceiling and then looking at Susan said, "Your husband is one hell of a salesman. You have your airplane Mr. Murphy. I'm going to sell the rest of the clubs on the idea. Hell, I'm going all the way to the family in Jersey. Since we are friends, you call me Al and I'll call you Mike and Susan. Whenever you are in the club you have my permission to kick the shit out of any obnoxious person, and I mean any, and Mike you can help take out the rest of the trash. On occasion we have a bunch of bikers come in who raise hell. We eventually get them out but not until they have caused thousands of dollars in damage and molested and raped some women. Do you think you could handle that situation?"

"I think Susan and I could quell the riot before it turned into a riot. It would be fun, don't you think, Susan?"

In her Barbie Doll voice she said, "Sugar, just the thought of all that excitement and sweaty bodies make my li'l ol' heart go pitty-pat, pitty-pat."

Al laughed and said, "I'm almost tempted to call up them bikers just to see the show. Too bad I couldn't sell tickets to it."

"Al, have your cashier make the check to Angel Flight and see that Steele gets the tax deduction. For the beating and humiliation he took he earned it," Mike stated. He offered his hand to Al and received a firm handshake.

"I guess that means it's a deal," Al said. "I guess you're right," Mike smiled.

Susan said, "Pardon the pun, Michael, Angel Flight is taking off. So far today you've gotten two birds and I think there will be more, so you are going to have to start recruiting airplane drivers."

"Since this is also our wedding night, I'm going to get a bottle of Asti Spumonte to celebrate with."

"Careful, you know how wine affects me."

"I'm counting on it. We haven't had this kind of opportunity since Galveston, and after all this is officially our honeymoon."

With the combination of wine and guilt reliever of the marriage license the happy couple, who were sincerely in love and not in heat, spent over two hours sipping wine and expressing their mutual love.

The phone rudely woke them from a blissful sleep at 7:30 a.m. It was Al Cimono.

"Mike, there's been a shooting at The Mirage. A patron's wife has been shot which is no big problem, but she has a heart condition and a rare blood type. Chi-town is the closest hospital that can do her any good."

"We'll throw some clothes on. Have your limo at the door in ten minutes. Tell the ambulance to go to the air park and get ready to transfer the patient to Angel One. Wheels up in thirty minutes or less. Gotta go, bye." Smacking Susan on the butt he said, "Get up, we've got to go to Chi-town now."

Al was waiting at the limo door with a sack. "Bagels with a schmear, OJ and coffee. I think you just got another plane."

The ambulance was waiting when they arrived. Mike started the APS and then exited while Susan supervised the transfer of the patient from the ambulance to Angel One.

Mike went to settle for fuel and parking. The cashier stopped him, saying," The Mirage said this was on them. I took the liberty of getting a weather report for you; here it is."

"Thank you. What is your name?" "Kathlene Kely with one L."
"I'll be in touch."

Mike made his walk-around inspection and got on board. "Welcome to Angel One." We will be taking off immediately so make sure your seat belt is securely fastened. The lady in jeans is a very capable and qualified nurse. Your wife could not be in better hands. What is your name, sir?"

"Bill Goldsbery, and that lady with the tubes stuck in her is my wife of 50 years. This was our anniversary."

"Try to relax, Bill. We will be at Chicago's Midway airport in three and a half hours. The hospital chopper will be waiting for us so there will be very little time lost. Nurse, I need you up front."

Susan closed and locked the cabin door and took her place in the co-pilot's seat. She went through the check off list and soon had both engines up and running. The wheel chocks were pulled and she called ground control for taxi clearance. "Angel One, requesting priority one clearance. We have a medical emergency on board."

"Roger, Angel One. You have priority. The rest of you just sit and let her go by."

"Angel One. This is the tower. There is a United 707 on approach. As soon as he clears, you are cleared for take off."

"Roger, tower. Thanks for all your help."

The 707 touched down and Susan waited until it was in the clear. Then she checked again, turned onto the runway, lined up, and eased the throttles forward. "Angel One rolling," she announced. At 175mph, she eased back on the yoke and started skyward.

"Listen to what I'm going to say, then execute," said Mike. "You are going to turn and bank to the left until your compass reads 15 degrees. Ease down on your left rudder pedal; at the same time turn the control to the left a little. The rudder will swing the tail around and get you pointed in the right direction, but you will be skidding like a car on ice. When you drop the wing, you stop skidding. It takes practice and experience to coordinate the two moves, but you can and will do it. When the compass heading is what you want, return both controls to neutral. When you reach 21,000ft ease forward on the yoke and level out. That was well done, Susan. Getting us from the terminal to airborne was an A. Climbing turn and bank rates a B. A few more lessons and I'll be a passenger."

"I think not," Susan retorted. "If you have rested enough from last night so that you can take over, I'll get our coffee, OJ, and bagels."

Al Cimono wasn't cheap about his breakfast sack. A half gallon of coffee, a quart of OJ, six bagels with a schmear, and a half dozen donuts. Susan give Mr. Goldsberry coffee, OJ, two donuts, and a bagel. She showed him where the restroom was and took Mrs. Goldsberry's vitals. After assuring her husband everything was okay, she retreated to the cabin with her sack of breakfast goodies.

"Everything is okay back there. I'll set up breakfast."

"Good plan," Mike said as he switched on the auto pilot. "We've picked up a nice tail wind which will cut some time off. There is a front moving toward Chicago so we may get wet before this is over."

Just over Des Moines, Mike saw the clouds and lightning ahead of him. He called air traffic approach for landing instructions.

"Angel One. The weather here is getting worse as the minutes wear on. You are priority one to Midway. We have you on the scope and will bring you in on radar, until you have visual."

"Roger, Traffic Control. Starting my descent now. Susan go back and secure the Goldsberrys and stay with them. Make sure everything is tied down, locked up, and put away. Then sit down and strap yourself in. We are going to experience considerable turbulence and buffeting and hit some down drafts but it is nothing to be afraid of. It will be scary but not really dangerous."

"Angel One. This is Midway Tower. There will be an escort vehicle waiting for you. You will taxi to Delta gate 6. Can you transport a family of three to Cheyenne? The patient, a 40-year-old man had transplant surgery and was just released. His wife and teenage daughter are with him."

"Can do, Tower. Have them ready to board as soon as we get our patient off loaded. I want to get out of here as fast as possible. I'm going to refuel in Omaha."

"The hospital Med-fly is grounded due to weather, but their ambulance is here with a police escort. Our radar says you are 15 minutes out and right on glide path."

"Thanks, tower. I'm going to be busy with the bird so you just keep me out of trouble."

"On glide path, 5 minutes out. You should have visual any second now."

"I have you visual, Midway."

The escort was waiting with its orange light flashing. Mike fell in behind him and was soon at Delta 6. It was raining hard. The medics brought tarps to keep Mrs. Goldsberry dry. Susan pressed some cash into Mr. Goldsberry's hand along with a business card. "If you need anything call us please."

"Okay."

Susan took him by the arm, turned him around, and gave a kiss on the cheek. "Promise you will call, to at least let us know. We were married yesterday so we have the same anniversary date. We will meet you in Vegas next year."

CHAPTER 54

A tall wide-shouldered man in a black Stetson boarded followed by two women that looked more like sisters than mother and daughter. Susan secured the door. Mke had already fired up the engines.

"Would you like to lie down on the gurney, sir?"

"Ma'am, my name is John Bodie. I've been flat on my back long enough. If you don't mind, I'll just sit here and stretch my legs out."

"That's fine with me sir." Please fasten your seat belts and keep them fastened until we get the okay from the captain. We are going to encounter some severe turbulance before we get above this storm front. You two ladies look so much alike a person would be hard put to be certain which was the mother, but since you have a wedding band and she doesn't, I'm sure you're the mother."

"Thank you for the compliment. I'm Virginia Bodie and this is our daughter Laramie."

Mike had started to roll, so Susan went forward and took the co-pilot's seat.

"We're good to go. There are no inbounds and we are the only one on the ground ready. Midway Tower, double check your scope for another aircraft on approach. I can't see any, but that don't mean they're not there."

"Roger, Angel One. Not a creature is stirring, now get out of here."

"Angel rolling," Mike announced. "We're going to test these engines by climbing a lot steeper than normal, to get above this mess as soon as possible."

The Gulf Stream and the Rolls Royce engines were a perfect match for each other. In just a matter of minutes, they were above the storm and into a bright blue sky. Looking down they could see lightning flashes. The storm was breaking up and had just passed Peoria.

"You can unfasten your seat belts now. We will be landing in Omaha to refuel in an hour," Mike announced. "If there is any coffee left, I would like to have a cup."

"I'm sure there is. I'll get it for you."

As she passed Ray, he asked her if he could sit up with the captain.

"I'll ask him when I take his coffee to him."

"It's okay with me," Mike said to Ray. "You might sit in the front seat just in case, and keep that thermos of coffee handy."

"I'm Ray Bodie, Captain," he said as he seated himself in the co-pilot's seat. He scanned the instruments with a practiced eye. "You seem to have all the bells and whistles. This Gulf Stream is one sweet bird. What do you have under the hood. She went upstairs like a homesick Angel."

"You do know something about airplanes, Ray. I'm Mike Murphy. I've been flying since I was sixteen. Went to Pensacola where I learned to fly jets. Landing in that storm was a piece of cake compared to an aircraft carrier at night in 16 ft seas.

"I was an air Force pilot. Had a tour in Nam and then went home to raise cattle. God and I built a 15,000 acre spread where I raise Angus cattle. I've got somewhere between 800 and 1,000 head. My daughter, Laramie, has leased some land next to mine. I gave her ten heifer calves and a bull calf I bought from a neighbor. That was five years ago. She sells the calves and is learning the cow business from the ground up. The only help she got from me was the ten heifers and the bull. She is determined to pay her own way through veterinary school and is working hard and saving all she can. She does artificial insemination she learned from our vet,

Doc Eckert, and has the reputation of being one of the best around. Would you trust me to land this bird in Omaha?"

"You seem to know what you are doing so take over. It's your airpane. When you call air traffic, we are Angel One."

Ray took the yoke and broke out with a smile. "This is what I'm going to miss the most. The FAA lifted my ticket because of my heart, so I'm grounded."

"The FAA is pretty strict about some things and maybe for good reasons. You could be second seat with me anytime. I'm supposed to have a co-pilot when I have passengers so Susan sits there. She is learning the routine from checklist to wheels up and does a little flying. I hope to have her ticketed before we have an unexpected inspection. I have fought for this country for ten years but have since learned that to our senators and congressmen, we're just not important enough to spend any extra money on. Unless, of course, it fattens the wallet of one of their buddies, who would drop a hundred Gs or so for their campaign so they can continue to screw the public. We, the people, could legally overthrow the government every two years by voting out all the congressmen and one-third of the Senate, but we don't. It seems when the people have to make a choice between a screwing or the unknown they would rather be screwed. I only answer the question. I never volunteer information. If they asked me if you were qualified to fly this aircraft, I would say, yes. They would have to ask me specifically about your ticket. I hope what I just said doesn't offend you, but you opened a door I can't help but walk through."

"Mike my friend, you and I are on the same page. "Fasten your seat belts ladies. We are about to land in Omaha," Ray announced.

"We can all walk away from the aircraft, so it was a good landing," Mike laughed. "Taxi over to Sky Harbor. We'll fuel and use the restrooms."

"Michael, we're hungry. Can we get some lunch?"

"We are only an hour or so away from our spread, Virginia said. "We could have a steak, and if you folks wanted to, you could bunk with us tonight."

"How far is the airport from your spread?" Mike asked.

"I've got a 7000 ft concrete strip on my spread. We can taxi right to the house."

"Let's get some milk and donuts," Laramie suggested, "and build an appetite for a slab of Angus."

"Now that's what I call a plan," Mike stated.

An hour later, Ray was approaching his spread. "Okay, Navy. Show me a Navy landing," he said taking his hands off the yoke. "It's your airplane."

It was one of Mike's best landings. The strip was glass-smooth. The only indication they were on the ground was the scream of protest from the landing gear. Mike smiled in satisfaction.

"That was not a carrier-type landing, Ray, that's so the patient on the gurney isn't bounced around more than necessary. I've never had a runway as smooth as this. What is your base?"

"Sherman Hill granite, concrete, and a lot of sweat, and worth every bit. You must be just about out of hours by now, if you started in Vegas. Why not bunk here tonight? You can park in the hangar next to the house. There's plenty of room"

"If it wouldn't be any bother, we'll take you up on it," Susan answered

"No bother, Susan. We don't get much company out here, and it will be nice to have somebody to visit with, rather than watch disgusting TV," Virginia said.

Ray opened the hangar doors and got the mule to put Angel One away. There was a sky blue Cessna 310J sitting off to one side. Ray parked Angel One in front for easy access.

"That's a nice looking bird, Ray. Now that they've lifted your ticket what are you going to do with it?"

"Up until today, I hadn't given much thought to it. Virginia has been on my back about getting rid of it for some time. I was planning on trading it in on a Lear. That's why I put so much runway in, but since my ticket is gone, that plan is out the window."

The ringing of the dinner bell diverted their attention. "Dinner is ready," Laramie announced.

"That is R Bar A beef," Virginia said. "You can only get it here. We raise it here, butcher it here, age it here, and eat it here. R Bar A is Ray's Bar Angus."

"A good steak with a baked spud, salad, a nice wine, good coffee, and good friends. Life doesn't get better than this," Ray said. "Out here people are few and you learn to make friends quick."

"We don't invite just anyone to bunk with us," Virginia said. "Nor do we turn anyone away without them being fed. On occasion, a hunter will get snowbound or lost and find their way here and we take them in. That's what Jesus told us to do, so we are just obeying orders."

"Mike, would you have any use for that Cessna you saw out there?" Ray asked.

"It would be nice to have a plane big enough for family and luggage. How much do you want for it?"

"I was figuring on giving it to Angel Flight. You don't need a semi to haul a bale of hay. There are times you need to get somewhere that can't accommodate a jet, so that little Cessna would fit like a turd in the snow."

"I'll accept it on behalf of the corporation and give you a receipt for it. How much is it worth?"

"I don't rightly know Mike, somewhere around a hundred and a quarter. It's all fueled up and ready to go. Why not take a test drive in the morning?"

"That will be fine with me. Are you sure you want to do this, Ray? It's a very generous gift."

"From what I know about Angel Flight and what you folks are giving, what I'm doing is a drop in the bucket. Let's take our coffee out on the porch."

It was a moonless night. The stars seemed just barely out of reach, and a warm zephyr from the southwest was keeping the insects away. In the distance, a coyote howled and a mama cow called her calf.

"We are remote," Laramie said, "but the little time I spent in Chicago told me I could never live in a city. We have three big dogs that are free to run. They are not pampered pets but working pets. They keep the predators at bay. The only things I have to worry about are snakes, and they warn you before they strike. Any man I hook up with is going to have to love this solitude or our relationship won't work. I may have my mother's looks but I've got Daddy's bullheadedness."

"Just listen to the sound of nature," Virginia said. "You can't hear a car or truck unless they are coming here. The planes are so high you can barely hear them. The only sound is the sound of nature which, I think is the voice of God."

"The Southern folks talk about Southern hospitality. You folks don't talk about it, you demonstrate it," Susan said.

"Out here it is a necessity. You never know when you are going to need help or be asked to help somebody. You don't ask why, you just go and do what is needed. A cattleman will help a sheepman and vice versa without the publicity you would get in the East. It's just the neighborly thing to do," Ray stated. "We know, personally, everyone in a fifty mile radius from here. There aren't that many neighbors, but people in the city most often know the one next door or across the street. Maybe that's why the crime rate is so high in the cities, they don't watch out for each other. Out here we have to because our law officers are spread too thin.

A few years back my neighbor, Bill Hughes, east of here about ten miles, came home and found his door open, the freezer gone, and a calf they were going to butcher missing. We knew who didn't do it and we narrowed it down to two suspects. The first had an alibi. Bill and the Sheriff called on the second suspect and found the remains of the calf in a ditch and in the freezer on the porch. They found a man who had lost his job and couldn't feed his family, so Bill gave him the freezer and asked him if he had a dollar to pay for the calf. The man broke down and said all he had was a dime. Bill said since he didn't have to butcher the calf, a dime was good enough. Bill hired the man on the spot and moved him and his family to a house he had on his place that needed a family and some work. He is now a top hand and Bill's ranch foreman. He and his wife cleaned the house, fixed it up, and have four of the best behaved kids you will ever see. All he needed was a chance and a job. Going to jail would have put his wife on welfare and hardened him. With a record, he would have a hard time finding a job and would end up doing the same thing. All that time, taxpayers would be footing the bill. It cost Hughes a calf, a freezer, and maybe $200 in food. Look what his return is on his investment; a damn good man that everyone, including me, has tried to hire. He just says no. It's not the money, it's the family that took him in. We all benefited. We have one more honest hard-working man to call on. That is just doing what our Lord commanded we do. Who do you think felt better for it - Bill or his new hand?"

"Ray," Susan said, "I know I speak for Michael when I say we are so glad to know you and your family. It is amazing how close our philosophies are. We don't have the extensive view you have but we do have the voice of God, as you put it, and Mount Hood. We have a cougar and the bubbling river for our night song. If I can use your phone, I need to call dispatch and home so our children will know where we are. Then I would like to shower and go to bed. I'm suddenly very tired."

Virginia led Susan to the den where she could make her phone calls in private.

"I'll get your room ready, and lay out fresh towels," she said, closing the door.

Ray and Mike did some hangar flying then decided to turn in. Laying in bed with a warm breeze and listening to God's voice, they soon were in a deep, peaceful sleep.

The sun was well up in the eastern sky before Mike nudged Susan awake. "I guess we were more tired than we thought. I'm going to have a wake-up shower and shave before I have breakfast, or lunch - whatever is on the menu."

"While you are doing that, I'll pack our bags and get your clothes laid out. I'll join you after I dress."

There was a note on the table under a coffee cup. "We are choring. Help yourself to whatever you want. Juice, fresh eggs, bacon, sausage, and hash browns in the fridge, bread in the drawer under the toaster. See you later."

Mike and Susan had just finished doing up the dishes, when Ray and Virginia came in.

"You didn't have to to do the dishes," Virginia said.

"That's why we did them," Mike countered. "I can't remember when I've slept so well and for so long."

"You two were really snoring when I walked by at 6:30," Virginia said.

"And still going strong at 7:00," Ray laughed.

"Let's take a test drive," Mike said. "Do you want to go, Susan?"

"No. I think I would like to just sit and get to know my new sister and niece, if they have no objections," Susan answered.

"Auntie Susan," Laramie said, "I would like that a lot." "So would I," echoed Virginia.

Ray and Mike rolled the Cessna out. Mike admonished Ray to be careful because of his recent surgery.

Mike walked around inspecting everything. He checked the oil and fuel levels, then went back to look at the floor where the Cessna had been sitting - searching for any signs of oil or hydraulic fluid that might have leaked. Finding none, he climbed in and fastened his seat belt. He found the checklist and carefully went through it.

"Well, now all I have to do is figure out how to get this thing off the ground," Mike laughed. The twin Continentals whined and sputtered into life. Mike waited until the engines were thoroughly warmed up before committing to flight. In the thin air at that altitude, Mike allowed plenty of room to gain airspeed. When the wheels were up, he asked Ray, "Is there any place you want to go, or shall we just bore holes in the sky?"

"Just bore some holes, Mike. You are a cautious airplane driver."

"Just as you would be if you were not familiar with the aircraft. This is a sweet flying bird Ray, and just the right size, great for commuting."

It was a day meant for relaxing. Mike and Susan had been under stress for several days, and a chance to take it easy for a day didn't come very often. They flew over Denver and noted how it all but disappeared in the polution.

"I don't see how you can call it progress when you can't breathe the air or drink the water or eat the fish," Ray commented.

"Man will destroy the earth; God will destroy the worldly. That's the way I've got it figured."

Back at the R Bar A, Susan was talking to Carl on the phone. "I rode Scout today and he didn't even buck. Lizzie and Marie are playing with dolls Faun made for them just like the Indians did long ago. Grandpa Bear made bows for Robbie and me. We're going to hunt for stuff to make arrows out of after lunch. Grandpa Murphy and Mr. Henderson went fishing and they each caught a big sturgeon. We're going to have them for supper tonight. Momma, me and Marie are so glad you are going to marry Dad. We are so happy and having so much fun. We love Dad. Tomorrow, Bear and me are going to town for some horse feed. When are you coming home?"

"We will be home late tomorrow evening. Around eight o'clock. We love you two and I'm glad I'm going to marry Michael. Say hello to everybody for me and let me talk to Marie."

"Hello, Marie. We miss you children a lot and we'll be home tomorrow. Bye."

CHAPTER 55

Bear loaded Carl and Robbie into the pickup and headed for Wasco County Co-op to get feed for the horses. "They have plenty of grass," he said, "but they need grain too. Not a lot, just a little every day."

Bear backed up to the loading dock and went inside followed by two very curious boys. Bear inquired about the quality of the various products. He decided to have Wally Mathis, the manager, custom mix and bag 200 lbs.

"We're going to Mary's for coffee and soda," Bear said. "We'll be back later to pick it up."

Wally spoke to a short, stocky, Latino man with a beard and sunglasses. He had a bandana on his head and a Notre Dame sweatshirt over a pair of dirty, ill-fitting jeans. "Ray", he said, "get the two-wheeler and bring those five bags of mix and dump them in this hopper."

Ray was not the most ambitious person in the world to begin with, and 100 lb sacks of grain were a strain for him, but he needed the money and this was the only job he could find, so he took it.

Bear sat across from his son and introduced Robbie to "My Son, the Police Chief."

Pride showed itself in every word. "How's it going, Pop?"

"This brave little man has already got two of his ponies broke to ride and will soon have the other two ready. If I didn't know better, I would swear he is pure Shoshone, the way he and his ponies connect."

Carl could hardly contain the pleasure of hearing such words about himself.

"Carl," Hawk said, "your dad is my best friend. I know how much he loves you and Marie and your mother. If anyone ever tries to do any harm to one of you, they will answer to me."

"And me," Bear interrupted. "In Shoshone justice. We just came in to get feed for the ponies, Son. Come out when you have a chance. Your mother and I miss you."

The feed was on the dock. Ray was sitting on some pallets catching his breath, when Bear backed in for loading. He went inside to pay Wally, while Ray struggled to load the feed. Ray saw Carl and opened the door of the truck to pull him out. Of course, Carl screamed in protest that drew Bear's attention. Ray had spent all of his life as a parasite, sucking a living off anybody he could. His soft flabby body was 5 ft. 6 in. tall, at 275 pounds.

Bear had spent his entire life working to make a living for his family. He stood 6 ft. 3 in. from the soles of his moccasins to the top of his head. With a small waist and massive shoulders, he weighed in at 250 pounds of bone and gristle. He had developed a huge chest by trying to break rawhide with chest expansion flexes.

Placing a big hand on Ray's shoulder, and spinning him around, he demanded in a calm clear voice, "Who are you? What are you trying to do to my grandson?"

"I'm his father. He and his sister were stolen from me, and I'm going to take them back to Cuba with me."

"You may have been the sperm donor but you never have been a father," Bear retorted. "A father doesn't treat his children the way you treated Carl and his sister. If you want to take this up with Carl's mother and dad they will be landing at eight o'clock tonight. In the meantime hear me, and hear me well. If any harm comes to any one of the four, even an ingrown toenail, anything at all, it is the custom of my people to take the scalp of our enemies. Your scalp will hang from my lodge pole and the wild creatures of the forest shall dine on what's left of you. Is there anything you don't understand? You are a stranger on my land. Get off my land."

It was impossible to hide the hate in Ramon's eyes and face. He slithered away thinking to himself, *"They land at eight o'clock; by nine they will both be dead. Then we will see who is Poppa."*

"Sorry about running off your hired hand, Wally."

"No big loss, Bear. He just couldn't cut the mustard. I was about to fire him any way."

Carl, visibly shaken by the encounter, sat between Robbie and Bear. Bear felt Carl shivering, put his arm around him and drew him up close.

"Don't worry about him, Brave Little Man. I'll alert the council and he will be watched. My son wants to arrest him for murder but won't until he has positive proof. He doesn't want to take a chance on some silver-tongued lawyer getting him off. When Hawk wants him, we will know exactly where he is. I will teach both you boys to move as silently as a cloud, and how to be so still, deer will eat at your feet. I never had the time to teach my son Shoshone ways and have often been sorry about it. He was more interested in the Paleface ways. When I have taught you all the Shoshone culture and customs you will be able to survive in the wilderness, living off the land. It is not easy but it can be done. Next summer when school is out and you are Shoshone, we will go into the wilderness and survive. You will do it all. I will be there in case of an emergency. We will not discuss what happened at the co-op. No need to worry anyone."

"I think the only one who should worry is that man back there," Robbie commented.

"When you get used to riding, Robbie, you and Carl could learn to team rope."

"What's team rope Grandpa?"

"It's where two cowboys rope the same calf at the same time. One throws a loop over the head and the other catches the hind legs at the same time. It's a timed event. They award trophies and cash to the winners. It takes a lot of practice and hard work. You have to teach your pony what to do. He is part of the team. A good pony makes the difference between cash money or going home broke. We will go to the Pendleton Roundup this summer and you can see what I'm talking about."

"Are you going to make us Shoshone or cowboys?" Carl asked.

"Shoshone cowboys. You will fear no man. You will respect others, especially your elders. You will walk with pride, but not proudly. You will know the joys of hard work and enjoy the rewards that come with it. You will not speak with forked tongue. If you work for a man, you will give him the best that you have. Get to work early and be prepared to work. Do the little extras like empty the trash or sweep the floor, restack bags, whatever you see that needs to be done and do it cheerfully. Your reward will be the good feeling on your insides. That is a reward money can't buy. Your employer may pay you extra but don't do it for the money,. Do it because it needs to be done. When you do those things you earn the respect of others, and that is another thing money can't buy. I'm sure you don't fully understand what I'm saying because of your young age, but it is in your mind and will emerge as you grow older."

Ramon grabbed his coat and hat and slithered into the alleys and back streets to his lair, under the old docks at the port of The Dalles. He was still seething. *"Who was that big Indian to tell me to get off his land? I did learn that the bitch and her lover are arriving at eight o'clock tonight though,"* he said to himself. *"I'll be waiting for them and they won't know what hit them. Then, I'll grab those brats and go back to Cuba and if that Indian gets in my way, and I hope he does, I'll kill him too."* He opened a can of baked beans he had stolen from the Safeway store and washed them down with a half cup of cold coffee left from his breakfast. After eating, he decided to take a nap. He had a lot to do later and needed to get his rest.

The sun was dropping behind the Cascades when he woke up. He had a strange feeling that he wasn't alone but couldn't see or hear anything, only the rats scurrying around in their endless quest for food. Back in the shadows, as still as death, stood one of the council men. He had the loaded clip of a Baretta in his hand, plus one round that was ejected from the gun. He substituted an empty clip for the one he had.

Ramon, again using alleys and back streets, found his way to his buxom blonde and demanded the keys to her Hummer. When she refused, he pulled his gun. He was about to shoot her when he realized the noise would bring a crowd, so he slapped her across the face with it and knocked her unconscious. Stealing her keys, he said, "I'll be back to deal with you later, bitch."

It was coming up on eight o'clock and he had to hurry to get in position to carry out his plan. The Hummer is a large vehicle and the short, fat Cuban was having difficulty maneuvering it. Plus he was driving pretty fast. The airport came in sight, so he shut off the car lights. The county had done some road work so when Ramon turned onto the airport road he didn't see the pile of gravel. The Hummer swerved and crashed into the power pole causing the feed into the airport to dislodge. The sign saying, "Danger 7500kv," stared him in the face. He shuddered at the thought of electrocution but since the line was down he would use it to pull himself out of the car. He thought he heard the jet coming in, so swinging over the ditch and steadying himself with the transmission line, he was working on plan B.

"Gear down and locked," Susan reported. "Punch the remote and turn on the lights."

There was a brief flash, up near the power pole when the lights went on.

They landed without incident and put Angel One in the hangar.

"It's good to be home," Susan said. "I didn't think much of the three mile high club initiation ceremony. I prefer the ground zero club."

"Maybe it was me. That's the first initiation ceremony I"ve ever conducted."

"I've been initiated, but I don't think I'm going to any meetings," Susan laughed. "And you are not going to conduct any more initiation ceremonies."

The new road to the new terminal building and office space was now opened, and they didn't see where the flash came from.

Everybody was up and waiting to greet Susan and Mike. Marie came flying out of her room at the sound of Mike's voice and jumped into his arms.

"Hi, Daddy. I missed you, did you miss me?"

"You don't have any idea how much I missed you, especially the good-night kisses. I'm not used to this kind of homecoming, but I believe I can get used to it very quickly. Unless my sense of smell is all confused, I think I smell applesauce cookies."

"Your sense of smell is okay," Winnie said. I just took the last batch out of the oven when you walked through the door."

"Fresh applesauce cookies, cold milk, a loving family, and a circle of friends more like family THAN FRIENDS. IT JUST get any better," Mike said choking back a tear. "Thank You Lord."

"Walt! Do you have to get back right away or can you stay a while? I've got some things to discuss with you in regards to Angel Flight."

"We can stay just about as long as you can stand us, Mike. Margaret and I have retired, I think. Anyway Henderson Manufacturing is no longer my responsibility. I can sit in the sun and do nothing,

"If you can be comfortable in our camper, move in," Murph stated. "I would prefer to have it out here than in the storage lot. That way if Winnie and I want to get away, we can come here and antagonize Mike and Susan. And you would have a place to stay while you're in town."

"That sounds good to me Murph. Is that okay with you Margaret?"

"That sounds fine to me, but I'm not going to be treated like a guest and neither are you. You can cut grass and help Bear and I'll help Faun. You can still take time to fish, or whatever, and I can do needlework or read or whatever I please. Lizzie can run and play with Marie and enjoy fresh air and grass and trees. She doesn't have those things in Portland because of the pollution. We have to fertilize the yard, and it smells of chemicals. Out here there is no pollution. The air is fresh, the water cold and safe to drink.

I'dbetter shut up or I'll talk myself out of going back to Portland at all."

"Murph, it sounds like Margaret is considering your offer," Walt laughed.

Murph and Winnie moved their belongings from the camper to their car, while Walt, Margaret, and Mike moved the Hendersons into the camper. Murph and Winnie left for home. Margaret and Susan made up the bed and got the Hendersons settled in. The children were all in bed asleep, leaving Mike and Susan alone on the patio.

"This past week has been very eventful," Susan commented.

"Yes it has. Would you like a glass of wine?"

"Indeed I would. Are you willing to take a chance? You know what happens when we have wine at bed time."

"I'm counting on it. As a matter of fact, I'm going to be sure we have plenty of wine on hand. I want to get back to ground zero."

The pine-scented soft breeze wafted over the sleeping lovers while the cougar screamed, the owl hooted, and the river gurgled and splashed on its way to the Pacific.

CHAPTER 56

Awakening to Susan singing softly in the kitchen and smelling fresh coffee brewing, Mike closed his eyes in prayer, "Father God, Brother Jesus, I don't know how You determined I should be so blessed with such a beautiful and loving wife and the children she brought with her. I thought this much happiness was only written about, never really lived. I thank You for Your grace. Amen."

He presented himself to Susan showered, shaved, and dressed - ready to take on the world. Taking her in his arms and kissing her tenderly on the lips, he whispered, "I love you so much. I'm going to have my regular shootout with Hawk this morning, then go see Red and tell him about our new Cessna. I'll also let him know we are going to be getting two or more planes for Angel Flight. This thing is coming together faster than I thought it would. We need to recruit pilot and nurse teams. Think about what would be the most effective way to advertise. There are not a lot of people with the qualifications we need that are looking for work."

"Michael darling, after a good-morning greeting like that, how could I say anything but yes. It is amazing what a glass of wine at bedtime does. More couples ought to try it. I'm going to shop for bunk beds for our cowboys. I'll meet you and Hawk for lunch."

"Good morning my brother," Hawk said. "Are you ready to get beat and buy lunch?"

"I'm ready to shoot and let the chips fall where they may. Let's get 'er done."

Hawk was perfect; Mike lost by the slimmest of margins. As they were leaving, Miss Johnson handed Hawk a large manila envelope.

"You will find this very interesting" she said. "You also, Mr. Murphy."

Hawk glanced at the report on top and put it back in the envelope.

"Where's Susan?" he asked

"She's meeting us for lunch."

Susan was waiting for them in Hawk's booth.

"Before we order lunch." Hawk said, "I have some good news and I have some great news. Which do you want first?"

"You got the report; you tell it like it is," Susan responded. "Okay, first the good news. We found Ramon. Not that we didn't know where he was. He was driving that big Hummer and skidded into your power pole knocking your feed line down. For some reason he grabbed hold of it and took 7500kv and electrifRied himself. His watch stopped at eight o'clock so we figure that was the time of death. The mystery is, what he was doing out there at that time of night with an empty gun. Now the good news. Finding him and checking ballistics solved Aggie's murder so that case is completely closed and the transient we found shot was shot with the same gun. And last, but not least, the mystery of stolen clothes from the clothesline is solved. He was wearing a Notre Dame sweatshirt. And now I don't have much of anything on my plate, so I'm going to visit Mom and Pop."

"I think we should have a thanksgiving picnic," Susan said, "not one with turkey and dressing but one with burgers and franks, and baked beans, etc. That kind of dinner. Let's do it Sunday. You will be the guest of honor Hawk, for what you have done for us. Bring your wife, and as many in the department that can come. We will have a real celebration."

"My wife and I will be there and I'll ask the sheriff if he will put some extra people on to keep the peace. I can cover the cost of the sheriff's patrol from my contingency fund."

"Since you beat me fair and square, I'll buy lunch," Mike said. "You should have seen him shoot. He was perfect. We're getting too close to each other's level; maybe we should use smaller-sized targets."

"We'll talk about that later, but for now, I want a pork tenderloin sandwich on wheat bread, fries and sweet tea."

Lunch was over and the trio were just catching up with each other when Ramon's busty blonde came in and walked up to the chief. Her face was swollen; it was obvious she had been crying. "Sir," she said through swollen lips. "I want to report my car being stolen and that I have been pistol whipped. The guilty party is Ray Romaine. I want to file charges against that Cuban bastard."

Hawk moved over and invited her to sit down. "This is Mike Murphy and this is Susan Romaine Murphy, the ex-wife of the accused. You tell me all you know. These folks will attest to the facts as you relate them, in the event any charges are pending against you. Officially I can say I don't know of any, so start anywhere you like. Would you like something to eat?"

"My mouth is so sore I don't think I can chew, but a bowl of chili and a large glass of cold milk sounds good. Thank you," she said. "My name is Rose Mary Nugent. I want to be fingerprinted and a search of my background done. To the best of my knowledge I have no wants or warrants on me, but I have been strung out on drugs for so long I'm not sure of anything. I've reached the bottom of the barrel and the only way out is up or die. I've got to attone for the bad things I've done. I'm on my seventh day free from drugs. I've put myself through hell, and I want to help in any way I can to stop anyone from going down that path."

"Rose, we found your Hummer early this morning," the chief explained. "Ramon lost control and knocked down a power pole, out by the airport. He grabbed hold of the feed line and was electrocuted. Your Hummer needs some front end work to make it driveable. Your insurance should cover most of it."

"All I have is liability. Is there someplace I could leave it until I find a job and get it fixed?"

"We can put it in our impound lot. I'll waive the fees, as long as you are working on getting it fixed. In the meantime, I'll have to take you into custody until we finish our investigation. You were seen with Ramon, so until you are cleared you will be a guest of the city. We have a clean jail, where you can shower in private. I will make you as comfortable as possible under the circumstances."

"That's more than I expected."

"I'll get you some clothes and underwear and personal items, Susan said. "What size shoe do you wear?"

"Size seven, but these shoes are okay."

"You're starting fresh so you are going to be a new person with new clothes," Susan answered. "In the very early days, when a person was baptized they were held under water until they almost drowned, symbolizing a new birth. They were then given new clothes and all their sins and debts were forgiven. That's what is happening to you, except for the drowning. Just imagine when you are showering, that you are washing away all your sins and debts and are a new person. We've got to go. I'll bring your clothes to the jail and will talk to you later."

Susan finished her shopping and left the items she bought for Rose at the jail and drove to the ranch. Mike went to the office of Mike Murphy and Sons to tell Julie and Murph the good news about Susan being cleared beyond any doubt, in Aggie's murder.

"The transfer switch didn't work," he told Murph. "Call the electrical contractor and tell him, so he can get it replaced. He has the replacement on order and maybe by now it's in. That's what fried Ramon. He grabbed the loose feed line, the generator kicked in and sent 7500kv back up the line. When Ramon grabbed the wire he completed the circuit. End of story."

He stopped at the Plantarium to check on Aggie's prized rose bush. The proprietor told him the rose showed good signs but he would like to keep it a day or two longer.

"Could I pick it up late tomorrow or early Saturday?"

"Early Saturday would be the best. I open at seven a.m., so anytime after that will be fine."

Mike drove into the garage a little after five. He opened the door to the kitchen and was greeted with the aromas of home; fresh coffee and supper cooking. There was no way to put in words what that does to a man. Susan greeted him with a loving I'm-so-glad-you're-home kiss and a cup of fresh brewed coffee.

"Supper at six. If you like, you have time to shower before we eat. We need to plan the celebration festivities sometime today. We don't have much time."

"Let's do it after supper. Have you told Carl and Marie about their father?"

"No, I haven't and was wondering if I should," Susan answered. "They never mention him. I think it's best not to tell them now. Let them think he's back in Cuba. When they do ask about him I'll just tell them he died."

After supper Mike and Susan sat at the kitchen table and worked out plans for their celebration. Susan worked on the menu while Mike prepared the guest list.

"You'd better start calling now so people can make arrangements to come. This is a spur-of-the-moment event so it'll catch every one off guard."

Mike called Ray Bodie. "Ray, Susan and I are having a celebration bash on Sunday and want you, Virginia and Laramie to help us celebrate. I'll come and get you and bring my chief mechanic, Red along to fly the Cessna back."

"We will be pleased to come Mike. I've got a side of Angus just looking for a place to barbeque. It'll take some time to cook. You should start it Saturday." However we have to be here Saturday morning. Laramie sold some calves and they're going to load up Saturday morning around seven a.m. Your mechanic can stay the night on Friday and fly us back in the Cessna on Saturday. Kind of a farewell flight. I'm going to miss her, but knowing it's for a good cause, and that she'll be in your hands makes it easier to let go."

"That'll work. We'll be there tomorrow around noon. That will give me time to get back and get the barbeque set up. Thanks for the beef. See you tomorrow. Bye."

Mike called Red and told him of the plans and asked if he and Yale could bring the Cessna home.

"And how can I say no, to an offer to bore holes in the sky with such a fine flying machine I ask. You did say it's a 310-J," Red said.

"Yes, that's what I said. Is nine a.m. too early for you and Yale?"

"Nine a.m. is just fine, me boy. See you then. Bye."

Mike called Julie, Hawk, Bubb, Bob Koch and everybody else he could think of.

"Susan! here's the list of those I've called. If I have forgotten anyone, write the name down and I'll call them tomorrow or Saturday. The Bodie's are giving us a side of beef for barbeque and I have to get it tomorrow. I'm taking Red and Yale with me. Red will fly them back Saturday. I'm tired. I'm going to bed."

"Me too. I don't think I need any wine tonight, but if you want a glass it's okay with me."

"Believe it or not, as good as that glass of wine tastes, I think I'll take a rain check on it."

"You can redeem your rain check any time sweetheart, just any time you want."

When Mike got to the airport, Red and Yale had already loaded their gear on board and had the APU up and running.

"I've got the weather report, Red said. "It looks like a fine day to bore holes in the sky."

"Then let's do it," Mike replied. "Who wants to ride shotgun?"

"Let Yale do it, boss. He's got a few hours in the piper and is a quick learner. I think he's a natural. Good coordination and a lot of common sense."

"Okay, Yale," Mike said, "it's time to get your feet wet. You make the walk-around inspection. I'm only going to observe. When you are finished, we'll board and then I will critique your inspection. Relax and don't be intimidated, just do what feels right."

Mike followed Yale, watching CAREFULLY NOTING THAT everything was as it should be. Then he pulled the chocks and stowed them away. He waited for Mike to board, then closed and secured the door. Yale took his seat in the co-pilot's spot and adjusted the seat to accommodate his long legs, then fastened his seat belt.

"Yale, that was letter perfect. I can't find one thing you missed. Red is right - you are a quick learner. Get the preflight checklist and go over it very carefully. It is written out so you don't forget anything. You must rely on training and instincts, not memory.

While I was in flight school there was a film of a Marine F4U Corsair taking off the deck of a carrier with his wings still folded. Of course, he crashed when he turned. He forgot. Can you imagine forgetting something as important and basic as being certain you've got wings before you fly? That's what I mean about training, instincts and memory. When I go over a checklist I touch each gauge and dial as I go through it, that way I know everything is as it should be. When you have finished the checklist, shut down the APU and start the engines. The door is on the starboard side and I like to start the port engine first. It doesn't make any difference which you start first. When the first engine is running smoothly, and the instruments are reading normal, start number two."

Yale completed his checklist and commented, "There's a lot more stuff to check here than there is on the Piper. Both engines are up and running smooth; all instruments are reading normal. Now, what's next?"

"Release the brakes and taxi to the assigned runway. At most airports we fly out of there is a standard of communications. You will learn this by observation and common sense. When you are ready to leave the gate, you ask ground control for clearance to taxi. They will give you clearance and assign you a runway. When you get to the assigned runway, you call the control tower for take-off clearance. They will give you clearance and assign you a heading and altitude according to the flight plan you filed. You will be passed off to one controller or another until you are switched to the ATC (air traffic control) for the area you are in. It seems like a lot of passing off, but at the speeds of today's aircraft, it takes plenty of eyes to watch over us. The sky is big but it's getting crowded.

Put your hands on the yoke, and follow me while I get this thing off the ground."

It was 12:15 p.m. MST when Mike set down at the Bodie ranch. He introduced Ray to Red and Yale. Bill Hughes and his ranch foreman were there to help load the beef. It was wrapped in butcher paper and plastic so it wouldn't contaminate the passenger compartment.

"I've got time for a cup of coffee before I leave. Red and Yale are at your disposal, Ray. If you need an extra hand, use them."

"Laramie could use a hand with the loading tomorrow and maybe some help now, rounding up the strays," Ray said, winking at Mike.

Laramie came from the corral leading a buckskin gelding all saddled and ready for action. Yale's eyes were on Laramie but he tried to show an interest in her horse.

"That there is a real beauty," he said and turned crimson with embarrassment. "I can ride some and would sure like to help if I can. They say I'm a quick learner. If you tell me what to do, I'll try my best to get 'er done."

Laramie was using all the ploys only women know to rope in a Maverick.

"Let's go get you a mount. There's an Appaloosa stud that needs work. If you want to try him, we'll throw a saddle on him. He will probably object, so be prepared for a wild ride."

The Appy was reluctant from the very beginning, but after a struggle he was saddled and ready. Laramie held the Appy's head while Yale eased into the stirrups. The fight was on. The Appy fishtailed, first in one direction then the other. He bucked and tried everything he could to dismount that stubborn rider. Finally, through a combination of exhaustion and resignation to the fact that the rider was a stayer, the Appy gave up and trotted to Laramie.

"You said you could ride some. I'd say that was some ride."

"I did do some rodeos. Saddle broncs and steer wrestling. That there Appy gave a good ride. What do you want me to do ma'am?"

"You can start by calling me Laramie, and I'll call you Yale. We need to find a few strays and get them drifting back to the ranch. Then we'll check the water holes."

"If it's all the same to you Laramie, I'd like to call you Amy. Laramie is too big a name for such a nice young girl, and besides it's the name of a city. I once knew a man called Paris because his last name was France, and his sister they named Florence. They were teased about their names. When Florence married, her teasing stopped, but Paris is still teased to this day.

"Okay, I'll be Amy and since college students are sometimes called Elys, I'd like to call you Ely."

"That suits me just fine. Amy and Ely."

They found seven strays bunched up in an arroyo with plenty of grass and water. It took a lot of coaxing, but they finally headed out for the ranch. By the time the last water hole was checked, the sun was disappearing behind the Rockies. It would be a moonless night, but the horses knew the way home so there was nothing to worry about. The stars began to show as darkness moved in. It was one of those nights when the stars seem just an inch too far away to touch.

Amy broke the silence. "I had no idea we would be so late. I'll bet you're starved. I'm sure hungry."

"I'm hungry that's for sure, Amy, but time has gone by so fast I never even noticed until you mentioned it."

"You are a good hand Ely. If you ever thought of doing ranch work, I'd hire you.

There is not much pay, the hours are long, and the work is hard. But at the end of the day, there is a satisfaction I don't think you can get anywhere else."

When they got back to the ranch Laramie said, "Ely, you tend to the horses and I'll rustle up some grub and meet you on the patio."

"That's a plan I can live with Amy."

Laramie had made sandwiches from leftover roast beef cut thick and laid on homemade wheat bread. She also served potato salad, cold milk and fresh apple pie.

They ate in silence, watching the stars and listening to the coyotes.

"I reckon this is what they meant, whoever wrote, "God's in his kingdom and all is right with the world," Ely opined. "We know there are a lot of bad things going on in the world, but at least in our little world right here, everything is all right."

CHAPTER 57

Virginia Bodie rang the dinner bell for breakfast at 6:30 a.m. "The day starts early and ends late out here. That was quite a show you put on yesterday Yale. How do you feel this morning?" "A little saddle sore and stiff from riding, but I'll work my way out of it Ma'am. Good morning Amy," he said as he rose to his feet.

"Good morning, Ely. Yale told me he likes the name Laramie but thinks it's too big a name for such a sweet young girl. He doesn't think people should be named after cities. He knows a man named Paris France who has a sister named Florence, so that's why he calls me Amy. I call him Ely because college students are sometimes called Elys.'"

"You two seemed to hit it off real good," Virginia responded. Amy excused herself and went outside to see what the weather was like.

Yale, continuing his conversation with Virginia said, "Yes Ma'am, we sure did. I've never met anyone like Lara... er, Amy, and would consider it an honor if you would accept me as her friend. Not a boyfriend, just a friend. I'm older than her and don't have much to offer, except an honest and true friendship."

"Ely or Yale. We would all consider it a privilege to count you as one of our friends. Laramie needs a friend to talk to about things she doesn't feel comfortable talking over with her father or me."

"Thank you Ma'am. I'd best get saddled up and get to work. Some of those critters carry a mean streak and will lay a hurtin' on you the first chance they get."

The loading was going as well as could be expected when dealing with animals that had free range all of their lives. Now, all of a sudden, somebody was telling them where to go and they just naturally rebelled. Laramie had dismounted to adjust her stirrups when one of the steers decided to show it's mean streak and went charging towards her. The gelding spooked and ran off, leaving her helpless with no place to go. Ray watched in helpless horror as the steer bore down on his daughter. Yale, seeing what was happening, spurred the stud and caught up with the steer. He left the saddle and grabbed the steer by the horns, his long legs stretched in front trying to stop the charging steer. His sneakers were not made for dogging so the steer was winning the contest. "Not today, you ornery cuss," he said. Using all of his 180 lbs., he twisted it's neck and flopped the steer on it's side a few feet from the terrified Laramie. Someone threw a loop around the steer and led it away.

"Good morning again, Amy," he said. "Fine day to load cattle, don't you think? I believe you lost your horse."

"Ely, I don't know what to say, except thank you. If you would bend down a little, I want to kiss you."

"Amy, that ain't necessary."

"Quit arguing and just do it," she snapped back.

Yale bent down and Laramie laid a kiss full on lips that said more than words. Not being used to this, Yale clumsily tried to return it. Laramie read the sign and squeezed his hand.

"Let's go fetch my horse and put our mounts away. The cattle are loaded and I've got some paperwork to fill out."

"You do the paperwork and I'll put the horses away. Then I'd like to shower and shave before we leave for The Dalles."

"Mom has towels and everything laid out for you. I'll see you later."

Virginia and Ray were having coffee with Red when Yale came into the house. Virginia threw her arms around Yale and hugged him. "Thank you for saving our little girl."

Yale looked down embarrassed at the attention, and said, "Shucks, Ma'am weren't nothin' special. I just done what had to be done."

Ray spoke up and said, "Yale, I've been around cattle all of my life and have seen bulldogging done by pros who train and practice daily. I have never seen it done in a life or death situation until today. You would be a top hand on any ranch you wanted to work on, including this one. I want to shake your hand and say thank you. You can hang your hat on our peg anytime. I saw Laramie thank you, and whatever happens between you two is perfectly okay with us."

Yale turned beet red and excused himself to clean up for the flight back.

Yale and Laramie sat in the back, Virginia and Ray in the center row, and Red sat in the driver's seat.

"Them continentals sure sound sweet," Red stated. "This is a nice bird, Yale. Work on your ticket so you can get qualified for multi-engines."

"I sure do like to fly. That's a fact, and I do want to qualify for multi-engines, but it's not on the top of my priority list. By the way, Red, what did you do while I was rounding up cattle and breaking broncs?"

"I just sat and rested and watched you. You are a credit to our clan and I'm proud of you. We've got better than four hours of flight time so relax. If you need a pit stop, let me know. I can set this bird down most any where."

Laramie leaned on Yale's shoulder and shyly took his hand and held it in her lap. She had a hero, and like Susan, felt safe and secure in her hero's presence.

After Mike's flight home, he topped off the fuel tanks and checked the fluid levels so Angel One would be ready to go. He put the side of beef in the back of the pickup and went to the office to see Julie and his Dad.

"Just the man I wanted to see. Howard and I are getting married and wondered if we could do it at your picnic. All our friends will be there and his sons will come."

"I think that's a great idea, Julie. Call Susan and get things started. There isn't much time to get ready."

"I've been getting ready since Howard took me to the ball game. I've got my wedding dress and everything. Look at my engagement ring."

"That's a nice rock."

"Howard bought a really big diamond, but I told him a smaller one would suit me fine, and I really didn't need to have an engagement ring. The one I really want is a simple wedding band. Your folks are the closest thing to a family that I have. I want Winnie to sit where my mother would sit and I want your dad to walk me down the aisle and give me away. I'm going to ask Susan to be my maid of honor. I'm so happy, I don't know what to do. Howard is such a gentleman. I want him to put a move on me, but he won't and I'm not going to start anything that he won't finish. But on our wedding night, if I have to make the first move, I will. I don't think I'll have to instigate anything, but I'm ready if necessary."

"A glass or two of wine before bed works wonders for us."

"So far your advice has been right on target. I'll remember that."

"Sit on the couch in your night clothes. Sip your wine and do a little necking, more wine and more necking. A little touching and feeling. Then the clothes come off and ecstasy is moments away. Don't fake anything. Hang in there until that ultimate explosion. Of course, if you don't get it right the first time, try again. Practice, practice, practice. That's what it takes, practice. Howard may need a little help, but you will know how and when. I love you, Julie, and pray that you and Howard are as happy as Susan and I are."

"I love you too, Michael. You've been a combination son, brother or whatever I needed you to be at the time. Get out of here before I ruin my make up."

"You okay Pop?" Mike asked as he stuck his head in the door of Murph's office.

"Never better son, never better. How are things going out at the ranch?"

"Busy, busy, busy. I'm going to take a welder home. Ray Bodie gave us a side of Angus for barbeque and I have to make a rack and spit to cook it on."

"Help yourself. Take anything you need. It's going to be quite a whing ding Sunday, with Julie and Howard getting married and all. I saw the doctor this morning and he can't believe the change in me. I've lost all my excess weight, and gained some muscle. The old pump is as good as ever, if not better. I've learned to control stress. The doc says that I can do whatever I want. Tonight, Winnie gets a surprise."

"You horny old fart," Mike laughed.

"No son, I'm not horny," Murph corrected. "I'm in love with your mother and an important part of a marriage has been missing for awhile because we were both afraid of another heart attack. But the doc gave me the green light. All systems go."

When Mike got home, Susan was full of news. "Everybody we've asked is coming. Howard's sons are coming for the wedding. I've hired a band for music and found a square-dance caller. I've booked the motel for guests that want to stay over. Get your dress whites and shine your shoes. We are going to renew our vows while Howard and Julie are repeating theirs. Walt is going to walk me down the aisle, Margaret is going to sit in Mom's place. Do you have any ideas about what you want?"

"I want Hawk to be my best man. I think Marie should be one of your attendants and Carl one of mine. Lois and Virginia should be included somehow, as well as Bob and Ray. Since all that is required to legalize a marriage is a license and public announcement, how about Bear doing the officiating? Imagine that 6ft. plus native in traditional dress and his booming bass voice presiding."

What wonderful ideas. Supper's ready, let's eat. We can make a game plan after supper."

Mike took time to talk to both Marie and Carl and told them about the upcoming wedding and asked if it was all right with them. "I want to adopt you two and give you my name. Is Carl and Marie Murphy okay with you?" Marie bobbed her head up and down several times in approval.

Carl said, "Yes, yes. I want people to know I am your son and I promise to never do anything to make the name Murphy look bad. Here is my hand on it."

Susan beamed with pride as she listened to the conversation. Mike was trying hard to keep a straight face.

Finally he said chokingly, "Thank you. I don't know where you learned to respect and honor your mother, after all, you had not seen her in several years. You must have had a wonderful teacher."

"Grandma Romaine taught us respect and honor. Each night we prayed in front of Momma's picture so we would know her when we saw her. And we always asked God to watch over us all and bring us together again, and He did."

"Thank You, God," he said, raising his eyes to Heaven.

"Your mother and I have a lot of planning to do. When you get the table cleared off, leave us alone 'til bedtime. Then we'll have bedtime treats."

Marie climbed into Mike's lap and arms and laid a big juicy child's kiss on his cheek followed by, "I love you Daddy."

"Before we get started on our game plan, there is something I have to do. I wasn't going to tell you, but after thinking about it, I feel you should know and will approve. Aggie had a prized rose bush. I think that was the only thing on earth she loved. Ramon and his crowd drove over it time and time again, until it was just a stick in the ground. I cared about Aggie but I didn't love her. I dug up the bush and took it to the Plantarium. They somehow salvaged it. I want to plant it out here and put her ashes in with it. That way she will be with it. I'm doing it out of respect. She died a horrible death, now she is at peace. This will be just a reminder that she and the bush are one of God's creations, deserving respect and dignity."

"I've got just the spot for it, by the patio where it will get full sun and be protected from the wind. It'll give off a nice fragrance while we are sitting out there and it will be easy for me to take care of, and I will. I don't feel threatened by the memories you may have. That bush will always be a reminder to me of how much you care about people. I've seen you in action, making certain that people have enough resources to get through an emergency. You give without question. You are the kind of a man every parent would like to have their children grow up to be. We'll plant it together."

"I'll have to make a spit to cook the beef on tomorrow and get plenty of dry, hard wood for fuel. It will have to cook all night to be ready for noon Sunday. I'll scrub down the garage floor and driveway for dancing and make signs telling folks where to park. I'll get a small log we can pad and cover with a sheet for a kneeler. Bear can have his back to Mount Hood while he officiates. Any suggestions?"

"We are going to be way short of chairs."

"There is too much work for you to do even with the voluntary help from Mom and Margaret and the rest. I'm going to ask Mary to close for Sunday and post a sign inviting her customers out here. We can use her tables and chairs, and dragging a few logs around, we should have enough seating and eating places. We'll have trash cans around to keep the place reasonably clean and no booze except to toast the bride and groom. With the Chief and his officers wearing their uniforms, I don't expect any trouble."

Marie came running into the kitchen in her pajamas and clutching her teddy bear.

"Cookies and milk time," she said, as she climbed into Mike's lap.

Mike drew her close. She was fresh out of the bathtub, and the sweet smell of innocence that all fathers recognize filled his nostrils. He kissed her tenderly on the cheek. "I love you Marie." Silently he prayed, thank you God for bringing these three extensions of Your love into my life. Amen."

Carl came in and saw Mike and Marie and had a longing look in his eyes. Mike picked up on it immediately and said, "Carl, I've got two arms and two knees. I have plenty of room in my arms, on my knees, and in my heart for you too. Boys are not as openly affectionate as girls are, and I understand where you are coming from. I don't know how to explain what I mean, but I love you every bit as much as I love Marie, and here is my hand."

Carl came to Mike, shook his hand and sat on Mike's right knee. "Can I have my cookies and milk here please?"

"I wouldn't have it any other way," Mike answered.

The children went to bed, and Mike and Susan did the dishes. "I won't need any wine tonight sweetheart," Susan said with a gleam in her eye, and she didn't.

She showered first and while Mike was brushing his teeth, she slipped between the sheets wearing only "Wind Song" perfume.

Mike climbed into bed wearing his sleeping shorts. Susan rolled over and kissed him on the lips and slowly ran her fingers down his stomach until she felt his manliness start to swell. Mike slipped out of his shorts and Susan opened the gates of paradise.

"Michael, I love you so much and the love you demonstrate towards Marie and Carl is overwhelming. It seems the only way I can express my love is like this. If there was a better way I would use it."

"Susan you show your love to me in so many ways. My coffee is always ready. If I want something, it's there. We're always together on things. There's nothing wrong with this way of loving each other, and like I just said, we're always together. I guess we are both trying to make up for what we missed in the past. When we get into our 70's we'll slow down to once a night. Pop saw the doctor today. His health is better than it's been in years, so he can do anything he wants. Pop said Mom is in for a surprise tonight."

"That old fart," Susan said. "Go for it."

The forest breeze blew softly across the sleeping couple, the owl hooted, the cougar screamed, and the Columbia River gurgled and splashed on it's way to the Pacific.

The smell of coffee brewing, sausage sizzling in the skillet, and Susan softly humming "You'll Never Know Just How Much I Love

You" woke Mike from a sound sleep. He hurriedly completed his grooming and dressed.

"Good morning sweetheart," Susan said, while pouring his coffee.

"Good morning to you too, honey. This is what I was talking about last night. You get up first, my coffee is poured and breakfast is ready."

Three eggs? Got to keep things running," Susan answered. "You are always singing or humming," Mike continued.

"It's because I'm happy and in love with a man who loves me and my children. Life is good."

"Do you think Grandma Romaine would like to get out of Cuba?" Mike asked.

"I'd not even thought about it. She has no family there and no one to turn to for help. From what I remember about her, she had practically disowned Ramon. I think she would welcome the chance to get out of Cuba and be able to see her grandchildren. Where would she live or have you thought about that?"

"We need to build a place for Bear and Faun before winter, so why not build a two-bedroom duplex? One side for Bear and Faun and the other side for, what is her name?

"Beatrize."

"For Beatrize, we'll find a way to get her out if she wants to come. I've got a lot to do today so I've got to go." With a goodbye kiss and a pat on her butt, Mike was out the door.

Mary liked the idea of closing on Sunday and immediately posted signs to that effect and invited her patrons to Mike and Susan's wedding, barbecue, and dance. NO BOOZE in block letters finished the sign. Mike then went to the Police station to catch Hawk before he left for the day.

"How, my brother." Hawk said

"How, yourself Hawk. I've got two questions to ask you. First question, would you stand up with me Sunday? Susan and I are getting married and I'd like you to be my best man."

"You're finally going to make her an honest woman, are you? I would be proud to stand with you. You said you had two questions to ask. What's the second?"

Noticing Rose cleaning the office, Mike said loud enough for her to hear, "Do you have any jailbirds who can help Mary with the food for the party?"

"I've only got one Mike. I think she has learned that crime doesn't pay. I'm going to release her as soon as she can find honest work. I'll have her at Mary's place ready to go to work whenever Mary wants her there. Is that all right with you, Rose?"

"I can't believe how decent you have treated me. I've been in jail before and had to get on my back and spread my legs to get anything. At those times, I wanted to have Aids or the Clap so I could give something back. Your offer is better than all right. I will not let you down."

"I'll arrange for a room at the motel. It's just a short walk to Mary's, and you start there Monday morning. She opens at 6:00 a.m.," Mike said.

"I'll be there at 5:30. I can help set up and learn the ropes."
"Susan has some clothes for you at the ranch including shoes.

We'll make sure you get what you need and can find room for. We'll keep the rest for you until you find a house or apartment of your own. I'll see you both tomorrow."

The next stop was the Plantarium. "Your rose is alive and doing well. Keep it watered and protected and it will bloom profusely next year. I hope you don't mind, but I took a root off and started one for myself. What is it called?"

"Agnes Murphy. I'll trade you your work for the rose root, but any profit you make, ten percent goes to Angel Flight."

"Fair enough, sir. My name is Harold Elliot."

"I'm Mike Murphy. Agnes was my late wife. I'm going to replant it and mix her ashes with the soil around it. That way she can still tend it."

"What a charming thought. Have a good day, sir, and thank you."

Mike and Susan planted the rose where Susan suggested. While they were on their knees Mike took Susan's hand, bowed his head, and said. "Aggie, I know you are now at peace and - now know those thoughts about me being unfaithful were untrue, until I met Susan. I forgive you for all the unkind things you said about me. I've always cared about you, but finally realize the difference between caring and loving. I hope you have forgiven me for all the things I didn't do, but should have and those things I did, that I shouldn't have. Amen."

"With Ramon and Agnes both gone it closes the book on the past and now we can look forward to our future" Susan remarked. "And what a wonderful future we have to look forward to."

"Susan, the future is not the destination; it's the everyday journey. Today is yesterday's future. We must make the most of each heartbeat because that's all we are guaranteed."

They stood up, Mike took Susan in his arms and tenderly kissed her on the lips. "I love you, Susan Murphy. Here's to tomorrow."

"Mike, sugar, my li'l ol' heart is about to bust with all your wooing and cooing. And I love you, too. If we don't stop this necking we are never going to be ready for the party. Go get the barbecue set up while I do my stuff. Lunch is on your own."

With Bear's help and expertise about those things, they soon had a crude but workable barbecue. Mike had located a used gear motor that turned slow enough and was powerful enough to turn the side of beef for perfect cooking.

"When the picnic is over, I'm going to refine this barbecue. We could cook a pig," Mike said.

"Or a deer or elk. Cougar was the favorite of the mountain men," Bear said. "We could smoke salmon. There are many things and many ways to cook outdoors. My people did it for many moons. Buffalo hump is very good. I'm getting hungry just talking about it."

"I'll take Carl and get a load of wood for cooking. Faun is making clothes for Carl and Marie to wear for the wedding. I thank you my son, for asking me to officiate. I didn't get the chance when Hawk got married, too many rules and regulations for my liking. Faun will probably cry. She told me she loves Susan and you as much as she loves Hawk. Hell! I feel the same way. Now get out of here before I make a fool of myself."

"Carl," Bear shouted, "get your gloves and get in the truck. We are going to be lumberjacks today."

Mike cleaned out the garage and washed it down with the garden hose, then tackled the driveway after barricading it from traffic. Next he made and posted signs indicating parking places.

He found a suitable log for the kneeler and a small rustic table with hand-hewn legs to use for an altar. He fashioned a cross from two small branches using a wild grapevine to lash them together. A small slab about six inches across and an inch thick served as the base. He enlarged a knothole to accommodate the stem of the cross. *"Pretty neat, if I do say so myself,"* he thought to himself. *"A pad and cover for the kneeler and I'm done. Something's missing but what? Candles. I forgot candles."* Mike went to the woodpile and found a log about four inches in diameter. Using his chain saw he carefully cut two slabs about an inch thick. He found two huge pine cones which he fastened to the slabs using a combination of white glue and screws. Using his adjustable pliers he removed just enough pine nuts to accommodate the candles. He sealed each candle in place by letting melted candle wax drip down and surround the base of the candle. He had just finished when the "Old Dog' landed down by the river.

Red got out first and explained, "They ain't never rode in a chopper so here we are. What kind of a party are you having? A revival?"

"No, Red, we're having a wedding party, with dancing and all the trimmings."

"Who's gettin' hitched?"

"Julie and Howard and Susan and I," Mike answered. He turned to greet Ray, Virginia, Laramie and Yale. "Virginia, Susan wants to talk to you and Laramie. Things are really popping around here. Here comes the firewood and chef so let's get this beef on the spit."

With the help of Red and Yale, and following instructions from Ray and Bear, the beef was ready to cook. Bear laid up the fire and when it was ready to light said, "I will now show you palefaces how this Indian starts a fire by rubbing two sticks together. It doesn't take much skill or patience. The most important thing is to be sure you have plenty of kindling. Then it is very easy, especially if one stick is a match. ..... Gotcha."

The kindling caught fire, then the larger pieces and soon the whole pyre was ablaze. When it had turned to glowing embers, they put the beef on the rack and started the motor. The spit turned slowly just like Mike hoped it would.

"We will add wood a little at a time, Bear said. "We don't want a lot of flames. We want a lot of heat. Most people would call this a bonfire if we weren't cooking on it. It is really a bond fire. History tells us that many tribes or clans would come together and make peace talks among themselves. There were no lights or candles and the talks lasted many hours. When everything was decided, and remember, these were enemies; no one got everything they wanted. There was compromise on all sides, but deciding it was better to live in peace than die in war, they smoked a calumet

- or peace pipe, to you pale faces - and bonded over the fire. It is a bond fire now because we are bonded as one family to celebrate the bonding of two other families in marriage. We need to set a watch schedule for the night." Soon the two-hour slots were filled with Mike volunteering to take over at four a.m.

Susan brought a huge pot of cowboy coffee, and Virginia coming right behind, with ham sandwiches, potato salad, and chips.

"There's soda and ice tea in the cooler, if someone wants to bring it out here," Virginia said. "Laramie, let's let the men tell the jokes and fish stories without worrying about a bad word now and then. Susan and I need your help in the house."

The men listened to Red tell of his childhood in Ireland. "I miss the old sod and someday I'm going back,' he said wistfully.

Ray told about how his life growing up on a ranch made him appreciate neighbors. "You never know when you're going to need a helping hand or a horse. Even though the fella you call doesn't particularly like you, there's no hesitating; get the job done and argue later."

Mike told of his Navy days, especially Top Gun competition and the tour with the Blue Angels. The programs were planned and practiced until it was almost automatic. You followed your leader. He told of an incident where the leader's controls malfunctioned while he was in a dive. He dove straight into the ground and his wingmen did the same, but the show went on anyway.

Bear Claw related his childhood following fruit harvests. "My mother had no education in white man's ways, especially dealing with money. When she went to the store to buy groceries, she would take one item at a time and pay for it, then get another until she had everything she needed or ran out of money. Most of the merchants treated us fairly even though they didn't want us in town. A rancher's wife saw a storekeeper cheating my mother by charging her too much and short-changing her. That rancher's wife let the man know the days of taking advantage of the Indians was over. 'We stole their land. You raped their women and you're still trying to screw them, but it stops here and now,' she said. 'This whole town will know what kind of a person you are, because I am going to write an editorial for my son's newspaper telling folks about the thief in the grocery store. You can't sue me for libel because it's the truth and I can prove it. Also none of my rancher friends' wives will buy from you. I tell you this; I will do without or drive miles away to get what I need, before I would walk across the street to buy from you.' "She taught my mother as much arithmetic as she could and all but adopted me. I went to white man's school where I was out of place and made fun of for a while. I didn't understand the language but she taught me to read. A whole new world was there for me to learn about. One day the biggest kid in school called my mother a dirty squaw. I stood up and asked him to apologize. He laughed in my face and asked what I was going to do if he didn't. He out-weighed me and his father was the biggest and richest rancher in the state. I told him I was first going to whip him, then hog-tie him, put him on the back of his horse, and send him home. He really laughed then, but I put all my 130 lbs. behind a solid right to the mouth and then a left to the wind. His nose was bloody, and he was trying to catch his breath.

'Do you want more?' I asked him. He shook his head, no, and I was reaching for a rope when someone said, 'Apologize to the man, son. When you get home you and I are going to have a come to Jesus talk about respect.' Then his dad looked at me and said, 'thank you for teaching him a lesson I've been trying to teach for five years.' I've learned more about Shoshone ways from books and listening to my elders. An Indian may speak with forked tongue to a paleface because that's what they are taught, but an Indian will never lie to another Indian. So when my elders speak of Custer and how he massacred Chief Black Hawk's old men, women, and children, that is what happened. It is getting late. I'm going to go home and go to bed; I'll see you all tomorrow. Good night."

"There walks a man you don't want as your enemy," Ray remarked. "I could spend hours listening to him talk. You would never expect him to be so intelligent."

"It comes from reading," Red remarked. "I think our fine Irish president, John Fitzgerald Kennedy, once said, 'The only thing worse than not being able to read, is to be able to read and not read.' Like Bear just said, books open a whole new world."

One by one, they went their separate ways, thinking over the stories they heard and realized they were closer now than they were earlier. This was indeed a bond fire.

Mary led a convoy of trucks with tables and chairs, a van was loaded with cooking equipment, including a portable steam table. At the wheel, with hair combed and make-up applied to perfection, was Rose. She was smiling, showing a perfect set of teeth. "I wore my jailbird clothes, because I didn't want to get mine dirty. I need to hug you, Mike. You and Susan and the Chief are the first people that haven't treated me like the trash I am."

"Rose! Forget what people think of you. In God's eyes, you are like the Prodigal son who came home. In our eyes, you are one of God's creatures who needed help. You are not, nor ever have been, trash and a hug won't do what a hug and kiss will do. He hugged her tightly and tenderly like a brother, kissed her on the cheek. Don't forget, God loves you and so do we."

"Mike, quit lollygagging with my waitress and let her get to work," Mary shouted. "I've got sausage gravy, fresh biscuits, eggs, bacon, pancakes, hash bowns, juice, and coffee, so ring the dinner bell. I'm going to open a family restaurant in your new building. I've talked to the architect and the plans should be ready in a week or two."

The breakfast was cafeteria-style giving everybody another chance to mingle. Bob and Lois Koch arrived along with Robbie, who dove into the sausage gravy and biscuits like he hadn't eaten in a week. Faun and Bear joined the others. Bear checked the beef and announced it would be done to perfection by noon. Bubb and his wife came with a huge cooler in the bed of his pickup. "Brats, franks and hamburger in case you need them." Hawk and his wife came directly from early church. The band came and set up. By ten-thirty the party was getting started. Julie and Howard came in Howard's car, followed by a stretch limo with his sons and their families.

Bear called Howard, Julie, Susan and Mike together to rehearse the ceremony. "It will be in Shoshone so you will not know what I am saying. When I look at you and speak, I am asking the traditional questions. I will stop and nod, you say I do. When it is time to present the rings, I will hold them up to the Great Spirit who will bless them. I will then offer them to you and will clasp my hands. You will put the ring on the finger and say, 'with this ring I thee wed,' then kiss the bride, and I will present you to your friends. When you get to the altar the four of you will kneel for a blessing. Do you have any questions? If not, I will go get ready. Its 11:30, how about one p.m. for the ceremony?"

"Sounds fine to me," Susan said. "How about you, Julie, okay with you?"

"I'll make the announcement," Mike said. "The band has the music," Susan said.

The people arranged their chairs for a good view of the ceremony. Mike had managed to find two comfortable benches with backs that he set up for Walt and Margaret and Murph and Winnie. The band softly played "Unchained Melody." Red in his full Irish tenor voice, sang beautifully. The bridesmaids reached the altar as Red finished. Walt and Susan came down the aisle followed by Murph and Julie. The band accompanied Faun in her clear alto voice, as she sang, "There's a Time for us." When Bear asked, "Who gives these women to these men?" the entire crowd said, "We do." Howard, Julie, Susan, and Mike knelt for the blessing. The Tribal Council, who were seated on the ground behind Bear, began a soft rhythm on their Tom-Toms. The band played the Lord's Prayer. Bear raised his hands and threw his head back and in a trained, bass voice, sang the prayer in Shoshone. The cloud that had shadowed Mount Hood moved away, and an eagle flew over the wedding.

Out of nowhere, Mary brought out two small wedding cakes and some sheet cakes.

Susan wore a long, white, leather skirt, slit up both sides to above the knees. It was trimmed with beadwork and she wore a matching jacket over a white dickie. She was stunning, with her hair in two long braids, and held by turquoise-trimmed clips to match her dangling gold and turquoise earrings. Her belt was a rawhide strap with turquoise tips, and moccasins completed the ensemble. She looked very Native American. Mike, in his Navy dress whites with his ribbons, also attracted some attention.

Julie with her dark red hair flowing loosely down her back wore a copper colored dress, slit up both sides to the upper thigh. A simple gold necklace, that belonged to her grandmother, nestled in her cleavage. Long, dangling, golden earrings, with a little rhinestone set off her hair. Gold-colored slippers, made for dancing, adorned her size seven feet. Howard, in a traditional black tuxedo, also drew some looks from widows who wondered how he got away.

After champagne toasts to the newlyweds, the fun began. Rose was dancing with one of Hawk's officers. Hawk asked Susan for a dance and Mike danced with Hawk's wife. The band took a break and Max Jenson called for square dancers. It took a little time, but Murph and Winnie, along with Walt and Margaret, Lois and Bob Koch, and Rose and her officer partner filled out the square. After a lot of starts and stops and laughing, they finished the first dance.

The band started up with some slow country ballads. Howard's sons all danced with Julie. Each in his own way expressed how pleased they were to see their father laugh and smile again, thanks to her. She told them she was their father's wife and would not try to take the place of their mother.

"When Mother's Day comes around, do something for someone's mother, like go to a rest home and spend some time with her. Time with your mother or father is more valuable than any gift you could buy. When Father's Day comes, take your dad fishing or to a ball game or just sit and talk. Remember the fun things you did as children and dig up some old photos to share with him. Give him yourself. That's the gift only you can give. He is a dear, sweet man and I truly love him. I won't let anything come between you and him. You are welcome in our home anytime. I don't know how to be a mother, but I would like to learn to be a grandmother. Which one of you wants to square dance with me?"

"I'd like to Ma'am," Howard Jr. said.

"Why don't we start by you calling me Julie, like everybody except your father does? He calls me Julia."

"They're calling for another square, Howard, let's go."

Hawk and his wife, Robbie and Marie, Carl and Lizzy, and Julie and Howard Jr. completed the square. Mary was coercing her customers to "Get in on the fun," and soon there were three squares. More laughing, starts and stops, and restarts. It was hard to tell who was having the most fun, the dancers or Max the caller.

After the dance was over, Susan and Mike sought out Bear and Faun. They were sitting with the Tribal Council and Hawk.

"I'm not good at speaking," Mike said, "so I'll just say what's on my mind. Bear and Faun, you made chills run up and down my back with your singing, and the ceremony was beautiful. I am honored to have the Council here to take part in the ceremony. Words cannot express how I feel. Just know, that this is a day I will cherish forever, not only as an anniversary, but for the love you all expressed toward us."

Bear replied, "The great spirit smiled and watched over you today, as he does every day, but today he gave you a sign. The cloud moved away from our sacred mountain as I prayed, then an eagle flew over. Your marriage vows are blessed and you will be very happy."

Mary was gathering her equipment. The people were leaving. The side of beef was just bones. Bubb's cooler was empty.

"You folks sure know how to party," Mary said. "Rose is a hard worker and I'm glad to have her. Unless I miss my guess, she will manage my supper club. I think she has found someone who cares about her. She and that cop have danced every dance and I haven't noticed any suggestive moves on either party. They are friends now, but I think romance is in the offing."

The band played "Good Night Sweetheart." Mike and Susan led the dance with Julie and Howard following. After they circled the floor, Walt and Margaret, Murph and Winnie, Red and Vonnie, Carl and Lizzie, Robbie and Marie, and Bear and Faun - who got a round of applause - joined in for the last dance.

"Heap good Pow-Wow for a pale face," Bear commented.

Faun punched him in the shoulder and said,"It was a wonderful party and we both were thrilled to be a part of it. Bear has never sung as beautifully as he did today. I was very nervous. I haven't sung in years. I said a little prayer and let it go. I believe the Great Spirit did shine on us today, that's why everything went so well. Good night. Come on Bear, let's go home."

"Ugh" Bear grunted.

Everybody had gone home or to the motel, leaving Mike and Susan alone. Howard and Julie came by to thank Mike and Susan for sharing their wedding with them.

"Let's go sit on the patio and have a glass of wine," Susan said. "It always helps me to relax and sleep better."

"I know," Julie replied. "Mike told me how it works."

The foursome chatted over their wine, when Julie announced, "Suddenly I'm very tired."

Howard said, "I'm just getting warmed up."

"Great," Julie responded. Mike, do you have an extra bottle of wine I could have? I'll replace it when we get back."

"Take it as a wedding present," Susan said. "Where are you going to honeymoon?"

"Timberline Lodge," Howard answered, heading for the limo. Julie, waving the wedding present, said, "The honeymoon is going to start in about ten minutes. Thanks again and good night."

Lying in bed with her "Wind Song" on and nothing else, Susan rolled next to Mike, enjoying the warmth of his body. He was wearing "Brut" for pajamas. The wine, the closeness of each other, and the relieving of the tensions of the past months, coupled with the real wedding led to the inevitable.

"Michael, if I had had all the time I needed to plan my wedding, it wouldn't have come close to what we had today."

Mike rolled over and kissed her breasts as her nipples rose to attention. He moved his hand slowly down her stomach reaching the door to paradise, which opened so he could slip in. Susan let go a soft, low moan, "Oh Michael! I love you so."

The owl hooted, the cougar screamed, the river gurgled and splashed on its way to the Pacific, and the pine-scented breeze blew softly across the sleeping couple. They didn't hear God's voice or smell His sweet breath.

I've had this story in my mind for 40 years and tried to find some one to write it for me since my handwriting is illegible. Then I decided to learn to type but I'm not a good student and that didn't work out, so one day I decided to punch it out, hunt and peck style on the computer, which worked better because I think faster than I type; therefore, I didn't have to go back and change too many ideas.

What I learned was, "writing" is fun and it amazed me how I would introduce a character in one place and they would show up later as an integral part of the story. If you have a desire to write just sit at your word processor and start. The story will flow out by itself. At least that's the way it happened to me. My wife asked me who wrote the book because the grammar and descriptions didn't sound like they came from me.

The story is set in The Dalles Oregon. I had an uncle who lived there. His ranch was west of town with an enormous pine tree in the front yard. In the early 40s my dad and I (I was 14 at the time) spanned the tree. As I recall it took us 4 or 5 times to go around that tree. We started at a chalk mark stretched finger tip to finger tip until we reached the original chalk mark.

CPSIA information can be obtained
at www.ICGtesting.com
Printed in the USA
LVHW011217100720
660328LV00005B/380